THE LIES BEHIND CAMBRIDGE MINDS

The Lies Behind Cambridge Minds

Published by The Conrad Press Limited in the United Kingdom 2021

Tel: +44(0)1227 472 874
www.theconradpress.com
info@theconradpress.com

ISBN 978-1-914913-36-5

Typesetting and Cover Design by: Charlotte Mouncey, www.bookstyle.co.uk
The Conrad Press logo was designed by Maria Priestley.

Printed and bound in Great Britain by Clays Ltd, Elcograf S.p.A.

THE LIES BEHIND CAMBRIDGE MINDS

JAMES HAYES

To Barbara and Tom for their
unconditional support in all my endeavours

- 1 -

Forcefully pressing his index finger against his left nostril, and snorting callously with the other, the white powder propelled through the rolled-up note, deep down the tube of Harry's nose, as he dragged it along the stained surface of the oak table. His heart stepped up a gear, like increasing the speed on a metronome.

'I love this game!' roared Harry to assert his dominance in the room.

Harry stood up. The intensity in the room was increasing with each passing second. He aggressively grabbed his luke-warm Heineken beer, which at this point was being carried around as a prop, and made his way through the crowded room. The room was filled with energy as the partygoers were dancing freely to Robin Thicke's 'Blurred Lines'. Blasting music; shouting; singing. Harry was oblivious to the noise as he bounced through the room; he only had one thought pounding in his mind.

A quick scan of the room enabled Harry to scout out the talent and see who he would be taking upstairs that evening. He strode with intent; everything about him oozed confidence despite the spilt beer on his pale blue Ralph Lauren shirt.

He ran his large hand through his thick long blonde hair and headed towards the kitchen where a group of three girls, all of a similar age to Harry, had congregated. Sniffing the final remnants of cocaine up his nose, he put on an approachable smile and locked eyes with one of the girls.

It was evident from Sarah's seductive red dress that no church could ever tame her. She took an immediate liking to Harry, opening up the circle to invite him in. She fiddled with her long brunette hair, which she had clearly spent some time straightening, and held her strong gin and tonic in the other hand. This was not her first drink, and as the night had progressed, the alcohol content had steadily increased, as she free poured her Gordon's gin into her American-styled red plastic cup. Like Harry, it was evident that she was here for a good time.

'Hey there, I'm Harry, nice to meet you'.

The girl smiled with deliberate provocation and responded simply, 'Sarah.'

There was an immediate connection between them and a flirty tension in the air. Harry wasted no time in steering the conversation towards capitalising on this mutual lust. The two spent what was only a matter of minutes engaged in small talk before Harry made the lunge, gripping Sarah's waist and pulling her closer in.

Eyes closed; they were both in the moment. The packed house now felt empty, as if they were the only two souls in the building. Harry gripped her firm buttocks tighter and tighter, like a boa constrictor taking hold of its prey as he felt her tongue go deeper into his mouth. It seemed as though nothing would be able to break this new-found connection.

The sirens got louder, and Harry was convinced that he just heard noises in his head, so he continued kissing Sarah undeterred. That is until the front door flew wide open. It almost came off its hinges with the sheer force imposed on it by the red battering ram. The music fell silent, and the ebullience that filled the room was quickly displaced with panic.

'POLICE! NOBODY MOVE!' barked the sergeant with beaconing authority.

There was a feeling of confusion and fear for the young adults at the party. This was Harry's chance to escape.

He pushed Sarah away and scurried through the crowded kitchen, where he bolted through the back door. He didn't look back as he knew this would only serve to delay him.

The sergeant instinctively set foot in pursuit, hunting the boy down like a bloodhound. This is what he lived for; he relished at the opportunity of clamping down on youthful delinquents. He shoved his way through the horde of individuals and left the other officers to take control of the scene at hand.

In Harry's rushed state, he clattered into a chair outside, stumbling to the ground. He could see the bulky sergeant's hi-vis jacket gleaming in the corner of his eye, so he quickly picked himself up and headed towards the back of the garden. The officer had the momentum and was gaining on Harry, trying to capitalise on his blunder. The torrential rain made the grass somewhat of a marsh, and both men were causing significant splashes with each stride. The conditions led to the officer's flat peaked cap flying off of his head to reveal his shiny bald head, but this just served to increase his determination. He was within touching distance of Harry and contemplated taking a dive at him.

Harry felt no pain from his earlier collision. The adrenaline pulsing through his veins kept him running in a similar fashion to the cocaine stimulating his mind earlier. The garden was only short, but to Harry, it felt as though he was in a 100m sprint, where the punishment for losing the race would be more catastrophic than any other contest.

'STOP!' barked the sergeant, while panting for breath but continuing in the hunt.

Harry ignored the orders and with one big spring hopped straight over the back fence and came tumbling down, further adding to his injuries. Knowing that he had no time to think about what was happening, he continued sprinting down the dark alleyway, his tunnel vision focused on getting as far away as possible. His hair was soaked and started to whip him in the face as he ran, but his athleticism enabled him to travel down the passage at some speed.

The sergeant had given up the chase, defeated by the six-foot fence panel. He knew he had to help his colleagues diffuse the situation, so he stormed back down the garden, frustrated in his attempts. On his way back, he picked up his sodden cap from the muddy grass and slapped it back on his bald, wet head. He trudged back to the house; his failure would fuel his fury towards the partygoers in how he dealt with proceedings.

2

The sun was beaming brightly on what was a glorious autumnal Saturday afternoon as Harry made his way down the Fulham Road, sporting a rugged dark green Barbour jacket and a slate grey flat cap. His style gave off a crossover between a Peaky Blinder and a wannabe Made in Chelsea star. Perhaps, with his newly acquired limp and bruises from last night's antics, he would fit in nicely as a Tommy Shelby's right hand man, but Harry certainly was not from Small Heath. He's London, born and bred, and proud of it too! His electric blue eyes sparkled in the sunlight as he approached two of his closest pals, Michael and John, outside of the Redback pub.

'Afternoon chaps!' Smirked Harry with a tone of smugness and superiority in his voice.

'What sort of time do you call this? We were supposed to have a couple in the boozer before the game,' said Michael, who sounded disappointed but deep down knew Harry would be late. He always seemed to be late, thinking his time is more valuable than the rest of the world.

'Apologies gents,' responded Harry, 'shall we get walking? I quite fancy a swift one in the ground if I'm honest.'

'Yeah, alright,' grunted John, who was a much quieter individual than the other two, more a follower than a leader. Lethargically, John set off, dragging his feet as he walked. The pavement's width only enabled two people to walk side-by-side; John was quickly overtaken and left to trail behind.

'Where did you shoot off to last night then?' Michael asked while staring at Harry, eagerly awaiting his response.

'I'll tell you when we get a pint,' said Harry.

It was not a long walk to the stadium, about five minutes or so given the length of the men's strides. Although if Michael had it his way, the journey would likely have taken twice as long. This stroll to the ground was a familiar one that the boys had been doing ever since the turn of the millennium when they were just little nippers. On the way over, Harry dug deep into his Levi pockets, rummaging around to see what change he had and handed over a two-pound coin and two fifty pence pieces to pick up today's programme. Buying the matchday programme was somewhat of a superstitious ritual for Harry, who never seemed to do any more than flick through the pages before getting live updates from Chelsea's Twitter page. A fairly procedural game, if there is such a thing in the Premier League, lay ahead for Lampard's men against Brighton.

The boys bustled their way through the ever-growing crowds like a pinball whizzing around a machine, colliding into what-ever was in their path to get to their destination. They approach the turnstiles in the Shed End, which operated like traffic lights with the green light signalling that the supporter could enter the ground. As his season ticket was in his grandad's name, it meant that an orange light would instead be displayed whenever Harry passed through the gates, indicative of a concessions ticket. As a student, he protested against forking out the full price for a ticket, and the stewards either did not care or were not being paid enough to stop this fraudulent behaviour, probably the latter.

The three boys headed straight to the bar, 'Three pints of Singha please love,' said Harry, ironically spending almost seventeen pounds on these drinks yet refusing to pay the full amount for his season ticket. It is incredible how the student mind operates; they can be so parsimonious with day-to-day living yet so frivolous with their money when it comes to alcohol.

'Go on, tell us then,' said Michael enthusiastically.

Harry took a large gulp of his beer, 'Ahh, that is bloody well refreshing!'

There were a few seconds of silence before Michael impatiently butted in, 'Stop being a dick and tell us.'

'Well, I gave the officer the smoke, didn't I! Piggy had no chance of catching me,' exclaimed Harry, with Michael hanging dearly on his every word. The two had gone to school together in Harrow, not the posh school, but a comprehensive one nearby, and since then, had taken very different paths in life. Michael, who always struggled at school, worked as a labourer on building sites scraping together whatever money he could. In contrast, Harry was heading into his final year at the University of Cambridge. Michael was in awe of Harry's intellect and looked up to him as an icon. He always knew that Harry would be successful when he was older and was grateful to have him as a friend.

Even though all that happened after the chase was the party being shut down in an eventless manner, Michael could not stop grinning as Harry told the story. He perceived the escape as fearless when, in reality, it was much more an act of cowardice and a dodging of responsibility. This was Michael all over, always electing to see the positive in everything Harry does. In contrast to Michael's exuberance, John appeared rather disinterested in Harry's story, given that he had not been invited to the party in the first place. He quietly sipped on his beer and checked his phone to see the team line-ups. Harry continued, 'The feds weren't even the worst thing about last night. I was necking on with some absolute worldie before they turned up!'

'Who was it?' asked Michael.

'How am I supposed to remember her name? I got with two other girls beforehand,' replied Harry braggingly.

'A hat-trick! You really are unplayable when you're in form,' remarked Michael.

John, who had somehow managed to grab himself a greasy burger while the other two were nattering away, hesitantly butted in, 'Do you guys mind if we head up? I think the teams might be heading out soon.'

With one final gulp, Michael was the last to finish his lager, and the three of them headed towards gate six. The atmosphere was beginning to build around the stadium, and the chants were flowing. There would not usually be an electric vibe like this against a team like Brighton, but the early season buzz was still present, and Chelsea's new manager and club legend Frank Lampard was yet to get his first home win. It is the energy and passion that draws the boys to the stadium every other weekend. The feeling when that ball goes in the back of the net and Stamford Bridge erupts is unrivalled.

'COME ON CHELSEA!' roared Harry, with Michael quickly joining in to show his support. Harry, filled with excitement, felt goosebumps as the boys headed up to the top of the stand and located their seats. 'What are we on today then lads?' asked Harry.

'I've got a tenner on Tammy to score in the first half! Love seeing the youth get a chance under Lampard,' replied Michael.

Shaking his head in disapproval, John remarked in a monotonous and dull tone, 'Betting is a fool's game.'

'It's free money mate. Chelsea and Manchester Shitty in an acca, you can't go wrong,' laughed Harry, whose betting patterns replicate his approach to life: minimising risk and being tactical in everything he does.

The game kicked off, and the spectators settled down in their seats. This did not stop Harry and Michael from putting their vocal cords to work, bellowing loud chants, replicating opera singers in their support for their club (except the pair were not quite as tuneful as professional singers). The two boys, as with most supporters, sung deep and powerfully as if to prove their masculinity. John, on the other hand, never sung at games. To him, it was a football match, not a concert, and he was always profoundly focused on the more intricate elements of the game.

About fifteen minutes had passed before the first real chance of the game. Tammy Abraham had been fouled over on the left wing, and the fans leapt up out of their seats, roaring ferociously at the referee to give the Brighton player a caution. Willian ran over the ball as a decoy before Mason Mount whipped in a sumptuous delivery, which Abraham soared towards but completely missed from close range before the ball bounced on to hit the post. A chorus of groans was let out by the crowd as they eased back into their seats.

'Fucking useless twat! How's he not scored? He can't have been more than two yards out,' yelled Michael in frustration while slamming his seat.

'It's amazing how a bet can make you turn so fast on our youngsters eh Michael,' chirped John with his eyebrows raised, a little happier for once.

The first half had ended goalless. Michael stormed down the aisle to empty his bladder and buy his round of beers, 'Absolute joke,' he muttered under his voice, knowing that these drinks will effectively cost him ten pounds more. To make things worse, he'd be lucky if he even managed to buy the drinks before the second half kicked off, given the mammoth size of the queues for the toilet.

The game had concluded with Chelsea taking all three points home, scoring two second-half goals without response. Michael had forgotten about his losses, and the boys filled with delight had returned to the Redback to sink a few more pints to celebrate. When they had eventually left the pub, just prior to seven in the evening, the sun had nearly gone into hibernation for the day, and a cool breeze began to sweep through the streets of London.

Despite the euphoria of beating Brighton, the boys fought off the urge to spend the night drinking in the pub. One of Harry's closest pals from school, Daniel, had decided to throw a little shindig to send Harry off before he went back to Cambridge. He lived near Harry in a small village on the outskirts of London, called Hatch End, and the boys had to take the Overground train to reach their destination. They decided to walk to West Brompton station, to avoid the hassle of getting the district line for one stop, and naturally popped into a local newsagent to pick up a few tinnies for the walk.

'That Jorginho step, you honestly can't beat it,' remarked John, who had found his voice after sinking a few drinks.

'It just screams confidence,' agreed Michael.

The boys merrily tapped through the barriers, hiding their open beer cans under their coats as they walked past the TfL staff and progressed towards platform 4, where they faced a fourteen-minute wait until their train towards Stratford arrived.

'This is what makes me proud to be a Blue!' said John in a somewhat confident passion. 'Up the Chels!' he exclaimed while pumping his fist in the air. Now that the game was over and Chelsea had their victory, John was more than happy to sing in support of his side. In fact, he even went so far as to start a chant off himself, which Harry and Michael swiftly joined in with. They were unreservedly carefree, and their songs were infectious, with fellow Chelsea fans on the platform joining in harmoniously. However, this chanting served as the spark for the chaos that was about to ensue. Had John's retro Chelsea shirt, stained in tomato ketchup from the chips he had sloppily managed to consume between the pub and arriving at the station, not given away that the group were Chelsea fans, their obnoxious shouting certainly showed their affiliation.

The Blues' supporters were met with a ferocious response from across the platform, 'YID ARMY!' A group of six Tottenham fans, on a high from beating Southampton by two goals to one (despite having a man sent off), were keen to show that their club was the superior team in London, off the pitch at least. After some angry words were exchanged from across the platform, the Chelsea fans had decided that they didn't want to settle this with just words; they wanted blood.

The Chelsea fans had exploded down the platform and ploughed over the bridge. Without even a second thought, Harry and his pals, influenced by their intoxication, decided that they had no option but to follow the herd to fight for their club. Michael had dropped the bag of beers and made way for the overpass. Storming not as an army but rather a bundle of overweight men, the Chelsea Headhunters came running down the steps, two at a time, ready to fearlessly fly into those who opposed them. The Tottenham fans were bouncing on their feet in preparation for the imminent war.

'Come on then!' shouted Harry, in an attempt to instil fear into his foes. However, his shouting came from the back of the group, and even the overweight John was ahead of him in the siege. Harry wanted to appear the alpha male with his battle cry but strategically placed enough distance between himself and the conflict to avoid getting hurt. The other two were just as tentative to get involved by the time they had actually reached the brawl. Five older men were fighting Chelsea's corner, exchanging blows with their outnumbered Tottenham counterparts. Although at this point, Harry, Michael, and John were of little value in the fight. It was not until it was clear that the Tottenham fans were getting a pummelling that the three youngsters decided that now was their time to enter the fray.

One younger Tottenham aficionado, bloodied-faced, was lying on the floor, taking a thumping from a skin-head Chelsea fan covered in tattoos. He was trying to protect his face to reduce the extent of the damage done, but the man was relentless and showed no mercy. 'Stop! Please!' yelled the cowering boy as he tried to get up to run away.

John uncharacteristically gritted his teeth and saw the vulnerable fan as his chance to inflict some damage. Harry and Michael watched on in incredulity as their peer ran up and swung his foot wildly towards the helpless man's face. John's heavy boot connected cleanly with his nose, crunching loudly as it did so. As his body slumped onto the cold platform surface, John shouted in disgust, 'Fuck off you Tottenham scum.' His friends were startled at what they had just witnessed. This was a side to him that they had never seen before.

One of the Spurs supporters had pulled out a glass bottle of Budweiser from his black plastic carrier bag and, without hesitation, took a momentous swing, striking the bald Chelsea fan's head as an act of revenge for his comrade. The glass shattered on his skull, and the man came crashing down onto the floor like a tumbling giant. Deep red viscous blood poured out from the ultra's head. It was at this point that the trio decided to bail. They were all up for a scrap, but even they knew that they were out of their depth. Their train was approaching on the opposite platform. Without speaking, relying solely on eye contact, they retreated, eager to vanish from the scene.

3

'Jesus! Did you see the amount of blood that was coming out of his head? It was like a slaughterhouse,' said a horrified Harry from the comfort of his brown and orange train seat. The adrenaline from the fight had dissipated, and the boys were too shaken up to conversate. All three of them were staring blankly out of the windows, relieved at their safety. The boys disembarked at Willesden Junction for their connecting train. It was as if somebody had flickered a light switch, drastically changing the mood of the evening. The electric atmosphere in the pub not so long ago was rapidly replaced with an eerie one. The beers that they had planned to drink on the journey were slowly warming. Alcohol was the last thing on their mind, given that it was a significant contributing factor to the scenes they had just witnessed.

They dragged their feet through the underpass to get the train that would bring them to Hatch End. At least John was content at the pace they were travelling at. A harsh wind attacked them when they got to the platform, and they were somewhat relieved to get back into the warmth when their train pulled in. In a similar fashion to the speed that they had been walking at, the boys slowly made their way through the remaining beers in Michael's carrier bag. It was not until they got to Wembley Central station that they finally broke the silence on the events which had unfolded before their eyes, doing so in meticulous detail. The twenty-minute train journey back to the fringe of London felt much longer than this, but the boys had decided, undeterred, to continue with their night. They unanimously decided that the massacre would not be brought up at the leaving drinks in fear of spoiling the party ambience.

The train pulled into Hatch End, which was precisely what you would expect for a suburban station. It was small, just two platforms, and one employee working there to ensure proceedings went ahead smoothly. The train station matched the personality of the sleepy village. It was only a minute's walk from tapping out of the station to being on the high street, which instead of being packed with exciting clubs and bars, as is the case in central London, was lined with restaurants and coffee shops to suit the needs of the elderly population that resided there. Despite the steady speed of consuming beers, the boys had been drinking all day and stumbled as they made their way down the street, passing the odd person giving them sinister looks.

'Beers for the legends, I reckon,' exclaimed Michael, eager to bring the night back on track. They walked into the local off-licence, Mili's, and decided that splitting a bottle of Captain Morgan's spiced rum was probably more fitting for the party they were set to attend. Of course, a two-litre bottle of Pepsi Max was the obvious choice for the mixer. It was an absolute steal at 99p. Always seeking the next level of intoxication, Harry had picked up a 660ml bottle of Birra Moretti so that he could continue to drink on the walk.

'I'm so gassed to see Georgia! She's a naughty little treacle,' said Michael. An extended pause had followed before he muttered, 'shame her boyfriend is such a meathead.' The other two laughed at Michael's frustration, knowing that he never stood a chance with her anyway. They continued to progress towards Daniel's house, with Harry lighting up a Camel Blue cigarette and sipping on his beverage. They did not know who to expect at the party since Daniel had messaged them directly instead of creating a Facebook event. This mystery led to them all excitedly predicting who would show up.

A few minutes later, the boys reached the front door. John had grasped the silver-coated lion head knocker and came crashing down on the door to inform the others of their arrival. They thought it strange that they could not hear any music playing, or indeed much noise at all. Before the door was even fully open, John had stormed past Daniel, grumbling about his desperation to alleviate his bowels.

'Well, it's nice to see you again John,' said Daniel sarcastically.

'How are we doing buddy?' asked Harry rhetorically before grabbing Daniel in for a friendly embrace. Michael opted for a fist-bump and a nod, not bothering to engage in the niceties of conversation.

'Beer?' asked Daniel hospitably.

'Actually mate, we've bought some rum and coke, have you got any ice?' said Harry.

Daniel had shepherded the two boys into the desolate kitchen and fetched them a glass each. He opened his freezer door and grabbed some ice from what looked like an endless pile of bags. Harry had been distracted in sorting out his drink and was completely oblivious to the quietness that enveloped the house. It was only when Michael asked where the others were that Harry realised how poorly attended the so-called *party* was.

'How was the match then lads?' asked Daniel, who was clearly excited by the arrival of his new guests. Harry spoke of his delight with the result but even while doing so was looking over Daniel's shoulder to see if there were more people to talk to. Michael was nodding away in agreement with everything Harry said, like a puppet who had his voice snatched away from him. Daniel wasn't a massive football fan. He followed Brentford because that's the team that his father supported but was glad that the boys were in such high spirits. 'Come on, let's head on through to everyone else,' said Daniel leading the way to the back room. By the time John had finished in the toilet, the kitchen was empty, and he was frustrated that he had to pour his own drink.

As the boys approached the living room, the music gradually came into earshot. The tunes were coming out of a small speaker, the sort of thing that you would pick up for a few quid from Flying Tiger, or even Poundland. At this point, Harry realised the boys would have been much better off in the Redback, boozing away in central London. There were about ten people dotted around the room, engaged in civilised conversation. Granted, they were school mates of Harry's, but this was not quite the send-off that he had hoped for. A quick examination informed Harry that there was only one girl in the room, which came as a disappointment. Tonight certainly would not match last night's antics.

As it transpired, it was quality that presided over quantity. The girl nestled into the worn armchair was utterly remarkable, instantly clutching Harry's undivided attention. She had a certain look of innocence about her. Her skin looked soft, and her soul looked pure. Harry recognised the girl, but he could not put a name to the face. She looked over to him, and he got lost in her mesmerising blue eyes, which contrasted with her simple yet elegant white dress. He was entranced by her beauty, as if she had cast a spell over to him, one which he did not want to be broken. Realising that he was gawping away at her without saying anything, he quickly diverted his eyes away and struck up a conversation with John, who had just entered the room.

John was rambling away about his disappointment at the lack of food at the party, but his words were going in one of Harry's ear and out of the other. Harry did not care for what John was saying, he just wanted to head straight over to the girl and introduce himself, but his confidence evaded him. This was most unusual for Harry, who was always a hit with the ladies, but something was intimidating about her that sucked away his self-assurance. The girl had gorgeous curly blonde locks and was giggling away at a joke that someone in the corner had just cracked. In fact, come to think of it, he did not recognise the man who had made the joke, which was most strange considering that he knew everybody else in the room. Harry was somewhat jealous of the mystery man, who was engaged in conversation with the only female present. He was also getting bored of John's monotonous voice and thought that now would be a good time for another smoke.

John was midway through a sentence when Harry decided to turn around and head to the garden, much to John's befuddlement. He traipsed back through the kitchen, opening the French doors and stepping out onto the garden patio. Harry did not bother telling anyone else that he was going for a cigarette for two reasons. First, most of his friends did not smoke as he did, but second, and more importantly, he wanted to be alone with his thoughts. He took out a cigarette and began to inhale the tobacco into his lungs. After a few puffs, he pulled out his phone to check the time and considered getting the last bus back home to Pinner. While his house was not far away, he certainly did not fancy the trek back, and the thought of his warm bed outweighed any deliberations about staying at this lousy event. With one last drag on his cigarette, he threw the butt to the floor and stamped firmly down on it, all set to make take-off without alerting the others.

That was until a soft voice called out from behind Harry, 'Hey, have you got a spare cigarette?' To his delight, he turned around and saw that it was the girl from inside. Harry was once again caught in a trance, staring in admiration at her, completely lost for words. A few seconds had passed before Harry reached deep into his pocket to grab his deck. He drew out a straight and handed it over to her.

'Sorry, have you got a light too?' she had asked in a polite manner, 'Oh, by the way I'm Elizabeth'. Harry shunned the lighter in front of her, still unable to conjure up any speech. She lit her cigarette, took a deep inhale, tilted her head backwards and blew out a large cloud of smoke.

'Party sucks right,' said Harry, who had finally found his tongue.

'Wait, aren't you the one that Daniel is throwing this party for?' asked Elizabeth quizzically. Harry felt embarrassed and tried to shift his reasoning onto the poor choice of music, but Elizabeth saw right through him and knew that he was not enjoying the vibe of the evening.

In an attempt to steer the conversation in a new direction, Harry deflected, 'So tell me, what do you do?'

'I'm actually going to Cambridge to study English,' responded Elizabeth. She did not feel at all conscious about making this statement; rather, she was proud of her achievement. Harry tended to wince at telling people that he too studied there in fear of coming across as pretentious.

'Oh, no way!' remarked Harry, 'I'm going in for my final year of Economics at Trinity College.'

'I know, Daniel told me. I was hoping that I'd get the chance to meet you this evening,' she said with a smile. Elizabeth had heard all about Harry and, in many ways, looked up to him.

Harry was excited by her positive energy but also a little caught off guard that she knew who he was. He felt as though he was on a roll now and kept the conversation flowing, 'What college are you going to?'

'Girton,' responded Elizabeth with a little cough as she inhaled too much smoke at once.

'Oh, so you're not *really* going to Cambridge then,' said Harry provocatively, 'you had better book your flight tickets if you fancy visiting the city.' Harry unleashed an arrogant chuckle, and you could almost see that a little part of Elizabeth had been crushed. She was shy at the best of times and did not know how to respond to a situation like this. Despite feeling belittled by Harry, she was also strangely attracted to his dominant personality.

Harry lit up another cigarette as an excuse to stay and chat with Elizabeth, and the thoughts of the last bus drifted out of his mind. He now had a much better offer. They delved into a lengthy conversation with Harry teaching her the ropes of what to expect at Cambridge, demystifying the strange traditions at the eight-hundred-year-old institution. Elizabeth hung onto his every word, enthralled by the fact that she would be studying here for the next three years.

As the conversation ebbed and flowed, Harry increasingly found his stride, and his confidence was back once again. Needless to say, the fluidity of the chat was aided by Harry's seemingly endless supply of spiced rum, which he had nipped back into the kitchen to grab. Elizabeth was drinking from Harry's cup, and this was an indication to him that he should think about how he was going to seal the deal. As Harry fed her more and more alcohol, the spark between them was getting hotter. It was as if there had been a complete role-reversal from earlier in the night, and it was now Elizabeth that was caught in Harry's spell.

After the voluminous amount of alcohol taken in by Harry, his bladder got the better of him, and he was now bursting for the toilet. 'Don't go anywhere,' he said while pointing a demanding finger at Elizabeth. She bit her lip and shook her head. Harry waltzed off in a chuffed mood after his flirty conversation. It would have been impossible to wipe the smile off of Harry's face as he headed to the lavatory; it turns out that tonight was a brilliant party.

However, when he pondered back to the garden, Elizabeth was no longer standing on the patio. He stepped outside to see if she was hiding, but she was nowhere to be seen. Harry thought it was most strange but presumed that she had gone back into the living room with everyone else. He could faintly hear Amy Winehouse's 'Rehab' as he approached the room. Harry stepped in and searched for his new-found crush, but on first inspection, she could not be seen. That was until he looked again, this time more closely. To his dismay, he saw the dark-haired boy kissing Elizabeth on the armchair in the corner. She was sat on his lap, and they were not holding back despite the rest of the onlookers in the room.

Harry was devastated, dropping down on the sofa next to Daniel. Once again, he was completely lost for words. Elizabeth let out yet another giggle as she pulled away from the man for air.

That should have been me, thought Harry, who now felt conned that he had provided her all that alcohol and cigarettes.

'So, are you excited for your final year in Cambridge?' asked Daniel.

Harry was in no mood for conversing, still shocked at what he was seeing, feeling entirely out of control. 'Yeah, I guess,' he said bluntly.

'Yeah, Elizabeth can't wait to start,' said Daniel while sipping on a homemade mojito. He was clearly having a great evening, even if the rest of the guests were getting bored by this point.

'Sounds nice mate,' said Harry automatically, with no regards to what his friend had just said. 'Wait. Elizabeth?' enquired Harry frantically.

'Yeah Elizabeth, my sister,' said Daniel whilst pointing across to the other side of the room. It all suddenly made sense. That is where Harry had vaguely known her from. He had been close friends with Daniel since secondary school but did not know him well enough to know his siblings.

'Who's the bloke?' asked Harry trying to contain his disgust.

'Oh, that's her boyfriend Matt. They've been dating since the start of Sixth Form. Really nice bloke actually,' said Daniel. His words only served to shove the knife deeper into Harry's heart.

Harry's jealously took over him as he stared on; she was the perfect girl in every way. It was not fair that Matt got to be with her and not him. He desperately desired her. He would be a far better companion for her than Matt. Feeling rather intoxicated and fed up, Harry had decided to call it a night and booked an Uber to take him home to Pinner. It wasn't until gone two in the morning that he stumbled up the stairs and collapsed into bed.

4

Thunderous banging on the bedroom door shocked Harry into a harsh awakening. He rolled across the bed and looked at the alarm clock, which displayed a time of nine-sixteen in the morning. Light was seeping through the poorly drawn blinds, which must have been too much of a struggle for Harry to sort last night in his drunken state. His mouth may as well have been the Sahara, and his head was pounding as if he had just lasted 12 rounds with Anthony Joshua. Desperate for hydration, he went to grab his glass of water that he religiously puts on his bedside cabinet before sleeping each night. It wasn't there, and upon further scrutiny, Harry found the glass lying defeated on its side on the worn grey carpet in a puddle of water. The image forced an unwanted flashback of the Tottenham fan lying on the platform in a pool of his own blood. Harry winced at the thought of last night's antics. The sight of the empty glass could have made Harry cry, except he was too dehydrated to produce any tears. He faced a dilemma. On the one hand, he was completely shattered from the lack of sleep and would love to get a few more hours under his belt, but on the other, he was desperate for water and to alleviate his bladder. He lay still contemplating life for a few minutes, wishing that he could be in somebody else's shoes right now, Matt's shoes would be nice, if he could choose anyone. Just as he was drifting off into an unconscious state from his inactivity, he was greeted with three more loud thuds on the door and yelling from his mother for him to get up. At this point, his decision was clear; he had to begin the day.

It was a sombre and rushed breakfast for Harry, who was getting an earful from his mother about his lethargic behaviour. They had agreed to head up to Cambridge early today to settle in for the term, and his mother was least impressed at his state. Despite Harry only going up to university for an eight-week term, he managed to fill the white Range Rover Evoque; it is hard to comprehend just how much stuff one person could need! Harry squeezed into the front seat, placing a bag of miscellaneous goods on his lap and a box filled with his pots and pans by his feet. Despite how full the car was, Harry brought a pillow from his room to catch up on some much-needed sleep on the journey. It was at this point that his mother appreciated the delicate state he was in and thought that there was simply nothing to be gained from shouting at him. She let him sleep peacefully, putting on BBC Radio One for company and headed up the A1.

The pair had arrived in Cambridge just after midday, and Susan, Harry's mother, gave her son a nudge to let him know that it was time to wake up. With an imposing stretch and a muted but wide-mouthed yawn, Harry was slowly coming back to life. When he opened his eyes, his mother had already left the car and was at the machine on Queen's Road to pay for the parking. Seeing this set a spark off in Harry, who thrust himself out of the car to chase after his mother.

'What are you doing mum? This is miles away from my room!' remarked Harry.

'Oh, I've bloody paid for the ticket now, it was so expensive as well! Why didn't you tell me this beforehand?' Susan asked, with a bit of anger creeping into her tone. She now sensed that Harry was in a better place than he was this morning, so thought it suitable to shout at him again.

Harry was reluctant to say that he did not tell her because he was asleep since this would only spur the argument. So, he conceded, 'I'm sorry'. A few moments had passed, and after the tension had died down, he proceeded, 'The whole purpose of coming on Sunday was that we can go down Trinity Lane and not have to carry my bags so far. I'm sorry that I didn't let you know sooner, but it will be significantly easier if we head over there. Especially with all this crap I've brought up with me'. Harry was a lot more careful with his language around his mother.

They both chuckled, and Susan had gotten over her initial frustration. They got back in the car, and with a smirk, Susan said, 'You really are an idiot aren't you. I don't know how on earth they let you in here.' It was only a short drive, but the atmosphere in the car had significantly improved. They headed towards the centre of Cambridge and pulled into Trinity Lane, which was one of Harry's favourite streets in the city. To him, this street embodied Cambridge as a whole. The long narrow lane is an ancient part of the city's street plan and is lined with old beige-brick houses, each with a towering chimney erect from the roof. The pathway was far too narrow but added to the street's rustic feel, with students often opting to walk in the middle of the road. Crooked buildings and uneven surfaces are typical of the city and provide character and individuality to each street. The gothic architecture in Cambridge is truly stunning and makes it an incredibly attractive place to live. However, the design flaws serve as a reminder that while the city may be beautiful, it is not necessarily functional.

Susan pulled up outside Queen's Gate, and Harry sat in a moment of reflection. Each time he had arrived at Trinity College, he had felt an array of different yet positive emotions. When he had arrived as a fresher, he had the pure excitement of starting a new adventure but was filled with nerves about meeting new people and establishing a new life. He could not believe that he was going to be studying at the University of Cambridge and questioned whether he truly belonged there. Yes, he achieved impeccable grades in his A-levels, but in his mind, the university was reserved only for the absolute elite. When people think of Cambridge, they think of all the great people that had studied there: Prince Charles, David Attenborough, Steven Fry, Steven Hawking, Albert Einstein, Isaac Newton, Charles Darwin, the list is endless. Harry initially felt so out of place; what was some kid from Pinner, a small town in the suburbs of London, doing at a place like this. It did not add up. It did not make sense. He felt almost intimidated by the university and the people that he thought he would be interacting with. It is safe to say that when he initially arrived, he suffered with *imposter-syndrome*. This emotion is something that many other students had felt and is certainly something that never fully goes away. Instead, as time progresses, it slowly erodes away. Students become more confident in their surroundings and feel like they deserve to be where they are. Embarking on his final year, Harry still felt incredibly lucky to be in the position that he was in and could not wait to get back to his studies, or rather the student life that came with it.

The ballot system at Trinity College meant that students who achieved the highest grades during the previous year had the best choice of accommodation room, and topping the *tripos* for Economics helped Harry land one of the top rooms that the college had to offer. The tripos is one of many obscure word from Cambridge's arsenal of jargon, simply referring to the examinations for a BA honours degree. Its etymology may be traced back to the three-legged stool candidates once used to sit on when taking oral examinations.

Harry's room was a matter of meters away from Queen's Gate, which certainly helped with all his luggage that he had to take in. Both Susan and Harry grabbed as much as they possibly could. Weighed down by the bags, they slowly made their way towards staircase M. He was situated on the ground floor, which was certainly a relief for the pair as they were struggling to keep moving, and a glance at the small blackboard on the door displaying '*H. Baldwin*' in chalk told them that they had arrived. The door was conveniently left open and the keys placed on the desk by the window for the arrival of the new tenant.

'Flipping heck! This is some room,' exclaimed Susan dropping the bags on the floor. Most student rooms resemble a budget hotel, with long lifeless corridors and small bland built-for-purpose rooms inside, but this was something else. It felt as though it belonged in a castle fit for a King! The door led straight into the living room, which boasted a high ceiling and an extravagant gold chandelier. Sizeable cast stone windows invited the natural light to beam in. The combination of the traditional oak flooring and large grey block wall certainly did not give off the most welcoming vibe but provided a unique and studious living environment. Across the other side of the large living room, there was a completely different tone to the room. A traditional coal fireplace was surrounded by a faded Sacramento green leather sofa, and a worn rose fabric wingback armchair. Despite the seats not matching, the two somehow worked perfectly together. Perhaps it was the complement of the large patterned Tunisian rug running underneath them or the oak coffee table matching the floors.

Startled, Susan opened the door at the end of the room and made her way into the bedroom. She could not believe her eyes. It was like something you would see on television; she felt like she had just walked into a scene from *The Crown*. A king-size four-poster bed made of mahogany wood was pushed against the back wall, with the rest of the interior replicating the same prestigious standards as the living room. Harry had joined her in the room now, slightly less in awe than his mother since he had been in similar rooms during his time at Cambridge. The pair stared out of the window, which overlooked Trinity's famous Great Court, reputed to be the largest enclosed courtyard in Europe. Harry's room had a prime view of what Cambridge had to offer; the lawns were immaculate, the fountain stood tall in all its grandeur as the centrepiece of the courtyard, and the chapel in the background only served to enhance the aesthetics.

Time almost stood still for Susan, who couldn't help but be amazed by her surroundings. On the other hand, Harry had begun unpacking his things, wanting to get the stress of moving out of the way.

'Shit!' yelled Susan. Harry looked confused at her sudden panicked state and gave her a blank stare. 'The car,' she exclaimed. Harry had suddenly remembered, and his eyes opened wide. They had left the hazard lights on and were only supposed to be stopping temporarily to unload his belongings. They rushed back through the college to the Range Rover, which was blocking the entire street. Susan had got there first, but it was too late. On the windscreen lay a white packet with 'Cambridgeshire County Council' written on it. Her heart sunk at the sight of the penalty charge, and despite not saying anything, she felt more bottled-up anger towards Harry as if this was entirely his fault. She grabbed the packet and headed towards the driver's seat.

'You grab the rest of the bags while I move the car,' she said in a bitter voice, 'I'll see you shortly'.

Harry unloaded the rest of the gear from the boot, ready for his second run back to his room. Disgruntled, Susan drove off, without even knowing her destination. Parking in Cambridge was an absolute nightmare, so she decided to go back to where she originally parked on Queen's Road; it looked as though she would be able to use her original parking ticket after all. When she finally parked up, she opened the notice, which revealed that she was the recipient of a seventy-pound charge. She took a deep sigh and headed back to Trinity, this time in a more direct route down the Avenue.

As Susan approached Harry's room, she heard a distinct

chatter taking place, and when she finally emerged into the living room, she saw a tall, dark-haired man of a similar age to her son. The two locked eyes in silence, and that's when Harry butted in, 'Oh yes, right, this is Raymond. He was just helping me to get settled in.' He then looked back towards his Italian friend and said, 'Raymond, this is my mum.'

'Pleasure to meet you Mrs Baldwin,' said Raymond with a firm handshake. Noticing that Susan was carrying the pots and pans that Harry had forgotten, he jumped in again, 'Are there any more bags that I can help you bring in?'.

'No, no, this was the last of them,' responded Susan with a pleasant smile. Despite just meeting Raymond, he had given off a good impression. Maybe it was the way he maintained eye contact or his helpful offer. In fact, Susan always took more of a liking to Harry's Cambridge friends, despite seeing much less of them than his home friends. She thinks that they are a good influence on her son and wished that he would hang around them more often. 'Well, it looks like the pair of you have got things under control here, I'm going to head off, need to sort the roast for this evening.'

'Come here mum,' said Harry, before pulling his mum in for a firm embrace, 'thanks so much for helping me to get settled in today, sorry about the ticket earlier.'

'Oh, don't be silly,' said Susan as the two finally broke from their long hug. 'I'm much more worried about you! I'm going to miss you loads!'

Susan turned and headed towards the door. She had only walked a couple of steps away before, before Raymond turned and said to Harry, 'I'm going to have some people over at mine for drinks before this evening if you're game?'

Susan instantly turned around and glared at Harry. 'You surely cannot be thinking of heading out again can you?' said Susan in a jokey but somewhat disappointed voice. 'You must be absolutely shattered,' she remarked.

'That's what power naps were invented for,' said Harry with a smirk, 'besides, I'm not heading out, we've got our start of term formal dinner tonight'.

Susan sighed and responded, 'God, do you ever stop! Just make sure you stay focused. You know how important your final year is and I would hate to see you throw it all away at the final hurdle.' She paused and looked around the room one more time, 'Well, you landed this room with your grades, so I guess you must be doing something right.' She was cautious and perhaps a little overprotective of her youngest child, but she meant well. She always wanted best for all three of her children.

5

The rays from the Lumie alarm clock were getting progressively brighter, replicating the sun rising at the start of each day. Except it was not the start of the day; in fact, it was close to 6pm before Harry had been 'naturally awoken' by the artificial beaming light. Yet he did not want to get up quite yet and lay there blank-faced staring at the bed's patterned tester, as if a frozen creature, waiting for the sun's blaze to melt away the ice he was trapped in. But for his need to alleviate his bowels, he could've stayed in bed a lot longer, but knowing this was a battle he could not win, he knew he had to get a move on. After all, he did not have long until pre-drinks for the formal dinner. He stepped into his navy slippers waiting for him by the side of his bed and plodded towards the door, where he chucked on his matching bathrobe to cover his naked body. He thought it best to open the curtains to allow the last of the Autumnal sun in for the day, then headed out of the room.

One of the strange things about Harry's (and indeed a significant amount of Cambridge's) accommodation is that inhabitants were often left sharing a bathroom with other students, despite the grandeur of the rooms. Thankfully Harry did not have to walk too far, just a couple paces from his room, and he was there. Deciding that he probably ought to shower before the formal, he jumped into the first cubicle and hung up his robe on the Britannia silver peg. At this point, he was bursting. He did not even have time to turn on the shower before he started pissing on the door and let out a monumental sigh of relief. The warm urine, which at this point was now dribbling onto Harry's feet, was a stark contrast to the ice-cold water blasting onto his back. The freezing water was certainly sufficient to blow him out of his sleepy state. He bent down and picked up a purple bottle of body wash. Of course, this bottle belonged to someone else with who he shared the bathroom, but this never bothered Harry. He always took what he wanted.

Refreshed, clean, and feeling ready for the night ahead, Harry headed back into his room, not before a little detour to grab a beer from the fridge, which Raymond had kindly brought for him earlier. Harry always enjoyed getting ready. He grabbed his UE Boom speaker from the draw and started playing some grime tunes to fuel his excitement. He pulled his tux from the cupboard and began to dress in front of the gold-plated full-length wall mirror. For a man, Harry always takes a while getting ready. Not only is he slowed by constantly sipping his beer, but he takes this opportunity to check himself out in the mirror. He follows a set order whenever getting ready; the trousers always go on before the shirt to ensure maximum time can be spent looking at his abs from all different angles. He took one last gulp of his beverage before he decided it was time to button up his winged collar dinner shirt. He adjusted his shiny silver cufflinks before pulling out his black bow tie from his drawer, which he proceeded to tie impeccably in front of the mirror – it was clear that he had attended many a formal dinner over his duration at Cambridge. After brushing through his hair and putting on his dinner jacket, Harry spent a few more moments glancing at himself in the mirror. This was one of his favourite suits, which he had tailormade while travelling in Vietnam on his gap year. The velvet fabric was stitched together in a serene coastal town called Hội An, where the people were friendly, and the lifestyle was bliss. The perfectly fitting suit was at great odds with the memories of freedom that it brought Harry.

Turning off the speaker, Harry grabbed his gown and threw it over his shoulder as he headed out of his room once more. While many of Harry's friends thought the Cambridge gowns were a bit snobbish (none more so than Raymond), Harry relished all of the traditions at the university and thought that was what made the institution so spectacular. After all, if you strip back all of these ancient rituals, Cambridge would be a depressing place, all the work without the fun. Harry headed to the kitchen to grab the rest of his beers, and on his way out, he bumped into two of his close pals.

'Gertrude! Sabrina! Long time no see!' said Harry, embracing them individually.

'It's so good to see you again! We're just heading over to Raymond's now,' said Gertrude.

'Oh perfect! I'll come with you then,' replied Harry. The three of them made their way up the staircase to Raymond's room, who lived just above Harry on the first floor. 'You two are both looking stunning, I must say,' said Harry with a smile.

'Thank you,' let out Sabrina in a nervous giggle. She returned the smile, with her cheeks blushing ever so slightly. Harry always was a charm, and Sabrina had developed a bit of a soft spot for him over the years.

Harry, now leading the way, had reached Raymond's room and stormed straight in without knocking. The two had got to that stage in their friendship where polite knocks were not required. 'Bonjour Raymondo,' said Harry.

Dressed in his finest dinner suit, Raymond grinned and replied, 'Back from the dead are we', before placing his almost-full crystal whiskey tumbler on the table. The pair embraced in a deep hug, and it was only then that Raymond had seen the girls standing rather awkwardly by the door. 'Oh gosh, yes, girls, come on in,' said Raymond in a rather flustered tone. He had not anticipated the arrival of the girls just yet and frantically rushed around the room to clear the mess. The room was an absolute bombsite, with the chairs covered in a rubble of clothes. For someone hosting pre-drinks, you would have expected him to have at least had a little tidy. He scampered around, picking up as much as he could to make space for the ladies to sit down.

'New year, new you then Raymond,' joked Gertrude before asking, 'Have you got any cups?'.

'Yeah, there's a stack on my desk over here, I'll grab you one,' Raymond took a large swig of his Jameson whiskey, grabbed the whole lot of cups and brought them back over to the table and chairs where the others were sitting. He had taken these plastic cups from the college bar earlier as he thought it foolish to buy his own reusable cups when he can get them for free. The room was of a similar style to Harry's, but substantially smaller, and while Harry's boasted a separate living room and bedroom, the two were combined for Raymond. This was because Raymond had only achieved an upper second class result last year, and the ballot system meant that his room was not quite the crème de la crème.

Raymond had just sat down when he heard the laughter echoing up the staircase, which meant that the arrival of the other boys was imminent. He finished off his drink, sending a burning sensation down his throat and leapt to his feet to greet the new guests, 'Hello, hello dear friends, how I've missed your ugly faces.'

'That's rich, you look like Danny Zuko with your hair slicked back like that,' remarked Aaron, who headed straight over to the table to secure one of the few remaining seats.

Mo clumsily followed Aaron with his beers clanging in his Tesco carrier bag; he was somewhat of a goofy but loveable individual, with thick round glasses serving to magnify the size of his eyes. His black suit trousers were just a bit too tight on the leg, and the cummerbund played an essential role in his attire. Without it, the trousers would likely be bursting at the waist. One can only imagine how much tension his trouser button was under.

Cuthbert, the last of the boys, was still at the door with an outstretched hand to Raymond. 'Don't be ridiculous,' said Raymond, who batted away the palm before him and pulled Cuthbert, who looked rather uncomfortable, into a hug.

'Hello again Raymond,' said Cuthbert while readjusting his white silk tuxedo scarf after his informal greeting. Cuthbert proceeded to join the others around the table, but unlike the rest of the boys drinking beer, he had brought a bottle of

Dom Pérignon. 'Have you got any champagne flutes?' said Cuthbert, wincing at the thought of drinking from a plastic cup. Raymond shook his head as he headed over to refill his glass. 'Excellent,' responded Cuthbert sarcastically with a roll of his eyes. As an Eton alumnus, Cuthbert was about as posh and pretentious as they come. Rumour has it that he had to have surgery when he younger to remove the silver spoon from his mouth. Given his family tradition of attending Cambridge, he knew he belonged there and despised that the institution was becoming more accessible to what he called 'common folk'. To him, the acceptance of people from different backgrounds only served to taint the pure blood of the university, and he was truly disappointed that after three years of studying, his friendship group consisted of a mix of people from private and state schools.

The group were drinking and catching up with what they had all been up to over the summer. While they had met up sporadically over the three-month break, including a weekend getaway to Paris, they all live in different places across the country, and indeed even across the world. This made it a challenge to keep up contact. The contrast is strange; at university, they live in close proximity, with intense daily interactions, yet when this commonality disappears, they live such different and separate lives. Some spend the break working odd jobs to earn enough money to fund their lifestyles at university, while others go on the most exotic holidays one could ever imagine, others still, more career-driven, have spent the past 12 weeks completing strenuous internships with the goal of a glorified graduate job at the end of it. Each person in the group does their own thing over the summer, but when they come back to Cambridge, their goals intertwine once more; the only thing that is on their mind is achieving a sought-after first-class degree.

There was much excitement in the room for the beginning of the new academic year, especially since classes were not starting for a few more days. This enthusiasm usually wore off once the term had begun and the hard graft commences, but for now, the group were carefree, the drinks were flowing, and the R&B music was filling any void of silence. In fact, everyone was having such a good time that they had nearly lost track of time, that was until Gertrude proclaimed, 'Guys, it's seven-twenty, we better get a move on, dinner starts in ten!'

Alarmed by this, everyone swiftly got up and prepared to make their way to the hall, leaving an even bigger mess for Raymond to tidy later. As everyone was heading towards the door, Raymond grabbed his half-empty tumbler and, with three large gulps, emptied its contents before slamming it back down on the table. 'Right, let's get a move on then shall we,' slurred Raymond in a stumble towards the door.

The group made their way down the staircase and headed out onto the Great Court, where their chatter was being over-powered by the sound of the stilettos and boy's shoes clattering against the cobblestone path. Gertrude was spearheading the group, walking a few paces ahead of everyone else with intent to ensure that they were not late. Thankfully, by the time they had got to the hall, there were still a few people queuing up and the group tailed onto the back of the line.

Gertrude was the first through the doors and stopped on her way in to pick up her vegetarian card. She spotted a cluster of empty chairs on the far table and thought that was the most suitable location to choose. Mo and Aaron were tussling away at the back of the line, trying to get in front of each other. Given that they were a group of seven, it meant that one person would be sat opposite a stranger, attempting to cling onto the conversation among the others, and these two both thought that this was a prospect worth fighting for. With one big shove, Aaron had become the victor, storming into the hall to secure the inclusive seat. Mo waddled along, accepting defeat and stood next to Harry. 'I hate you,' mouthed Mo to Aaron, who simply grinned in return.

As everyone in the hall stood in silence, awaiting permission to be seated, Harry took a thorough inspection of the candle-lit dining room. He stared at the arched wooden beams running across the ceiling and let his eyes wander to explore the magnificence of the room. It was the little details that Harry always fixated on, the colourful stain glass windows, right down to the patterns engraved in the woodwork. Colossal portraits of the former principals of Trinity College lined the walls and were so meticulous, creating an intimidating arena for students and serving as a constant reminder of how fortunate they were to be in their position. The pinnacle of the artwork always stood out to Harry, a portrait of none other than Henry VIII, who founded the college in 1546 as one of the very last acts of his life. The painting depicts the promiscuous former King in his equitize garments in a powerful stance, with his fists clenched, pressed firmly against his waist. The painting stands alone behind the high table to overlook all of the students. The silence allowed Harry to reflect on how far in his life he had come but reminded him that he still has a long way to go to fulfil his potential and follow in the footsteps of the greatness that came before him.

The gong was struck, sending a deep echoing chime through the hall and turning any faint whispers into absolute silence. Suddenly, the college choir, dressed in black and standing in front of the high table, burst into life. Although very few could understand the Latin they sang, their voices were angelic and added to the formality of the occasion. After the conclusion of the choir's hymn, the principal, George Draw, stood up to say grace, also in Latin.

'Benedic, Domine, nos et dona tua, quae de largitate tua sumus sumpturi, et concede, ut illis salubriter nutriti tibi debitum obsequium praestare valeamus, per Christum Dominum nostrum.'

Which loosely translated to blessing the Lord for the nourishment that they were about to receive. After he finished reciting the grace, he took a long pause before declaring, 'Please be seated'. The sound of chairs being dragged across the stone flooring and conversation piercing the silence resuscitated the room back to life.

'Thank god that nonsense is over,' remarked Raymond, 'I don't get why they feel the need to do everything in Latin. Nobody bloody understands the language'.

'You're the Italian,' said Sabrina provocatively, 'Where is your sense of pride in your country?'

Getting a little wound up, Raymond responded, 'What benefit does Latin have at all? What am I going to do, phone the pope up and have a chat with him?'

Cuthbert chimed in, 'Well, I for one, rather quite like the use of Latin. It is traditional and forms just part of what makes this the best university in the country. You'd do well to remember that'. Cuthbert was stern and cold with his words.

'Oh, shut it Cuthbert! You probably know the pope well enough to have that chat with him,' said Raymond, who now felt under attack.

Using this discussion as a distraction, Mo reached over and swapped his brown bread with Aaron's fresh white roll. He had been planning this manoeuvre for quite some time. 'Oi, give it back!' shouted Aaron. Before Aaron could reach over, Mo took one big lick of the bread to mark his territory and claim the bread as his. This small victory had made him feel good after being snubbed in the seating arrangement for the evening. Of course, it was childish and totally inappropriate behaviour given the formal setting, but Mo did not care one bit about this.

The catering staff swarmed the hall like a hive of bees around honey, bearing thick mushroom soup to be served to all of the students. The staff were clearly well trained, serving each individual from the left-hand side and avoiding any engagement of informal conversation with the students. Feeding 180 people simultaneously is no easy feat, yet the catering staff always delivered to the highest standard. Resembling a military operation, the service was unbelievably efficient, with everyone being served in a matter of minutes. The soup was placed in front of Harry, who thanked the waitress kindly, but just because he had his food did not mean that he could commence. As per formal dinners, guests are expected to wait until everyone has their food before starting, but given the size of tonight's feast, it was conventional to follow a rule of six when dining. That is, you must wait until all those immediately surrounding you have their food. This also gave Harry the time to study the table layout, which may be confusing for a 'first-timer'. There was an abundance of different objects in front of each guest, from the soup spoon to the fish knife, the two different wine glasses to the water glass, not to mention the various knives and forks to choose from, but to a seasoned diner like Harry, this was no longer an intimidating sight.

'Let's get this party started!' said Raymond while reaching out for an uncorked bottle of Châteauneuf-du-Pape. 'Who's on the red then?'

He began filling the glasses of Gertrude and Sabrina before proceeding to fill up Aaron's glass and finally came back to his own, tactically giving himself just slightly more than the others. No sooner had he finished filling his glass did Sabrina reach over a drop a single penny into his drink. The coin sank slowly to the bottom of the glass and was lost in the deep rogue liquid. 'Thank you, Raymond,' said Sabrina with a tilt of her head, 'now I want to see that wine polished off'.

'Oh excellent! How I've missed pennying,' said Raymond, who reached out and grabbed his full glass of wine. He proceeded to chug down his thick red wine, demolishing it in a matter of seconds. With his last gulp, he finished the remainder of the liquid and leant over the table to spit the penny out. 'Keep your eyes peeled Sabrina, I'm coming for you!' said Raymond in a playful yet sinister voice.

The wine continued to be replenished after each bottle was consumed, serving to exacerbate the raucous conversation in the hall. After the salmon main course had finished, the gong chimed once more, and the room fell silent. George stood up to give his speech for the evening. 'Good evening everyone.

For those of you new here to Trinity College, I want to extend my warmest welcome and sincerest congratulations for getting into the University of Cambridge. It is quite some achievement and you should be incredibly proud. For those of you coming back, it is, as always, a pleasure to have you all with us tonight. The college has been incredibly empty over the past few months without your presence.' Everyone was hanging onto his every word; George was a powerful speaker and always inspired all the students. He paused strategically to draw his audience in closer. 'Those of you who have been with us before know how challenging studying at this institution can be, so expect no easy ride. The hard work commences now. But this brings me on to what I want to talk about this evening. Cambridge is an institution where you have plentiful opportunities to stand out and excel, but too often people become overly fixated on academia and blend into the crowd. Attending university is not just about studying, it is about so much more: finding your passion in life, stimulating innovation, experimenting with new things. You should use this once-in-a-lifetime opportunity to explore who you really are, you might be surprised with what you find. There are almost eight billion people on this planet, and you are not going to stand out by blending into the crowd. Greatness never came to those who waited for it. Be bold, be brave, don't fear putting yourself out there. Greatness comes from within, and often our biggest failure is not trying at all'.

George took another long pause to allow his words to sink in, and it was at this moment that Raymond stood up, knocking his chair over in the process. He hastily grabbed the two wine bottles in front of him and started clanging them together to get everyone's attention. He continued smashing them together until eventually, they shattered, spilling wine all over the table and guests in the proximity, ruining their formal wear. 'Whoop de bloody do dar. Oh everyone, look at me, I'm the principal and I know Latin,' blurted Raymond in his drunken state. He expected rapturous laughter from his fellow students. Instead, his remarks fell on death ears. 'You think you're so special sitting up there on your high table,' he said while pointing directly at George, 'well you're bloody not. You're just old and a pretentious waste of space'.

Harry was grappling with Raymond trying to pull him back to his seat to save the embarrassment, but Raymond shrugged him off and continued with his rant, 'You and this institution are an ego-centric *disgrace!* You care about nothing other than consolidating your power and holding it over the students. You don't care about us or our mental health, you care about your status and personal affluence'. The rest of the hall was stunned into silence, and Raymond, angry that he didn't have their support shouted, 'Well, fuck all of you! You're all blind and can't see what's going on around you!' Without any hesitation, Raymond picked up his chair and, in his infuriated and intoxicated state, hurled it over towards the principal. A guest on the high table ducked just in time to avoid the chair as it came clattering down on the table just short of the principal, smashing everything laid out in front of George. Raymond stormed out of the hall, slamming the door on his exit.

- 6 -

'You look a right state. What got into you last night?' asked Harry as he plunked himself down onto one of the empty chairs in Raymond's room. The room was still a pigsty from pre-drinks last night, and it was evident that there had been no attempt to clear the mess.

'Just don't,' replied Raymond, 'I feel a lot worse on the inside. My head is pounding, and I've thrown up twice today, I feel an absolute shamble of a man. I've just had a meeting with the dean, and it wasn't good,' he remarked while rubbing his head and delicately taking a seat on the corner of his bed as if he was a fragile object.

'Oh yeah, she didn't deem that you were an inspiration and praise you in all your glory?' joked Harry. It was clear that Raymond was in no mood for Harry's mockery.

'Far from it,' responded Raymond, 'she gave me a two-hundred-pound welfare charge'.

Harry chuckled, 'Well that supports your theory about the college being money-centric'.

'That's not even the worse part. If the Dean would have had it her way I'd be packing my bags as we speak. She was leaning towards making me leave college accommodation, but I pleaded my case that this was a one-off event and would never happen again,' said Raymond as he opened his tattered plastic bottle of lukewarm water and began to drink it in a desperate attempt to rehydrate.

'So, what will happen now?' remarked Harry in a much more concerned tone. He certainly did not want to lose his neighbour and one of his closest friends.

'Well, we came to a compromise. I had to agree to take weekly anger management therapy,' said Raymond whilst making tired air quotes with his fingers, 'as well as abstaining from alcohol for the rest of term.'

'Ouch! I mean they can't *really* monitor if you're drinking alcohol or not, so I'm sure you'll be able to get around that,' said Harry perkily in an attempt to cheer his pal up, 'it's not that bad all things considering. I mean, after all, you did throw a chair at George,' there was a brief pause before Harry continued, 'and missed may I add. I think you ought to join the cricket team to improve that arm of yours.' The boys both laughed, lightening the heavy atmosphere. Harry was ever an optimist, trying to make the most of any bad situation. 'What's your plan for the rest of the day? Fancy grabbing some lunch from Hall?'

'I couldn't think of anything worse to do. One thing is for sure is that I won't be showing my face much around college until all this has blown over. I've got to go apologise in person to George this afternoon. Christ, I'm not looking forward to that,' said Raymond.

'Oh, to be a fly on the wall in that room. Good luck with

that mate,' remarked Harry as he picked himself up from the chair he was lounging on, 'Right, I'm off to unpack the rest of my belongings. You ought to tidy this room too.'

'Don't fancy giving us a hand, do you?' asked Raymond.

'Not really, no,' said Harry as he waltzed out of the room. He had slept well last night and was in a rather jolly mood, delighted to have avoided a hangover from last night's dinner. He wanted to organise his room and do any admin work before the new term commenced in three days. Before he had even moved a single box, he opened up his MacBook with the intent of messaging his friends on Facebook to see if they fancied a kickabout in the afternoon. The screen lit up to his Hermes inbox, and since he was already there, he thought it best to quickly flick through his emails. It was mostly junk, but he saw one email entitled 'Paper 14 Supervision Essay 1', and his heart sank. Seeing this email completely changed his plans for the day. What would have been a chilled football session in the sun had suddenly unfolded into a day of intense studying in the library. It was clear that the term was not really beginning in three days after all.

Deciding that there was no point in dwelling on the matter, Harry packed his satchel for the day. It is remarkable how student essentials have changed over time. Previously students would have had a pen, paper and some books, or even a quill if you go far enough back in time. Now, all Harry picked up was his laptop with its charger, his baby blue Chilly flask of water, an apple for sustenance and his packet of cigarettes as an excuse to take breaks from work and get some 'not-so-fresh air'. He never tended to eat the apple he packed each day, but at least it fooled him into thinking that he was being healthy.

He headed out of his room, determined for a productive day. There was simply nothing Harry hated more than wasting his time. He was always active and constantly had to be occupied. In fact, Harry's desire to permanently be busy was bordering on a mental illness. Free time was his greatest enemy. He paced down the corridor in his Nike tracksuit bottoms, fresh white trainers and his Trinity College jumper. He was rather fond of wearing subtle stash at university, from puffer jackets to sports clothes, but of course, he did not want to be seen in anything displaying the crest and 'Cambridge University' in large letters; those were reserved solely for tourists. His casual studying attire provided a great juxtaposition to last night's black tie, but he always felt more productive if he was comfortable when he had his nose in a book.

As Harry headed through into Nevile's Court, he passed a couple of fellow students in his year from the college who he knew well enough to nod at but not quite so much to stop and chat to them. This is what the collegiate system at Cambridge does, students create a vast network of acquaintances from living in such close proximity to others. These people are seen everywhere, and perhaps on a night out, one might even stretch so far as to talk to them, but after university, they are never to be seen again, only following their life updates on Facebook or Instagram. While they are usually interesting characters, if you stopped and spoke to them all, you would achieve nothing all day since it is impossible to go anywhere in Cambridge without bumping into someone you know.

The sun was beaming brightly through the arches as Harry made his way through the cloisters. He was heading to the college library, egotistically named after its legendary designer

Sir Christopher Wren. The Wren Library is an architectural masterpiece finished just before the turn of the eighteenth century. The building has the pristine court on one side, with the River Cam running along the other in all of its beauty. Harry made his way into the historic library and searched for a space to call his own for the day. Walking on the black and white marble tiles, Harry felt as though he was on a chess-board. A King ready to conquer. Except he was here to take on a supervision assignment, as part of the continuous cycle of students repeating homogeneous essay questions year on year. Making him more comparable to a pawn – there to make up the numbers instead of achieving true greatness. The first three booths were taken, and Harry was already beginning to fear that the library was full before the term had even started. However, there was room at the inn after all. A space was available in the booth with IV inscribed high above on the old oak bookshelf, and Harry tossed his bag on the floor next to an uncomfortable-looking wooden chair.

The desk was enclosed by three identical bookshelves and a plaster cast bust of a notable writer; the surroundings of which Harry had got so used to that he hardly even noticed their splendour anymore. Before he sat down, Harry walked over to the books to stroke their leather spines and skim over their titles before picking up an ancient book that intrigued him the most. This was a routine for Harry before commencing with any work, or perhaps it was inadvertent procrastination. Either way, he was always fascinated by dated books, this one enti-tled *Tractatus Logico-Philosophicus* by Ludwig Wittgenstein, an Austrian-British philosopher. He skimmed through the pages. The complex equations made this book seem as though it was written in a different language. Harry wanted nothing more when he was older than to have a large living room with an oversized globe, snooker table and an aesthetically pleasing wooden bookshelf filled with ancient books similar to the one before him. A space where he could entertain guests with whiskey and a cigar. Despite his interests in books, he seldom read out of leisure, focusing instead on academia to ensure success in life, which served as a reminder that he ought to begin reading for his essay.

Opening up his laptop brought Harry straight back to the assignment emailed to him, a three-thousand-word essay on the value of public participation in a democratic society, as part of his Planning Policy module he had chosen for this year. The deadline was not until Friday, but Harry was always keen to get his work done promptly. He gathered some initial thoughts on the topic and wrote them into a word document before opening up the PDFs of all of the required readings. He had an incredibly efficient system for essay writing, where he worked smarter, not harder. Instead of reading the entirety of all of the papers, he only ever read the abstract, introduction, and conclusion, which served to cut the reading from around five hundred pages to less than twenty. His logic behind this approach was that realistically students were never expected to bring in more than two or three sentences on each reading in an essay, so Harry saw no point in wasting time reading the whole thing. Plus, this gave him more scope for creativity and original thoughts, which he knew all too well distinguishes the best essays.

As the day proceeded, Harry ploughed his way through the academic papers, working relentlessly to take in demanding concepts, all the while formulating his own opinions on the matter. It was only when Harry had taken a brief break to check his emails once more that he realised he had completely forgotten about lunch; he had been so focused on his work that his hunger had evaded him. Knowing that food would no longer be served in the hall and that he had not yet got any food in himself, his only option was to head to the bar to grab a snack. He could have headed out to Sainsbury's, but that would have wasted valuable time that could be spent in the library. He grabbed a couple of odd books from the bookshelf and spread them across the desk to mark his territory and ensure he could return to his space after he ate. After swiftly repacking his bag, he departed.

Harry's thoughts were still on his readings as he made his way across the college. Not even the fresh air could take him away from his work. He was trying to get his head around Arnstein's ladder of citizen participation and was so deep in the zone that he completely missed one of his friends giving him a nod as their paths crossed. The bar was surprisingly empty, given that it was situated within a university and term had not even started yet. Granted, it was early, but in most other universities across the country, you would expect anywhere serving booze to be heaving in Fresher's week. However, Cambridge is not like other institutions. Work always comes first here and more often than not, the libraries are busier than the pubs. There was one pair sitting in the corner quietly playing a game of chess and another reading a book by the fireplace; even when the students were not studying, they were still stimulating their minds.

'Hi there, can I have a pesto chicken panini to go please?' asked Harry with a smile. He was always polite regardless of who he was conversing with, 'oh, and these too,' he said while tossing an upmarket packet of sea salt and cider vinegar crisps on the counter. He would have actually preferred a packet of Walkers or McCoy's but using fancy crisps meant that the college could get away with charging £1.20 a pop.

'Scan here,' said the bartender, who clearly was not happy at the restart of the new term and being back working in the world's quietest bar. Harry pulled his CAMcard from his wallet, which doubled up as a collegiate credit card as well as a form of student identification, and did as instructed.

It was only a matter of minutes before Harry had his food and headed back to his room. He withdrew his laptop from his bag and set it up on his desk to watch some Netflix as he ate. He only ever watched a series with short episodes in his lunch breaks to not waste too much time watching television in the day. Series with longer episodes were reserved solely for before bed to help him switch off for the day. Disciplined in everything he does; Harry never takes his phone with him to the library as he knows how much of a distraction it could be. He enjoyed his breaks mindlessly scrolling through his phone while having a comfort episode of *Friends* on in the background, acting not just as company but also as a timer for his downtime.

Relaxing only served to tire Harry. He could feel his delayed hangover slowly kicking in and knew he needed to get back into the library immediately before he crashed and lost the rest of the day. He nipped into the kitchen and put the kettle on, heaping eight spoons of instant coffee granules into his gigantic silver flask – fuel to keep him ticking over. He added the boiling water and stole some milk from one of his neighbours before stuffing the flask into his satchel, ready for round two in the library.

It was not long until Harry was reunited with his study spot, blasting his way through the rest of the readings, which he finally finished at around 8pm. The coffee had undoubtedly worked in stimulating Harry, who was motivated to finish the essay before bed. It had been a while since Harry had written an essay, so he was a bit rusty to begin with, but soon got back into the flow of things while planning his essay. Harry never wanted to waste too much time writing his supervision essays since they are just formative and do not actually count towards the final grade, yet he was adamant about maintaining their quality. A day of reading, two hours of planning, four hours of writing and thirty minutes to run it through Grammarly to format the essay; that was Harry's winning formula. With today's plan taking just over three hours, Harry was slightly behind schedule and knew if he wanted to get it done today, he would be working into the early hours of the morning, nothing uncommon for him. Happy with his progress, he decided to quickly flick through the various social media sites on his laptop as a reward. There was nothing of notable interest on Twitter or Instagram, but when he opened up Facebook, he saw that he had a message from Raymond.

Zoot?

It was short and sweet but enough to plant a gigantic smile on Harry's face. The message had been sent about twenty minutes ago and despite the silent room was music to Harry's ears.

Thought you'd never ask. In Library atm, meet downstairs in 10?

Harry's message was met instantly with a thumbs-up emoji, and he started packing his bag. As much as he wanted to get his essay out of the way, the term had not even started yet after all, and he could always get back to it tomorrow. The hard work was done; writing the essay was always easy once you had finished the preparation. Despite being in the final hour of the day, the library was still reasonably busy with students looking to get ahead with their work, making Harry feel a bit guilty and weak with his early finish.

'Yes Raymondinho!' chirped Harry, who was delighted to be out of his prison cell studying all day.

Raymond was not in quite such a good mood as Harry as he rhetorically murmured, 'Alright?'.

As the boys headed outside towards the back of the college, Harry was hit by the bitterly cold night air. It had been sunny all day, and he foolishly assumed the evening would follow suit, leaving Harry feeling rather underdressed in his jumper and tracksuit bottoms. He was shivering as the pair headed over the bridge towards their smoking spot, a bench down the tree-lined avenue - out of sight and out of mind.

'Here, have some of this, it'll warm you up,' said Raymond, handing over a half-empty hip flask. Harry knew all too well that this meant that Raymond had already made a start on the alcohol. He did not even need to open the flask to know its contents. It was always whiskey for Raymond.

'Thought you were on an alcohol ban?' joked Harry as he unscrewed the lid in a jittery fashion. The pungent smell seeped into Harry's nostrils like fumes at a petrol station.

'It's been a long day,' replied Raymond, 'I just want to have a chilled smoke and drift off to sleep forgetting everything that's happened'.

Harry reluctantly took a swig of the whiskey, sending a burning sensation down his throat. He winced and slowly shook his head in disgust at the strong beverage. 'You couldn't have just got us a couple beers, could you?' said Harry while handing his friend back his poison.

Raymond smirked and took a large gulp. The whiskey went down like water for the Italian and appeared to have no impact whatsoever on him, 'Now where would be the fun in that?'

The two had finally reached their usual smoking spot, a tranquil space where they would be left undisturbed. Of course, they had to avoid the college's designated smoking huts, given the contents of what they were smoking. As Raymond lit up the joint, Harry asked him, 'So, how did it go with George earlier?'

Raymond took in a deep inhale of the cannabis, blew out a large cluster of smoke and replied, 'It actually went a lot better than I thought it would, he took it really well,' with a surprised look, Harry nodded along. 'Well, it was definitely better than my talk with the dean, that's for sure! He wanted to understand my frustration as opposed to blindly punish me for my actions. Or maybe he's just trying to butter me up so that I don't speak out against the college or escalate my concerns about the institution.'

Raymond took another two puffs before passing the joint to an arms-crossed Harry. Not sharing Raymond's concerns and not wanting to get into an in-depth discussion on the matter, Harry was quick to change the topic, 'Ahh it feels good to be getting high again.' He was hit almost immediately with a head rush and requested Raymond to put on some reggae music on his phone, a cliché that they had grown to love.

They had smoked just over half of the weed when the effects really started to kick in. They both mellowed out and slouched on the bench, talking utter nonsense to each other. Harry was rambling on about the possibility of aliens being among us in space, which was met by Raymond suggesting that it was instead humans that are the aliens and the rest of the animals in the world that were the normal ones. Raymond kept pushing his theory, 'Look, all I'm saying is that we pick and choose which animals to slaughter, package up and eat. Sounds a lot scarier than the aliens we depict in movies.' Despite the quality of the conversations going off on a tangent, the drugs provided the much-needed escapism away from the real world. It took Raymond's mind off of yesterday's actions, and Harry was certainly no longer thinking about his essay.

'Mate we should definitely get some Dominos,' said a ravenous Harry, 'I haven't had dinner yet.'

In complete agreement, Raymond replied, 'Maaaate, what a shout.' He opened his phone onto the website, and the two browsed around customising their pizzas. In their intoxicated states, they continued to add all sorts of toppings, not forgetting the stuffed crust. They ordered the food to the top gate on the Queen's Road to avoid having to go past the porters to pick up their delivery. A forty-minute wait was expected, and from the moment Harry had suggested it, the pizza was all they could think about.

Harry had relit the spliff, which had gone out whilst arranging their pizzas, and took another long toke, when suddenly a torch was beaming over in their direction. Both the boys turned and were left like a rabbit caught in the headlights. They could not work out the figure making their way towards them but assumed it to be a porter patrolling the college. Thinking fast, Harry dashed the remnants of the marijuana to the floor, trampled on it and quickly rustled around his satchel. He pulled out his opened packet of cigarettes and handed one over to Raymond, muttering, 'Here, take this. And cut the music.'

As the figure approached them, it was clear that their hunches were right. It was indeed a porter, 'Good evening boys.'

Both startled and not in the best state for conversing, they looked at each other and over to the porter without much of a plan. 'Evening,' replied Harry as he lit up his cigarette.

'And what are we up to out here at this time of night?' asked the porter dressed immaculately in a suit with the college crest sewn on the breast pocket.

'Just having a cigarette and getting some fresh air,' said Harry. Raymond was clearly flustered and did not want to chip in in fear of giving away the truth. He had been in enough trouble today and certainly did not want to add to this.

The porter now lowered the torch and stared directly into their eyes, knowing that they were lying. 'You know the smoking area is back closer to college and you shouldn't be smoking anywhere else,' he said sternly, 'look I'm a reasonable man, and I'm just going to give you a warning this time.'

'Apologies for this, we'll come over to the smoking area now,' said Harry.

'Sorry,' said Raymond, who had finally plucked up the courage to speak.

'Good,' responded the porter, who now turned around and

it was going to be tight. While taking the route down the backs was actually a little faster, Harry tended to take the more scenic route down the King's parade. Not only was it a more picturesque walk, but it enabled him to pass Fitzbillies, his favourite coffee shop, en route. Given his rush, it would have made more sense for him to take his bike, but instead, he strode swiftly down the King's parade. He did not have time today to stop and take a picture of the King's chapel for his Instagram story, and thought that the grey skies did not do it the justice it deserved anyway.

Thankfully there was not much of a queue in the café, and Harry picked up his usual caramel latte to go. The coffee, while delicious, was very overpriced and small, but Fitzbillies was the sort of shop that people want to be seen in. Students around the city are rather snobbish and whichever coffee shops they go to acts almost as a personality trait. Besides, Harry thought the coffee on Sidgwick site was ghastly, and he despised waiting in the extensive queues for the budget coffee. He paced down Silver Street, where the pavements were far too narrow for their daily footfall and the buildings all stood rather crooked, which added to the quaint nature of the city.

Harry was nearly ten minutes late to the lecture when he came storming in with his coffee to hand. He had to hike up three flights of stairs to get to the dated Economics theatre. Harry tried to sneak in silently but was out of breath from his trek. The layout of the lecture hall was not ideal for any late-comers, who had to make their way past the lecturer and ascend the theatre to find any available seat. The lecturer stopped mid-speech and gave Harry a piercing glare, yet this did not bother Harry, who was frequently late to classes. He simply

headed back to where he came from. After he had taken a fair few paces away, Raymond blew out in relief and withdrew his flask from his jacket pocket, taking another large drink to calm his nerves. Not wanting the situation to escalate, the boys tranced back over towards the smoking hut, knowing that they had gotten away with one. They did not actually know the consequences of taking drugs on college grounds, but they were sure as hell glad not to find out. They waited quietly in the hut for the pizza to arrive and decided it would be best to take it straight to their rooms when it came.

- 7 -

The weed must have been stronger than usual, or perhaps it was Harry's intolerance that had built up over a relatively abstinent summer break. Either way, the effects lasted quite some while, and it ended up being a late one for the boys. Harry decided to spend an extra hour in bed to compensate for last night but was still rather ratty with his 'ganjover' when his alarm went off. He again spent the day in the library, turning his miscellaneous thoughts into a well-articulated argument but was frustrated that his work was not up to his usual high standards. Harry reasoned with himself that his quality had slipped because he was sleep-deprived, which may have been true, but he was also out of practice and writing an essay did not feel as natural as it did at the end of the last academic year. No sooner had he finished his essay and submitted it online did he find himself being set two further essays to be completed within the week. The academic monotony was kicking in as the start of year excitement quickly wore off.

Harry settled into a routine where he was either studying

or sleeping, with little spare time for any other hobbi[es] the term commenced, he felt like he was slowly drifting from his friends, living amongst them, yet feeling very is[olated] in his lifestyle. Harry was incredibly sociable by nature, the start of the term, his motivation for success outweigh[ed] urges to mingle with others. It was only when he started g[etting] weighed down under the pressure of his academic lifesty[le] he thought his constant studying was becoming unh[ealthy] He knew he had to socialise a bit more and find a way t[o take] time off.

Harry was just leaving the college when he bumpe[d into] Bertie, the captain of the college football team. It wa[s clear] that he was a sportsman from his athletic frame. He [was] taller than Harry, with broad shoulders. It looked as t[hough] he did not have an ounce of fat on his body. 'We reall[y need] you against Girton this weekend mate,' pleaded Bertie, [we've] lost our first two games and are starting to fear relegatio[n. The] new centre-mids that have come into the team are usel[ess.]'

'You know I've hung up my boots,' said Harry, who [was a] crucial player in helping the team to win the second di[vision] last season, 'it's third year and my studies have to come [first.]'

'Come on, you know how much you're missing it! Loo[k, you] need to stay fit, and taking a break from studying may a[ctually] do you some good. You're always cooped up in that li[brary,]' said Bertie convincingly.

'As much as I love you and the boys, my final answer [is no,]' proclaimed Harry, who strode past his dear friend leavin[g him] standing disappointed.

Harry glanced at his watch and saw that he only h[ad ten] minutes until his lecture was set to start over at Sidgwic[k.]

avoided all eye contact and sat down swiftly.

There were few seats available in the hall, given that they were only a few weeks into the term. The number of people attending lectures tended to drop as the academic year goes on, but October offered a fresh start and people came with the right intentions. Eagle-eyed, Harry scanned for a spot where he could park his rear end for the next couple of hours and could immediately tell who did not want to be in the room. Many sat fiddling on their phones underneath the desks, just waiting for the lecturer to stop rambling on, feeling that by attending the lecture they had been productive, even if they took absolutely nothing in. Others looked like absolute zombies, who had clearly gone out last night and were battling with their hangovers to stay awake. He found a spot on the bench next to someone he recognised but did not know well enough to conversate with. Harry adored the traditional lecture halls. While the wooden benches were rigid and cold, and the attached desks were impractical in size, this added to the charm of the academic arena. He admired how passionate the professors were about their field, scribbling complex algebra in chalk onto the blackboards, which quite frankly nobody in the room could follow. He felt honoured to be in a room where some of the world's greatest minds have learnt.

Despite Harry's fascination over the design and beauty of the lecture halls, his preparation and eagerness to actually study really had declined since he began university. As a fresher, he would always print out the lecture slides in advance, read through them as well as any other readings set, arrive early and listen keenly to what the scholars had to say. Now he would merely turn up and make a few notes on anything he found particularly interesting. He often paid attention for the first twenty minutes or so before opening up Facebook on his laptop to distract his friends in the room with messages about how dull the lecture was.

The lecturer rambled on about Coase Theorem and drew out an elaborate Edgeworth box as Harry stared mindlessly out the window, looking at the birds and imagining what it would be like to have that freedom. Harry turned to examine the ticking clock behind the lecturer, which felt as though it was moving in slow motion and informed him that the midway break was well-overdue. Like the rest of the students, Harry always looked forward to the break, not that he does anything different in this time, just that he can feel less guilty about scrolling through his Facebook timeline. Others around him would use this break to chat to those around them, perhaps nip to the loo or even get a quick coffee, but after two years of being a student, Harry had grown sick of the small talk and did not want to engage in these needless niceties.

The lecture dragged on for ten minutes longer than planned, but when it had finally finished, Harry wasted no time in fleeing the building. He looked around and saw his only two real friends from his course were already engaged in conversation with people that he hardly knew, and he certainly did not fancy sticking around. He desired only to get back to college and crack on with his essays.

In the first three weeks of Michaelmas term, Harry managed to complete nine out of his sixteen essays set for the first eight weeks. He was quite some way ahead of schedule but was eager to finish the rest of the essays in the next fortnight to give him plenty of time to focus on his dissertation; he planned to have completed his first draft over the Christmas break before he returned for Lent Term. To say Harry was an organised student would be an understatement. When he made a plan around his studying, he stuck to it meticulously, allowing nothing to get in the way of what he wanted to achieve.

When Harry got back to college, he decided that today he would work from the comfort of his own room. He usually opted to work in the library, which, in his eyes, created an environment where you feel pressured to perform. He made himself an extra-strong coffee in his 'Keep Calm and think of May Week' mug, which he topped up with a splash of cold water since he did not have the patience to wait for it to naturally cool down. Although he got this mug as a joke present from his Secret Santa last year (which he and his friends from college do annually), its words rang true. It gets him through the dark days of being a student snowed under with work, knowing that there is a light at the end of the tunnel and that light certainly shines lustrously. There is nothing quite as spectacular as May Week in Cambridge, the one time of the year when tension and stress are banished from the city. The festival vibe chimes through the city. In the day, students drink at various themed garden parties, and by night, they dress up in black tie for astonishing formal balls. If there was one thing motivating Harry to persist in all his endeavours and ensure him that all sacrifices will eventually be worth it, it was this week after exams had finished.

Harry was efficiently ploughing through the readings in his room, perhaps because he had locked his phone away in his drawer in the kitchen and put on an app on his laptop to stop him from visiting any social media sites. He enjoyed the convenience of only having to walk a few steps from his door to put on a microwave carbonara for dinner before getting back to work. In fact, he had worked so well in his drawing room that night that he decided he would spend Saturday typing up his essay from the same spot. Indeed, Saturday was a productive day in terms of work accomplished, but he did not leave his room all day. Harry was relishing the comfort of working in his chamber a little too much; it was beginning to become unhealthy.

On Sunday, Harry rose early once again and started preparing for his next essay. He was tasked with evaluating the economic benefits of urban agglomeration. At this stage, he was in full academic swing, at the zenith of his productive potential. It appeared as though nothing could stop his flow. He had once again spent hours reading. However, without a break, he finally burned out. His brain had become completely frazzled, nothing he was reading was going in, and he was beginning to get frustrated that he was not fruitful. It is no surprise that he struggled to focus this morning; he had not been outside for nearly two whole days or interacted with a single other soul. No amount of coffee seemed to pull him from this slump, and Harry was starting to think that he needed a change of scenery.

As he paced around his room trying to restore his concentration, his bright pink football boots on his shoe rack caught his eye. He sauntered over to them, and hesitantly picked them up. Football was indeed his biggest passion in life, but these boots had not seen action in quite some while, given that Harry had decided to give football up in his final year to focus on his studies. He knew the fresh air would do him good, and he wanted nothing more than to be out on the pitch again, but put them back on the rack again, knowing how much time football takes up.

He sat back down at his desk and stared at the words, which at this point were now floating around the page before him. Nothing was going in. His mind was completely blank, 'Fuck it,' he said to himself as he went to get his phone from the kitchen.

Any chance of a game today?

He had left messaging Bertie late; kick off was in a matter of minutes, but he thought it was worth a shot. Instantly Harry's phone vibrated.

Absolutely! Get down here immediately. Over at Girton's pitches.

Buzzing, Harry ran to his room to pack his bag in a matter of urgency that was certainly missing when he was running late for lectures. Grabbing his grey Nike sports holdall from underneath his bed, Harry started flinging in all the essentials. Two litres of water, bananas, his Chelsea tracksuit top, energy gels, deep heat, paracetamol, sock tape and of course, his precious Adidas Predator boots. He dressed swiftly, chucking on his college top with *BALDWIN* written in white above the large number eight on the back of the shirt. Rummaging around his draws, Harry pulled out a packet of dissolvable Imodium, placing one on his tongue as he ran out of his room to counterbalance the red bull that he drank while leaving the college.

Harry always cared about his appearance, and his bike was

no exception. When he started at Cambridge, he wanted to get a suave racing bike to look the part, but given how expensive they were, he ended up getting a second hand one from Facebook Market place. Except this bicycle certainly was not second hand; it looked to be more fifteenth hand. The bright yellow bike boasted a roaring red saddle with matching handlebar wraps. Even if the bike was past its use-by date, its vivid colours ensured that Harry got noticed wherever he went. The fresh respray acted as a façade. Harry's bike was on its last legs or rather last wheels. The chain was rusty, the breaks barely worked, and to top it all off, Harry could not even change gears on it. However, this was all part of the rustic charm that Harry loved about the bike. In his eyes, it got him from A to B in somewhat style.

Harry pedalled frantically down the Avenue, past his smoking spot and out of the back gate. It was quite some cycle (well, at least for Cambridge standards) to get to Girton College. He got to the college about twenty minutes after setting off and considered this journey to be his warmup. It was clear from his breathlessness that he had not done any exercise for a while. Harry wasted no time locking up his bike and heading straight over to the pitches, breaking into a jog to get there as quick as possible.

As he was running over, he saw someone he recognised but could not quite remember where from. He stopped running so as not to look a fool, and upon closer inspection, realised exactly who it was.

'Elizabeth,' said Harry in a surprised tone.

'Well, well, well, what are you doing down my neck of the woods. I do hope you have your visa to be this far out of

Cambridge,' she said with a chuckle and a sip of her Starbucks coffee.

Confused, Harry stared at her blank-faced until he remembered his obnoxious behaviour when they met a few weeks back, 'Ah yes, well I'm actually here for a football match.'

'Sporty and smart, the best combo.' Elizabeth locked eyes with Harry and started to play with her curly hair. It was this flirty behaviour that warmed Harry to her so much. She was dressed in nothing fancy, but her beauty shone beyond the garments she wore.

Nervous from her presence, Harry did not know how to react. He wanted to say so much, yet so little came to him, 'Thanks'. He was usually resoundingly confident around girls, but Elizabeth was different; she took this power away from him. When they first met, Harry had a fair bit to drink, and the conversation was flowing effortlessly, yet without this liquid confidence, Harry was struggling. 'How are you finding Cambridge?' jittered Harry.

Elizabeth proceeded to tell Harry about her experiences so far, but he could not focus on what she was saying. He was enchanted. All Harry wanted to do was ask about her boyfriend, praying that they would have broken up. However, he knew it would crush him if they were still together, so instead, Harry adopted the 'ignorance is bliss' philosophy. Speaking to Elizabeth made him forget about all his other stresses. He completely forgot that he was running late for the match. That was until Elizabeth asked, 'So what time is your game then?'

At this point, panic overcame Harry, bringing him back to reality, 'Shit, the match. I'm actually running really late. I've got to go!' He wanted to stay and keep chatting and was frustrated that the pair did not have more time together.

'Well good luck, or not actually! I supposed I had ought to support Girton,' said Elizabeth with a smile.

As Harry ran over to the pitches, his mind was far from the game at hand. He was in absolute awe of Elizabeth and wished that he could see more of her. Harry saw the team huddled by the side of the pitch, and it was clear that he had made it for half time. The vice-captain Joel Lockhurst, who looked remarkably like Bart Simpson, was giving a speech to the boys, 'We need to take our chances up top lads,' he spoke in an uninspiring tone and was really struggling to fire up the team, most of whom lying flat, exhausted from the first forty-five minutes. 'We've been solid at the back, nil-nil, this game is all to play for,' barked Joel, hitting most of the clichés as he spoke.

'Harry! Get in there!' chimed one of the lads on the floor. His arrival seemed to perk up the team far greater than Joel's dreary speech.

'You good to go?' asked Bertie. Harry nodded his head. 'Excellent! Right Marcus, you're coming off, great performance lad,' lied Bertie to the fresher who looked disheartened to be hooked at the interval. 'Harry, right in the centre of the park. You can dominate this game, don't be afraid to carry the ball and create some chances,' said a passionate Bertie. Once more, Harry nodded his head in acknowledgement. He was a some-what quiet player on the field and preferred to let his football do the talking for him.

Both sides made their way back onto the pitch, and the ref blew his whistle to commence the second half. The ball was played immediately back to Harry, who took a heavy touch and was dispossessed by an oncoming forward. This was not the start that Harry wanted. Nothing had come from his mistake, but it was a clear sign that he had some cobwebs to blow away.

As the game progressed, Harry was really struggling to stamp his mark on the game. He was blowing heavily, unfit from a lack of action and his touch was not quite up to his usual high standard. Harry was frustrated because he knew that he was significantly better than he was currently performing. Wanting to get more into the game, he decided to play a few simple passes to feel more comfortable. Receiving the ball in the middle of the pitch, he turned back towards his own goal. Harry was under a bit of pressure from a Girton player and saw Joel, the right-back, in acres of space, so he knocked the ball over to him. Joel took a touch and looked around at his options, plenty to choose from. The Girton winger started sprinting at Joel, who panicked at the sight of him. Joel rushed over to the ball but slipped while trying to get there, leading to the winger dispossessing Joel and running in one-on-one with the keeper. Joel slowly picked himself up and chased the Girton player but was far too slow to keep up with him. Without hesitation, the attacker placed the ball into the corner in what was a simple finished.

At the sight of the ball hitting the back of the net, Joel dropped to the floor once again, embarrassed by his mistake, as the rest of the Girton team ran past him to celebrate with the goal scorer. 'Oh, for fuck sake Joel!' belted Bertie in anger. This was not the first time Joel Lockhurst had a howler. His mistakes had cost them dearly in the previous two fixtures.

The entire team looked defeated as the match restarted. They were in a rut of poor form and conceding a goal as easily as this certainly did not help their spirits. There was about a quarter of an hour to go, and Bertie tried to motivate his team to raise their game but, deep down, knew that this would be another defeat to add to the tally.

Harry was frustrated with his lacking performance and decided that he was going to be more positive in his play for the rest of the game. A Girton midfielder, who had the better of Harry all game, drifted past Harry, and instead of letting him run on, Harry sprinted back, flying in with a huge sliding tackle to take back possession. Typically, in this game, he would have just opted for a simple pass, but this time he decided to go alone. He picked up the ball just outside of his own area and dribbled with intent down the field. Determined in his run, he refused to be tackled, despite attempts from the opposition. He shrugged an opponent to the floor and used his pace to get past the next two. A defender came charging towards Harry with malice as he carried the ball over the halfway line. As he came flying in, Harry skilfully nutmegged the player and carried on with his run. *This was more like it*, Harry thought. The Girton defence was out of shape, and Trinity had the numbers in support. Using this advantage, Harry threaded a perfectly weighted through ball to his striker, who took it round the keeper and blasted it into the back of the empty net.

The rest of the Trinity team chased after their striker to celebrate, but Harry was too exhausted from his run to join in. He was instead met with a big high five from the striker, grateful for the assist, as the team made their way back to their own half.

Following the Trinity equaliser, the game shifted entirely back in Girton's favour. They were bombarding the Trinity goal, really testing the ability and resolve of the defence before them.

Girton thought they had won it when they finally managed to beat the keeper, only for the goal to be ruled offside. There was not long left, a minute at most, when a miscommunication between the Girton defender and the goalkeeper resulted in Trinity getting a corner kick.

Torn between two minds of holding what they had or going for glory, Bertie made the tough decision to send up the big men from the back to attack the delivery. There was tussling and shirt tugging as the Trinity players tried to lose their markers. They were just praying for a decent cross to at least give them the chance of the win. Harry was not small by any stretch but was marked by the tallest player on the pitch, towering over him. The cross had been delivered right into the danger zone, and with a quick spin, Harry had lost his man. He was steaming in at full speed towards the ball and came in with a towering leap above everyone else in the box, meeting the ball with a bullet header at the near post. The ball soared at incredible speed and had too much power for the keeper, who could only push the ball into the roof of the net.

Letting out a ferocious roar, Harry had done it! In the dying embers of the game, he pulled out an undeserved victory. Harry went storming towards the corner, flying into a massive knee slide to celebrate before being bundled by his teammates. This is what he missed, the sheer passion and elation of scoring a goal, that dominating feeling where you are the centre of attention. This is what he lived for. The ref blew his whistle, and the boys had picked up their first points of the season.

There was an electric vibe in the dressing room after the match, the tunes ablaze from the speaker and the team jumping up and down, clattering the ceilings as they chanted away in celebration. The tinnies were being handed out left, right, and centre and the celebrations were well and truly underway. This may have only been college football, but this winning feeling is unrivalled at any level. Even Joel Lockhurst was dancing around the dressing room with a can of Fosters in hand, completely forgetting about his dreadful mistake.

After getting everyone's attention, Bertie bellowed out, 'Right, we're going big tonight lads!' which was met by a loud cheer of agreement from the rest of the team, 'Meet in the bar as soon as we get back to college, we'll get the pints and pizzas in watching the United Liverpool match, then head on out to Sunday Life.' The singing and dancing continued as the boys got dressed. Even Harry thought he deserved to celebrate after today's result, forget his essay, that can wait for another day.

The boys had reassembled in the bar after showering and getting ready back in college and wasted no time continuing their celebrations. They were reminiscing over their victory and talking over the highlights and indeed lowlights of the match. Naturally, Joel was getting slated for his shaky performance at the back, but praise was going to the goal scorers in their valiant efforts on the pitch. Some of the boys dropped off as the night progressed, but most stuck around ready to hit the town in the evening, and Harry did not need much convincing to head out with the team. With all his recent academic endeavours, he had not been this jubilant for a long time and dancing the night away with his pals reminded him of how much he missed this lifestyle.

Harry's head was pounding the next day as he woke up; far too many VKs were consumed last night. The dark room he found himself in felt much smaller than he remembered. Confused by the situation, Harry inspected the room further to find clothes thrown all over the floor. However, there were not just his clothes in sight, but also some women's clothing too, lying beside a used condom with its contents seeping out. It was at this moment that Harry realised that he was not in his own room and must have spent the night with a stranger. He tried to remember what had happened in the club last night, but his memory eluded him. Rolling back around revealed a petite figure whom Harry did not recognise lying asleep next to him, and he thought it best not to disturb her. Quietly making his way out of bed, a stark-naked Harry began collecting his possessions from all around the room and swiftly got changed in the darkness. Once dressed, Harry grabbed a pen and paper from the desk and wrote a note to his mystery companion. Not knowing her name, he omitted it from the note:

Hey,
Last night was great. You were asleep this morning, and I
had to rush off for a lecture.
Harry x

He left the message on the desk and crept towards the door, cautious to escape undetected. At that point, the woman rolled over, half-asleep and mumbled, 'Harry, is that you?'

Not wanting to engage in what would have undoubtedly been an awkward conversation and the possibility of having to stay around for any longer, Harry ignored the woman's call and snuck out of the room.

Harry made his way down the staircase, still absolutely clueless of his location. To make matters worse, his phone was out of battery. Leaving the building in his hungover state wearing last night's clothes, Harry was shivering as he tried to gather his bearings. He could tell by his surroundings that he was in one of the colleges but did not recognise it. He was just hoping that it was not Homerton or Girton, as that would have left him with a mammoth trek home. Still ill-informed of his whereabouts, he asked a passing student where the Porter's Lodge (or plodge as the students called it – effectively the college's reception) was, and he headed in that direction to evacuate the college as quickly as possible.

Upon arriving at the Porter's Lodge, he discovered that he was, in fact, in Pembroke College, so the walk back to Trinity would not be so long at all. His throat was parched, and he needed a drink immediately, so he headed into the newsagent next door to grab an ice-cold Oasis. It was only upon leaving the shop that his hangover was kicking in, and Harry felt a sudden urge to alleviate his bowels. Fearing being caught by his one-night stand, he decided to nip into Peterhouse College across the road to use the toilet. As a student, nobody took a second look at him as he snuck into the college on the brink of explosion. He frantically scoured the college in sheer desperation and eventually found a toilet outside of a fellow's office. It was a grim, dingy and cold toilet, but that did not matter to Harry, who felt a tremendous sense of relief as the toxins left his body. To him, excretion was a vital part of the ritual for a morning after a night out to rid a hangover, accompanied by drinking plentiful liquid and taking a cold shower.

Feeling satisfied, Harry began his journey back home. He had already missed the start of his 9am lecture and thought that the best call of action was to get back and sleep. Besides, he had a supervision in the afternoon, and given the intensity of these discussions, it was always paramount to be in top condition. After his nap, Harry felt well-rested, and he arranged to meet up with some of his pals for lunch in college. Raymond still did not want to show his face at the scene where his temper had flared a few weeks back, but Mo and Aaron were around to grab something to eat, and the trio met outside of the hall.

Battered tempura prawns were on the menu, which always went down a treat. While Harry and Mo only went for a small lunch, Aaron stocked up with extra prawns, some vegetables on the side, a side salad, a brownie for dessert and a can of diet coke to top it all off. 'What are you two looking at, it's basically free if you're using the CAMcard,' said Aaron after the two boys were staring in disbelief at how much food he was planning to eat, 'I haven't had any breakfast either,' added Aaron in an attempt to justify his colossal meal.

The boys put their trays of food on the long tables, and Harry headed over to grab some water, glasses, and condiments for the group. 'How was last night then Harry?' asked Mo as Harry finally sat down at his seat.

'It was good actually! Well, I'm assuming it was pretty good,' said Harry whilst pausing in thought, 'I can't remember much of it, I was off my face, but I've just got back from Pembroke, so it must've been good,' he said with a little grin.

'Oh, do tell,' said Aaron while scoffing down a prawn drenched in sweet chilli sauce.

'Well, there isn't really much to it,' replied Harry, 'I don't know the girl, or her name for that matter,' he gave a facial expression of distress, but beneath the surface, he was quite proud of his venture, 'she looked pretty good last night of what I can remember.'

It was at that point that Gertrude and Sabrina pulled up next to the boys plunking their trays down, 'So what are we talking about gentlemen?' asked Sabrina chirpily.

'Harry was just telling us about a lucky woman he spent last night with,' blurted Mo.

Sabrina's mood suddenly sank, and she was filled with disappointment as she responded, 'Oh, right. Well done Harry I suppose.'

Harry could tell that she was upset about his licentious activities and quickly tried to change the topic, 'Shut up will you Mo. It was nothing. What have you been up to today Sabrina?'

The group nattered on for quite some time about the stress of final year and the ever-growing pressure to succeed. They competed on who had spent the most time in the library and yearned for the end of the academic year when this stress would finally be lifted once and for all.

'Speaking of work, I've got to make a move,' said Harry picking up his satchel and now empty tray, 'I've got a supervision over in Catz and don't want to be late.' He headed on, leaving the rest of the group to continue in conversation and enjoy their break from work.

Harry made his way across the Great Court, striding past the infamous fountain, much more wrapped up than when he left Pembroke earlier. He nodded to the porters on duty as he made his way through the lodge. As he made his way past Newton's Apple Tree and headed onto Trinity Street, he pulled out a folded piece of paper from his pocket. Harry's essay was crammed onto the single piece of paper in an incredibly small font, and he began skimming through his articulated thoughts. It seems strange that he keeps his work folded up and stuffed in his pocket when he bears with him a bag designed to carry books, but this was all part of Harry's routine. He would always print out his essays and cram them into his brain right before any supervision. After all, he had submitted the essay a few days back and had forgotten some of the nuances of his work. This week's essay was on the advantages and disadvantages of microfinance as a tool for promoting economic development. It was imperative to Harry that the topic was fresh in his mind to ensure that he could deliver a masterful performance. This was what he lived for – his chance to shine. To be in the spotlight and flex his superior knowledge and creative approaches to any questions put before him. He thrived on standing out and discussing complex theoretical issues.

Harry was tranced by his work as he walked down the King's Parade towards St Catherine's College. Other pedestrians were weaving around Harry, as his eyes were fixed solely on the page. He was mid-way through his paper, refreshing his mind on housing microfinance used in Pakistan, when a voice bellowed out to him.

'Spare some change?' said a rugged man on the floor sporting an overgrown beard and tattered clothes. The man was wrapped in a sleeping blanket to protect him from the harsh autumnal wind and had an old McDonald's cup to collect money.

Harry had walked a few paces beyond the man when he stopped and folded his paper closed. He walked back slowly towards the man and pulled out his wallet. A twenty-pound note was staring at Harry as he opened his wallet, but he ignored this and unbuttoned the coinage compartment. He shook his brown leather wallet around and pulled out a quid. 'Here you go bud,' said Harry as he leaned down to give the man the coin.

'Thank you, sir!' said the beggar.

But as Harry made his way back up, he saw how little was already in his cup. A few coppers and some other small denominations of change. Seeing this made Harry empathise with the struggles of the homeless man. He knew that the man was not begging by choice and would have been through some hardships in his life. 'Actually, here, take this,' said Harry as he drew out the pink note.

The man's face lit up, 'Thank you! Thank you so much! That is incredibly generous of you.' Harry smiled in response and pulled out his essay once again. 'You have a great day sir!' shouted the man who had now risen to his feet.

Harry always had time for other people, regardless of who they were and knew that the money would help make that man's life a lot better than it could make his own. Harry continued in stride and picked up where he had left off with his essay.

Harry had just about finished reading through his essay as he made his way up the staircase towards his supervisor's room. He could hear indistinct chatter coming from above, which was slowly becoming clearer as he ascended. He folded the paper away and stuffed it back into his pocket, not wanting his fellow course mates to see him cramming in information minutes before the supervision.

Harry awkwardly greeted the two girls, who fell silent at his arrival. It would be a stretch to say that they were his friends; rather, they were acquaintances. They could engage in deep discussion and riveting debates about the economy in a controlled environment, yet trivial conversation was always just that little bit uncomfortable when waiting outside for the supervision to commence. The three of them now stood in silence, waiting for the current session to end so that they could displace their fellow students hidden beyond the door. Strangely, Harry had spent so much time in the proximity of these two girls, from lectures to supervisions, he had likely even been in nightclubs with them, but he did not know anything about them in the slightest.

The previous supervision had overrun by a few minutes, but eventually, it was time for Harry's group to enter the arena; and what an arena it was. This was a true Cambridge seminar room. Bookcases spread around the entire room, filled with ancient books. It was clear that some of these books had not been read in hundreds of years, but their atavism served to complement the aesthetics of the room. An array of heterogeneous sofas and armchairs were set up around a fireplace, each unique and looking as if they had their own stories to tell. The grand piano in the corner added to the subtle extravagance of the place. The room was incredibly cosy, yet the menacing look of the professor in his dated double-breasted black suit created an intimidating environment. The ageing man did not rise to greet his students, in fact, he did not say anything, just making eye contact with each individual and waiting for them to take a seat. As Harry stared back at him, he thought that the supervisor looked as if he did not have a musical bone in his body but knew never to underestimate anyone in Cambridge, for they always seem to have secret talents and obscure capabilities.

Once the three students had settled down, Professor Williams, a northern academic who had devoted his life to studying the power imbalance between the north and the south in the UK, finally broke the silence, 'Who are you?' he asked rudely and openly to the group.

'I'm Harry Baldwin.'

'Yes, I know who you are Harry,' interrupted Williams, 'You two, names?' he asked once more. Harry was not sure whether to take it as a compliment that the professor knew who he was. Normally he would have been ecstatic to be the one that is known, but the sharp tone and snappy voice of the professor made Harry take this remark as somewhat of an insult.

'Diya Patel,' said the girl sitting on the sofa opposite Harry. *Ahh, that's her name*, thought Harry.

'And erm… my name is erm… Sarah Valentine,' whispered the last girl, who was clearly petrified for the hour ahead.

'Speak up girl,' roared Williams in frustration.

'Sarah Valentine,' she said louder but still lacking confidence. The supervisor was jotting down the names on some scrap paper, clearly some sort of register to tick off those who he had seen today.

'Let me grab your essays,' said Williams as he reached down towards an untidy stack of papers, sifting through to try and find the names he had just jotted down. He leant over and handed the first one to Diya, 'Disappointing,' he said without any remorse. Diya's face sunk as she saw 2.ii scribbled in red ink at the top of her essay. 'Sarah, here you go,' said Williams, handing over her essay. Harry peeked over, always curious about how other students got on, but she kept her paper very close to her chest, and he could not quite make out the mark at the top of it. Despite being a shy individual, Harry knew that she was smart on paper, so no doubt it would have been a strong essay. Harry had been so focused on trying to see her mark that he ignored William's outstretched arm. It was not until he barked his name that Harry took his essay off of his supervisor. The lack of communication between Harry and Williams would give off the impression of a poor result, but when Harry looked at the top of the page, he saw that he had received a first-class result. This was no surprise for Harry, who had been used to achieving the highest grades with quite some ease. However, he was always particularly chuffed when he got a first from Williams since he is renowned for being a harsh marker.

'Right, well let's get started then,' said Williams. The two girls reached into their bags and pulled out their laptops to take notes on. Harry, on the other hand, was more old-school, opting to use a leather bounded notepad and an ink pen. He thoroughly believed that he could remember anything that he had physically written down far better than when he mindlessly types away on a computer. Professor Williams had begun proceedings with a ruthless ploy by asking Diya to start by discussing her essay. This was an inevitable trap and one with no escape for the poor girl. She had got no further than her introduction when the supervisor had already begun to shoot her down, contradicting everything she had said, digging deep into the flaws in her arguments. Williams had spent about ten minutes tormenting the girl, who was clearly desperate to get out of this situation until eventually he was bored of tearing Diya's work apart.

The other two students summarised their work, Harry somewhat more confidently and coherently than Sarah. After the earlier bloodbath, both were extremely cautious not to put a foot out of line and leave themselves exposed to William's wrath. Unlike many students, Harry truly loved the theoretical discussions in supervisions, always striving to push his intellect further. This was actually one of the things that he relished most about Cambridge, going toe to toe with some of the world's leading academics. He loved this space in supervisions to explore his own thoughts and learn new things. This was far better than the mind-numbing lectures, which lacked the engagement that Harry sought in education. These intense meetings were a chance for Harry to go above and beyond what is expected on the course. His fellow students may have loathed how much he venerated this environment, as they always tended to look bad in his company, but this was his theatre. They were his audience. He was the star of the show. He never held back; he never shied away.

While the time flew for Harry, the supervision felt like it was never-ending for Diya, who had not spoken since her interrogation. In fact, the tutorial somewhat resembled one of Blair's bilateral meetings. Instead of being an open discussion, it became more of a competition of wits between Harry and Williams. The two girls typed frantically away to get down everything that the pair said as if they were stenographers in a courtroom. They would be leaving the room with pages of notes. On the other hand, Harry had not written a single word, with just the title heading a blank page. The supervision ended up going far beyond the allotted hour, with Harry and Wilson losing track of time in their deliberations. It was not until there was a knock on the door that the pair finally broke their heated debate.

'Yes, yes, we're finishing up now,' shouted Williams to the group awaiting their session outside the door. 'Well, we had better end it there,' he said, now speaking to the three students in the room. Diya and Sarah were quick to pack up their belongings and rush off without any delay. Harry, in no hurry, put his notebook back in his satchel and chucked on his jacket. 'Exquisite work today Harry,' said Williams shaking the young student's hand. It was the first time that he had ever recalled getting a compliment from his professor.

'Thank you, professor. Your supervisions are always a pleasure. I look forward to seeing you again in two weeks,' responded Harry with a straight face. It was not until after Harry had left the room that he broke out a huge smile, grinning from ear to ear. The students waiting outside of the room looked perplexed at his enthusiasm. Nobody ever left a supervision with Professor Williams with a smile. He marched on past the next set of course mates without saying a word.

The sun had now broken through, showing the true beauty

of St Catherine's, and immediately after Harry had left the college, he lit up a cigarette to ease the tension in his body. He could now finally relax and allow his performance to sink in as he walked merrily back home.

- 9 -

The second Saturday in November had been a miserable day. The weather was somewhat undecided on whether to spit raindrops or just darken the city with deep grey clouds. There was no prospect of sunshine, but that did not matter to Harry. Not even the drizzle could dampen his spirits today, for it was the day that he turned twenty-two years old, and he was filled with excitement. He had been woken early by Raymond, who came waltzing into his room with a fresh fruit salad, bursting with bright colours, while singing an out of tune rendition of *Happy Birthday*. He went out for a boozy brunch with his friends from college at The Ivy, where no expense was spared. It was nice to dress up in a suit and feel like a king on his birthday. While dining at a fancy restaurant was a pleasant treat, Harry was most excited by his home friends coming up for the evening. It had been about six weeks since he had seen any of them, and he could not wait to have a big old sesh with them in Cambridge. He had worked relentlessly over the past couple of weeks to justify taking his birthday weekend off as he just wanted to focus on his mates when they came up.

Harry went to *Mainsbury's* (Cambridge's main Sainsbury's) to pick up the essentials for the evening. Two bottles of spiced rum, some mixers, and a large crate of Fosters (he was still a student, after all, so he did not splash out on the expensive beers). It took a monumental effort to lug the liquid back to his accommodation. He placed the mixers and all bar two of the beers into the fridge to get nicely chilled. He chucked the other two beers directly in the freezer with the rum, as he wanted a drink now. After he showered and got ready for the evening, he headed back to the freezer, grabbed a now ice-cold lager, and went back to his room for a facetime with his parents. Naturally, his mum was concerned that he was drinking beer at 3pm, but Harry ignored her remarks, knowing that there was little she could do to stop him from all the way back in London. His parents wished him a Happy Birthday and were melancholic that they could not see him on his special day. They were perturbed that their youngest son had grown up and now enjoyed the company of his friends more than his parents (or at least that is how they saw it). However, they insisted that they would come up next weekend for a belated celebration in lieu of today. Not long after Harry had finished speaking with his parents did his phone vibrate once more. It was a message from Daniel.

We've just parked up! Walking over to your college now mate.

He jumped off of his desk chair with vim and vigour, finishing off his beer before heading to the Porter's Lodge to meet them. Harry had polished off a fair few drinks already but certainly was not showing any signs of slowing down. He made his way through the main gate and saw his two mates looking a bit lost outside the college. Daniel was on the phone, clearly calling Harry to let him know that they were outside, but Harry ignored the vibrating phone in his pocket. 'Yes fellas!' he shouted, and they turned towards him. It was now clear to Harry who the other figure was, Daniel must have given Michael a lift up.

'Oi, oi, Happy Birthday Sunshine,' said Michael, who was looking even lankier since the pair had last seen each other. Harry was almost worried when they embraced that he might snap him in half if he squeezed too tight. Harry went over and hugged Daniel too after he had put his phone back in his pocket.

'Here you are, let me give you a hand with those,' said Harry, who picked up the boy's bags, leaving them with their beers to carry. 'Are you sure you've packed enough for the night?' he joked to Michael, who had an excessive amount of luggage.

'Yeah, well the thing is, I needed to take a couple of different outfits as I wasn't sure what to wear. Like, I dunno what the vibe is. Was torn between a jumper or a t-shirt and didn't know whether to go for my blue jeans or ripped jeans. Plus, I need all of my hair stuff for after my shower,' said Michael.

'Christ, did you pack your tampons too yeah?' remarked Harry, which was met by a snigger from Daniel. Harry had given them strict instructions not to act suspicious when going past the porters, and the pair remained silent as they went through the lodge. The college was preposterously strict about guests. Students were expected to sign any visitors in and were limited to one guest at a time. However, Harry had invited far more people to come and stay than that. In fact, he was not actually too sure as to who was coming up in the end. Since most of his friends had been students, they did not mind slumming it and sleeping on the floor for the night to save them booking a hotel or Airbnb.

The boys successfully made it past the porters undetected and walked out onto the cobblestone path. 'Fuck me, this is alright isn't it!' exclaimed Daniel while staring out at Trinity in all of its glory, 'This is where you live?' he asked rhetorically. This was the first time Daniel had been up to visit Harry in Cambridge and was absolutely startled by it. In contrast, Michael had been up many times to visit in an attempt to live the student lifestyle that he missed out on by going straight to work after school. However, Cambridge offers no ordinary student experience. Its quirks and traditions make the university so unique. It is what makes it the second-best university in the country, behind Oxford, of course.

'Wait until you see people storming around in their gowns,' said Michael, who thought himself a bit of an expert on Cambridge culture. However, even Michael had only been exposed to a fraction of the weird and wonderful events that take place in the city.

'Can we all wear a gown when we go out tonight?' jested Daniel. Harry just shook his head and started chortling along with the other two.

The boys got to Harry's room and were amazed at his *student accommodation*. Daniel put his beers on the floor by the door and invited himself around for a tour of the place. Like a child, he was running around, touching whatever he saw. Daniel ran his hand along the mantlepiece, tried out the sofa for comfort; he was even fascinated by the heavy velour curtains of all things. Eventually, he made his way over to the bedroom, and when he opened the door, he could not believe what he saw hanging on the back of it. His jaw dropped, and his eye opened wide. Daniel did not say anything. He just grabbed it and flung it on over his back. He darted back across the room, jumped on the table and shouted with sheer excitement, 'Look at me, I'm Harry Potter,' while flicking an imaginary wand to mimic the wizard casting a spell. Harry could not help but burst out laughing. He had forgotten how jejune but entertaining his home friends could be. Of course, Daniel would love Harry's gown. Harry had missed mucking around with his home mates and could not wait for the night ahead.

Harry's friends arrived in dribs and drabs from all over the country over the next few hours, some by train, others instead opting to drive. Alfie, one of Harry's newer friends, who had only joined the close-knit group about three years ago, made a four-hour trip the whole way from Newcastle. The train ticket from where he studied would certainly have set him back a fair few pounds, but he would never miss a link-up with all the boys. The room slowly started to clutter up with bags, and the drinking had commenced as soon as people set foot in the room. There was no time to waste in catching up with each other. This was predominantly the reason why all the men made the journey to Cambridge, not necessarily to celebrate Harry's birthday, but because it felt that as they grew older, they saw less and less of each other as everyone drifted off doing their own thing. Only John bought Harry a birthday present, the rest of them claiming that their presence was the best present Harry could ask for. Indeed, Harry did not care for materialistic things; he was just content to have his friends up with him today.

As the night ticked on, the boys were getting stuck into an array of different drinking games, and their behaviour became increasingly raucous. The tunes were ablaze, and undoubtedly the group would be disturbing anyone trying to study in rooms nearby. But Harry did not care; it was his birthday after all. He jumped up onto his table and managed to grab everyone's attention to run through the night's itinerary. 'Gentlemen, gather around,' the seven others around him fell silent, paying respect to Harry, perhaps just because it was his birthday, but nonetheless, he proceeded, 'the plan is simple. We get drunk!' Which was met by a collective cheer, 'We go clubbing.' Another group cheer, 'We get food,' fists were being pumped as the group cheered along as a support act, 'We go home.' This last item on the agenda had not been met with the same eagerness and enthusiasm. Instead, it had been greeted with a chorus of boos and jeers. Harry paused to allow the dissatisfaction to sink in, before shouting, 'But then we drink more when we come back home!' This was met by the loudest response yet to really gear all the boys up for the night ahead.

The group continued on their mission to become intoxicated. The boys were drinking an assortment of different concoctions to get as drunk as possible for as cheap as possible. This was a vital part of any night out; only a fool would be caught paying excessive amounts to get drunk in the club. As the time crept towards 10pm, Harry thought that now was a suitable time to head to the nightclub. In most other cities across the country, one would not dare to enter a club before midnight, but things are done differently in Cambridge. The nights start a lot earlier and end earlier too, as if it was tailored for the students, to allow them to go clubbing, but also make their 9am lectures the next day. However, it was a Saturday, and Harry had no worries whatsoever about studying the next day. He was taking the boys to Cindies, Cambridge's 'best' nightclub. For all the things they have got right in the city, it falls far short with its nightlife. The club was grimy and dingy, boasting two unimpressively small rooms. But it was where all the students went, although Saturdays tended to be more of a local's night. However, Harry made sure not to tell his friends this information in fear that it may deter them from coming to visit.

Everyone made one last drink for the road and got ready to leave. It was at this moment that Daniel blurted out, 'Oh shit, where's Paisán?' The boys looked around in disbelief. They had been having such a good time that they had not realised that Garcia Paisán was not present.

Alfie pulled out his phone and remarked, 'I've got a message from him saying he is five minutes away.'

'Oh right, we'll just wait for him then,' said Harry.

'Yeah, but he sent me this message twenty-five minutes ago,' said Alfie in utter hysterics. This was typical Paisán, always late for everything. He had somehow managed to arrive over six hours after the first guests. Harry could not wait to hear what excuse he would pull out this time. The rest of the boys were hedging their bets on why he would claim to be late. From train delays to babysitting to being stuck at work, everyone came up with their own guesses.

'Right, let's just crack on,' said Harry, 'tell him to meet us outside of the Porter's Lodge.' He did not have the patience to be waiting around all night for Paisán. The herd of boys bounced their way through college, and Harry had to remind them to turn it down a notch when they went through the lodge. But in their drunken state, it was far from easy to listen to Harry's command, as they proceeded to be rowdy.

A figure was jogging over to the group, and despite the dark, Duncan, who had travelled with Harry with on his gap year, had just about made it out to be Paisán. 'What sort of time do you call this fella?' asked Duncan, a tall boy with slicked jet-black hair, with just a bit too much gel in it. Rocking a salmon pink Tommy Hilfiger shirt with dark grey suit trousers, Duncan was far overdressed for the evening, and the boys were sure to let him know this.

'Ah mate, it was a nightmare,' said Paisán in a Spanish accent, 'basically, I had to get a trim, but my barber wasn't working today. I phoned him up, but he wasn't answering my calls. So, I had to go to his house and knock on his door. It was so long man,' whined Paisán.

'Who had getting a haircut down as their bet!' yelled Michael, with the rest of the group breaking out into laughter.

'I haven't even had time to pick up any drink. Do we pass a shop on the way?' asked Paisán.

'Nah mate, we actually don't,' said Harry, 'but here, have this,' he said, passing him an unopened can of beer.

'Got anything a little stronger? I'm sober as a judge,' said Paisán. Harry nodded and pulled out his hip flask from his back pocket. Paisán unscrewed the lid and winced as he took a sip. 'That hits the spot,' he said.

The group made their way down Trinity street, and Harry

thought that he would take them down a more scenic route past King's College to see the chapel, unequivocally the landmark building in the city. He enjoyed being the impromptu tour guide and telling them a few useless facts about the place. 'King's College was founded in 1441 by Henry VI, just one year after he founded its sister college in Eton. Originally, the college was just for Etonians, and it wasn't until 1865 that other people were allowed to study here,' said Harry. A couple of people in the group were interested in what he had to say, but most were too drunk to listen to all of Harry's nonsense. He continued to spew out the facts anyway, 'In the 2012-13 academic year, the college's annual wine budget was over three hundred and thirty-eight thousand pounds.'

'Let's go and raid their wine cellars then,' shouted Alfie, 'I'm sure we can find some booze for Paisán in there.'

'Well, I wouldn't do that if I was you, you aren't even allowed to walk on the college's lawns, let alone raid the bloody cellar,' replied Harry.

Taking this almost as a challenge, Alfie leapt straight over the low-lying wall and ran onto the lawn beneath the chapel, 'Doesn't look like there's much that they can do to stop me,' slurred Alfie, waggling his hands in the air.

Suddenly, two porters emerged from the lodge and shouted, 'Oi! Get off of the grass,' while running over to the group of boys. It was at this point that the boys knew they were in trouble. Panicking and not knowing how to react, they turned around and started sprinting away from the college staff, dispersing in all directions. They ran without any delay, not even daring to look back. However, the porters had succeeded in their goal of shooing away the delinquents.

The boys had been split up into different groups. Duncan and Daniel stuck with Harry, and Harry thought it was best to send a message into the group chat to assemble them again. He told them all to meet in the market square and shared his location for the others to find them. 'Well, that'll certainly keep us fit,' said Duncan.

'Really didn't fancy doing any exercise except dancing on my birthday, if I'm being perfectly honest,' said Harry.

Daniel was not too stressed by the whole ordeal and was receiving a call, presumably from one of the other boys. He answered it and started to drift off from the other two. Slowly the boys arrived in the market square and were all breathlessly discussing the events that had just happened. No surprise, Paisán turned up last with John ten minutes later than the rest of the boys, who had somehow managed to get themselves a bottle of Disaronno to Harry's shock.

'Where on earth did you manage to get that?' asked Harry.

'Well, when we ran away, we just kept running and we ended up going past a Sainsbury's,' said a chuffed Paisán.

'You had better drink up,' said Harry, 'the club is just around the corner.'

After their adventure, the group made their way towards Cindies, subtly finishing off whatever drinks they had left in the queue, cautious not to have them confiscated by the bouncers. It was only when the boys were nearing the front of the queue that Harry noticed that Daniel had just hung up the phone. All of the boys were together, so it must not have been one of them that he was talking to. Harry made his way to Daniel at the back of the group, 'Is everything okay mate?'

'Yeah, everything is good,' Daniel replied, clearly not wanting to get bogged down on the details.

Harry was curious and persisted, 'Who was that then?'

'It was just my sister. She's basically got into a massive fight with her boyfriend and is a bit upset,' said Daniel sheepishly.

Harry's eyes lit up, 'Ah that's not good to hear. Have they broken up or something?' He spoke with a little too much excitement and quickly wiped the smile from his face to hide his emotions.

'Nah, nah, they just had an argument. I think she said that she's going to go out with the girls tonight to blow off some steam. I think they've been struggling a bit with the distance, that's all,' replied Daniel solemnly.

Harry was a bit disappointed to hear that they were still together. He thought now was the perfect chance to start something with Elizabeth, but that was clearly not the case, 'Fair enough mate, I'm sure she'll be just fine. Now let's get in, get some drinks down us and boogey the night away. It's my birthday so you're buying the first round.'

The boys had made it into the club, and amazingly, nobody was turned away for being too drunk and disorderly. The club was heaving, and the beating music sent vibrations pulsating through Harry's body. The group headed directly to the bar to sort out some beverages. Rather than doing one big round, they split up into smaller drinking groups. Harry could tell who the experienced clubbers were against those who simply did not have a clue. Naturally, his choice of poison was an Orange VK, a drink widely recognised as the symbol of the student. Plus, it was four for a tenner, so you really could not go wrong. It had the sugar to keep energy levels up on the dancefloor while having the same ABV as a beer, so you would get just as drunk in the process. The plastic bottles made them an ideal drink to hold while chucking some shapes and meant that you could just drop the empty bottle on the ground when finished with it – an absolute no brainer. However, Michael, who was a bit more inexperienced, opted for a draft lager. While it may be a stellar choice in a pub, the contents of his glass were being spilt everywhere as he tried to barge his way through the crowd – a rookie error from the kid.

The group had occupied a space right in the centre of the dancefloor and really made it their own by forming a sizeable circle. They took it in turns to jump into the middle of the ring and show off their questionable unrhythmic moves. It did not matter to them what they looked like to others since they did not know anyone else around them. They were just here for a good time. It was only Harry that may bump into someone he knew, but he was far too drunk to care what anyone thought of him.

After working up a sweat from a mixture of dancing and lack of ventilation in the club, the boys had the urge for some fresh air. Or rather, the smokers in the group wanted a cigarette and a chance to chat up some Cambridge girls outside. Harry was handing out the cancer sticks to all the part-timers, those who called themselves 'social smokers', but somehow never managed to buy a packet of cigarettes themselves. In their inebriated state, nearly all of the boys decided that they wanted to get involved. Daniel went up to a stranger and asked if he would take a picture of the boys, and within a few seconds, they were all arranged for the shot. Harry looked over and saw Michael and Duncan immediately putting their hands behind their back to hide the fact that they were smoking. They lived in constant fear of their parents finding out about their nasty habit and could not possibly take the chance of being photographed with a cigarette in their hand. They had family members on Facebook and were concerned that this might somehow leak back to them. Harry thought it was ridiculous that they would blissfully be photographed off their rocker but had an irrational fear of being caught smoking. He considered calling them out on it in front of the group but thought better of it, not wanting any drama on his birthday.

Harry had finished his potation and his cigarette and realised that it was probably his turn to grab some drinks. He decided to go to the bar on a solo mission as he knew that it would be a much faster way to get service. Leaving the group chatting outside, he headed back inside, making his way once more through the busy crowds. He had finally shoved his way to the front of the bar, where to his surprise, he saw a familiar face standing next to him. It was Elizabeth. She looked absolutely stunning as per usual.

'Hey, how's it going?' shouted Harry in order to be heard over the blaring music.

She smiled at the sight of Harry and leaned towards his ear to avoid having to yell, 'I'm good.'

Harry saw this movement towards him as some sort of a sign of interest, so asked Elizabeth, 'Can I buy you a drink?'

Elizabeth leaned in once more, and Harry thought that he was in luck. 'I'd rather have the money,' she said. The bartender handed her the drink that she had been waiting for. She waved at Harry and turned away to make her way back onto the dancefloor. The bartender looked over to Harry, awaiting his order, but Harry did not want a drink; he wanted Elizabeth.

Harry turned away from the bar and went in pursuit of Elizabeth. He was looking frantically for her and eventually, whilst scanning the dancefloor, saw her curly blonde hair. She was alone and seemed to be looking out for her friends. Harry rushed straight over to the lost girl without formulating a plan of what he wanted to achieve. It seemed frighteningly apparent that she was not interested in him, but that just added to the challenge for Harry, making it a more desirable goal. He tapped her on the shoulder, and she smiled when she saw him.

'What do you want?' said Elizabeth.

'Just one dance with you,' he said with a smirk.

Secretly she was giddy that Harry came after her, and she nodded in consent. The DJ was playing a slow RnB song, and Elizabeth was moving her hips mesmerizingly. She could dance, and she was not afraid to show it. Harry was focused on ensuring that his dance moves were more palatable than earlier in the night, eager to impress Elizabeth. Harry smoothly put his hands on her waist and danced in synchronisation with the flawless woman, slowly pulling her towards him. Their bodies were now rubbing up against each other, and this had gone slightly beyond a platonic dance. Elizabeth raised her hands, linking them around Harry's neck, and stared deep into his eyes. This was it. This was his moment. Fearlessly, Harry leant in and touched Elizabeth's lips with his own. He had made the leap. Initially, Elizabeth was reluctant but eased in to greet his warm presence. The dancing between them had come almost to a halt; instead, it was now Harry's tongue that was slowly dancing away in Elizabeth's mouth.

Realising what she was doing, Elizabeth suddenly pushed Harry away in a panic. She would never have kissed him if it was not for that stupid quarrel with her boyfriend. It was not a long kiss, a few seconds at most, but Elizabeth instantly regretted what she had done. Not knowing how to react, she turned away from Harry to vanish into the horde. How could she have been so unfaithful to Matt? Harry shouted after her, but it was to no avail. His voice was drowned by the overbearing music. He again went to chase after her, and it was at this point he bumped into a stumbling drunk Daniel.

'Where are the drinks at man?' asked Daniel. Harry knew he could not go after her; the last thing he wanted in the world right now was Daniel to find out that he had just kissed his sister.

- 10 -

The drinking throughout the night had been incessant, damaging not only the boy's brains but also their wallets. There is no doubt that they would have spent the night partying away in Cindies until close, if it was not for Michael going overboard and throwing up outside in the smoking area. The bouncers kicked Michael out for his antics, and rather than leaving him to suffer alone in the cold, the boys decided that it was right to call it a night in the early hours of Sunday morning.

'Come on Michael,' said John, 'let's get you some food.'

Michael was staggering around, so John ran over to him and insisted that he put his arm around him for support, 'I'm not even drunk,' slurred Michael.

Despite the mess of the man, John knew that there was nothing to be gained by disagreeing. Instead, he entertained him, 'I know mate, I know.'

The boys made their way out of the club and headed down the stairs onto Petty Cury street, an empty pedestrianised road lined with shops that were all now closed for the night. As with any night out, the men were ravenous and eager to get some greasy food in them as soon as possible. While some of the group wanted to go to McDonald's, Harry had insisted that they try the local delicacy, where all Cambridge students go. Students tend to be split between two late-night eateries for food, a glorified Greek chicken shop, Gardies, and a trailer in the market square, Van of Life. While the trailer seemed a bit makeshift, it had been serving drunk students for almost thirty years and provided more of an authentic Cambridge experience. Harry played the 'birthday card' and managed to persuade his friends to dine from the dark blue van. He recommended cheesy chips, and if the boys were feeling a bit more adventurous to get it smothered in gravy.

It was not until the boys were halfway to their destination that Harry realised that one of his friends was missing. It appeared that Duncan must have had some success in Cindies and would not be slumming it in the room with the other seven tonight.

Daniel was scrolling through his phone when he suddenly remarked, 'Oh no way,' he paused while the others turned and looked at him, 'it turns out my sister was still in that club with us. I must have just missed her.'

Pouncing on the opportunity to see Elizabeth again, Harry quickly jumped in, 'Well, why don't you ask her to meet us at Van of Life and grab some food.' Daniel typed away to his sister, who probably would not reply if she was in the club with her friends.

The boys had finally reached the trailer and were met with an orderly yet long queue of students. With nothing else to do, they joined the back and discussed what they were going to order. Alfie was bouncing around filled with energy, clearly still over-intoxicated and not ready for the night to end. Harry told the boys that the van was cash only, which sent three of them to the back of a different line to withdraw money from a nearby ATM.

After Paisán and Alfie had taken their money from the machine, it was at last John's turn. Alfie was lurking behind his friend as he typed in his pin. No sooner did John finish typing in the last digit did Alfie swiftly reached around him and hit the 'Withdraw £200' button on the screen and confirmed the transaction before John could even react. Alfie let out a high-pitched cackle at the mischief he had managed. John was fuming that he had been mugged off but stayed reserved. It was not as if any harm had been done. It was just an inconvenience and, quite frankly, a bit of a worry to be carrying around so much money.

The boys, now with cash to hand, re-joined the others near the front of the queue, leaving punters behind annoyed at them pushing in. Alfie and Paisán did not care, but John, feeling a sense of guilt, slowly waddled to the back of the line.

'So, what did Elizabeth say?' asked Harry.

'Let me check,' said Daniel as he pulled out his phone. He read the message on his lock screen out loud, quickly deciphering the typos from his drunken sister as he went along, 'Hey bro, I decided that it was best just to go straight back to Girton. In cab with friends. Bye.'

Harry was clearly disappointed by this message, 'Ah, that's a shame.'

'Nah, not really,' said Daniel, 'I'm going to get lunch with her tomorrow before I leave.' Harry had meant more that it was a shame for himself. He really wanted to see her. Of course, Harry had no idea what he would actually say to her; he had not thought that far ahead, but he just wanted to know what was going on. He could not believe that he had finally kissed her, and now that he had a taste, he wanted more. The uncertainty was killing him.

All of the boys, bar John, now had their food from the truck, with most of them taking Harry's suggestion of cheesy chips. Paisán went rogue with a vegetable quesadilla, and Daniel, watching his weight, decided to completely skip out on the late-night snack. Alfie was running around like the menace he was, stealing chips from his friends despite having his own large portion. Although Alfie tried to be sneaky, in his inebriated state he was far from discrete in his ventures, and the other boys were beginning to find him a bit of a nuisance as they tried to peacefully eat their food. Michael was monotonously getting through his chips, his face almost buried in the gravy, utterly oblivious to his surroundings, making him an easy target for chip theft. Neither did Michael notice or care about Alfie's actions since he was so focused on getting his chips into his mouth, using the carbs to aid his long journey back to sobriety. While the group were nattering away, reminiscing over the events of the evening, Harry spotted something out of the corner of his eye. Two men were intimidatingly towering over a man on the floor, giving him abuse for begging on the streets. Harry recognised the overgrown rugged beard of the homeless man; it was the same man he gave twenty pounds to not so long ago.

Harry was disgusted at the way the two bullies were

tormenting the vagrant and ran over to do something about it. 'Leave him alone,' barked Harry.

'Listen mate, I've had enough of all these beggars on our streets. Trying to take my hard-earned money,' said one of the men in a husky voice. It was clear to Harry that this was not a Cambridge student; rather, it was a local (or 'townie' as the students called them). These townies had a reputation for being rough around the edges and disliking the students who thought they owned the place. The clashing rivalry between the two groups, 'Town vs Gown', could be seen frequently on nights out.

Harry tried to diffuse the situation and persuade the two locals to leave the beggar alone, but it was clear that they were riled up and had an agenda against the homeless. 'Look, he's clearly been through some hard times, there's no need to make things any worse for him,' said Harry in a calming voice. Harry's friends had come over to the scene, perhaps out of curiosity, but nevertheless were now there in support. 'There is nothing to be gained from belittling him further, just walk on,' urged Harry. It seemed that he had finally got through to the two men, or perhaps they stood down given the escalated situation.

The two men turned around and started to walk away from the scene. Harry immediately breathed a sigh of relief that things had not spiralled out of control. He turned the other way to gather John, who had only just been given his box of chips. The men were only a couple of paces away when Alfie chirped up, 'Yeah that's right, jog on lads,' in a cheeky manner. Perhaps the two men would have let that remark slip if it was not for the fact that when they turned around, Alfie was staring straight at them with a middle finger held firmly towards them.

This obscene hand gesture was the catalyst – converting the men's anger into action. One of the men turned back with his fists clenched and headed towards Alfie, who was too drunk to realise what was happening. He pulled a grimacing face and, with an almighty swing, threw a firm punch, connecting full-on with Alfie's jaw. The sheer force of the blow sent Alfie's box of chips flying through the air and pouring down like heavy rain onto the floor. Replicating his chips, Alfie was also sent through the night's sky and landed on the concrete with a heavy thud.

Realising that they were outnumbered, the two men immediately took off after this sucker punch, fleeing from the scene that had unravelled in a flash before them. Caring more about their friend's well-being than seeking vengeance, the boys immediately rushed around Alfie to comfort him. Alfie was discombobulated and could not truly comprehend what had just happened. He screamed in agony, despite the alcohol acting as a painkiller. When he was eventually lifted to his feet, probably not the wisest move from his friends in hindsight, his jaw was completely displaced, hanging loose over on the right side of his face. Blood was dripping viciously from his mouth, splattering on the cold floor, and from a quick inspection, Harry saw that he had a chipped front tooth.

'Right, we need to get him to a hospital,' remarked Harry, who had somehow managed to keep a cool head despite the distressing event.

'Well, we surely don't all need to go,' remarked Paisán.

'You're right,' said Harry, 'look we just need one other to go with him to make sure he's alright, you can just jump in a taxi to the hospital, it's not far.' He looked around at his friends, but they were all avoiding eye contact, shying away from responsibilities as they now wanted nothing more than to be back in Harry's warm room and heading to bed. 'Well, I obviously need to go back to the room, I don't trust leaving you lot alone in there. God knows what you'll get up to. And we can't send Michael, look at the state of the man,' he said pointing over to Michael, who was drunk as a stick, walking around in circles, staring at his feet and mumbling gibberish to himself.

Alfie groaned away in pain, clutching onto his jaw as if it was going to fall off any moment. There was a prolonged silence as nobody wanted to spend the next few hours waiting in A&E. Finally, John stepped in to fill the void and tentatively said, 'Fine, I'll do it.' John was still annoyed at Alfie for making him withdraw £200 earlier, and in some ways thought that his injury was a form of instant karma, but John could not believe that he was the one stuck taking him for medical assistance.

'Great,' said Harry, who directed them to the taxis lined up outside the nightclub they had come from.

The group split and went their separate ways. This was not the ending to the night that anyone had hoped for.

11

It had been an uncomfortable night's sleep for the boys, four of them had bundled into Harry's bed, and the day started far too early for any of their liking. Harry checked his phone and saw that he had five missed calls from John and a message reading:

> *Tried calling, but you must be asleep. I wanted to come back but will just spend the night here with Alfie. He's broken his jaw and will need surgery tomorrow.*

Harry would have felt a sense of guilt for not picking up his phone, but his raging hangover was the only thing occupying his mind. The boys rose in waves, some taking showers, while others opted for a little longer in bed. They headed to the hall to get some brunch down them before splitting up to do their own things. Michael decided that it was best to just get the train home since he wanted to be fresh for work on Monday, and Daniel went to meet his sister for lunch. There was still no word from Duncan, who presumably was still with his new found lover (either that or his phone had died, and he had no way of contacting the others). It was just Paisán and Harry who ended up getting a taxi to see Alfie in the hospital.

En route, they picked up some Lucozade and grapes for Alfie, as one does when someone is in hospital. Yet, funnily enough, he was in no mood for eating or drinking given the state of his jaw, so they just shared the treats among themselves and John. Alfie was gutted when the boys came to see them. He informed Paisán and Harry that he was going to have surgery to fix his jaw and that his parents were on their way up to take him back home once the procedure was done. Alfie's parents were naturally mortified at what had happened to their youngest child and certainly did not want him travelling back up to Newcastle for his post-op recovery.

It was always an eventful occasion when Harry was with his home friends and his birthday weekend was no exception. Getting a little stressed that he had not done any university work in a while, Harry headed back to college and sent the remaining boys on their way. Except Duncan who showed up in the late afternoon to pick up his belongings and shared quite some stories about his venture with a girl from Downing College.

Another year older, another year wiser; Harry's birthday had come and gone once again. However, there was no time to dwell on his ageing years, he had to revert his focus back to his studies. We all know how Steven Toope loves his academic rigour, and Harry's ambition was to never disappoint the Vice-Chancellor of the university. As the days ticked by, Harry struggled to readjust back to his usual academic prowess. Having his home friends up was a form of escapism from the illusive Cambridge bubble. His essays were taking far longer to write, and his concentration was no longer there. Harry yearned for the real world where he could finally reap the rewards of his studies. But he was not there yet, only seven more months until freedom.

***

'Come on, let's get a move on. We're going to be late if we don't leave now,' said Mo, nagging Harry to walk with him to their Economics lecture. This week they had a guest lecturer, Daron Acemoglu, an infamous Turkish economist from MIT, who would be talking about his book *Why Nations Fail*. Mo was animated and did not want to miss out on this opportunity. Unfortunately, his enthusiasm was not shared by Harry.

Harry was nose-deep in a textbook, with his possessions spewed across the table in the college bar. He sat comfortably on the sofa, showing no signs of a man in a rush, 'Yeah, I'll meet you there,' said Harry, 'I'm going to finish up with the reading for the Macro essay.' Mo was disappointed by his response, knowing that in all likelihood, this would be another lecture where Harry would play truant. Mo wasted no time storming out of the college bar towards the city centre.

Harry's attitude towards attending lectures was at a complete juxtaposition to Mo's. Harry only attended if he thought the topic was particularly interesting. Mo was a religious attendee who had not missed a single lecture in his three years at university. Mo treated them as compulsory, yet Harry preferred to learn directly from books instead of people talking about such texts. He saw this as direct learning. In truth, he was still undecided as to whether to attend today's lecture. On the one hand, Acemoglu was a true expert in the field, and Harry had read a lot of his work. He was also curious to match a face to the writing, since he would often spend hours mulling through an academic's work without ever knowing what the creator looked like. However, on the other hand, the realist in Harry knew that this session would be an extra-curricular one. Given that he was a guest lecturer, the contents, while interesting, would be beyond the remits of the syllabus.

Harry spent around thirty minutes trying to understand an empirical study on the Phillips Curve but simply could not comprehend its intuition. He up re-read the pages multiple times, but his neurons were exhausted. Not even multiple coffee trips could stimulate his brain. The words just simply refused to go in. Frustrated at his lack of productivity, he decided that he needed a break; some fresh air would serve him well. He packed up his things into his trusty brown Hugo Boss satchel, and with a nod of gratitude to the barman for his services, he left the bar.

The sun was beginning to set as Harry wandered mindlessly through Cambridge. Usually, he would leave college and head to a nearby café, but at this point, his body was sixty per cent coffee. With no real destination in mind, Harry decided that he would head to the market square and get himself some fresh orange juice. He despised rambling with no purpose; this way, he would have achieved something on his walk and maybe even have a chat with the friendly street vendor.

It was only a short stroll to the market, but then again, everything is close by in Cambridge. That is the beauty of the place, especially if you reside in a central college like Trinity.

Despite the juice being far overpriced (one could have easily gone to *Mainsbury's* and picked up a whole carton for a pound), Harry was now looking forward to his refreshing beverage, a sweet treat before he resumed his dreary Economics readings.

As Harry passed Gonville and Caius College, he took a moment to stop and stare at the towering building, basking in all of its glory. There was not anything specific that could be attributed to its beauty. Rather, it was the individual elements combining that made the building so extravagant: the gothic beige blocks, the contrasting grey slate tiles on the steep roof, the flag whistling away in the wind high above bearing the college's crest, the meticulous stone statues of the three founders of the college facing out onto the King's Parade. Harry wondered when Stephen Hawking, a notable alumnus of the college, would be getting his statue built. This led him on to thinking that he had never actually seen a statue of someone in a wheelchair, and he wondered whether a statue in his honour would be sculpted of him before or after the tragic effects of motor neuron disease had kicked in. It was not so long ago that Harry had seen Hawking live at the Cambridge Union. The chamber was packed to the rafters with students desperate to see arguably the greatest modern theoretical physicist in the flesh.

The city was steeped in history and served as host to some of the world's greatest minds. Harry's own mind retroceded to the beauty of the city, and he acknowledged that it was all too easy to grow accustomed to the magnificent surroundings that Cambridge had to offer. Almost all of the colleges were spectacular in their architectural design (except Churchill and Robinson, of course), making it difficult to rank any individual building far ahead of the rest. Students were often too busy frantically studying away to really appreciate the stunning nature of the city, and their time at the great university always flew by rapidly.

Harry had been so fixated at the college that he had almost forgotten what he had come out for. He was caught in a reverie, that was until someone called out his name. 'Harry!' shouted Aaron as he approached his close friend, 'What on earth are you doing?' he said in reference to Harry standing alone in the middle of the street staring up at the sky. Harry was embarrassed and caught off guard. He had a blank expression and was lost for words. 'You really are a strange one,' said Aaron.

Finally, Harry came back to earth, 'Aaron, how's it going mate?'

Now a little bit concerned, Aaron replied to his question with another question, 'Are you okay mate?'

'Yeah, yeah, just a bit tired today, not really with it,' said Harry.

'Where you headed anyway?' asked Aaron, who seemed to be filled with questions.

Harry shrugged his shoulders and replied, 'Nowhere in particular, just needed to get out for some fresh air.'

'I'm heading back to college if you fancy joining?' offered Aaron.

Harry considered this proposition, but now that he had the thought of getting some juice, it was the only thing occupying his thoughts. Not wanting to seem impolite, he responded, 'Nah, I'm going to have a little walk and pick up a drink, but I'll be back later if you fancy doing something this evening?'

Aaron pulled a wincing face, 'Ah mate, I'd love to, but I've got an essay due in at midnight. It's going to be a long night ahead in the library.' Secretly Harry was happy that Aaron had an excuse. He only offered to do something out of courtesy; he had his own work to be getting on with tonight. 'Well enjoy your drink,' said Aaron, who swaggered away.

'You too,' said Harry, who immediately after saying these words felt like a complete imbecile. He shook his head and carried on his journey to the market square. As Harry strolled down the cobbled street towards the market, the light was slowly bidding farewell to the day. It was not until he passed the four red telephone boxes that he saw the vendors packing up their stalls. Harry's heart sank. Despite having just decided that he wanted the fresh juice, he really had developed an emotional investment in having the beverage and was gutted that he would be denied what he desired. He thought he would try his luck anyway, in the hope that the stall would miraculously still be open, but upon arrival at the far end of the market, the vendor was nowhere to be seen.

Fed-up with the seeming futility of the walk, Harry pondered what to do next. He considered getting some juice from the supermarket but knew that simply would not suffice. Harry contemplated heading back to his room to continue with his reading, but the thought of going back to study was not an attractive one. He sought to achieve something now that he had left the college and eventually decided that since he was already outside, he may as well head to the lecture by Acemoglu. It was taking place close by at the Mill Lane lecture halls, which meant he would not have to make the trek over to Sidgewick Site. Knowing that he would have missed the first half of the lecture but not caring anyway (since it was scheduled to be two hours long), Harry started to walk towards Mill Lane at a pace just marginally quicker than his previous meander.

Harry opted to walk down the backstreets and made his way past the Eagle pub, where Crick and Watson famously announced that they had discovered DNA in 1953. As he turned the corner, he glanced at the shining gold Corpus Clock, which looked too modern and dreadfully out of place in the city. The huge gold grasshopper rocked back and forth at the top of the clock, and the blue laser lights confirmed that Harry was running very late for the lecture indeed. The pavements were relatively empty as the day fell dark; the tourists did not tend to flood into the city until the weekends. While making his way down Trumpington Street, Harry started to get excited by the lecture he was about to attend. His curiosity as to what Acemoglu looked like would finally be satisfied. He could have just looked him up on Google, but there was more of a climactic feeling with seeing him in person for the first time. Harry imagined all academics to be old, balding, white, middle-class men and was often surprised when he saw them in the flesh.

Harry made his way past St Catherine's College, where he reminisced over his supervisions with Professor Williams. When he got to Ede & Ravenscroft, London's oldest tailor and robe maker, he stopped to admire the graduation gowns in the window. It was not long until his day would come, where he had the chance to wear that very gown, which differed slightly from his current gown boasting a part-lined white fur hood. He was so excited for Graduation. He passed Fitzbillies and fought off the urge to buy another over-priced coffee from the café he loved so dearly and finally headed down the narrow pavement of Mill Lane. Bike parking spaces were minimal, indicating to

Harry that Acemoglu's lecture would be well attended.

Harry scoffed at the plaque on the outside of the building, which stated that the lecture rooms were for Land Economy, a desperate attempt of a subject to imitate Economics. The 'wannabe Economics' had a reputation for being a more accessible route into Cambridge, and Harry ridiculed people that studied the discipline. He was sure that it was just a glorified farming degree and those who took it were not worthy of their place at the institution. Upon entering the building, he looked up at the electronic board to find out what room the lecture was taking place. Unsurprisingly it was taking place in Room 3, the largest hall. Harry swung the door wide open and casually walked into the room. Entering was a big mistake.

As he burst into the packed room and looked around to see if there was any space available for him, Acemoglu fell silent mid-speech. The entire room turned to look at him with glaring eyes. He suddenly found himself in a stand-off with the Economist at the front. Panicking at the disruption that he caused, a red-faced Harry was now frozen to the spot. Acemoglu finally broke the silence and barked directly at Harry, 'Do you think it is acceptable to interrupt me midway through my lecture?' Harry knew this was a rhetorical question and chose not to respond. 'Do you think that your time is more important than the rest of ours?' shouted the Turk in an American accent. Harry had been half right about what the academic would look like. He was white and middle-class, but he was not old or balding. Quite the opposite, he was energetic and filled with passion and fury. Unfortunately for Harry, this fury was directed entirely at him, and there was no way to deflect Acemoglu's wrath. Harry stood there and took his punishment like a man. He glanced over at Mo for salvation, but Mo looked away in disdain.

Harry stood paralysed halfway down the aisle, not knowing what to do with himself. 'Well, get out of my lecture,' shouted Acemoglu in a commanding voice. In some ways, Harry was relieved to be told to leave; at least now he knew what to do. He did not need to be told twice and turned around to make his way to the exit at the top of the lecture hall. This reprimand reinforced why he did not bother attending lectures. Acemoglu certainly came across a lot better on the page than he did in real life!

12

Mo took considerable pleasure in informing the rest of the gang about Harry's scolding. It was a story that was always met with rapturous laughter. There was nothing Harry could do but laugh it off as his friends would imitate him freezing in the lecture hall. It became a bit of a running joke if anyone was caught out that they would be 'doing a Harry', and as much as he abhorred it on the inside, Harry had to act as if he was unphased by their mockery.

Week six and seven of the term seemed to drag on for an eternity, with all of the students weighed down under their seemingly endless piles of work. But they had eventually made it to the last week of term, and as final essays were handed in, it was as though the tension on the city was lifted. Given that the undergraduate students tend to go back home at the end of November, this final week was somewhat of a Christmas celebration to get everyone into the festive spirit. The 25th November was called 'Bridgemas' across the university, and like most things at Cambridge, celebrating the birth of Jesus a month early made very little sense, but everyone rolled with it anyway.

The students would spend this final week catching up with their friends before saying farewell for the Christmas break. Harry and his peers made their obligatory visit to the North Pole (Cambridge's annual Christmas event held in Parker's Piece), where they enjoyed mulled wine and overindulged in expensive minced pies. They took to the ice rink, and while Gertrude danced away with such precision in her movements, Mo looked more like Bambi on Ice, clumsily making his way around the rink, hanging dearly onto the sideboards. The week marked a well-deserved celebration for surviving Michaelmas Term in one piece. Even Harry, with his regimented study plan, managed to find time off this week to relax. He was already well ahead of the game, and research for his dissertation could wait until he was back home in London. There were, of course, some scrooges who worked away relentlessly in the library, but it was not because they were so committed to their work; rather, they were the people who did not have any friends to celebrate Bridgemas with.

Each day Harry would go to his pigeonhole (where letters were posted for the students) and find it replenished with treats and Bridgemas cards. Harry himself gave a bag of chocolate coins with each of the cards he posted to his friends. There was something quite special about this time of year, having a few lie-ins, going for drinks with friends in the evenings, watching all of the cheesy Christmas movies in bed with an extra-large mug of hot chocolate; it almost felt as though they were *normal* students for once.

Harry entered the college bar in the early afternoon, which was more of a common room for the Trinity students. The bar was almost unrecognisable with all of its Christmas decorations, tinsel lining the walls, a glowing tree with fake presents underneath it, mistletoe hanging from the ceilings. The college staff really had put a lot of effort into ensuring that all students felt festive. They were even serving mulled wine and mince pies all day in the bar. It was a lot busier than it usually was throughout the year since the term had nearly come to its conclusion. Sabrina and Gertrude were sitting on the sofas in the corner by the fireplace, and Harry headed over to them.

'Hallo Gertrude, wie gehts?' said Harry in a German accent with a swing of his fist as if he was holding a large beer stein. Gertrude was less than impressed at his attempt to converse in her mother tongue and ignored the question.

Sabrina, on the other hand, let out a cute little simper and responded in her friend's place, 'Hey Harry, why don't you come and join us? We were just talking about our predicament about what to wear to the dinner tonight.' The students had been left with the option of whether they wanted to come in formal attire or Christmas jumpers for the Bridgemas feast.

'It's a no-brainer,' said Harry, who stood tall above the seated girls, 'Bridgemas comes once a year, you have to wear the ironically hideous jumper.'

'See!' said Sabrina to Gertrude before returning back to look at Harry, 'She just wants to wear her new dress, but I keep telling her that she can wear that whenever, we have enough formal dinners throughout the term.'

Looking a little upset that she was being tag-teamed by the other two and feeling outnumbered, Gertrude replied in a whiny voice, 'Yeah, but this is the last formal of term, I won't get to wear it for ages otherwise.'

Realising that he was stepping on toes in this argument and

not wanting to be the cause of any bickering, especially during Bridgemas, Harry backtracked a little to remain neutral, 'Yeah, well if you want to wear the dress, go for it. Do whatever will make you happiest.' This was the response that Gertrude was looking for, and she tried to hide the smile that had just slipped out. Sabrina just did not want to be the only girl wearing a Christmas jumper, but she thought that at least the boys would be wearing the absurd jumpers, so did not push Gertrude further on the matter.

'Come and sit,' said Sabrina while patting a space next to her on the sofa.

'Ah I can't,' said Harry, swerving the invitation, 'I only came in here to pick up a coffee. I've still got to buy a present for my Secret Santa later.'

'What time do you want us?' said Gertrude, who was now a lot higher in spirits.

'Ab sechs Uhr,' replied Harry in his broken GCSE German to indicate that the girls should arrive at his from six o'clock. Gertrude's smile quickly turned upside down, and Harry briskly spun away to avoid her playful rage. He picked up a gingerbread latte to go and headed towards the town centre to pick up his gift.

Each year Harry and his friends would do a Secret Santa between them before the Bridgemas formal. It was only a bit of fun, with a spending limit set at ten pounds, but it was always nice to get an early Christmas present. This year Harry had pulled Raymond's name from the hat and was lost for ideas about what to get him. He would usually just order something off of Amazon, but since it was the last year they were all together in Cambridge, he wanted to get something more personal.

Harry mulled around the Lion Yard Shopping Centre trying to pick out the perfect gift for Raymond. He searched everywhere, from beauty stores to clothes shops. While he enjoyed seeing all of the latest retail stock, pretty much everything was out of his price range, so he tried Flying Tiger Copenhagen, a variety emporium that sold just about anything you could imagine. Harry walked around the store, grabbing whatever caught his attention: a head massager, a miniature version of Connect 4, phone cases. This was surely a haven for finding a whacky Secret Santa gift, yet as Harry made his way around, nothing really jumped out at him.

Leaving the shopping centre empty-handed, Harry was still lost for ideas. To make matters worse, it had started spitting when he got outside, and Harry thought that he would just make his way back to college and have a good think about what to buy. He made his way down the narrow St Edwards passage and caught a glimpse of King's College in the distance. As he stared at the Corpus Christi college playroom, the weather took a turn for the worse, and the light drizzle turned into a full-fledged rainstorm. The downpour was relentless, pounding down on the exposed student. Foolishly he was wearing a jacket without a hood. Harry contemplated running like a lunatic back home, but it was still quite a distance to get to the safety of his college. He frantically looked for shelter but could not find any cover in the passage. In his attempt to evade the rain, he saw one shop open in the passage and scurried straight to it.

It was a quaint, old-fashioned bookshop, which almost blended into the scenery despite the matching bright red painted door and window frame. Harry must have walked past this shop a hundred times over his three years in Cambridge, yet never noticed it until now. It was like the room of requirement in Harry Potter, only appearing when a person was in great need of it. The shop was minute but boasted a large square window stacked with exciting books to entice customers into the shop. Harry did not have much time to analyse the shop or even question how he had never seen it before, but as he came bursting in, he caught sight of its name on top of the window, 'The Haunted Bookshop'.

Thinking nothing of the name and quite frankly not having any other alternative, Harry was glad to be in the warmth of the shop. It was eerily quiet inside the bookshop. The floorboard creaked as Harry made his way around and realised that he was the only person in the store. 'Hello,' shouted Harry tentatively, hoping not to scare an employee who might be in the back of the shop. But there was no response. He made his way around the shop and saw a wooden plaque engraved with white writing up on the wall:

The Haunted Bookshop in St Edward's Passage is so named because of the two ghosts rumoured to reside on its premises.

Harry did not believe in ghosts but was beginning to feel a little uncomfortable being alone in the store. He was here now, so thought that he might as well inspect some of the books chaotically stacked on the shelves. There was no system to how the books were presented. Rather, they were crammed onto the shelves, struggling to breathe. It was clear to Harry that this was a second-hand bookstore that had received far too many donations to handle, yet they did not want to turn any contributions away. The books were piled high on the floor, with additional trollies alongside the existing shelves to provide extra capacity. It was a struggle for Harry to make his way around the clutter. He ran his fingers across the spines of the cloth hardcovers, tickling them as he went. He stopped at a book that intrigued him, a deep rouge book with golden raised bands. There was no name in sight on the spine. Drawing it out slowly from the shelf revealed a layer of dust on the book's top edge. There was no writing on the front cover, nor blurb on the back. Turning the first page, Harry learnt that the book had been printed in London in 1848. His curiosity about the history of the book grew. Who had read it? Where had it been? How did it end up here? Turning the pages further revealed the title of the book, one that Harry instantly recognised. He engrossed himself in the book and started reading the first page. The lighting batten on the ceiling above him flickered, making reading more strenuous. He got so lost in the words that he completely forgot his surroundings and about the storm outside. As he turned the page, his eyes followed its flowing movement, shifting from right to left, and that was when he saw a figure in his periphery vision.

The old woman dressed in black was silent, observing the student's perusal of the book. She gave Harry a dreadful fright, but he contained his propensity to shriek in fear. Harry did not know how long she had been standing there staring at him, but he knew he did not like the situation he found himself in. With the storm in full force outside of the door, he was effectively locked in with the harrowing hag. He decided that the book in his hand would be the perfect gift for Raymond and headed to the till to pay for it. Now face to face with the woman, she reminded Harry of Nanny McPhee. She was cursed with a humongous nose, imposing warts on her face, a wild monobrow, and goofy teeth. Harry tried to resist staring at her impediments, but they were simply unavoidable. She had large beady eyes, and despite Harry's efforts to engage in small talk with her, she remained silent. She scanned the book and took his money without a word. The book itself was fourteen pounds, a little steep for a second-hand book, but it was so magnificent that Harry was willing to shell out beyond the budget.

The storm had mellowed, and although it was still raining, Harry thought that he would rather brave it than spend another minute with that creepy witch. He was pleased with his gift and equally relieved to be out of the bookshop. No wonder it blended into the scenery – who would possibly want to go there? Harry tucked the book inside his jacket to protect it from the rain and began marching back to college. His Bridgemas spirit was taken away from him by the strange encounter in the store, but it was soon restored upon arrival back in college, where he passed yet another Christmas tree in the Porter's Lodge. He wondered how many trees were scattered around the college and how much effort went into putting them all up. He recalled a tree in the bar, one in the library, and now this one in the Lodge. The most extravagant one was always put up in the Great Hall, and Harry could only imagine the person who had to climb the tall ladder to decorate it.

Harry had spent a bit longer than planned in town looking for his gift and was now soaking wet from the rain. He flicked his wet mop of hair back, which had been growing increasingly longer as the term proceeded and headed straight to his room to have a protracted warm shower in the communal bathroom.

By the time he had washed, he realised that he was tight for time and quickly scrambled to wrap up his gift for Raymond. For all his talents, Harry could not for the life of him wrap presents. Even a regular item as simple as a book was a struggle for Harry, who scrunched the reindeer-decorated paper around the edges of the book. He Sellotaped all around the wrapping paper to stop it from falling apart. Mastering the art of gift wrapping was not important to Harry. Nobody cares about *how* the present is wrapped; they just care about its contents (or that was what he always convinced himself).

He had only just chucked the abysmally wrapped present under his desk when Raymond came storming into the room, 'Harry my dear man!' Raymond certainly did not disappoint in his attire for the evening, bright red trousers like Santa himself, a god-awful Christmas jumper with a combination of every colour you could imagine, and what Harry liked most, he had even decorated his beard. It was dyed green and covered in glitter, like tinsel on a Christmas tree, and he even had miniature baubles hanging from his thick facial hair.

Harry was howling at the sight of him, 'Raymondo! You've out-done yourself this year,' he said while inviting his friend to take a seat. Raymond had brought a bottle of red wine with him, which he had every intention of drinking in the room before the dinner. He was in the final week of the college-imposed drinking ban, so this would be his only opportunity to get intoxicated. Seeing Raymond starting to drink and not wanting to let him do so alone, Harry nipped into the kitchen to grab his chilled beers.

By the time he returned to his room, Sabrina and Aaron had already made themselves at home, lounged out on Harry's sofa.

The pair were wearing Christmas jumpers, although not quite as extravagant as Raymond's. 'Hey, Harry,' said Sabrina, who looked rather cosy and cute in her simplistic white Christmas jumper bearing a solitary reindeer on the front. 'Where's your jumper?' she asked.

Harry rushed over to his desk where his woollen garment was tossed over his chair and scrambled to pull the cheap jumper over his head. 'How does it look?' asked Harry while giving the other three a spin to model the jumper.

'Oh, love the twirl! You belong on a runway son,' said Aaron. Unlike the other two, Aaron came along empty-handed.

'Beer?' asked Harry.

'Yes, please mate if you've got one going,' said Aaron. Despite not being as affluent as his friends, Harry was always generous and shared whatever he had with those close to him.

Mo and Cuthbert came in next, and Cuthbert clearly did not get the memo about wearing a Christmas jumper. He was wearing a rather extravagant red and black patterned tuxedo jacket and looked a hell of a lot smarter than the rest of the gang.

'What's all this about then?' asked Aaron, who seemed lost at Cuthbert's fancy get-up.

'Oh, I could not bear to be seen in one of those ghastly Christmas jumpers. The very sight of them makes me cringe,' Cuthbert responded. The rest of the group felt vaguely insulted and attacked by his words, but this was just who Cuthbert was, blunt and to the point. He continued, 'Besides, the jacket I am wearing is rather festive. This is no ordinary tux you know.' He proceeded to bore the group about the quality of the fabric and how the finest tailors in the country made it. Harry hated it when Cuthbert went on these pretentious tangents; it really magnified the difference between him and the rest of the group.

'Where is Gertrude?' asked Mo, who found himself without a seat; instead, making do with sitting on the rug on the floor.

'She's still getting ready,' said Sabrina.

'Well, can someone send her a message? I want to do the Secret Santa presents,' said Mo.

Harry shook his head in disbelief at the man's impatience, 'You really are such a kid, aren't you?'

At the very mention of Secret Santa, Aaron swiftly rose from his chair and said, 'Ah shit, I've left my gift in my room. I'll quickly run up and grab it.' As soon as Aaron got up, Mo sprung to his feet to take the vacant seat. When Aaron rushed out of the room, he swung the door wide open, and the wreath on the outside of the door flew into the room. 'Sorry,' he shouted back into the room, with no intention of picking it up.

Harry walked over to replace the Christmas decoration on the door. He bent down to pick it up, and when he got back up, Gertrude was standing in the door frame before him. She was dressed in a sparkling black dress, showing just the right amount of cleavage, and the slit down the dress revealed her long bronze legs. Gertrude was already tall, but her heels brought her nearly to Harry's height. She wore a simple silver necklace matching her glamorous earrings. Just a touch of make-up helped her keep a natural look. Her brunette hair was straightened and touched the arch of her bosom. Harry was taken aback at her startling beauty, 'Wow. No wonder you wanted to wear that dress,' he said while leaning in to give her a kiss on each cheek.

Her heels clambered on the floor, and she commanded the attention of the entire room without even so much as opening her mouth. She walked over to the rest of her friends and lay her small gift down on the table. Sabrina certainly felt overshone by her German friend and was jealous that she was not getting the same attention from the gawping boys.

'Mo, get up man,' ordered Raymond, 'let the woman have a seat.' Annoyed at the hypocrisy, Raymond could just as easily have given up his own seat, but not having the energy to fight it, Mo vacated his seat and returned once more to the floor. Gertrude was grateful for Raymond's intervention and took a seat on the sofa.

Aaron came running back into the room, panting for breath as he held a rather large unwrapped brown box above his head. 'Where should I put it?' asked Aaron.

'Just pop it by the table, I'll grab mine now and we can do the presents,' said Harry as he walked over towards the desk to retrieve his book for Raymond.

Everyone was enraptured receiving their gift from a mystery individual and subtly watched the reaction of the person they themselves had gifted. Harry was playing the role of the mother hen, handing out the gifts to all of his friends. He went around the circle and handed them out one by one, putting the gift that he had received to one side. He had finished giving out the parcels, and everyone but Mo received one. There had only been six gifts, not seven. The others were too excited to realise the missing present, but Harry brought it to their attention, 'Guys, we're missing a gift, Mo has not got a present. Did anyone forget to bring theirs with them?'

There was a prolonged pause, and Aaron spoke up, 'This is really shitty from whoever has done this. Look its best if we don't whittle down to find out who the culprit was, just make sure you get Mo a gift tomorrow. Maybe leave it in his pigeon-hole'. The rest of the group were looking around suspiciously to see who the guilty party was, as if they were playing a game of 'Among Us'.

Mo looked glum, and Harry could not handle seeing someone so upset. He breathed out a deep breath, 'Here, take my present,' said Harry while pointing to his gift.

Mo could not hold it in anymore, 'I got you! All of you,' he said with a belly full of laughter. The others looked confused, and Mo went on to explain himself, 'I drew my own name from the hat.'

'Well why did you not say something,' said Sabrina, still bamboozled by his actions.

'I did not want to mess up the whole Secret Santa,' said Mo, 'plus, this way I got to get myself a gift that I really wanted!'

'What was that then?' asked Harry. Mo reached deep into his pocket and pulled out a full packet of cigarettes, looking very smug at how it all went down. Exactly as he had planned. There was a collective sigh of relief that nobody had missed out on getting a gift, and one by one, they started opening their presents.

Sabrina opened her present first and received a beauty face mask treatment. Aaron got a beer glass with his name engraved in it. Cuthbert received a grey pocket square, which he tucked straight into his tuxedo jacket to add to his elegant look. Gertrude got a copy of David Copperfield, a Charles Dickens novel that she had already read many times, but she at least pretended to be grateful for her gift. Harry opened up his small parcel, and it contained a plain stainless-steel cigarette holder case. He joked openly to his Secret Santa, 'Has my smoking habit really got that bad?' and then looked over to Mo, 'I bet you wish you swapped presents with me now.'

'No chance,' replied Mo, 'you can't smoke a case, can you?'

Raymond was the last to open his gift, 'What is this shocking attempt at wrapping?' he said while ripping off the paper. He was intrigued by the book that was now revealed in his hand, as were the rest of the group. He opened it up, and it revealed the title a few pages in:

Manifesto of the Communist Party: By Karl Marx and Friedrich Engels

Raymond was still completely lost as he read out the title to the rest of his peers.

'Let me have a look,' said Harry, who grabbed the book from him. He opened the book to the inside cover and acted surprised at what he saw, 'Oh look. There is a note written here,' knowing fine well that he had scribbled it there in blue ink not so long ago.

'What? Pass it here,' demanded Raymond, who was a little frustrated at his present. He read it out loud:

Dearest Raymond Verducci,

I thought that I would get you the Communist Manifesto in case you fancied any more radical speeches at tonight's dinner. You should find plentiful inspiration in this book.

Merry Bridgemas,
Your loving Secret Santa x

'Brilliant,' said Raymond knowing that one of his peers had just mugged him off. He was already apprehensive about showing his face at the dinner tonight, and this certainly did not help his nerves. The rest of the group cackled away and applauded whoever the mystery giver was.

Ever the punctual individual, Gertrude rounded up her friends like a sheepdog to make sure that they were not late for dinner. She wanted to make sure that they could take some nice photos to remember the evening. Gertrude had not gone to all this effort with her outfit to not get pictures of it. They made the short walk over to the Great Hall and had their names ticked off the guest list by the catering staff.

The hall had been set magnificently for the occasion, dressed up in sparkly Christmas decorations. Silver and white were the exclusive colours, giving the room a classy feel. The tables were filled with an array of cutlery, glasses, bottles of wine, and somehow, the catering staff had managed to find space for a shiny silver Christmas cracker in front of each place. A queue was forming in front of the ginormous Christmas tree as the students waited in turn to have their photo taken. The thirty-foot tree stood tall in the hall and almost reached the high ceiling. Harry thought that the white lights dotted around the tree would have cost a fortune to run but admired the effort that the college went to each year. Upon closer inspection, Harry saw that the white and silver baubles actually had the Trinity crest on them.

Ever the lover of college stash, Harry wanted to get his hands on one of the trinkets to put on his own tree back home. When it was his group's turn for a photo, he headed to the tree and turned around, pretending to adjust his jumper for the picture and sneakily stuffed one of the baubles down his pants. He did not know where else to put it. Aaron joked about sacrificing Mo to take the photo, but in the end, another student in the hall took their picture. Harry knew that this photo would be all over the gram by the end of the night.

Wanting to ensure the safety of his newly prized possession, and not wanting an extra ball in his pants all evening, Harry hastily headed back to his room to drop off the college bauble. By the time he returned to the Great Hall, his friends had already secured a space on the long table, and he realised that he had been shafted by the seating plan and was set to spend the meal opposite a stranger. However, this did not matter so much to Harry as he knew he was interesting enough to steer the conversation in his direction.

The choir had prepared somewhat of a concert and sang a few Christmas carols before the meal commenced (thankfully after the students had taken their seats). The wine was flowing, and the students were treated to a full three-course Christmas dinner with all the trimmings. The crackers had been pulled, and terrible jokes told as everyone wore their paper crowns, except Cuthbert, of course, who did not want it to ruin his hair.

Aaron had particularly enjoyed his joke and made sure to gather all of his friend's attention before telling it, 'How many letters are there in the alphabet at Christmas? And why?' he asked. After a few shots in the dark, they had not managed to guess the answer. Aaron put them out of their misery, 'Twenty-five,' he said as he started wheezing, 'because there's Noel.' He was slapping his knee, adoring the joke, but the rest of the group found Aaron's reaction more entertaining than the written humour.

The Bridgemas feast was truly a blissful ending to the term. Harry could not be happier with the friends he had made during his time at the university. They were an odd bunch, for sure, but he loved each and every one of them with all of their little quirks. The group began to discuss their plans for the holiday. 'I'm going to Switzerland to go skiing for a week,' boasted Gertrude, 'my father owns a chalet in St Moritz.'

'Oh, how lovely,' said Cuthbert, 'I went to watch the Snow Polo World Cup there last year. It was fabulous.'

'Are you coming again this year?' asked Gertrude.

'No, no,' he said with a shake of his head, 'It's Whistler this year for us. Papa wants to improve his off-piste skiing, and well I just want to drink champagne in the hot tub.'

Aaron interjected, 'Christ, I could not think of anything worse than a ski break. It's cold enough here in England, why would you possibly want to be even colder?' He topped up his glass with red wine, leaving enough space for it to breathe, 'I'll be spending the break in Australia. The whole family are flying over to see Uncle Rick. Who knows what we'll get up to? Swimming in the day, fighting Kangaroos at night,' he laughed.

Harry listened enviously to all the others and their exotic-sounding breaks, and eventually, he was asked the question that he had been dreading. 'What are you getting up to Harry?' said Raymond. Suddenly, all twelve eyes turned to Harry in anticipation.

Harry knew that he would be spending most of the break locked away, focusing on his dissertation. He should have thought of an answer when they were rambling away, but all he could muster up was, 'I'm just going to be at home really.'

'Where's the fun in that? You deserve a break after this draining term,' said Sabrina.

'Well, I love being back home with my family and seeing all my friends. I feel like I hardly know them anymore,' said Harry.

'Suit yourself,' said Aaron while scoffing down a pig in blanket.

Harry had felt a little sorry for himself that he would not be having as impressive of a break as his peers, but he quickly moved on so as not to let it ruin his night. As the feast was drawing to a conclusion, Principal Draw stood up to give a speech, which, thankfully this time, Raymond did not interrupt. He congratulated all the students for making it through another term, as though their education that they were paying for was a burden and wished them all a Merry Bridgemas. After another one of Draw's trademark speeches, he thanked the catering staff, who received a hearty round of applause from the dining students, and proceeded to say, 'The festivities do not end here. There will be jazz in the bar after dinner.'

After the Principal's speech, the students began nattering away again as the caterers collected the plates and began to clear the tables. The students grabbed whatever was left of the bottles of wine and carried it with them as they migrated towards the bar.

'That was a sensational meal,' said Aaron, 'I'm stuffed to the brim.'

In agreement, Harry said, 'Too right, I'm going to struggle to walk over to the bar with all this food in me'.

The seven of them toddled across the courtyard like the dwarves in Snow White. They made their way into the bar, which was slowly beginning to fill up as if the music were a magnet attracting the glutted students. Upon arrival, they were each handed a complimentary glass of port. Even Raymond managed to sneak down a quick glass, who had been dying for an alcoholic beverage all throughout dinner. The port was not to Harry's taste, who took one sip of it and decided to get a proper drink instead.

The jazz was blaring away, and the students felt carefree for the first time in a long while, dancing the night away. Mo was just bopping his head away to the music, whereas Aaron and Harry danced with natural rhythm. Gertrude was struggling to dance in her high heels, so rather let her hands do the dancing while wiggling her petite waist.

Harry took Sabrina's hands and spun her around in a whirl in sync with the sound of the saxophone. She smiled as Harry pulled her in close. She stared up at the leafy plant on the ceiling and said to Harry, 'Look! We're under the mistletoe.' Harry looked up at the plant and smiled. 'You know what that means,' she said, hoping that Harry would lean in to kiss her.

'Oh, yeah,' said Harry laughing the indication off. He let go of Sabrina's hands and headed back to the rest of the group to dance. This was not the response that Sabrina desired, and she was dismayed by this blatant rejection. Sabrina was an incredibly attractive girl. In fact, she was Harry's type, but the two of them had formed such a strong friendship over the past three years that he saw her as more of a sister than a potential lover. Besides, Harry still had only one girl on his mind from his birthday kiss: Elizabeth.

- 13 -

After Bridgemas, Harry spent a few more days partying away with his friends before it was time to bid farewell again. He had developed a habit of slipping away unnoticed as he did not care much for emotional goodbyes. Much to Harry's frustration, he spent his final morning packing up all of his belongings to take home. He would have loved to leave his possessions in Cambridge over the break, but the college rented out the rooms to guests over Christmas, meaning that the students had to clear everything. Harry ignored all of the messages on the group chat asking when people were leaving. He thought it would be easier to send a long message when he got home, wishing everyone a pleasant break. Harry met his dad, Alan, outside Queen's Gate, carrying as many of his belongings as physically possible.

'Harry! How's it going? Here, let me grab those off of you,' said Alan while reaching to help his son with his bags. He stored the two large suitcases that Harry was carrying in the boot of the car, and Harry walked over and popped his rucksack in the back seat.

'Alright dad, how's it going?' said Harry. Both of them had asked the same question, yet neither of them actually received an answer. The question was more of a greeting between the two before they embraced. It had been quite some time since Harry had seen his father, well, two months, but a lot had certainly happened in that time for Harry.

'Got much more stuff to come?' asked Alan.

'Well, if we both go, we should do it in one run,' said Harry.

The Range Rover, which Harry's parents shared, was completely blocking the narrow street, 'Right, let me just pop the hazard lights on and we'll quickly grab the rest of it then,' said Alan with a quick jog around to the driver's seat of the car. He opened the door and pressed the two red triangles. 'Let's go,' he said.

The men made their way to Harry's at a pace somewhere between a walk and a jog and quickly gathered the last of Harry's things. Neither of the men were keen to stick around Cambridge. They both wanted to get back to stream the Chelsea match against West Ham at three o'clock. Thankfully there was no oncoming traffic when they returned to the car. While Alan was carefully organising Harry's things in the boot, Harry recklessly chucked what he was carrying into the back seat of the car and hopped into the vehicle. Alan spun the car around, and they were on their way back home to London.

The pair exchanged stories about what they had been up to over the past couple of months. Of course, Harry kept his tales innocuous but nonetheless had much to tell. Chatting to his father made Harry realise how much he missed being home: the cooked meals, family, friends, nightlife – he could not wait to return to the capital. They had just got onto the M11 when

Alan reached over to the digital screen and put on a song from his playlist. It was none other than Chris Rea's 'Driving Home for Christmas'.

Harry buried his face in his hand in disbelief in his dad's choice, 'Could you get any cringier?' said Harry.

'What, it's not like I get the opportunity to play this song often,' he said while nodding along to the piano symphony, 'lighten up a little will you, not too long until Christmas now anyway.' Harry grinned. He loved his dad, even if he was still a kid at heart. The roads were relatively clear, which meant that it did not take much more than an hour to get back home to Pinner. Alan pulled into the crazy paving driveway. Alan detested that the ugly grey slabs were the first thing people would see of his home and was adamant that he would replace them with something a bit more modern but had never gotten around to it. The irony was, Alan was a bricklayer and could have easily sorted his driveway out, but he was always too busy working on other people's homes to focus on his own. Harry got out and grabbed his miscellaneous possessions from the back seat of the car, whereas Alan went straight to the larger suitcases in the boot. When they opened the door to dump Harry's stuff in the hallway, Susan and Harry's two older brothers were standing there to greet him.

While Harry was tall, he was dwarfed by his giant brothers, who were both nearly six foot and five inches. Ethan, the oldest by five years, had long blonde hair tied up in a messy top knot. Timothy, the middle child, and just one year older than Harry, had a completely different look to his older brother. He cut his dark hair short, arguing that if it was any longer, it would serve to obstruct him on the building sites. Timothy wanted to be like his father and work in construction, but Alan insisted that his son got some form of qualification, so they met in the middle and Timothy went to college to study to be an electrician. His dad used his contacts to help Timothy get work initially, but he was so proficient at his job that he soon no longer needed his dad's nepotism.

Both Ethan and Timothy rushed out to grab the rest of Harry's things while Harry was being squeezed to death by his mother, who had missed him dearly. In truth, there was not too much more to gather from the car. Ethan carried Harry's suits and his large box of tinware, leaving Timothy walking rather awkwardly back with a very light drawstring bag.

'Where should I put all of my stuff?' asked Harry to his mother.

She had a quick glance and replied, 'Well, you can leave the things that you aren't going to use in the utility room, and I think Timothy has made some room in his wardrobe for your clothes.'

Timothy butted in, 'Yeah, that's right. I've cleared out the top draw of the chest of drawers, and you should be able to hang a few bits up in the wardrobe.'

Harry wasted no time in grabbing his belongings and storing them away. First to the utility room, then upstairs to Timothy's bedroom. As it transpired, Timothy had hardly made an effort to make space for his younger brother. There was not enough space for his suits, let alone the rest of his clothes, but somehow Harry managed to squeeze in his things and headed back downstairs. He could hear the commentators speaking loudly from the front room. The boys always had the television blaring when Chelsea were playing.

Susan was waiting at the bottom of the stairs, ready for an extensive catch up with her son, but Harry did not want to miss any of the match. 'I'm going to head in and watch the game,' said Harry feeling peccant as he had not seen his mother in such a long time, 'we'll have a proper catch up at dinner?' he asked, although it came across as more of an instruction.

'Yeah, that's fine,' said a disappointed Susan. Football always took priority, she thought. 'We're going to order in a Chinese as a treat for having you back,' she said.

Harry's face lit up; what a welcome back indeed! To top it all off, Alan had just walked past him bearing four ice-cold green bottles of Heineken. 'Sounds phenomenal,' exclaimed Harry in a rush to get to the telly. Susan headed to the kitchen, where she occupied herself for the next couple of hours. As she strode away, Harry jumped in one last time, 'Oh, mum, what are the sleeping arrangements?'

Since Harry had left for university, his parents converted his bedroom into a home office. They stripped the room completely, which made Harry feel as though he was surplus to requirements back home. In his eyes, it was harsh that he was the only family member without his own room, but he did spend most of his time in Cambridge, so it was understandable. 'You're on the sofa,' said Susan with no remorse, perhaps because of the lack of affection her son had just shown her in prioritising the football. 'I've left a duvet and a pillow on the floor next to the sofa.'

Harry wanted to expostulate and contend that one of his brothers should be put up on the sofa instead of him since he was effectively a guest. However, he knew any efforts would be in vain. The decision had clearly been made in his absence and was not up for discussion. Of course, there were some perks growing up as the youngest child. Mainly that his parents were much more lenient with him than they ever were with Ethan. There was also an abundance of downsides of being the baby in the family. He had always had the smallest room in the house, he never got to sit in the front seat of the car, he never got new clothes (just hand downs from his brothers), and even now, when they were all adults, he drew the short straw and did not even have his own bed.

When Harry finally entered the front room, the game had already commenced and was two minutes deep. Harry took a beer from the modern glass coffee table and grabbed a backless stool to sit on. Alan was nestled cosily in his sky-blue armchair, exactly how he enjoyed watching football, from the comfort of his own home, where he would get the best view of all and as many beers as he wanted from the fridge. Ethan was sporting a replica of the latest Chelsea top and was sat alongside Timothy on the corresponding sky-blue sofa. Often Harry would go to watch the games at the stadium with his brothers. They preferred to soak up the atmosphere and watch the high-tempo sport live, but their grandad and uncles were using the tickets today.

All four of the men were yelling at the screen as Chelsea failed to break the deadlock. After a few more beers, Ethan had become somewhat gassy and let out a whopping fart on the sofa. 'Oh, for fuck's sake,' whined Harry, 'that's my bed you're farting on.' Not only did the sofa cause him great neck pains, but now it would reek of Ethan's poo particles. Harry was certainly humbled when he came home. His accommodation was fit for a king up in Cambridge, yet he was set to spend the next six weeks couch-surfing like a nomad.

It was a tough fought game, but much to the men's disappointment Chelsea ended up losing. The mood was far from euphoric when the family got together in the newly refurbished kitchen for the takeaway. So much for a celebration for Harry's arrival home. Susan opened a bottle of Villa Maria sauvignon blanc and began filling up her glass, 'Did Chelsea lose?' she muttered under her breath to Harry.

Alan interjected to speak on his son's behalf, and bluntly responded, 'Yes. They lost one-nil.'

Not wanting to cause any further upset but equally not knowing how to react to the boy's frustration, Susan remarked, 'Ooh, well that's not very good is it.' She sought to come across as sympathetic, but her comment felt sarcastic in its execution.

Alan, Ethan, and Harry were sticking to the beers, but Timothy joined his mother on the wine. After a few more drinks, the conversation gradually digressed away from Chelsea's performance and with this change in direction came a marginal improvement in the boy's spirits. Alan's stories from his week at work dominated the dinner talk, with Susan chipping in with anecdotes about her colleagues and complaints of their incompetence. Both Ethan and Timothy had their fair share of tales too. It was Harry that was always the quietest when the whole family was together. Ethan and Timothy had always been more assertive than he was, and he felt as though he could never get a word in. His older brothers were always the favourites whenever the Baldwin family were at any social events, and Harry rather lived in their shadow (quite literally too, given the size of them both).

Harry wanted to participate in conversations with the family, but he was always too hesitant to intervene, and when he did pluck up the courage to speak, someone else would invariably talk over him. The rest of the family never detected Harry's suppression because they were far too busy engaged in conversation amongst the four of them. Harry had a lot to offer. He was the most educated of them all (or was set to be, Ethan obtained a degree in Geology from the University of Lincoln), but all of his thoughts seemed to be locked away in his head when chatting as a group with his family. Harry loved his family to bits but preferred speaking to them individually rather than collectively.

After spending the night drinking with his ménage, Harry retired to his sofa, which was not as uncomfortable as he had imagined it would be. Although it is feasible that this perception was succoured by his tipsiness. When the morning came around, Harry was woken by his parents getting on with their day. The noise seeped into the living room far greater than it did with the bedrooms upstairs. A sleep-deprived Harry stretched out his body, and unsurprisingly, his neck was in agony from sleeping in an awkward position. Harry had not yet decided what to do with his day. There was always university work that he could turn to. As a student, it felt like there was constantly something extra that he could be doing for his studies, whether it was another reading for one of his classes or cracking down on his dissertation. However, he was not keen to dive straight back into work, particularly with his new-found headache. He never worked well the day after drinking, and after some deliberation, concluded that today he would shop for Christmas presents for his family in Westfield, just to get it out of the way.

Timothy was still in a deep sleep. He liked to use his weekends to have extended lie-ins to catch up on missed hours from the early starts he had each day during the week. Not wanting to disturb Timothy, Harry avoided going into his bedroom and simply put on the same clothes he wore yesterday. He devoured a hefty bowl of Crunchy Nut Clusters with chocolate flakes, his favourite cereal, before heading out the door. Harry popped on his heavy maroon Parka jacket over seemingly endless layers of clothes, slid on his plain black woollen gloves and adjusted his matching black hat to keep him warm. It was not a long walk to Pinner station, but the first day of December was a bitterly cold one.

Harry put in his Apple AirPods and was a little disgusted by the amount of earwax that had built up around the speakers but could never be bothered to clear it away. He chose a song from his grime playlist and made his way down the street. This was one of the subtle differences between being back home in London and being up at university. In Cambridge, Harry never knew who he might bump into, but invariably, he would see somebody he knew whenever he left college. This was part of the allure of the student city. It was small, and everyone seemed to know each other. People were more approachable and would greet others as they passed by. The same cannot be said for London, where the individual is lost among the masses. The constantly expanding capital absorbed people from all over the world and had grown so large and diverse that it was impossible to know everyone in the same manner as Cambridge. London's residents were so focused on their own paths, so busy pursuing their own ambitions, that they did not have time to be friendly. Therefore, Harry opted to join the others and block out the rest of the city by listening to his music. *If you can't beat them, join them.*

It was a fair old slog to get to Shepherd's Bush, but fifty-six minutes and two trains later, Harry had arrived. The sheer size of London meant that it took an age to get anywhere, unlike Cambridge, where everything was within walking distance (or a bike ride at most). Harry weaved his way around the busy plaza. It was clear that many others had the same idea as Harry to get their Christmas shopping done nice and early, and Sunday was a prime time for a bit of retail therapy. He had no idea what to get his family this year, so he window-shopped to see what lured him in. Everything seemed to be in the 'sale', but Harry knew that this was just clever marketing to trick people into thinking that they were getting an exceptional deal. Despite being a student, Harry went around splashing his cash on presents for his family. To Harry, his family was the most important thing in life (just edging his studies), and he wanted to make sure that they got the gifts they deserved, regardless of the price tag attached to them.

After a few hours shopping around and a coffee break to fuel his toil, Harry headed back home with bags filled with presents. It was actually a bit of a struggle carrying them all back. He wasted no time wrapping them up (poorly) and storing them under the Christmas tree in the kitchen. Besides, he did not exactly have anywhere to hide his presents, considering he did not have a room of his own.

While Harry loved being at home for the first few days, the novelty soon wore off. He had anticipated spending more time with his family over the break, but they all had full-time jobs. Harry could not handle the boredom of sitting around the house. The others would come in with fresh gossip about their day, and Harry once again would bring nothing to the table. His only saving grace was working on research for his dissertation, which maintained his sanity.

This year the ennui hit a new low. Usually, Harry would just meet up with his home friends during the day, and this social contact would be sufficient to keep him satisfied. However, unlike his friends, Harry took a gap year before going to university, which meant than they had all graduated and begun their careers. While most of his friends dreamed of securing a role on a graduate scheme in London, only Paisán had managed to do so. These jobs were like gold dust to come by, and the application process had been much more competitive that they had expected. This left the rest working in office jobs locally for now, but they still had ambitions to make it to the Big Smoke.

Despite all the stress Cambridge had generated in Harry's life, he yearned to be back in the city so that he could keep occupied and have a sense of purpose again. It truly was a love-hate relationship. Even after all the pains of studying, he wanted nothing more than to return. This extended six-week break seemed to be dragging on forever for Harry.

Timothy was the first to arrive home on the third Wednesday in December. Usually, Harry's family would not be back before dark, but today Ethan came bursting through the door, belting out some Michael Bublé at around lunchtime. 'It's beginning to look a lot like Christmas,' he sang in an operatic voice. The deep, beckoning voice was enough to disturb Harry, who was midway through reading an article for his dissertation.

Harry came rushing from the home office down the stairs to greet his brother, 'You're home early,' said Harry, 'and in a particularly good mood.'

'Why wouldn't I be in a good mood,' said Timothy with a

smile, 'I got off the job nice and early, and it's just a week until the big day.'

Harry loved seeing his big brother in high spirits. The reminder that Christmas was just a week away certainly served to perk up Harry's mood too. 'Have you done your Christmas shopping yet?' asked Harry.

'Nope,' said Timothy. He always left things like this until the last minute. He'd probably just get everyone a gift voucher from a petrol station on Christmas eve. 'Have you?' he asked Harry.

'Yeah, I went a few weeks back,' said Harry rather smugly, proud of his organisation, 'well, actually, I still need to pick up a present for Ethan. But I've got everything for the cousins, and the aunts, and uncles, and the rest of our ever-growing family. Us Baldwins really do breed like rabbits, don't we?' said Harry with a titter.

Timothy pulled a grimacing face, 'Haven't you heard the news?'

'No, what news?' asked Harry, bracing himself. He was always the last to find out any gossip in the family.

'Well, Auntie Bessie has fallen sick, so they've decided that it isn't suitable for her to be flying over from Ireland,' said Timothy.

'Oh, that's terrible to hear,' said a worried Harry, 'Is she okay?'

'Yeah, it's nothing too bad, thankfully, but it does mean that it'll just be the five of us for Christmas dinner.' Harry was disheartened by the news. He got on so well with his cousins, who certainly brought the best out of him. Now it meant that he would be spending Christmas day with his nuclear family where he would only get the chance to say about four words all day, and those words would probably just be 'Pass the turkey please'.

The one thing that he had been looking forward to the most had been taken away from him. Well, not completely taken away, but he knew Christmas would not be the same this year. Paisán's New Year's Eve party was the only thing keeping him in London at this point.

- 14 -

The frosty liquid collided with his parched tongue, stimulating the gasping tastebuds. The sensory organs cherished the hoppy and bitter flavouring. But the fluid did not spend long in the mouth. The first three-quarters of the palliative intoxicant was sent down the abyss with the first substantial gulp, and the remainder was seen off with a subsequent quaff. The drink served the paradoxical role of refreshing the desiccated body while simultaneously increasing its inebriation. The alcohol was being consumed faster than it could be broken down by the liver, slowing the brain cells down. While the depressant's negative side effects were inevitable, these were to be outweighed by the dopamine tonight. One thing was certain, this would not be the only beverage Harry would consume this evening.

'Another?' asked Paisán as Harry slammed down his empty Hop House 13 Lager. This question was met with an affirmative shake of Harry's head. There were now less than two hours to go until midnight. The start of a new year, a new decade, with endless possibilities. Who knew what it would bring? People were slowly arriving at Paisán's penthouse apartment in Greenwich, which overlooked the River Thames. He was the only one of Harry's friends who had moved out from home. Most could not afford to rent a luxury flat like this at such a young age, but as a risk analyst at a big Hedge Fund, this was pennies on the pound for Paisán. Although, he did not actually get to spend much time here as most of his precious hours were spent slaving away at the Headquarters in Canary Wharf.

'This is some flat you've got yourself,' said Harry, who was particularly enjoying the changing LED strip lights running along the covings. They really set the tone for the party and worked harmoniously with the strident music.

'Thanks bud,' said Paisán. He was an incredibly humble individual who did not like to gloat about his success. Instead, he switched the conversation back to ask Harry about his studies, 'How's Cambridge?'

'Yeah, it's all going well mate, obviously a bit stressful. Final year and all,' said Harry leaning in slightly towards his peer. He, too, did not really want to talk about academic work at a party; he would much rather spend the night drinking and putting academia to the back of his mind. 'When are the others getting here?' he asked.

'They're on the train now. You know how long it takes to trek over from North West London,' said Paisán,

'Yeah, took me over an hour,' said Harry in agreement, 'Is Alfie going to be coming along? I haven't seen him since he got punched.'

'Christ, yeah that was terrible, wasn't it? He said he's going to make it though,' said Paisán.

'Oh, that's good. Do you know how he's recovering?' asked Harry with genuine concern about his friend.

'He's made pretty much a full recovery. Think he had to eat through a straw for a few weeks and has a little scar where they operated,' said Paisán.

Harry looked distraught. He felt as though the assault was somehow his fault. His friends were up to visit him for his birthday after all, and this sense of responsibility had not left him since that night. 'That really is horrific, I hope they catch the bastard that did it,' he said.

'I think his parents are still a bit worried about letting him leave the house. I wouldn't be surprised if he came wrapped in cotton wool,' laughed Paisán.

The boys drank a few more beers and made their way around the flat to socialise. There were some people that Harry knew, but many that he did not recognise. Paisán introduced Harry to some of his workmates, but Harry found them lacklustre and cliquey; all they spoke about was their work. He was delighted when the rest of his pals arrived, and he could finally escape the conversation on merger arbitrage strategy.

'Yes boys,' shouted Harry, who leant back and had his arms wide open. Paisán's colleagues were least impressed at this boisterous behaviour, but Harry did not care. His friends had all arrived together, and Harry would have travelled with them, but for the fact that he was bored in the house all day, so decided to come over earlier to see Paisán. All of the crew were there except John. While Harry felt obliged to invite John to any social event since they had known each other for an eternity, Paisán did not care for the man. Paisán had not known John for as long and did not feel the need to extend his niceties to him. To put it bluntly, John was a leech on other people's conversations, offering little to nothing in a group context. He only served to take up valuable space in a room and quite a substantial amount of space too.

As Michael walked over towards Harry, the beers in his trendy River Island rucksack clinked. Despite working on a building site, Michael cared about his outward appearance and always made sure to drink bottled beers if he was in the company of girls as he thought it looked classier. Alfie and Duncan, on the other hand, came bearing cans of Sainsbury's Basic brand lager in an effort to get drunk for as cheap as possible.

'Guess how much these four cans of lager cost me,' said a chuffed Duncan, who brandished the simplistic orange and white cans in front of Harry's face. Harry stared at the cans, which looked as though they could have been designed by a seven-year-old on Microsoft Word. Before he could even answer, Duncan blurted out in disbelief, 'One pound ten!'

'Yeah, but they're two percent alcohol,' responded Harry, 'going to struggle to get drunk on that.'

Duncan immediately examined the can and was devastated when it informed him that Harry was correct. Alfie now pitched in for the first time, 'Oh for fuck sake, I told you that it was too good to be true.'

'Ah shit, we'll have to go to the shops and buy some more booze,' said Duncan.

No sooner had they joined the party were they on their way back out again, and Harry shouted out to them just as they got to the door, 'Lads, can one of you pick me up a packet of chewing gum. I'll give you the cash when you come back,' he said knowing fine well that they would never see that money.

'Those two are absolute clowns,' said Harry, 'so what have you got clinking in your bag then?'

'Oh, just a few bottles of Corona,' said Michael dismissively. 'But,' he said, building up the tension as he reached into the pocket in his jeans, 'while we may not have had a White Christmas, we've got snow tonight.' Michael pulled out a baggie of cocaine, and Harry's eyes lit up.

The buzz was beginning to build around the apartment. This was a combination of midnight looming but also guests becoming more intoxicated. Harry had gotten to the stage where he was beginning to slur his words. He approached Paisán, who was in deep conversation with his colleagues, and asked, 'Where are we doing the fireworks then?'

Paisán stepped aside, so as not to invite Harry into his circle, since his workmates were more clear-headed than Harry, 'What do you mean fireworks?' said a confused Paisán.

'You know, the thing that goes BOOM!' said an animated Harry, imitating a firework flying high with his hands and exploding as it peaked, 'It is New Year's Eve in case you forgot.'

'I live in a flat. Where on earth did you think I'd be doing them?' asked Paisán.

Harry conceded, 'Good point dear friend.'

'We'll head out onto the balcony for the countdown, I'm sure everyone around us will be having displays,' said Paisán before abruptly returning to his colleagues.

By this stage, Alfie and Duncan had returned from the corner shop. This time with a 700ml bottle of Glen's Vodka and a two-litre bottle of diet lemonade to share between them. Duncan held a packet of cool breeze chewing gum in an outstretched arm to Harry. 'Cheers mate,' said Harry.

However, as Harry stretched to grab the gum, Duncan quickly retracted it from his reach, 'Money please,' he said.

Harry patted his pockets and came up with the lame excuse, 'I don't actually have any cash on me. Look, I'll transfer it to you.' Duncan reluctantly handed over the chewing gum. He was still doubtful that he would see that sixty pence.

Harry enjoyed catching up with his friends who he had not seen since his birthday in November. It seemed that Harry had the lion's share of the stories. Since all bar Michael had graduated, they knew how exhilarating being a student could be and cherished Harry's tales about life in Cambridge. The group were nattering away. As usual, their conversation found its way to reminiscing about school days and how those really were the glory days. Usually, at parties, Harry would wander off and look for a companion for the evening, but nobody stood out to him tonight. In truth, no girl had grabbed his attention the way Elizabeth had. So, Harry spent the evening with the boys, which made a welcome change. He did not have to stress about making mistakes as he did with girls or putting on an act to seduce them. He could just relax, be himself, and enjoy the evening.

Harry took centre stage and began telling the story of how Alfie broke his jaw up in Cambridge. Duncan had obviously heard what had happened the next day, but not the full details. 'So, Alfie has given them the middle finger as they're walking away,' said Harry, who replicated Alfie's rude gesture straight to Duncan's face, 'and this bloke was having absolutely none of it.' Harry told the story with such enthusiasm; his hands were flying all over the place, and his facial expressions matched those he was talking about. Alfie stood scrolling through his phone, unamused at the story mocking him, not wanting to relive that traumatic moment. 'So, anyway,' continued Harry, who now turned to face Alfie, 'the geezer runs up, takes a huge swing back. And Wallop!' roared Harry, who re-enacted the punch, falling just short of Alfie's recovering jaw.

Harry had come so close to hitting Alfie that he flinched, scarred mentally and physically by what had happened to him last month, and his phone flew out of his hands, just as the chips did back in Cambridge. Alfie tried to catch it as it came down, but it went fumbling through his hands and came crashing down on the floor. The screen on his iPhone completely shattered, with tiny shards of glass scattering right across the living room. 'Fuck man,' said Alfie, 'What the hell did you do that for?' asked Alfie aggressively as he bent down to pick up his broken phone. The screen was blacked out. 'I did not need this man, my parents are going to kill me,' he said, closing his eyes and tilting his head up towards the ceiling. Alfie was the unluckiest guy that Harry knew. If anything unfortunate happened, it always seemed to happen to him.

Harry was apologetic, but in all honestly, it was not really his fault. If Alfie was not mindlessly scrolling through his phone, this would not have happened. Harry's attention was not with Alfie and his phone for long. He looked over to the door and saw that Daniel had arrived, and with him, his sister Elizabeth. She was radiant as usual, sporting a faux-fur brown coat with a tight black skirt. Harry was utterly beguiled. He had not seen her since their kiss but had been desperate to message her. He just did not know where her mind was. She knew that he would be here tonight. She wanted to see him, Harry convinced himself. By this point in the evening, Harry had consumed enough liquid lubricant to build up his courage to go and talk to her without delay.

Harry sifted his way through the crowd. It was only an hour until midnight, so he had no time to waste. She was finally going to be his; he would touch her lips once more at the turn of the year. His heart was racing, but as he approached, that's when he saw him. Matt appeared ominously from behind the siblings. Harry was in disbelief, crushed by the presence of Elizabeth's boyfriend. He was now too close to them that he could not turn away and cower back to his friends.

'Harry! How's it going?' said Daniel cheerfully at the presence of his dear friend.

'Very well,' lied Harry.

'You know my sister right, Elizabeth. And this is her boyfriend Matt,' said Daniel as he took off his coat and hung it up by the door.

Harry more than just knew his sister, he could not stop thinking about her, day and night. He nodded at Elizabeth, who avoided all eye contact, and leant in to shake the hand of the man he despised. It was not Matt's fault that Harry loathed him; the man had done nothing wrong. He just had the girl that Harry so desperately wanted. 'Hi, I'm Harry.'

It was met with a short but sweet response, 'Matt.' He had an incredibly firm handshake. Given how tight he was squeezing Harry's hand and how abrupt he was in introducing himself, Harry wondered whether Elizabeth had told him about their kiss.

Harry led the way back into the party, but it was just Daniel who followed. Elizabeth and Matt went into the kitchen, presumably to sort themselves some drinks. After Daniel had greeted Paisán, the host, he went over and joined the rest of the boys, who were ecstatic at his arrival. Daniel was quick to make his presence known, bringing fresh life updates. However, Harry was uninterested in what he had to say. He could not stop himself from looking through the crowded room to see what Elizabeth and Matt were up to.

Elizabeth was stuck to Matt's side all night, perhaps because they did not know many other people at the party. Even if Harry had tried to speak to her, he would never get the chance to be alone with her. Matt was like a guard dog, except flinging a cold slab of meat far away would not distract him from his duties. There was nothing suspicious about the couple's behaviour; perhaps Harry was just overthinking his introduction to Matt earlier.

Harry was distracted whenever his friends tried to converse with him. Even when one of Paisán's colleagues tried to flirt with him, he showed no interest. He contemplated flirting back with her to make Elizabeth jealous but knew that that would only serve to push her further away and into Matt's arms.

Harry was still part of the circle with his friends and had just lost sight of Elizabeth and Matt when Daniel asked him, 'Do you fancy another drink?'

'Nah, I'm alright for now,' replied Harry, who still had half a cup full of Captain Morgan's spiced rum and coke. He had switched over from the beer as after a few, he always felt so bloated.

'Right, I'm going to go and ask Betty if she wants one,' said Daniel walking off.

Initially, Harry did not know who Betty was but quickly figured that he was talking about his sister. Not wanting to miss this golden opportunity to speak to her, even if she was wrapped around Matt, Harry turned his cup upside down, emptying its contents into his mouth. He chased after Daniel and said, 'On second thoughts, it is New Year's Eve, what the hell.'

Daniel grinned, 'That's the response I wanted to hear!'

They located Elizabeth, who unsurprisingly was chatting away to her boyfriend. The music was not as deafening in the kitchen as it was in the living room where the speaker was situated, yet the room was no quieter. The bustling kitchen was instead filled with tumultuous conversation. Harry eyed-up Matt, who was slouched against the marble worktop and compared himself to him. Harry was taller, older, presumably more intelligent, much better looking (or so Harry told himself). *What did Elizabeth see in him? Why could she not just come to her senses and see that Harry was better suited to her?* As Harry and Daniel approached, Elizabeth stepped in front of Matt, who now stood tall and wrapped his arms around his girlfriend protectively.

'Want a gin and tonic Betty?' asked Daniel, who opened the fridge door in the hope of scavenging some tonic water.

'Go on then,' she answered.

Daniel had found precisely what he was looking for, a chic bottle of elderflower Fever-Tree tonic. There were even some pre-cut lemons on the first shelf, which he nabbed before closing the door. 'G&T alright for you too Harry?' asked Daniel.

'Yeah, nice one mate,' said Harry.

'Good,' said Daniel, 'because that's all I can offer you.' Daniel headed to the other side of the kitchen, where the plastic cups were stored, to start making the concoctions. He had forgotten to ask Matt if he wanted one but could always return to make another drink if he did. This left Harry alone with the couple.

'So, how are you guys finding the party?' asked Harry to be polite. There was so much more he wanted to say to Elizabeth that he could not say in front of Matt.

Matt spoke for the pair of them, 'Yeah good mate, don't really know anyone though, but I had nothing else planned for tonight.'

Harry was tempted to use this response as an excuse to get Elizabeth alone. Perhaps he could send Matt back with Daniel to meet their friends. He thought about the cunning plan but did not really have any faith that it would come off. He would just end up taking Elizabeth with him. No longer in the mood for games, he decided to direct a question straight at Elizabeth to force her to engage with him, 'How about you Elizabeth, are you enjoying your evening?'

Elizabeth bluntly replied, 'Yep,' while keeping her eyes fixed on the ground. You could almost cut the tension between them with a knife.

She was so bitterly cold and rude to Harry. It was understandable that she acted this way in front of Matt because she did not know how to react to the situation. Even though she was insensitive with Harry now, the spark they had when they first met was remarkable, and the fact that they were intimate not so long-ago convinced Harry that she was worth fighting for. Harry persisted in his endeavours, 'How are you finding Cambridge?'

Another question aimed directly at Elizabeth. This time, he was hopeful that it would invoke more than a one-word answer from her. For the first time all night, she plucked up the courage to look at Harry. Her vivid blue eyes captivated Harry, who quickly found himself getting lost in them. It was at this moment that he knew. This was more than lust. He loved her. Was it possible to love someone that you cannot have? Someone you hardly even know?

It was as if looking at Harry warmed Elizabeth up. She was no longer as icy as her eyes and was slowly coming out of her shell. Elizabeth spoke about how she found her first term in Cambridge, but Harry could not focus on her words. It was as if he was placed under a spell by her eyes. If Matt was not stood behind her, holding her, there is no doubt in Harry's mind that they would be kissing right now.

Daniel had come back from the other side of the kitchen, skilfully carrying three plastic cups together. He was grateful that he had not offered Matt a drink as he did not think that he would be able to carry four over at a time. 'Here you go,' said Daniel as he held all three drinks in front of his sister. Elizabeth grabbed one, and Harry lurched in to grab his cup. As he reached over, his hand brushed Elizabeth's. It was only brief, but he cherished the physical contact with her.

Much to Harry's surprise, Elizabeth raised her cup and said, 'Cheers.' Matt turned around to grab his tepid can of Magners cider from the worktop. Upon retrieving it, both Harry and Daniel had raised their plastic cups to meet Elizabeth's. Elizabeth stared deep into Harry's eyes, and the pair did not break this connection as they drank from their cups. Matt was too late to collide his drinks with the other three and took a solemn sip of his drink.

The kitchen had slowly begun to empty out as people made their way into the lounge. With a check of his watch, Daniel said, 'Gosh, we had better head out to the balcony for the fireworks. Only five minutes to go.'

There was not much room on the wooden panelled balcony, and Harry was actually a little worried that they might fall through it. Daniel nipped through the assemblage to join the rest of his friends, but Harry stuck behind with Elizabeth and Matt. He did not know what to expect at midnight, but he had rekindled his connection with the girl that he loved and sure as hell wanted to be around to find out.

Most of the people on the balcony were shivering in the biting winter's air but did not want to rush back inside to get their coats for fear of missing that vital second.

'TEN!' shouted out someone from the crowd. Harry did not know how they knew precisely the time. There was no clock in sight, and even if there was, it might not have been accurate to the second. Perhaps they got the exact time from their phone.

Nonetheless, Harry, as well as everyone else on the balcony, joined in on the countdown, 'NINE!'

Harry turned to look at Elizabeth, and to his surprise, the stare was reciprocated. 'EIGHT!'

Their eyes were locked together as they both shouted out, 'SEVEN!'

Surely this was not going to happen again. Was this the moment that Elizabeth was to become his? Was this the moment that she would leave Matt? 'SIX!'

She edged towards Harry, still keeping her eyes gazing into his. Harry froze, not just because of the cold night, but because he could not believe that this was actually happening. 'FIVE!'

Elizabeth lowered her eyes to Harry's lips, and Harry prepared himself for his magical midnight kiss. 'FOUR!'

Harry swallowed the salvia in his mouth; he wanted to make it a pleasant environment for Elizabeth to feel welcome in. 'THREE!'

Harry had goosebumps. He was going to do it. He was the man. It should be him that leans in. Or should he wait for Elizabeth? 'TWO!'

Despite the numbing temperature, his palms were sweating. His heart was pounding. Blood was rushing to his penis. He stood there erect as everyone shouted, 'ONE!'

Here goes, it was now or never thought Harry. Their eyes were still locked. He could not believe it. He began to lean in, but as he started to move, Elizabeth was swooped away by Matt, who buried his face in hers. At that moment, the party-goers collectively cheered, 'HAPPY NEW YEAR!'

The sky began to flood with colour as fireworks were set off all around the capital. Everyone was toasting with their plastic cups, which did not quite have the same ring to it as the clinking of champagne flutes, but nonetheless they were all rejoicing the turn of the year. Harry stared at Elizabeth as she passionately kissed Matt. They showed no signs of stopping, and Harry did not know how long this pain would go on. He could not believe it. That was his kiss, his moment, his girl.

When they finally broke apart, Matt said to Elizabeth, 'Happy New Year babe. I love you.'

Elizabeth smiled at her boyfriend and replied, 'Happy New Year!'

Daniel pulled in Matt to celebrate the beginning of the decade. He wrapped his arm around his sister's boyfriend and started rocking with him as everyone drunkenly sang 'Auld Lang Syne'. Harry could not bear it. How imprudent was he to think that Elizabeth would kiss him here in front of Matt?

Not wanting to be surrounded by joyous people, Harry turned away and stormed back inside. He paced swiftly towards the front door, just wanting to be back home to cry himself to sleep. Elizabeth saw Harry leaving in the corner of her eye and slipped off away from everyone else. Harry had just slammed the front door shut when she got back into the warm living room, and she jogged over so as not to let him escape.

Just as Elizabeth had got outside the flat, Harry angrily slammed his hand against the wall in the hallway. 'Harry, wait,' she said in a soft tone to prevent him storming off.

Confused that someone would leave the party to follow him, but instantly recognising the voice, Harry turned around. Tears were pouring down his face. Harry let out something between a groan and a shout, 'What? What do you want?' He had stopped in his tracks, and Elizabeth began slowly walking up to him.

'I'm sorry,' she said while consoling Harry.

'Sorry for what exactly? He's your boyfriend. You don't need to be sorry for kissing him,' Harry said, hoping that she would disagree.

'I'm not sorry for that,' said Elizabeth. Harry looked down in disappointment, but she carried on, 'I'm sorry for kissing you on your birthday.'

Harry looked utterly devastated. This was not what he was expecting her to say. 'What do you mean?' he sobbed.

'I should have never dragged you into this,' she said, grabbing his hands to comfort him, 'I really am sorry.'

Not believing that she did not love him back, Harry said, 'You cannot tell me that you don't feel this connection between us. We click, we have this buzz that I've never felt with anyone else before'.

'Of course, there is a spark between us Harry. That's what has been fucking with my mind these past few months.'

Harry shook his head, not able to comprehend the situation, 'I don't understand what is getting in the way. You know we are meant to be together. I love you Elizabeth.'

Elizabeth was caught off guard with what he had just said and instantly let go of his hand, 'The timing is just all wrong. I'm with Matt. I'm sorry Harry.' She turned away and headed back to the flat. Harry slumped down onto the floor; he was an emotional wreck, and being drunk only served to exacerbate this.

'Happy New Year to me,' said Harry gingerly to himself.

There really was not too much keeping Harry in London at the start of 2020. The festive period was over, his family and friends were all back to work, and worst of all, he felt as though his head was going to fall off if he slept one more night on that wretched sofa. It was time for Harry to head back to Cambridge for another rigorous term of studying, this time with a few extra fleeces from home to keep him warm. On the first weekend of the year, his mother, once again, drove him up and helped him to settle into his not-so-humble abode. Thankfully this time, she had dropped Harry off in the right place and avoided getting a parking ticket by remaining in the car. Despite the magnificence of Trinity College, Susan did not want to loiter in a cold Cambridge and headed straight back home.

The term was not set to start for another ten days, so the city was significantly more tranquil than usual. The college was particularly desolate. It felt as though the only other people on site were the Porters. They were almost part of the furniture in the college, there day and night, keeping the college secure all year round. Some porters were even held captive on Christmas Day, which Harry found tyrannical.

The dark winter days rushed by expeditiously. Harry spent most of them in bed, lacking the motivation to do anything. He was still dolorous over what had happened on New Year's Eve. His suffering was made worse by the fact that he was living in complete isolation. The only time he left his stuffy old room to get some fresh air was to do a food shop. Other than that, he was trapped inside like an aristocratic prisoner. Harry would go entire days without human contact, even virtual human contact. His friends back home were getting on with their careers, and his Cambridge friends were too busy having fun wherever in the world they were.

Trapped, with nobody else to talk to, Harry was alone with his thoughts, which was not a good thing given his current state. He kept replaying the events of Paisán's party; how he thought he would finally be with Elizabeth but how she played him and crushed his heart. Thinking back to it led to frequent outbursts of bitter tears. The intermittent segments of the day where Harry was actually conscious would be spent watching Netflix in bed and eating every unhealthy food you could imagine. He practically lived off takeaways, ice cream, and crisps, especially when his food stock was depleted. It was as if Harry had been through a tough *break-up*, but he was never with Elizabeth in the first place. He found himself in a strange paradox; could he miss something that he never had? When the pain got particularly bad, Harry often found himself stalking her Instagram account, but this only made things worse as he would see how happy she was with Matt. It was toxic looking at the girl he loved with someone else, but he could not resist the temptation of seeing what she was up to.

By the time his friends were beginning to arrive back in college, Harry's room resembled a dumping ground. His clothes were chucked wherever he had taken them off each night, empty Dominos boxes decorated the barely visible wooden floor, crushed cans of all variation lying around the room (from Pepsi to beer, there was even a tin of soup that had rolled under his bed), plates and mugs dotted all around too. The stench was building up in his room, and Harry was beginning to stink too, as he lacked the motivation to shower each day. He did not see the point if he was not leaving his room or interacting with anyone; he could not smell his own scent, so he often went days without washing.

Harry's dormant phone sprung back into life as his Cambridge friends were messaging of their return. However, Harry had no interest in going to see them. He had given up with the outside world, which was filled with indescribable horrors. No, he much preferred the security of his own room and did not desire social interaction. Harry fell completely silent on the group chat; he even ignored it when Raymond and Mo messaged directly to check up on him. For all they knew, Harry was still at home with his family.

It had been a couple days before Raymond had decided that enough was enough and came bursting into Harry's room to see if he was there. Raymond was in utter disbelief at the state of the room; he was on the verge of chundering on account of the smell alone. He heard a muffled wailing noise coming from Harry's room, so he slowly made his way through the living room. Raymond could have sworn that he saw a rat mulling through the litter as he approached the door nervously. As he slowly opened the creaking wooden door, he did not know what to expect, but he certainly was not anticipating seeing Harry curled up in a ball weeping away. 'Harry, are you okay?' said a hesitant Raymond.

Without turning to see who it was, Harry shrieked, 'Go away!' He pulled the blanket even further over himself as if to cover himself from the intruder.

Raymond was shocked at his response but knew he could not just leave. 'Harry, it's me mate, Raymond,' he said to succour his friend.

The identity of the individual did not matter to Harry as he remarked, 'I just want to be left alone.'

However, Raymond was having none of this. He made his way around the bed so that he could see Harry's face, but when he sat down on the mattress, Harry instantly flipped to the other side to avoid having to look at his friend. 'Okay,' said Raymond, 'you don't have to look at me.' There was a short pause as Raymond conjured up what to say next. He was not really good at this whole comforting business and wished that someone else had come into the room in his place. 'Can you at least tell me what's up?'

Harry did not want to be impertinent to his friend or unduly take his volatile sentiments out on him, so finally gave a proper response, 'I'm just not in a good place right now,' he knew this was not going to be enough to shake off Raymond, so continued with a sob, 'I don't want to talk about it either.'

Raymond did not want to push Harry any further and was relieved that he had been handed a golden ticket out of this situation. He stood up to leave the room, but as he was on his way to the door, he remembered what he actually came to speak to Harry about. 'Oh, we're having the termly meeting for the Drinking Society at the Eagle later. Are you going to be coming along to that?' Raymond made it sound a lot more official than it actually was. In reality, it was a chance to have a few informal drinks with pals and run through the term's agenda.

However, Harry was not in the mood to see other people, let alone come across in a presentable way at a 'meeting'. 'I'm going to give it a miss today,' he said, poking a fraction of his face out of the blanket, like a butterfly emerging from its cocoon after days of solitude.

It was when Raymond saw Harry's puffy red eyes and his damp face that he saw how crushed his friend was. This was when Harry needed him the most, before things got any worse. But Raymond did not want to spend the next hour of his life listening to his grieving friend, so he quickly looked away from Harry and headed straight out of the door without saying another word.

All of Harry's close friends were in his drinking society. It was not necessarily that they were close friends as freshers; rather, the society solidified their friendships because of what they had been through together. Now that they were in their third year, they were at the top of the hierarchy and called the shots. Drinking societies are another strange Cambridge quirk, loosely resembling American fraternities and sororities, but not quite as cringy. Each college would have at least one drinking society, separated by gender, and would meet weekly with another college's society in what was known as a 'swap'. The societies would go to shady venues and pay the owners to use the space to get as drunk as possible in their designated two-hour slot. It was said to be an opportunity to mingle with people from other colleges, but in reality, as inhibitions lowered with each drink, students were doing far more than just getting to know each other by the end of the night.

The Draggalbs, or Galbs for short, was Trinity's infamous drinking society. It was the oldest drinking society in the university and was notoriously difficult to secure a place in. Students did not choose to join the drinking society; instead, the society chose the individuals who would be invited along to select events and put through their paces to see if they were 'Galb material'. Those who passed the initial sift were put through the most outrageous initiations, which evolved and became more extreme with each passing year.

When Harry and his friends were initiated, they were pushed to their limits. It was not just drinking that they had to do, although that was, of course, a key component. In fact, drinking probably helped with all of the other gross things that they had to do. Harry still remembers (as much as he tries to forget) the Surströmming tinned fish he had to eat. Fish that had been fermented for at least six months and was once voted the worst smelling food in the world. He could just about hack the drinking, the ghost chilli peppers, and anything else thrown his way, but this was undoubtedly the vilest thing that had done in his short life. So, he certainly enjoyed making the freshers eat it on their initiations. He also particularly enjoyed kidnapping the freshers during their lectures and making them drink copious amounts of spirits before returning them in a drunken mess to their lecture halls. It was all 'just a bit of fun', or that was what they always told themselves. Although the freshers certainly did not see it this way.

The societies were undemocratic and exclusive by nature. As opposed to an election, the Presidents are appointed each year by the previous holder of the position, and this year Aaron was given that very honour. He had assembled a cabinet, which consisted of final year students, to ensure the smooth running of the Galbs. In Aaron's so-called cabinet was Raymond, Mo, Cuthbert, and Harry, and those were the people he summoned to the termly meeting.

With Harry still nestled in bed, wanting to escape reality, it was just the four men who walked down to the Eagle shortly after the sun had gone down. As a history student, Aaron loved all of the unique traditions that came with Cambridge. Perhaps that was why he rose to lead the Galbs. He was particularly fond of the Eagle, not just because it was where Crick and Watson 'discovered the secret of life', but also as it was the second oldest pub in the city, and you could tell. Thick wooden beams ran across the low ceilings, the floor was uneven and creaky, and there was barely enough space for punters to weave their way through the tightly packed tables to get to the bar. Most buildings in Cambridge were small and cosy, creating an intimate environment, whereas the Eagle was dark and dingey. It was also compact and rather uncomfortable by design. The interior was hideous; it was old-fashioned (but not the good kind of old-fashioned), looking as though a hipster cat had thrown up everywhere. The pub was the definition of impracticality, completely unfit for purpose, but that was what Aaron loved about the place.

The place was absolutely heaving that Saturday night, or so it felt, with the boys packed like sardines into the cramped pub. Aaron led the other three to the RAF bar at the back of the tavern, hoping to try their luck for service. During the Second World War, Allied airmen used wax candles, petrol lighters and lipstick to write their names, squadron numbers and any other doodles that came into their minds onto the ceiling, and this bar was Aaron's favourite drinking spot in the entire city. However, just one woman was working behind the small bar, running around frantically to try and serve customers with beverages. People were leaning over the counter, waving their money at the bartender with frustration at how long they were being made to wait. It was clear that there was no order of service, it was dog-eat-dog, and the boys joined in, shoving their way to the front.

It took what felt like an eternity for the boys to get served, especially since they bought their drinks separately in typical student fashion. Aaron was the first to be served and ordered a pint of Eagle's DNA, the special ale served by the pub to commemorate the discovery. Happy to have his jar of ale, he headed over to the corner of the pub where there was one poorly-lit table available. It looked as though it was made for two people, but they would find a way to squeeze all four of them around it.

Cuthbert came over next with his glass of red wine. His glass stuck to the table and was evidence that the table had not been cleaned following the last guests. This was no surprise as the bar staff were rushed off of their feet. 'Could we not have gone somewhere nice for drinks,' Cuthbert remarked as he reluctantly took a seat on the chair, worried that it might stain his pale red chinos.

Aaron shook his head, 'Cuthbert dear, this pub embodies everything it means to be a Galb!'

Cuthbert let out a small sigh, 'Oh but it is so ghastly and busy, we could have gone anywhere.'

Raymond made his way over from the bar next. He grabbed a stool from a neighbouring table and slammed his tumbler of Jameson down on the table. His college-imposed drinking ban was finally over, and he wasted no time in hitting the strong stuff. 'What are you on Cuthbert?' he asked, referring to his peer's drink.

Pulling his glass from the suction of the table, Cuthbert raised it up and said, 'This is just a Cabernet Sauvignon. I wanted to get a cocktail but would not trust one from here.' Raymond laughed at how pompous his friend was and took a small swig of his whiskey.

'Shall we get some grub?' asked Raymond as he picked up the menu, 'I really have a hankering for a burger.'

'I'd get on that,' said Aaron, nodding in agreement.

It was no surprise that Cuthbert looked disgusted at his peers, 'Absolutely not. I am not eating *pub grub* from a Greene King,' he emphasised, 'you can count me out'.

'Suit yourself,' said Raymond, who was now scanning through the menu, ignoring Cuthbert's opinion.

A fair few minutes passed before Mo was served. Unlike the others, he was waiting a lot more patiently for his drink. Unsure of what to get, he decided to copy Aaron and got himself a pint of ale. It was not until he took the first sip that he realised it did not suit his palate; he winced as he made his way through the crowd of punters. As he bumped and hustled his way through the throng, beer flowed over the edges of the pint glass. He was only a couple paces away from the other three when the glass slipped straight out of his hand and spilt all over the dark carpet.

Cuthbert leapt up in fear of the liquid splashing onto him. 'Nice one butterfingers,' remarked Aaron while laughing away at his peer's misfortune. This was typical Mo, clumsy as they came. Embarrassed, he bent down to pick up the glass, which miraculously did not shatter and headed back into the rabble to sort himself out with another beverage. Mo thought that perhaps this is why they had such a gloomy-looking carpet, so that any spilt drinks would camouflage into the fabric. Either way, it was such a waste of a fiver.

Mo came back a little while later, this time carrying over a large bottle of Hooch. Aaron was confused at this drastic change of drink, maybe it was easier to carry over, and he asked, 'Interesting choice of drink. Why the substitution?'

Feeling a little insecure about Aaron's comment, Mo responded, 'I didn't actually like the taste of that ale before. Thought I'd go for something a bit more flavoursome.'

'To business then gentlemen,' said Aaron, who pulled out his phone to get up his notes. He had already made all of the important decisions for the term but wanted to inform the others of the agenda and make them feel part of the society. 'This term, we are going to have swaps bi-weekly. I know last term we had a swap every single week without fail, but that was just so persistent.'

Mo chipped in, 'You're quite right. They almost felt like a chore towards the end.'

'Precisely, while they were all great fun, well most of them at least,' digressed Aaron, 'I've never met a more boring bunch than the Homerton Ha'Pennies,' he said as a passing comment before getting to his actual point at hand, 'I want to have swaps every other week so that we can really build up the excitement around them. Besides, everyone always seems a lot busier in Lent Term than Michaelmas, what with work and all.'

Raymond jumped in to support Aaron, 'Yes, that's a great idea. We can make sure that we can really do them properly so that everyone will attend.' One of the issues of having a swap every week is that they begin to lose their appeal and can become quite burdensome for the industrious students to attend. After all, these were Cambridge students, who study relentlessly.

'Exactly,' said Aaron, taking a sip of his beer before continuing where he left off, 'I have arranged our first swap with the Newnham Nobles. This is set to be a big one,' he said excitedly, 'they've got a reputation for being wild. So, we'll have to make sure all the boys are on top form.'

Mo could not help but grin as he added, 'Christ I'm excited, they have an abundance of talent.'

Cuthbert disapproved, 'That's not really an appropriate comment, is it now.'

Mo quickly tried to cover up his remark, 'No, no, what I meant was that they are very loud and witty.'

'Well, that's obviously not what you meant,' said Cuthbert.

Aaron could not tolerate their bickering, so he spoke over them to drown them out, 'In week 4 we have the Robinson Rockets. Week 6, we pair up with Clare Cats, then in the final week of term we're scheduled in with St Edmund's College.'

'St Edmund's?' said Cuthbert in a confused tone, 'Is that not a mature college?'

'Yep,' said Aaron.

'I do love an older woman. They just know what they're

doing. Got the experience, if you know what I mean,' said Raymond as he nudged Cuthbert with his elbow.

Cuthbert laughed, and Mo jumped straight in at his hypocrisy, 'Why do you laugh when Raymond makes a comment like that, but scrutinise me when I do it?'

'Because it is not as creepy when Raymond does it. Plus, he actually gets girls, unlike you,' said Cuthbert, taking a cheap shot at Mo, who was already agitated.

'What about Michelle? I slept with her after a swap,' said Mo trying to boast about his ventures with the fairer sex.

'That was in first year,' said Cuthbert.

'And the only girl you've slept with at uni,' added Raymond, rubbing salt in the wounds.

Aaron was getting fed up that they were drifting away from the agenda, 'Guys, that's enough, stop tormenting Mo.' Mo started to calm down now that Aaron was taking his side, but Aaron continued, 'We all know he can't get girls, but can we please get back on track.' Mo's smile quickly vanished. He considered standing up for himself but realised that he was outnumbered three to one, so let it go.

The burgers that Aaron and Raymond ordered had now arrived at the table, interrupting Aaron's flow. 'Thank you,' said Raymond as his food was placed in front of him, 'Can I grab some ketchup actually?' The bartender looked flustered at the request, it was clear that she was in high demand this evening, but ever the professional, she politely complied with the request.

Aaron had just finished his pint of ale when he took a large bite into his gourmet burger. His mouth dried as he began chewing away, and he wished that he had another drink to wash down his food. However, he knew if he went up to the bar to get one, his food would be freezing by the time he came back, or more likely still, his friends would have got stuck into it in his absence. Prioritising his food over running through the agenda, he asked an open question to the others, 'Themes gentlemen?'

Each swap would have its own distinct theme to make it authentic and allow the members to invest in the evening. More often than not, they would end up making their own costumes, which never turned out well, but it was *more entertaining* that way. Mo was the first to offer a suggestion, 'ToGalb party. It's nice and easy at least.'

'Could you get any more basic-uni student,' said Cuthbert, who did not fancy the idea of dressing up in his bedsheet in the freezing winter months.

'We'll put that one on the *maybe* list,' said Aaron, stuffing down his chips. 'I'm going to grab another pint, have a little think amongst yourselves,' he said while squeezing out from the table and preparing himself for the scrum at the bar. The others chatted away in his absence, running through different ideas, all trying to be creative and make a pun with some variation of 'Draggalb' or 'Galb' in it. Aaron had been served surprisingly fast, and when he returned, he said, 'A meal is only as good as its drink,' parading his freshly poured pint amongst his peers.

The other three whisked through some ideas that they had, but none of them were really what Aaron was looking for. That was until Cuthbert suggested, 'How about OktoGalbfest?'

'That's so stupid,' said Mo, who was clearly still bitter about how Cuthbert had treated him earlier.

'No, no. I think I like it,' said Aaron, who looked up at the graffitied ceiling in deep thought, 'It makes no sense to have an Oktoberfest theme in early February, but nobody would expect it. In fact, I love it!' Aaron raised his glass to toast Cuthbert for his idea. 'OktoGalbfest. We'll have that as our first theme with the Newnham Nobles.'

The boys spent the next few hours making repeated trips to the bar and moved beyond Draggalbs' business. They caught up on what each of the others had been up to over the Christmas break and enjoyed hearing the fresh new tales. They even spoke about why Harry was acting odd, but this topic was quickly brushed over, not wanting to put a downer on the evening. As the pub rang the bell for the last orders, the boys got in one last round of drinks to see them past midnight. Aaron once more brought the conversation back to the upcoming swap with Newnham, 'Right, we are all obviously going to have to be on top of our game. We want to leave a lasting impression,' he said while scanning each of the other three individually. 'It is also imperative that we invite some good freshers along. We cannot be having any weirdos coming and damaging our reputation. Raymond, I'm going to leave this task to you.'

Raymond loved serving the Galbs and went very serious in his tone, 'For sure. I think it's best we stick with freshers we've already had, much less risk that way.'

Aaron nodded in agreement, 'Yes. Two or three at most, not too many. We do want to make sure we can begin to integrate some of them into the Galbs.'

The bartenders were now doing the rounds to kick everyone out of the pub so that they could close up. Since the boys were in the corner, they were the last group to be told to leave, but they did so respectfully, finishing their drinks and heading home. The evening had been a successful one, and they could not wait to spread the word of the events planned for the term with the rest of the members of society. It was lining up to be an excellent term for the Draggalbs.

- 16 -

We get up each day because we feel motivated to achieve something, an internal light that guides us through life. Our goals are dynamic and change as we progress through our existence. We may be motivated to succeed in education, at work, in our love lives. It does not matter what this driving factor is; all that matters is that it gives us purpose. The brighter this light beams, the more ambitious we become. Yet, when this beacon within us begins to dim, we start to slip into a dark depression. For Harry, it felt as though this light bulb was completely shattered and that there was no way of turning it back on. Life was seemingly futile without Elizabeth, simply not worth living. What good is achieving a degree from Cambridge? Securing a good job? Earning his riches? It all meant nothing if he did not have the woman he loved by his side. Harry had truly slipped into a slump of depression at the start of the new year. A sense of hopelessness began to outweigh any opportunities that living could hold.

When Harry did pluck up the courage to leave his room, he

rarely engaged with others and could not wait to get back to the comfort of his own space. He no longer found pleasure in spending time with his friends; instead, he felt isolated in their company. This forlorn feeling and loss of interest in his own life had a drastic impact on his studies. While he missed a fair few lectures throughout his degree, he would always make sure he at least did the readings to keep up with each module. Now, however, lecture attendance was a rarity, and he slacked with academic papers too. Harry did not write his first two essays of term, nor did he bother to attend the supervisions. His inbox piled up with emails, overflowing to an unmanageable scale, and he chose to ignore them all. His friends tried to be there for him, but he pushed them away further and put on a brave face to hide his pain. The power of love is perplexing. We often do not realise our happiness until it is stripped away from us.

Raymond would often come down to chat with Harry. Even though he was uncomfortable with situations like this, he believed that he needed to support Harry. To help him through this rough patch. Raymond was the only person Harry had told about Elizabeth, and while he was sworn to secrecy, he soon told the rest of the friendship group to get their views on the matter. Whatever attempts Raymond tried to get Harry out of his room were always unsuccessful. Initially, Harry would go out for a cigarette with Raymond, but Harry had now put a sock over his smoke alarm and had begun smoking in his room.

Helping Harry seemed an impossible cause, his friends were also busy studying, wanting to secure a good grade at the end of the year. However, things changed when Harry received a message from Bertie:

Semi-final against Fitzwilliam this weekend. Absolutely massive fixture. I can't stress how much we need you for this one.

It was quite astounding. Harry's friends had tried painstakingly hard to pull him out from his depressed state, but all Harry needed was this message from the football captain. Bertie, of course, did not know of Harry's broken heart, but nonetheless, his short message had done the trick. Harry's love of the game seemed to be the one constant that was always there for him.

Trinity had been on a terrific cup run, just scraping past Queen's College on penalties in the Quarterfinals last term. The competition, called 'cuppers', was the highlight of the footballing season, where all thirty-one colleges would battle it out to get their hands on the silverware. Everything seemed possible in this competition; there always seemed to be a story of the dark horse that defied all the odds. However, Trinity really would need all of the Gods on their side to win this match. Fitzwilliam college, or Fitz, were renowned for their sporting prowess. In fact, they were accustomed to being more lenient with their admissions for those with outstanding sporting abilities. The Fitz football team was stacked with university-level players, and they had won cuppers for the previous three years. Trinity were indeed the underdogs for the fixture, but you just never knew what freaky result this cup could churn out. That was the magic of the cup.

The week flew by, and before Harry knew it, it was Saturday morning. He had a good night's sleep in him, ate porridge with a banana for breakfast and completed all of his pre-match rituals. He knew that he needed to be on top of his game today because he could make all the difference. Harry was certainly in the zone; his mind was focused solely on the fixture. He had never been more pumped up. It may have only been a college match, but Fitz were despised in sport by all other colleges. They had a reputation similar to that of Chelsea or Manchester City, buying their way to success. Today, Trinity had the chance to be the giant slayers, and a sought-after place in the final was at stake.

Trinity were playing away at Fitzwilliam's fortress, and this meant that a gargantuan crowd would be expected, a hostile environment for the Trinity men. Indeed, despite the drizzle, the supporters were already beginning to flock to the pitch when both teams headed into the changing rooms one last time before the match commenced. Fitz looked immeasurably more professional in their matching maroon tracksuits and ran over as a group to the changing rooms. Each player for Trinity was wearing a different training top, and they lumbered back to the clubhouse in uncoordinated waves, kicking a few footballs over with them as they did so. It was a typical away changing room, cold and unwelcoming. Spiders crawled ominously around the ceiling, and the players had to get changed on firm super-annuated wooden benches. The contrast could not have been greater with the home dressing room, which boasted heating and comfy leather seating for all of the players. It also came equipped with showers and a whiteboard for the manager to run through the tactics. This was all part of the mind games to get into the away team's head before kick-off. However, Bertie did not let the changing rooms affect him. As a third-year, he had played many a time against Fitz and knew exactly what to expect. He had never managed to prevail but was adamant that today would be the day that Trinity finally triumphed!

The tunes were popping off in the away dressing room to get the side mentally pumped up for the game. Bertie was eager to make sure that his side were louder from the off, to really impose themselves on Fitz, and fight back in the psychological warfare. Most of the team wore extra layers and put on gloves to keep warm for the match, but Harry did not believe in that nonsense. It was not that he liked the cold, but if he wanted to stay warm, he would just run around more. While his team-mates were messing around and dancing away to the music, Harry sat in complete silence, staring at the white-painted brick wall, waiting for Bertie to run through the team. He was trying to channel all of his emotions and internal aching about Elizabeth into his performance on the pitch. The team was announced, and Bertie gave the command to send his men out to the pitch like a general sending his soldiers over the top. This was met by war cries from the sportsmen in a final attempt to hype themselves up ahead of the match.

The crowd had built up significantly by the time the two teams jogged back over. While it was by no means comparable to the attendance of a professional match, there were enough supporters to make a connected loop around the entire pitch (at least a few hundred people or so). The ref blew his whistle, and the two captains went in to shake hands. Harry loathed the Fitzwilliam captain, Rodger. Harry remembered how the two of them were competing for the same spot in the university trials in first year, and how Rodger pipped him to the position. The Fitz man always seemed to score against Trinity in the league and would always gloat about their team's success. To make things worse, Rodger was sporting a top knot; he was arrogant enough as it was before making this dreadful decision about his appearance. Today was the final opportunity for Harry to take revenge on Rodger, the man who had haunted him for the past three years.

Bertie had won the toss and decided that he wanted his team to have the kick-off. He thudded his hands hard together and shouted, 'Come on Trinity, let's fucking go boys!'

The game started at a remarkably high intensity, and Fitz were really pressing on the Trinity men in dark blue, forcing them to make mistakes. It was clear that Trinity would have to sit in for a lot of this game and defend with their lives. Bertie's men were playing solidly and holding their own against the favourites. Thirty minutes had passed without any goals, although Fitz had come close striking the woodwork twice.

The Trinity keeper booted the ball long from a goal kick, and Harry went up to compete for the ball with Roger in the middle of the park. They had both got up high in the air, and it looked as though Harry was going to win the ball. Roger decided to take matters into his own hands and swung his elbow aggressively into Harry's face. Harry dropped straight down to the floor, and the Fitz man headed the ball onto an onrushing striker bearing down on goal. Harry was left holding his now bloodied face, but it seems the referee must have missed the incident, and the game continued. The striker took it around the Trinity goalkeeper but brought the ball out so wide to a near on impossible angle to score. Joel Lockhurst was sprinting back to defend his goal as the striker took his shot. The striker hit it firmly, but it was clearly going wide of the goal. Eager to make an impression in front of the roaring audience, Joel slid in along the wet surface to block the shot but ended up firing it into the roof of his own net from a couple of yards out.

The striker ran off to the corner flag and celebrated with a backflip as if he had scored the goal. The rest of the Fitz team darted over to join the attacker. Joel was left on the surface with both hands covering his face. He felt too humiliated by his feeble attempt at defending to face the cheering crowd. Harry was also left on the wet ground, holding his face in distress. The rest of the Trinity team surrounded the referee pressuring him to overturn the decision and award the foul. The referee stuck with his original decision and awarded the goal. When Roger came running back to his half, he passed the wounded Harry, leant in and said, 'Unlucky mate.' These two words were enough to rile Harry up, who wanted to pummel him right there and then. Rodger was camped in Harry's head, and it was clear that he was here to win at all costs.

The momentum of the game showed no sign of changing after Fitzwilliam took the lead. They were playing slick football and dominated possession. Fitz had a few more great chances and were denied increasing their lead through some phenomenal saves from the Trinity keeper; without him, the game would have been long gone. The Fitz *goalscorer* fancied his chances with a speculative effort from long range. It was heading right for the top corner, until the keeper's hand came from nowhere to tip it wide of the post for a corner kick. The effort was met with a collective groan from the crowd who thought their college were about to double their lead.

The corner was whipped in with pace, but Bertie was the first man to meet it, sending it well clear of the box. It landed at the feet of one of the Trinity wingers who had acres of space to run into. Fitz had committed a lot of men forward for the corner and now found themselves exposed to a counterattack. The winger took a few big touches to carry the ball up the pitch, and Harry was busting a gut to get there to support his teammate. They found themselves in a two versus two situation, by far Trinity's best opportunity of the game. The Fitz defender closed the winger down, leaving Harry open, and the winger played a perfectly weighted ball to find Harry, who was now one-on-one with the goalkeeper. Harry looked him in the eyes as he approached him and felt that he was too close to get a shot away. Instead, Harry threw in a step over, dropped his shoulder one way and went the other. He had completely fooled the goalkeeper, who was now left sitting on the floor. But as Harry went running onto the ball to tap it into the empty net, the keeper just managed to extend his leg and trip Harry up before he could get there. Harry plummeted to the floor, and the keeper rushed over to collect the ball.

The referee, struggling to keep up with the pace of the players, eventually made his way over to the two men. He blew his whistle and pointed to the penalty spot. To everyone's disbelief, he only brandished a yellow card for the goalkeeper, not a red one. Nonetheless, Trinity had a penalty and a chance to level the match bang on half-time.

The showers had now turned into a full-fledged storm, and the supporters were all pulling out their umbrellas for shelter. Harry picked up the ball. He won the penalty, so he would be the one to take it. Harry placed the ball on the spot and took seven steps backwards. He ran his hands through his floppy damp hair to make sure it was not in the way. Anyone else's heart would have been racing as the referee blew his whistle.

In fact, it seemed as though everyone else was more nervous about the next kick of the ball than Harry. He had ice running through his veins as the crowd were jeering and booing in an attempt to distract him. Harry ran up with intent, but as he went to strike the ball, he slipped on the wet surface, scuffing his shot off to the right. He still made a good connection with the ball, and it flew through the air but struck off the outside of the right post and out of play.

There was a monumental hurrah from the spectators and the Fitz players as Harry sat on his bum, burying his head in his knees. It was the final play of the first half, and the referee blew his whistle to bring a halt to proceedings. Bertie went to console Harry, but much like his friends trying to help him through his exigent mental health struggle, it was no use.

Both sides took shelter in their respective changing rooms once more, and Bertie had lined up a motivational team talk to encourage his team for the next forty-five minutes. 'Come on boys, it's only one-nil, we're still in this boys,' he said. But his words had little effect; Trinity were completely deflated at the break. Although they had been dominated, they felt hard done by. They were angry that the first goal stood despite the foul in the build-up, and although not saying it, they were gutted that Harry had missed from twelve yards.

The second half kicked off, and Fitzwilliam were quick off the mark. They were zipping the ball around adroitly on the wet surface and really making Trinity persevere to keep up with them. It was only a matter of minutes into the second half, where a clumsy challenge from none other than Joel Lockhurst led to the hosts being awarded a penalty. It was the captain Rodger who took the spot-kick and made no mistake in burying it into the bottom corner. The crowd went wild as Fitzwilliam planted one foot into the final. Rodger grabbed the ball from the goal and took it with him to get the game started again quickly. It was a clear sign that he was hungry for his team to annihilate Trinity. He deliberately ran past Harry, and as he did, he shouted, 'That's how you take a penalty mate,' before bolting back to the halfway line. Harry's temper flared up inside, but he knew that there was nothing he could do about it. It only spurred him on more to score a goal.

Trinity could not muster up more than a few half chances and showed no real sign of coming back into the game. The tide was with Fitz, the fans were with them, and the scoreline was in their favour too. There were less than ten minutes to go for Trinity to respond to the two-goal deficit, but matters were made worse when Rodger went on a silky run, beating three Trinity players, including Harry and bent the ball into the far corner. The fans went less wild for this goal as it was already clear to them that Fitzwilliam would be once again booking their place in the cuppers final. In celebration this time, Rodger ran directly to Harry with his finger pressed up against his lips to silence Harry.

Harry was aggrieved, 'Fuck off,' he shouted while shoving Rodger out of his way.

Rodger responded sarcastically, 'Oooh, it's only a game mate,' knowing that he had finally cracked his opponent.

By this point, Trinity just wanted the game to end so that they could go home. Their fate was inevitable, and there was not much point in playing out the final few minutes. The Fitz players were loving it, showboating with the ball and displaying exactly why they were the best sporting college at the university.

The fans adored the silky play and let out a huge cheer whenever a Fitz player pulled off another skill. Rodger had the ball in the middle of the park. His top knot was flapping above his head as he danced around the ball. Harry had enough of the taunting and wanted to dispossess his opponent. He came rushing in, but Rodger effortlessly flicked the ball through his open legs, resulting in the largest outcry yet from the buoyant crowd for the nutmeg.

That was it. That was the final straw. Harry could not take this anymore, the humiliation, the losing, being second best all game. It had all gotten too much for him and all the emotions he felt now channelled into one: anger. He came storming back towards Rodger with a one-track-mind. Harry no longer sought the ball. He wanted to lacerate the man. Harry had picked up some serious pace as he approached Rodger from behind. He soared through the sky with both feet in the air and targeted his calves. With all of his momentum and body weight, Harry flew straight through Rodger's unprotected left leg, which made a loud crunching sound upon impact.

Rodger let out a scream in absolute anguish. He had never felt soaring affliction like this in his life. As he glanced down, he could see the bone completely popped out of the skin of his leg, and he nearly fainted at the sight of it. Blood was pouring out of his leg, and Rodger's screams of pain soon turned into outright panic. He just wanted to wake up from this gruesome nightmare; he wanted it all to go away. With an injury as horrific as this, he may never walk again, let alone play football.

Harry got up from the challenge and sauntered away, feeling no remorse for the damage he had just inflicted. He could not get his revenge on Rodger by beating him on the field, but he indisputably had his revenge now. Harry's action had started a mass brawl on the pitch - even some of the supporters sprinted on to the pitch to shout abuse at Harry. The referee had no difficulty making this decision as he reached into his back pocket to give Harry a red card. Harry was not bothered. He did not care that he had been sent off, he did not care that the Fitzwilliam players and fans were harassing him, he certainly did not care for the man wailing on the floor. Harry was irate that he had lost, that others were rejoicing at his expense. Harry detested losing.

- 17 -

It had been another gruelling week for Harry, rounding off what had been a poignant month. He had slipped back into the comfort of his own company and shielded himself from the outside world. He knew that he could not go on much longer like this and decided that it was time to move on from his fixation on the taken Elizabeth. Harry had been messaging Gabriella, a girl from Downing college that he had a one-night stand with after a swap last term. The sex was disappointing, and he foolishly gave her his number as he scarpered away in the morning. It is not that she would have had any difficulty finding him on Facebook but giving out his phone number felt more personal. On social media, someone would have to make that first leap to start a conversation, yet having Harry's number invited her directly to build a connection. They had exchanged a few messages since the night they met, and Gabriella was keen to meet up again, but until now, Harry always seemed to find an excuse to get out of it. This time, Harry reached out to her, and she suggested that they headed to the Fitzwilliam

Museum (which is not linked to the college, only sharing its namesake). They arranged for the date to take place on the morning of Saturday 1st February. A new month, a chance for Harry to turn over a new leaf and get on with his life.

Harry was actually quite excited when he woke up, that was until he drew his curtains. Heavy snow was cascading from the sky and had settled on the ground. No longer could the grass lawns or stone paths be seen on the Great Court; instead, they were covered by a white blanket. While it looked aesthetically pleasing from the inside, Harry was well aware that walking outside today would not be enjoyable. He was a bit of a grinch when it came to snow. Most of his friends were likely to take the day off and have themselves a 'snow day', but Harry hated needlessly being out in the cold. He would much rather be cooped up inside by the fire, with a hot chocolate in one hand and a good book in the other.

The thought of sitting around the fire was certainly tempting, and Harry was on the verge of messaging Gabriella to cancel the date. However, he knew it would be unchivalrous to pull out at such short notice, so he headed to his wardrobe and layered up. When Harry left his room, he put on his hat and gloves and made his way across the Great Court. The crunch of his sturdy boots on the fresh snow was enough to send shivers down his spine, making him feel even colder. As Harry approached the Porter's Lodge, he took off his woollen hat. Even though he would only be inside for a matter of seconds as he passed through, he was brought up that wearing any form of headwear indoors was impertinent. Harry enjoyed the brief warmth of the lodge but continued on his journey to the museum.

As Harry made his way down the King's parade, he unexpectedly found himself walking right through the midst of a snowball fight. People were stood on either side of the road, hurling compressed balls of ice crystals at each other, and he just so happened to be in the crossfire. A snowball thumped him on his left shoulder, but he did not even feel it because of how thick his jacket was. He wondered whether it had been intentional but decided that it was not worth causing a scene. As he proceeded, he saw a bunch of students on the lawn outside of King's College rolling a prodigious orb of snow around. It was clear that they were constructing a snowman, but they still had quite some way to go. This was the same lawn that Harry's friends got shouted at by the porters for walking on when they came up to visit, but it seems that anything went when it was snowing. A little further on, he saw two girls lying on the ground, flapping their arms and legs like a bird trying to take flight. When he saw the girls making the snow angels, he questioned why people acted so odd when it was snowing. If they behaved like this without the snow, there is no doubt that they would be sent to a mental asylum.

The brunette girl was already waiting at the steps of the museum when Harry arrived. She called out to him, 'Harry,' and waved her gloved hand in the air. She had perfect olive skin and intense brown eyes and seemed to be completely unaffected by the bitterly cold weather.

Harry was not sure whether to go in for a hug or not. A handshake was far too formal, but he did not know the protocol for a first date. Despite his active sex life, he had seldom been on dates with women. Thankfully, Gabriella took control of the situation. She leant in and pressed her soft lips against Harry's bitterly cold cheek, then kissed his other cheek after. It had been a rather exotic greeting, which caught Harry off-guard, although he probably should have anticipated it since Gabriella was born in Italy. 'Shall we head on in?' asked Harry, both to get the conversation flowing, but more importantly, to head inside to get his blood circulating again. He felt as though his toes and fingers were about to fall off.

'Well, we could always go for a walk in the snow if you fancy?' said Gabriella in a slight Italian accent, 'It is so beautiful in Cambridge when it snows.'

This was an idea that Harry certainly was not a fan of, 'Maybe after.'

They made their way up the steps of the museums, and Harry stared up at the colossal columns at the building's entrance. This was another building that Harry always stopped to photograph on his iPhone. The gallery was magnificent and looked akin to the Lincoln Memorial in Washington, except the Fitzwilliam was more intricate in its design. Greek statues were placed on top of the pillars to protect the building from above, and four lions were located on the ground to guard it from below. It was said that at the stroke of midnight, the lions came to life, walking down from their plinths to drink from the guttering in the street before returning to their posts. All sorts of fables were made up about the stone statues in the city, and although obviously untrue, they were always intriguing. The museum was particularly aesthetic today camouflaged in the snow, and as much as Harry wanted to get a snap of it, he wanted to play it cool in front of Gabriella.

Once inside the Grade I listed building, Gabriella asked Harry, 'Do you have any preference of where you want to go first?'

Harry had not given much consideration to the activities of the date itself; he just wanted to see Gabriella, to have human contact. It had been her idea to go to the museum, and Harry had never been before, so he thought this was the ideal opportunity to see the place before he graduated. Harry was far from a cultured individual and had just expected to roam around the museum whilst getting to know Gabriella a bit better. To be perfectly honest, Harry was most excited about getting a novelty bouncy ball from the gift shop, but of course, he was not going to say that to his querida. 'Well, what are the options?' asked Harry.

Gabriella was shocked by this question, as if it was an insult to her personally. 'Options,' she said and paused before continuing, 'look around you Harry, the options are endless.'

They were only in the lobby, yet it was filled with splendour. There were all different shades of brown, gold, and green in the entrance hall, which were in complete contrast to the white stone exterior of the building. Shiny brown marble pillars, intricate gold patterns on the abnormally high ceilings, ancient Greek sculptures were all around them. It was clear that no expense had been spared in the building and decoration of this nearly two-hundred-year-old edifice (which is not actually that old by comparison to most Cambridge colleges). The careful artistic planning of the museum's interior design was an exhibition in itself worthy of admiration. Harry was certainly impressed by what he saw and was perhaps even more astounded that admission was free. He wondered why he had never been here before. 'It is quite extraordinary,' remarked Harry.

'Isn't it just,' said Gabriella, pleased to have converted Harry, 'it comprises one of the best collections of antiques and modern art in western Europe. Over half a million objects and artworks.'

'That certainly is a lot of options to choose from,' said Harry in the hope of breaking down Gabriella's tough exterior.

With no emotion, she responded, 'Quite right. The best thing about this museum is that you can see something new every time you visit.' This was a clear indication to Harry that Gabriella was a frequent visitor, and he suddenly felt very out of his depth.

'How about we look at some paintings?' suggested Harry. He thought that you could not go wrong with a good old painting. How wrong he turned out to be.

'Good idea,' said Gabriella, leading the way up the off-white stone staircase, 'they have a lovely gallery of Picasso paintings. Let's head there first.'

'Oh, I've heard of him,' said Harry, who perked up at his name, glad that he was no longer completely in the dark.

'Why do you sound as if that's an achievement?' asked Gabriella bitterly, 'He's one of the most famous artists in the world.' Harry felt belittled again and sensed that the date was heading south. 'The gallery holds pieces from all the best artists in the world,' she said before proceeding to list them. 'Monet, Canaletto, van Gogh, Constable, Rembrandt, Cézanne, Van Dyck.' Harry recognised some of these names, but not all of them. The last one stood out to him for some peculiar reason, but he soon realised that he was thinking of the Dutch foot-baller Virgil van Dijk, who certainly was not a painter.

There were only four paintings in Picasso's gallery, but they had been displayed exceptionally in the bijou room. Each canvas had an ornate golden frame and a minuscule spotlight above it, shining down to illuminate the artwork. Harry had not seen a painting from Picasso since school and forgotten about his abstract techniques. 'They're so wonderfully weird and whacky,' said Harry with reference to the painting of a person whose face had been broken up into pieces and rearranged authentically.

'That's one way of expressing Picasso's cubism,' said Gabriella, 'he was so ahead of his time, so, so futuristic.'

'Yeah, but it looks as though a six-year-old has drawn these, choosing colours at random to colour it in. This one has an eye completely disconnected from its face,' laughed Harry. Gabriella did not.

Gabriella started defending the artist, 'It's not Picasso's fault that you do not understand his artwork. He created more than twenty thousand paintings, drawings, sculptures, ceramics and other items in his long career.'

Harry continued to laugh, 'Well I'm not exactly surprised. If you gave me a box of crayons, I'd be able to knock out one of these pictures in six minutes.'

Gabriella was getting fed up with Harry's acerbic comments and was disappointed that he did not admire the beauty of his work. 'Look at it,' she said. Harry took a quick glance, then looked back at the Italian girl who seemed ready to explode. 'No, really, really look at it.' Harry inspected the piece for a few minutes. 'What do you see?'

'A poorly constructed face,' said Harry, confused as to the response she was expecting.

'You truly are a lost cause. Come on, let's go to a different exhibition. Perhaps you'll find the Egyptian coffins a bit more exciting,' said Gabriella storming out of the room.

Clearly not having any say in the matter, Harry said, 'Sounds like a plan to me.' The big-ticket items were probably more to his taste anyway – a bit more exciting than children's paintings.

Gabriella led the way around the museum, providing additional information on each of the artefacts as she passed. It was clear that she had done her research before the date as she knew so much more than what was on each plaque. As a historian, rambling away about the background of each object was second nature to her, and it was clear that she was in her element. She was clearly a very intelligent young woman, even for a Cambridge student, with a mind of her own. She was beautiful inside and out and certainly ticked a lot of boxes. But something was missing; there was no spark. The date seemed too formal, as if Harry was being taken around by a tour guide. Perhaps Harry's lack of passion about ancient oriental pottery was a contributing factor. Either way, there was a lack of amorous energy between the two of them.

When they had walked around the museum for what seemed like an eternity, they finally headed towards the exit. Gabriella could have stayed there for hours. In fact, Harry would not have been surprised if she came back to the museum after they parted. Harry himself was tempted to return just so he could get that bouncy ball he so desired. Not wanting to separate on an awkward note, Gabriella let out a wry smile and said, 'We should do this again sometime.'

It was palpable that she did not mean it, yet, out of politeness, Harry replied, 'Yes, we really should.' He knew that was the last time he would be seeing Gabriella. Well, the last time that they would be going on a date with each other, it seemed impossible not to bump into people you knew in Cambridge, however awkward the situation may be.

It had stopped snowing when Harry made his way back to Trinity, and the crisp snow had now turned into slush. The students had successfully erected a stout snowman with a quintessential carrot for a nose and twigs for arms. It stood tall next to the two snow angels on King's front lawn. The date certainly had not gone as planned. Rather than helping him move on from Elizabeth, she was now the only person he could think about. What if he was never to share that spark with another woman again?

Harry started drafting a long message to Elizabeth, saying how he just wanted to clear the air, to talk to her in person. He started professing all of his feelings in the message. *Maybe she would be different when she was not around Matt.* Harry was on the verge of pressing the send button, but he did not have the courage to have his heart broken again, so he deleted the memorandum.

- 18 -

'That bad was it?' said Aaron, who had just listened to Harry's painful experience on his tryst.

'I just could not have got away any faster. That's the last time I'm going on a date for a long while, I'll tell you that for free,' said Harry.

'Well, we've got the swap tonight,' said Aaron perkily, 'make sure you get yourself down for that. Could not be anything further from a date.' It was now Sunday, and the boys had their first swap of the year lined up with the Newnham Nobles.

'I'm not sure,' said Harry, who was still hesitant about going out socialising in large groups. His confidence was at its nadir, and the thought of having to be the centre of attention was not an attractive one at this point in time.

'Oh, come on,' said Aaron persistently, 'it's set to be a big one. All the boys are coming too.' Aaron could tell that Harry was sitting on the fence, he just needed a little shove to be convinced, and Aaron had one more bargaining chip. 'I tell you what, I'll let you have first pick on what girl you want to sit next to. How does that sound?'

Harry let out a cheeky grin. He knew that a swap was only as good as its company, 'Fine, count me in. I'll need to pick up some booze for later then.'

The evening came around fast, and after an hour or so of getting the three freshers absurdly drunk. It was time to head to the swap. The Galbs had a strict dress code for its members, a baby blue shirt tucked into a pair of tobacco brown chinos. It was also compulsory for the boys to wear a navy tie with pink and white stripes. Their uniforms were a symbolism of the middle class and matched nicely with the exclusivity within the society. Naturally, the freshers had not *earned* the right to wear this attire and instead had to dress up in Lederhosen, in line with the OktoGalbfest. They were put through their paces down by the Avenue, far enough away from the rest of the college. This was where any boisterous behaviour took place in the college. Tonight's freshers, who, of course, were trying to prove themselves to the existing members of the Draggalbs, had to do a whole assortment of challenges, including drinking port out of a condom and seeing off a litre bottle of Smirnoff vodka between them. Alcohol and any other costs were expensed to the Galbs' bank account, which was funded termly by its members but also relied on sizeable donations from the society's alumni. Once a Draggalb, always a Draggalb. Alumni often wanted to give back to Cambridge, but not to their wealthy colleges. They wanted their funding to be beneficial, to feel as though they were contributing to something meaningful in their eyes instead of adding a few gold coins to a large college pot.

Aaron decided that it was best to get taxis over to the swap venue, Sesame. It was in the south of Cambridge, all the way over by the train station. Almost all of the boys ended up getting in a Panther taxi, except for a couple of frugal second years who wanted to save a bit of money, deciding to walk instead. Sesame was a notorious venue in Cambridge for swaps, it doubled up as a fast-food Chinese restaurant during the day, but Harry was sure that nobody ever went there for the food. He was sure this *restaurant* was just used as a cover to get a license to operate the swaps.

When the taxi arrived outside the restaurant on Hills Road, David, the enthusiastic young Chinese waiter, was already waiting for them. David stood on the door like a bodyguard for a nightclub, collecting five pounds from all of the Draggalbs before letting them in. The money had to be paid in cash; using a card was not an option, which matched the shady nature of the restaurant. Sesame was by far the cheapest swap venue in Cambridge, you could pay upwards of twenty pounds at other restaurants, but you really got what you paid for here. The five-pound charge was supposedly there to cover the food, but the students rarely ate the horrible sustenance that was brought out. Instead, the levy was in place for the inevitable destructive and rowdy student behaviour, who effectively bought the right to disrespect the eatery.

Aaron had gotten to know the seedy David very well over the past three years, and while there were other swap venues available, Aaron exclusively used Sesame because the Draggalbs could do whatever they so pleased here. David led the group down the stairs, and they disappeared into the darkness. There were three rooms downstairs, which could only be described as dungeons, and the Galbs were in the largest prison cell this evening. The Newnham girls were already sat waiting for their men to arrive, with space in between each of them to ensure an alternation in the arrangement of the sexes. Arriving second was a typical tactic of Aaron's so that the boys could scope out the room before deciding which girl to sit next to. As promised, Aaron let Harry lead the way and have the first pick over whom he would sit beside. He did not have long to make his decision and tried to be subtle with his choice. There was a selection of good-looking girls, and Harry opted for a seat that would put him in the middle of the room to ensure he was totally involved in the night's events. After Harry had perched on the questionably sticky leather sofa, the rest of the boys chose where they would sit, in order of seniority, with the freshers being separated and placed in the corners of the room.

There were no windows in the basement. The only source of light was the florescent LEDs which glowed dimly on the walls, making it difficult to identify others in the room. The poor lighting tended to come in handy as people committed embarrassing acts throughout the evening, and it certainly helped to hide the dreadful quality of the food that was served.

The girl to Harry's left was quick to introduce herself, to get Harry's attention before her rival on his right. 'Hi, I'm Sofia,' said the brunette girl in a soft Eastern European accent.

Before Harry had even said a word to her, he reached over and dropped a penny into her small white plastic cup, 'Well Sofia, you had better finish that drink off.' While games like 'pennying', the act of dropping a one-pence copper coin into someone's drink compelling them to down it, had been cracked down on at formal dinners, it was actively encouraged at swaps. Sofia grabbed her cup, feeling rather uncomfortable being forced to drink by a man whose name she did not even know. She finished what was left of her cheap Tesco zesty white wine in two large gulps and sieved out the coin in her mouth before spitting it straight onto the table. 'I'm Harry by the way,' said Harry while holding out a patronising hand, which Sofia reluctantly shook.

Pennying was a brisk and elementary start to the evening, helping the students to get drunk. Like most swap venues, Sesame was a bring-your-own-booze affair, so it was not as though hefty bills were racking up with each drink that was forced to be downed. In fact, any awkwardness of mingling was swiftly overcome with alcohol. Aaron had managed to penny the shy girl opposite him three times before Raymond got things underway. Raymond was appointed the vice-president of the Draggalbs by Aaron and was eager to help wherever possible with the running of the society. Aaron thought that tonight would be an excellent opportunity to allow Raymond to take the reins.

Raymond stood up, grabbed two wine bottles in his proximity and began clattering them together to get the entire room's attention. This was certainly a much more suitable environment for this animalistic behaviour than at the introductory dinner in college at the start of the academic year. The clinking noise quickly halted the chatter, and about thirty people were now looking over at the tall Italian. 'I would just like to start by saying how beautiful you ladies are all looking tonight and how grateful we are that you chose to spend a night with us Draggalbs,' it was clear that he had not prepared a speech of any sorts but wanted to stamp his mark on the night and formally kick off proceedings. 'As you can see, we have brought three

213

lovely freshers with us, all attempting to dress in Lederhosen. That is because the theme for our Galblets, was OktoGalbfest.' There were a few sighs of realisation from the Newnham girls, who were befuddled at why three individuals were wearing fancy dress in contrast to the rest of the impeccably dressed men. 'As a thank you for your attendance, Johnny has written you a welcoming poem,' said Raymond pointing at the slumped fresher in the corner, 'take it away.'

The freshers in their drunken state were like puppets to the members of the drinking society, doing whatever they were told to do to leave a noticeable impression. Johnny had been completely caught off guard. He had not been expecting this; he had prepared nothing. He sat frozen for a few seconds before realising that he would have to do something; everyone in the room was now looking at him. 'Stand on your chair please,' heckled Harry from across the room.

Johnny nervously got up. Despite being hammered, he could feel the eyes piercing his skin. 'Errm,' he hesitated, while thinking what to say. He knew he had to say something and just hoped that the words would come to him as he went along, 'Oh dearest Magdalene.'

What a horrendous blunder he had just made, and he was sure to know about it. The girls all started booing at him, and Raymond stood up and shouted at him, 'It's Newnham you idiot. Say sorry and down your drink.' Feeling intimidated by the hostile environment, Johnny gingerly apologised and finished his cup in hand before returning to his seat.

Raymond took control once more and stood up to make another announcement, 'In line with our OktoGalbfest theme, we have an assortment of challenges for those wishing to challenge for captaincy. I will be starting as the Draggalbs captain, and the lovely Jessie will take the armband for the Nobles.' Jessie was the President of Newnham's drinking society, and Raymond had known her well since they both studied Natural Sciences together. It was this close relationship that Raymond had with Jessie that enabled him to secure the Nobles for this evening's swap. Being a captain was an arbitrary status symbol, which any pair could challenge for. This desire for captaincy would compel students to go to extreme and uncomfortable lengths to gain acceptance from their peers. It was awarded for the most outrageous behaviour, which only got more scandalous as the night went on, and more drinks were consumed.

Sofia turned once more to Harry to get to know him a bit better, 'So what do you study?' A classic small talk question used by all students across the land. She stared into Harry's eyes and held her cup in both hands to protect it from being pennied.

'Economics, and you?' asked Harry.

She smiled and took one hand off of her cup to play with her hair, 'Oh me, I study Classics.' The two quickly progressed past the small talk stages and were soon in deep conversation with each other. Harry had now completely turned his back to the girl on his right and was thoroughly enjoying Sofia's company. She intrigued Harry and could hold a conversation well. When Harry had let out a witty response to one of her questions, she released a raucous laugh and placed her hand on his upper thigh, keeping it there a little longer than someone using it purely for balance.

It was now one of the Newnham girls who stood up,

clattering wine bottles together. When she finally had everyone's attention, which was becoming increasingly difficult
as people started to engage in interesting conversations, she
shouted out without any decorum, 'Fine if you've ever wanked
off your supervisor in the Grand Arcade car park.' The fining
system replicated an enormous game of 'Never Have I Ever',
except more often than not, the fines were so tailored that they
were used to reveal the darkest secrets about others. People
would often be publicly outed for things that they had told
others in confidence, but if you had done the scandalous act,
you had to stand up and take a sip of your drink.

Sofia slowly took her hand from Harry's lap and felt embarrassed to have to stand up. She took a large gulp from her
cup as the rest of the room were shouting at her to reveal the
story. Instead, she fired straight back at her friend to deflect
the attention away from her, 'Fine if you've ever pissed on the
dancefloor in Cindies!' Her friend rose and took a drink. The
Galbs were roaring like beasts at the exposure of the women.
After these first two fines, the floodgates opened, and the skele-
tons were flying out of the closet. Raymond actually kept a list
of all the fines on other members in the Draggalbs to ensure
that all the girls in Cambridge would know about his peer's
dirty little secrets.

Raymond unscrewed the lid on his bottle of wine and
topped up his cup as he stood up and prepared to unleash
another fine. Given his presence in the room, it was easy
for him to command everyone's attention. Just as he started
speaking, the girl sitting opposite him reached over the table
and dropped an 'engineering penny' into his bottle of wine.
These were pennies that had been mechanically bent in half

by first-year engineering students using the workshop's metal benders (despite the sign put up in the department explicitly telling students not to use the machines for this purpose). The reshaped pennies were small enough to fit down the neck of a wine bottle, and the coin slowly made its way down the container until it reached the bottom. Everyone started roaring with excitement that Raymond had been caught out. The girl was particularly pleased with her efforts, given that Raymond was relentlessly pennying her all night. Like normal pennying, if someone put an engineering penny in your bottle of wine, it meant that you had to finish off its contents.

Raymond had no escape. Everyone in the room was looking at him, egging him on to finish off what would be his second bottle. 'Fair play,' said Raymond, who grabbed the bottle and began chugging away. The room was starting to fill with spurring chants as the bottle was emptying. The taste of the wine began to sting his throat; it certainly was not a drink that was made to be downed at pace. He did not manage to get it down in one hit, but over the space of about a minute and about three attempts later, its contents had finally been drained. Raymond pounded his chest like King Kong, letting out a loud roar as he did so to celebrate his perceived achievement. It was clear that it would be a wild night for the Great Raymondo, and there was no chance that he would be making his lecture at nine the next morning.

The drinks were flying down, and the event was degenerating into complete anarchy. It was not long until people were jumping around on the wonky tables, which had been battered from previous swaps. After about forty minutes or so, Sofia stood up and declared that she wanted to challenge for captaincy. This, by default, meant that Harry had been pulled into whatever task they had signed up for. It was at the discretion of the current captains to come up with the challenge, and Jessie, the Newnham President, decided to keep the first dare reasonably tame. 'To take the captaincy, you two must swap all of your clothes!'

This was a fairly common task and a good chance to inspect the other person's physique. With a tilt of her head, Sofia said, 'Challenge accepted!' She dragged Harry by the hand and led him towards the toilets so that they could have some privacy. Often the girls would change separate from the boys and maybe just exchange tops, but Sofia pulled Harry with her into the only cubicle in the woman's bathroom. She did not speak to Harry but began seductively undressing, first, by pulling her tight tank top over her head to reveal her red bra. Harry found himself gawping at her well-toned tanned body but quickly realised that he too had to disrobe. He started by doffing off his tie and unbuttoning his shirt. Sofia then dropped her skirt to reveal her matching red nickers. The pair still did not say a word. Harry mirrored her actions by undoing the buckle on his brown leather belt and unbuttoning his chinos. They put their clothes on the toilet seat to keep them off of the wet bathroom floor. Harry reached over to put on Sofia's skirt, but as he did so, she grabbed his hand and shook her head. 'Jessie said all of our clothes,' she said delicately as she put both hands behind her back to undo her bra. Her nipples were firm as her perky breasts were exposed in the air, and blood began rushing to Harry's penis too. She slowly lowered her panties and allowed them to drop to the floor.

Once again, Harry copied her and dropped his underwear to

reveal his erect penis. They both stood stark naked, their bodies close to each other in the small bathroom stall. Sofia put her hand forwards and stroked Harry's genitals once, before leaning over to give Harry a kiss on the lips. Excited by this turn of events, Harry went back for more action, but Sofia said, 'Only a taste for now, you'll get the rest later.' Now that Harry had seen Sofia naked, he wanted his way with her, but she kept him on a tight leash, teasing him to maintain authority. She began putting on Harry's Calvin Klein pants and buttoned up the shirt, which was a few sizes too large for her. Not wanting to be left standing naked for much longer, Harry put on the bra and squeezed into the tight tank top, worried that he might rip it. He only just managed to put on the skirt and was left struggling to breathe by the time he was now dressed in his new attire. Sofia unlocked the door and headed back to join the others.

It was absolute carnage when Harry made his way back into the dungeon, like a scene from the Riot Club. In one corner, Johnny had clearly gone over the edge with the amount of alcohol he had drunk and was now spewing up all over himself and the table. Instead of helping the drunk fresher, people either moved away to make sure that they did not get any sick on themselves or took pictures of the poor kid. Throwing up was pretty typical on a swap, and he was just ordered to move even further to the corner, ushered away so that he would not ruin other people's night. In the other corner, one of the Galbs was getting with one of the Newnham girls. Harry could not quite make out who it was, but it appeared to be one of the second-year lads. However, this was getting little attention. It was the three topless men lying on the tables covered in whipped cream that everyone stood up to watch. In fact, nobody had even noticed the fact that Harry had come back into the room wearing girls' clothes.

Upon closer inspection, it was actually Mo, Aaron, and one of the second years, Lewis, who were on their backs, each with a girl standing tall above them. The tables had been cleared of the bottles of wine to minimise the damage and potential loss of alcohol, and Raymond, who was stood on the sofa, higher than everyone else in the room, shouted out, 'It is the first girl to find the mini pretzel in the whipped cream that wins the challenge.' Harry assumed that the pretzel was another reference of sorts to the OktoGalbfest theme. Raymond continued, 'Remember, you cannot use your hands to find it, only your mouth!' Presumably, the girls were unaware where the small biscuit was hidden; otherwise, it would have been too straightforward. Raymond held his hand high and shouted, 'Three, two, one, go!' lowering his hand to signal the start of the race.

Two of the girls simultaneously buried their faces in the thick cream on the men's bodies, while Samantha, who was searching Aaron's hairy body, was a bit more tentative. The girl inspecting Mo rather lacked a strategy. Instead, diving in at random areas of his torso and licking away to reveal his skin. The tall girl licking Lewis' body had a much better strategy, working her way from his neck right down towards his chinos. Samantha, influenced by the peer pressure, eventually got a bit more stuck in, and the three girls were quickly left with a face full of cream as they frantically searched for the mini pretzel. Everyone else was cheering them on with such great excitement, and in the end, it was Mo's partner who hit the jackpot. When she felt the pretzel hit against her teeth, she quickly popped it into her mouth, then took her hand from behind her back to retrieve it off of her tongue. She jumped up in the air with joy to show her savoury trophy to the rest of the room.

'We have a winner,' shouted Raymond as everyone cheered. The other two girls were left disappointed that they had not found the pretzel but had enjoyed the light-hearted fun. Mo got up and high-fived his partner, who was reluctant to hug him, and the three boys headed to the bathroom to wash up and put their shirts back on before returning.

The beauty of swaps was that they offered an evening that was not bound by social norms. All rules went out of the window when you walked through the dingy old door. Sesame truly was the perfect place for this boundary-breaking behaviour. Its minimalist set up allowed Cambridge students to truly trash the place without guilt. Indeed, it offered an ideal escapism to experiment and replicate the childish behaviour that the students would have displayed in restaurants on school trips many moons ago.

The binge-drinking continued throughout the night, and the students were excited when David came in with what seemed like unlimited plates of spring rolls and undercooked chips. As people were drunk, they would dive straight into the substandard food, before immediately realising that it tasted utterly disgusting. David had not even finished serving the last tray of food, when Aaron stood up, grabbed a handful of spring rolls and chucked them straight across the room at David. As the Chinese delicacy hit David on the back, Aaron shouted, 'Food Fight.'

Everyone else in the room was quick to jump on board, mainly targeting David in the middle but opting to hit others with the food too. David shrieked, 'No, don't hit me,' as he ran out of the room. It was raining chips, and it was impossible to avoid being hit by a spring roll soaring across the room. The privilege of *eating out* reduced the food only to a backdrop, allowing debauchery to take precedence, the ultimate symbol of entitlement.

Eager to stamp his mark on the evening, Mo reached out and grabbed the two nearest wine bottles, which were now completely empty and struck them together. 'Fine if you,' he had only said these three words before Raymond had launched a spring roll at him, knocking his glasses off of his face.

'Shut up Mo,' said Raymond. By this point in the evening, people had grown bored of the fines and were far more excited by the various challenges. They all cheered at Raymond's successful shot.

The evening in Sesame was coming to a close, and it was almost time to head to Life, the nightclub where they would spend the rest of the evening. But before proceedings were wrapped up, Aaron stood up on the sofa and announced, 'I would like to challenge for captaincy. Samantha here is my partner,' he said while pointing to the girl who clearly was not consulted on this decision. She was a fresher, and this had been her first experience at a swap. This really was not her scene, and she had spent most of the night in her shell, looking forward to returning back home. Now all of a sudden, she found herself getting dragged into another task, as if licking whipped cream off of Aaron's revolting body was not enough.

Harry and Sofia were still captains, and they consulted on what challenge to make their peers do. Sofia whispered something grotesque in Harry's ear, but Raymond shouted across the room, 'Harry. You know what to do.' Harry was confused at what Raymond had meant. That was until he pulled out a thick German sausage from his rucksack and wiggled it in the air. Of course, the ultimate challenge for the OktoGalbfest.

Harry ignored Sofia's suggestion, stood up in his dark green tank top and skirt and declared, 'If you want to take the captaincy from us, so late in the evening, you will have to have a lovely German sausage eaten from your bum.' The girls were all left in disbelief at this request; surely the meaningless status was not worthy of this demoralisation.

'Challenge accepted,' shouted Aaron opening his arms wide. All of the boys began slamming down on the table to display their excitement except Johnny, who was now passed out in the corner. Some of the girls joined in with the slamming their fists as Raymond walked over to the President to hand him the large sausage.

Aaron grabbed the sausage from Raymond and first dipped it in his cup of wine, saying, 'A bit of lube to help it up there,' which received a fantastic response from the audience. He jumped back up onto the sofa, turned away from the rest of the room and lowered his trousers just enough to reveal his pasty white bum. He shuffled his feet so that they were shoulder-width apart and leant forward to rest against the wall. Aaron held the sausage in his right hand, and with his left hand, he spread his cheeks to reveal his hairy anus. Some of the girls looked away in disgust, but none of the boys' eyes moved. 'Here goes,' said Aaron, more to himself than the onlookers. He slipped the firm German sausage deep into his rectum, letting out a slight groan of pain as he did so.

Most of the room were now cheering on Samantha to eat

the sausage. You could tell how uncomfortable she was with the request and some of the other Newnham ladies were least pleased with the challenge that she was being pressurised into. They felt as though the Galbs had gone too far this time. But any concerns were being overpowered by the chanting men, goading the girl on. Jessie, however, was loving it. She pulled out her phone to begin recording the event. 'Come on you pussy,' shouted Jessie, 'eat the damn sausage!' Feeling like she had no other option, Samantha leaned towards the phallic object sticking out of Aaron's bum, wincing as she approached. Others had now joined in filming her, and the flashes lit up the dungeon, burning through the poor girl's soul.

Samantha opened her mouth and took a little nibble from the end of the sausage, and tried to sit back down, but the boys were having none of it. They began heckling her, and Harry shouted out, 'Eat the whole sausage!' It was clear that her initial effort would not suffice. She went back for a second round. This time she took a huge bite from the sausage and chewed away. All of the boys begun cheering loud, but the girls could see the pain in Samantha's face. They started telling her that she did not need to do it if she did not want to, but now she was almost determined to prove herself to everyone in the room. The final bite was the one that she was dreading the most. The majority of the sausage that remained was deep in Aaron's rectum; she did not even want to think about it. She leant in one last time, dug her teeth into the exposed sausage and pulled it from its holding. Samantha tried to eat the sausage, but when it was in her mouth, she began to gag. She dry-heaved multiple times before she could no longer hold it in, and vomit came flying out of her mouth. A concoction of meat and wine spewed across Sesame's floor.

Her vomiting invoked the greatest cheer from the Galbs that the dungeon had seen all night. The beasts were truly going wild, slamming the walls, ceilings, tables, anything they could to make as much of a racket in the room. Sesame was their playground, a space where these intellectuals could act like boys again.

- 19 -

Harry had an extra spring in his step the next day after his intimate encounter at the swap. While much to his disappointment, he did not end up sleeping with Sofia, since she got too drunk and left the club early, he did receive ample kisses in the club. This spark between the pair was an enormous confidence boost for Harry and served to substantially improve his mood over the next couple of weeks. Harry remembered just how much he loved to party and ended up going clubbing a lot more, maybe too much more, as Lent Term was rapidly disintegrating. If you want to be a successful Cambridge student, you can only have two of the following: good grades, a social life, or sleep. Harry was more frequently opting for the first two, as he spent many a tired day in the library.

Obsessing over Elizabeth was toxic, especially scrolling through her social media and stalking her every action. Every time Harry saw Matt on her Instagram story, it flared his temper and ruined his mood. Harry knew it was time to take back control; he wanted to enjoy his final few months at Cambridge and leave with no regrets. Harry certainly did not want to have wasted his time hopelessly pursuing a taken girl, so he took the decision to block Elizabeth on all forms of social media. Cutting her out cold turkey was the only option for him, and he felt all the better for doing so.

Once Elizabeth was out of sight and out of mind, Harry started getting back into a routine. He was eating better, exercising more, actually attending lectures for a change and submitting his essays on time. It is easy to falter at Cambridge, given the sheer pace that the degree moves at, and Harry realised just how far behind he was. Just as he would finish one essay that was already a few weeks late, another three would be dumped on him. It was relentless, but that was the Cambridge ethos, and why it has its infamous reputation. Diamonds are made under extreme pressure after all. Harry's supervisor had been worried about his dip in performance at the start of term, but Harry had pulled himself back and brought himself into contention to achieve a desired first-class degree.

Harry was using every single hour available to him each day to ensure he could study all day and party all night. It seemed as though he had an extra few hours in the day compared to everyone else. Downtime was not a thing for Harry and his hectic schedule. When the opportunity came to have fun with his peers, Harry could never turn it down. Fear of missing out, or FOMO, had always been a big problem for Harry; he could never turn down an opportunity to socialise, regardless of how busy he was. Raymond had suggested that the group took an hour off of work to go punting together.

As it turns out, that Saturday afternoon, in week 5 of the term, was one of the rare occasions that Harry took almost the entire day off from studying. Not only was he nursing a hang-over from Fleek Fridays (Cambridge's weekly RnB & hip-hop event in Cindies), but he justified taking some time away from his studies since Trinity did not have a football match this week. The final of cuppers was scheduled for this afternoon at the stadium in Grange Road, and Harry had absolutely no interest in attending.

Sabrina had accompanied Harry to listen to Sir Ian McKellen give a talk on his life as an actor at the Cambridge Union. The Union always seemed to draw the most incredible speakers from all walks of life, be it politicians, actors, athletes, come-dians, singers; the A-listers never seemed to stop attending. Events at the Union were an excellent way to gain insight into someone's life as they offered advice and stories about what they had been through. Harry thought that the life membership was well worth its price. 'Ian is just brilliant, isn't he? He's a lot more charismatic than I would have imagined,' said Harry.

'Yeah, he's great,' replied Sabrina. In all honestly, Sabrina did not care too much for Lord of the Rings or the actor. Instead, the only reason that she went to the talk was that she wanted to spend more time with Harry. But going to the Union was similar to a date to the cinema, besides a little interaction at the start and the end, most of the time spent in the company of the other was in complete silence, admiring the entertainment in front of you at the expense of admiring your date. And while Sabrina may have seen it as a date, Harry certainly did not.

The pair made there was back towards the town centre, where they were already running late for their 2pm meet. They had planned to hire the college punt, but frustratingly Trinity did not rent out their punts in the winter months, so they instead decided to go to Scudamore's on Mill Lane, which was open all year round, except for Christmas Day. Harry led the way down the left-hand side of Sidney Street, following the tall red brick wall. He always opted to walk on this side to avoid the man selling *The Big Issue* newspaper, who he thought was obtrusive and made him feel uncomfortable. The pavement was too narrow for Sabrina to walk alongside her crush, and she was instead left following behind, chasing Harry as he strode away with his long legs. When they got to *Mainsbury's*, Sabrina finally joined alongside Harry, walking on the street and asked, 'Shall we pick up some bits for punting? Maybe some crisps or sweets.'

'No time,' said Harry abruptly. A large white van came flying up the one-way street towards Sabrina, and she quickly hopped back to her position trailing behind Harry in single file. It was not until they got to Market Street that Sabrina re-joined and walked beside Harry. On this street, everyone seemed to walk right in the middle of the road, and it was the cyclists that had to avoid the pedestrians instead of the other way around. Despite the chilly weather, the market was buzzing, as people wrapped up in all their layers to shop local and support community businesses. The duo made their way around the market and headed towards the King's Parade.

'Isn't it gorgeous,' said Sabrina to Harry, who was fed up with the lack of conversation between the two of them.

'Isn't *what* gorgeous?' asked Harry, who was clueless as to what Sabrina was talking about.

'The Senate House,' said Sabrina as she pointed to the vast baroque building enclosed with spiked black fencing to cordon off the general public. The white Corinthian columns and pediment stood gleaming in the winter sunshine as it stood bold above its immaculately mown grass. It was yet another of Cambridge's many Grade I listed buildings and the ceremonial centre of the university, where graduations took place. 'I cannot wait for our day to come, to get our pictures by the iron rusted cauldron or on the steps of the Senate House,' said Sabrina as her mind drifted off.

'I'm more nervous about results day,' said Harry staring over towards the steps. 'I must admit, I do like the scramble when the class lists are posted on the notice boards and everyone rushes over to see what grade they have received.'

'God, I would hate that,' said Sabrina, 'think I'd have a panic attack. That's why I've always opted out and get my results online instead.' It had been traditional for every students' ranking and class to be posted outside the Senate House, but in recent years it has been dubbed as grade shaming and instead has been replaced with an opt-out system.

The conversation carried on as they headed towards Mill Lane, 'I live for that buzz. It's arguably one of my biggest driving factors to succeed,' said Harry. The sunshine was deceptive, and Harry put on his beanie and ski gloves to stay warm. He was gutted that he had left his scarf in college but had no time to head back now. Sabrina had just started to trail behind Harry, who was walking at a ferocious pace as they passed the Corpus Clock, 'Keep up will you, we are late enough as it is,' said Harry in a patronising tone. Sabrina felt guilty for slowing the party down and almost switched to a jog to keep up. They made their way beyond the lecture hall, where Harry had been humiliated by Acemoglu and finally arrived at the Mill pub where the others were already waiting for them in a huddle.

Sabrina was now almost completely out of breath as she panted, 'Sorry that we're late,' she exhaled a deep breath, 'the talk went on a little longer than planned at the Union.'

'Your apology is not accepted,' said Aaron in a sombre tone. Sabrina looked confused at this remark, and Aaron could no longer hold in his laughter, 'I'm joking, we're still waiting for Mo. He says he's not far away.' Aaron swivelled and continued, 'In fact, I can see him making his way down Laundress Lane now.' Mo was waving a floppy arm in the air as a signal of greeting as he stumbled into one of the many bins stacked in his path.

Harry took a step towards Aaron to glance down the narrow alleyway, and sure enough, he too could see that Mo's arrival was imminent. He was always fascinated by the dated sign hanging up high just below the street sign on Laundress Lane. It read: *No Thoroughfare for Carriages or Horses – 24th March 1857*. How times have changed, yet the city remained so constant, thought Harry. In the beginning, people walked everywhere, then they used horse and carriages, next was the advent of trains, followed shortly by automobiles. Harry knew it would not be long until the next mode of transport came along, maybe flying cars of some sort. Society is constantly evolving and seeking innovative solutions. Indeed, many of those solutions would come from the brilliant minds in this city itself. Regardless of these changes, Cambridge stood the same – a historic city steeped in traditions that it refused to let go of.

As Mo finally emerged at the end of the alleyway, Harry pondered how on earth a horse and carriage would ever fit down that Lane anyway; it would have been one hell of a squeeze. 'Yes guys, what's going on?' asked Mo rhetorically.

Gertrude was least pleased with his tardiness and ignored his arrival; instead, turning to head towards Scudamore's.

The six of them (punting was not really Cuthbert's scene) made their way to the floating platform and paid to hire a punt for an hour and a half. Since it was the low season, the rental price was slightly cheaper than usual, aided further by the fact that they were all students. After their substantial discount, it set them each back a fiver. Once the group had made their way past the kiosk, a man wearing a plain white shirt and a navy waistcoat with the Scudamore's crest stitched onto it, came to address them. He was shivering in his uniform, clearly underdressed for the weather, and a big gust of wind almost blew his straw hat right off his head. The man began to explain how to punt, but Mo rudely interrupted, 'Please. We're Cambridge students, we're seasoned veterans.' The employee looked relieved that he could rush back into the comforting warmth of the kiosk without giving them a demonstration.

Harry was the closest to the man who handed him the long pole, which was sticking out of the murky water. It came as a relief to Harry that he had his ski gloves on. Otherwise, the cold metal pressed against his skin would have caused considerable discomfort. 'Right, well we've put some extra blankets in the punt to keep you all warm. Have a good'un!' said the worker.

Bearing the pole in his hand, it was clear that Harry would be the first to punt. He made his way to the end of the boat, gripping firmly onto the pole for balance. The rest of the group made their way onto the punt one by one. Mo was the last to make his way on; his knees looked weak as he struggled for balance. He was uncoordinated enough as it was on dry land, so standing on a punt was particularly challenging for him.

Once he finally took his seat, Harry guided the boat out of the punting station. Harry was probably the most experienced punter and was best placed to navigate them towards the college backs. He stood tall above the others who were sat at water level and was isolated from the conversation taking place below him. The first challenge came with the low-lying bridge immediately after the punting station, but this was easy enough for Harry to overcome. One big push with the pole and a crouch later, they drifted elegantly underneath the Silver Street Bridge. The sunlight and noise from the traffic above temporarily evaded them until they emerged safely on the other side.

'I've never actually punted before,' said Sabrina.

'Really,' said Aaron, who seemed shocked.

'Well, I've been on a punt before, but there was always someone else doing the work for me. I think I'd quite like to have a go today,' she said turning to Harry with a smile. Harry was too focused on his task at hand and ignored Sabrina's attempt to incorporate him into the conversation.

'It's easy,' said Mo, who proceeded to give Sabrina advice despite the fact that she did not ask for any, 'you want to make sure you feel comfortable standing up, keep your knees bent and really become one with the punt.' Gertrude shook her head as she opened her pink Marc O'Polo backpack. Mo acting as if he was an expert yet could hardly balance on the punt was laughable. 'You want to drop the pole into the water down to the riverbed and push off of it, walking your hands up to the top of the pole and pulling it with you again.'

'It sounds awfully complex,' said Sabrina, who was growing increasingly apprehensive by the idea.

'Nonsense,' said Aaron, 'I'll show you how it's done before

you have a go. You need some good core strength, but I know you've got that,' he said leaning over and playfully punching her stomach a few times.

Grey clouds began to drift over inauspiciously to cover up the afternoon sunshine. What had been a glorious winter day was slowly degenerating into a menacing one. The dissipation of the sun brought with it a noticeable drop in the temperature, and the group just hoped that the rain would hold off since only Gertrude had thought ahead to bring an umbrella. Aaron grabbed the blankets that had been left on the floor of the punt. The one at the bottom of the pile was damp, but the rest were relatively dry. He offered them out to the rest of the group, and nobly kept the moisten one for himself. Gertrude had finished digging around in her backpack and pulled out a large silver flask, 'Who fancies a hot chocolate then?'. This question was met exclusively with positive responses, and she began to pour out the warm liquid into the paper cups she had brought with her.

Not only was Harry excluded from the conversation and without a blanket, but he also was not offered a hot beverage. He was beginning to find the punting tiresome and was hoping that someone else would volunteer to take over as the chauffeur soon. Nonetheless, Harry marvelled at the breath-taking views that the vantage point of a punt had to offer. They glided along towards King's College, and Harry was in complete admiration of the spectacular landscape. His right displayed the chapel in all its divinity. This remarkable architecture completely juxtaposed the natural setting on his left as the cows grazed on the common land. The beauty of punting in the winter is that the cold weather scares the tourists off, bringing a peaceful and quiet riverbed and allowing the stunning views to talk for themselves void of the chaos. There were no crashes, no tourists, no 'rush hour' river traffic. The six of them were left alone to enjoy the serenity of the River Cam. In truth, Harry would have still preferred to have been punting in the summer heat with a bottle of bubbly and some strawberries, even if this meant that he would be crashing into other punts like bumper cars. But for now, the tranquillity brought a new experience for Harry, and his isolation above his peers allowed him to be alone with his thoughts. He was incredibly grateful for his odd bunch of friends, appreciative that he could try new experiences, like winter punting, before his time at the university came to an end.

The group had been enjoying the experience so much (it was remarkably gratifying to actually take some time off of studying and enjoy each other's company) that they began to lose track of time. Gertrude, with her ever-persistent diligence was an exception, and at precisely forty-five minutes into their journey, she said, 'Harry, we are halfway, turn this ship around.'

'Hang on,' said Harry, who, instead of bringing the punt to a halt, increased the speed that they were travelling at. He was beginning to work up a bit of a sweat to propel the boat down the river.

'What on earth are you doing Harry? We need to head back to the punting station,' said Gertrude, who was becoming agitated by Harry's antithetical actions. Harry continued to ignore her muttering until she barked out his name, 'Harry!'

'Nearly there,' he said as he pushed the vessel past Trinity College. It was clear that Harry had some destination that he wanted to reach, but the others were befuddled as to what it was. The punt began to pick up some serious momentum as they headed towards Kitchen Bridge in St John's College. 'Hold on tight,' said Harry.

Gertrude was now getting hot-headed, and the others fell quiet to avoid getting involved in the confrontation, 'Turn the punt around immediately Harry! I've had enough of your childish games,' she bellowed in a commanding voice. Once again, Harry chose to take no notice of her, just as the group had been disregarding him for the entirety of the journey.

When they came out on the other side of Kitchen Bridge, Harry stopped punting. His arms were aching from the hard work, but that did not stop him from using his muscles to crack a smile of approval, 'There she is,' said Harry softly. Raymond and Aaron could see exactly what Harry was talking about since they were all facing the same direction as the captain of the punt. Gertrude was left infuriated and swivelled her neck one hundred and eighty degrees like an owl to see what all the fuss was about. Harry had been determined to make it to the 'Bridge of Sighs', before they headed back to return the punt.

The neo-Gothic bridge at St John's College was built almost two hundred years ago, and Queen Victoria herself was said to have loved it more than any other spot in the city. While the covered bridge was officially named 'New Bridge', it soon became known anecdotally as the Bridge of Sighs in reference to the famous enclosed bridge that connects the ducal palace to the prison in Venice. Harry had always set out to reach this checkpoint; he idolised the bridge. He believed that it epitomised the architectural brilliance of the city and stared on in admiration until Mo interrupted him, 'Come on then, let me have a go at punting. I'll show you how it's done Sabrina!'

Mo tentatively stood up, careful not to make any sudden movements so as not to lose his balance. Harry was delighted to be relieved of his duties and nestled himself on the edge of the punt next to Sabrina, where Mo had previously been seated. He was glad that Sabrina was in the middle blocking him off from a very disgruntled Gertrude. 'You must be freezing standing up there,' said Sabrina, 'here, come and get under the blanket with me.' It was a smooth manoeuvre from Sabrina, who managed to get herself some public intimacy with Harry. Internally Sabrina was ecstatic that Harry would be couped up tightly next to her for the rest of the journey. Sharing a blanket for now, but a bed in the not-too-distant future, she hoped. Sabrina shouted out to Mo, who was wobbling his way across the punt, 'Actually, I don't think I want to give punting ago today, it's a bit too cold for me. I'll do it in summer instead.'

As Mo finally reached the end of the punt, Harry gripped firmly onto the wet side of the boat. His waterproof gloves managed to keep any water at bay. Wanting to cause a bit of mischief and keep Mo on his toes, Harry used his weight to gently rock the boat from side to side. Mo responded calmly, 'Really funny Harry. You can stop it now.' His benevolent nature only spurred Harry to shake the boat more aggressively, and momentum quickly started to build. Mo began staggering on his small platform and, in a now panicked voice, shouted out to Harry, 'Don't you dare!'

Harry enjoyed tormenting Mo and mockingly shouted back to him, 'Just use that core strength of yours and you'll be fine!' Mo was now too alarmed to respond, and with one last thrust of Harry's weight, the unstable platform had become too much for Mo, who had now completely lost his balance. He was gripping onto the pole for support, but as he lost his footing, he was sent flying off the punt, pole-vaulting into the dark, icy water. Mo's body fully submerged into the water, and if the shock of the fall was not enough to wake him up, the glacial water certainly would have done the trick.

The rest of the group were cackling away like a clan of hyenas after seeing Mo plummet into the water. They could not hold back the laughter, but this attitude quickly changed when he finally emerged from the water. Instead of unleashing his anger at Harry, he shouted out to his peers in desperation, 'Help!' His glasses had fallen off of his head and had sunk to the bottom of the river. It was known that Mo had terrible eyesight and desperately needed his glasses to see, but what was not known was his inability to swim. His arms were flapping in the water as he tried to stay afloat. He was in an even more alarmed state than moments earlier. The mood had suddenly become serious, and what may have been a funny joke in Summer certainly did not feel that way now.

Raymond grabbed the small oar that was kept inside the punt and paddled over to Mo, who at this point was fighting for his life. 'Here, grab a hold of this,' commanded Raymond, while holding the oar out towards Mo's face. Mo could only just make out the blurry wooden object despite it being right in front of him. He grabbed it with both hands, and Raymond pulled his friend in towards the punt. 'Give us a hand pulling him on board,' said Raymond to Aaron. Mo was a fairly large individual as it was, and the added weight from his drenched clothes made it quite a challenge to bring him back onto the punt.

Mo laid spewed across the punt in the passenger seating area, shivering from his unplanned swim. Harry now felt incredibly guilty for what he had done and said, 'Take my coat,' as he unzipped his jacket.

Mo was unresponsive, and Raymond spoke on his behalf, 'No, not yet. I've read online that we need to get him out of his wet clothes first to stop him from getting hypothermia.'

Harry remembered a similar scene from *the Inbetweeners* where Simon fell into cold water and discerned that what Raymond was saying made sense. 'Wait, so we're going to strip him naked,' said Harry, who thought this was a bit demeaning.

'We'll let the man keep some dignity,' said Raymond, 'let's just strip him to his pants, then layer him up with dry clothes.' Harry was relieved that he did not have to see Mo's shrivelled penis and wondered why they did not do the same for Simon. Well, they did give him a sock, at least. Harry was relieved that he would not have to volunteer his own cotton for the cause.

Mo was breathing rapidly as the boys began to strip him. Gertrude, who was still more concerned about returning the punt on time, leapt up, grabbed the pole and started punting back towards Scudamore's. As Harry pulled off Mo's soggy trousers, he felt Mo's phone in one pocket, and wallet in the other and his compunction magnified. When he was finally stripped to his underwear, the boys began to bury Mo under piles of warm clothes. Harry was more than willing to give up his jacket, but they also used the blankets to keep their friend warm.

Gertrude was using all of her power to ensure the punt flew down the river. They had just passed Trinity and were approaching Orgasm Bridge (a bridge which got its nickname primarily from its steepness and the groans people made when they reached the summit) when Raymond made the executive decision, 'Stop the punt!'

'Why?' asked Aaron, 'We need to get Mo back as quickly as possible.'

Raymond could not believe Aaron's comment, 'Yes doofus, we'll pull up on the riverbank here and Mo can go straight back to his room now.' Aaron felt imbecilic, and much to Gertrude's frustration, she complied and pulled the punt over to the side. Mo continued to shiver on the cold wooden surface, but the thought of moving was not a desirable one. 'I'll walk Mo back over to college and take his wet clothes. Explain to Scudamore's what has happened and tell them that I'll be over shortly to bring back their blankets.' Raymond bent down to pick Mo off of the floor. If he had a lack of coordination before, this was now ten times worse. Back on dry land, Mo leant against Raymond as they lumbered back to college. Gertrude went full speed ahead to get the punt back in time; she only had twenty-five minutes left to avoid a late fine.

20

What on earth was Harry thinking? It really was a rush of blood that went to his head. For the entire journey back to college from Scudamore's, which had been a chilly one without a jacket, Harry could not help but ponder and stress about how Mo would respond when their paths next crossed. Harry felt ashamed by his actions, and his culpability was exacerbated by the continuous discussion about it on the walk back. He was torn between two minds on whether to check up on Mo straight away or allow this situation to diffuse and give Mo some space. He opted for the latter and cowardly sent Mo a message on WhatsApp when he returned to his room. There was no response all night from Mo, and Harry's guilty conscience grew so large that it prevented him from sleeping. The following afternoon, to gesticulate his apology, Harry decided to get Mo a crate of Heineken from *Mainsbury's* and carried it over to Mo's room in Blue Boar Court.

Harry knocked on Mo's door and tried his luck opening it simultaneously. Much to Harry's surprise, it was locked, and he was kept waiting for a few seconds before a very casually dressed Mo answered the door. Harry could not gauge from Mo's reaction whether he was fuming or not. Mo was neither jovial nor vexed, and Harry was just pleased that he was not already getting an earful. 'Come in,' said Mo in a monotonal voice.

Harry accepted the invitation into the unwelcoming room. Unlike Harry's palace, Mo had rather been shafted with his accommodation, which was located on the other side of the road to the main part of Trinity. The accommodation block was built in 1989 and was rather at odds with the splendour of the rest of the college. Harry had no doubt that the dated room's interior had not been changed since its completion over thirty years ago. Blue Boar Court was a spill over living space for Trinity, it had been rushed to accommodate the growing number of students, and there was a real lack of care in the design of the purpose-built rooms. Everything about the room looked cheap, from the uncomfortable looking single bed to the electric heater in the corner. To make matters worse, Mo had gone to no effort to make the place feel homely. There were no decorations or signs of the resident marking his stamp on the place. The bland white walls and empty cork notice board reflected the lifeless nature of the characterless room and its inhabitant.

'Here, I got you these,' said Harry, handing over the crate to Mo. Harry was sure that he had seen a little smile from his friend, but perhaps he was just being optimistic. Mo carried the crate and placed it on his desk, which was filled with his notes and a few empty coffee mugs. Mo's laptop was wide open on Microsoft Word, and it was clear that he was mid-way through writing an essay. When Mo returned, Harry looked Mo straight in the eyes and said sincerely, 'I won't stay long, I just wanted to say sorry for yesterday.'

'I have to be honest, what you did was really shitty. You know that I can't swim,' said Mo. This was new information to Harry who had only found out yesterday, but he did not want to seem like an even more callous friend so said nothing. Mo continued, 'but, how can I stay mad at you. You're my boy!' It had been a smile Harry had seen earlier, and now it was out in full display.

Harry breathed a sigh of relief and said, 'Come here man!' while pulling Mo in for an embrace. 'When I tried to message you last night and you didn't reply, I feared the worst.'

Half aggressive, half jesting, Mo responded, 'And why do you think I didn't reply. My phone is fucked!'

This realisation sparked further guilt within Harry, who superficially offered to help out with the cost of getting him a replacement. Thankfully for Harry, who certainly did not have the funds to buy a new iPhone, Mo confirmed that it was covered on the insurance and his new phone would be arriving in the next week.

'Well at least let me buy you a new pair of glasses,' said Harry, 'I'm sure they can't be on your insurance policy.'

'No don't be silly man,' said Mo persistently, 'they were a spare pair. I hardly ever even used them.' Harry was truly grateful for how well Mo was taking all of this. He had fretted all night that Mo would never forgive him and would be sending him a long invoice for the damage that he had caused.

'I can see you're in the middle of studying, so I'll let you be man. I'm glad we have cleared the air between us,' said Harry as he headed towards the door. Just as he put his hand on the door handle, Harry remembered that he had forgotten something, 'Can I grab my coat back?' asked Harry cheekily, who was worried that the timing might be wrong. Mo opened his stand-alone wooden wardrobe, which looked rather bare, and pulled Harry's black Ted Baker jacket off a green plastic hanger. Harry folded his coat over his arm and left the room.

When Harry stepped out onto Trinity Street, he took out his packet of cigarettes from his jeans pocket and lit one up, using his hand to shield the flame from going out in the wind. He crossed the road and sat on the low-lying stone wall in front of Newton's tree. He watched the cyclists whizzing down the street in front of him, most following the rules, but the occasional cyclist ignoring the one-way system, using the road as a shortcut to get to the North of Cambridge. The cyclists swerved around the sporadically placed tourists walking in the middle of the road photographing everything they saw, oblivious to their surroundings. Tourists were not so much of an issue in the winter months; it was when the city started to heat up that they became a real nuisance. The tourist boom in the summer months were welcomed by businesses, but the congestion on the streets in the city centre served to frustrate students. This pent-up anger was made worse by the fact that students are in full-blown exam mode and became increasingly stressed by any delays. Most cyclists ring their bell to alert tourists of their presence politely, others lose their temper and heckle tourists in their way. Given that Harry did not have a bell on his rusty yellow bike, he always opted for the confrontational approach.

With each toke of his cigarette, Harry contemplated what he was going to do with the rest of his day. He only had a few hours until he was set to attend a formal dinner with a difference over at Homerton college and wanted to ensure that he used his time wisely. He had a four-thousand-word essay on the suitability of Enterprise Zones as an economic tool to promote economic growth in deprived regions of the country, which was due on Tuesday at midday. He had not yet started writing it and thought it best if he spent a few hours mulling his way through the readings.

With one last drag on his Camel Blue dart, he chucked the cigarette butt on the floor, despite the bin right next to him and headed into college through the Great Gate. A nod to both of the porters on shift and then straight to his bedroom to gather his things for the library. He spent about three hours studying in the Wren Library and was a little annoyed that someone had taken his favourite spot. Harry wanted to make sure that he left himself enough time to prepare for tonight's formal. He had been invited along by his college wife, Alexandra, and while he was sceptical of attending at first, he thought that the dinner would be a great opportunity to visit Homerton, a college that he had never planned to visit.

A college spouse is yet another of Cambridge's bizarre quirks. As a fresher, you get married to a college peer that you are particularly close to. Of course, the marriage is completely platonic, and often people coupled up friends of the same sex to avoid any awkwardness. Despite the ethos of the tradition, some people went to extreme lengths with their proposals. For instance, as a fresher, Harry was told of the couple that managed to get on stage at a Scouting for Girls concert in a venue over by the train station and convince the entire audience that the proposal was real. That was always the ambition when asking for someone's hand in marriage, yet more often than not, for all of people's crazy ideas, they usually lacked the courage to go through with it. Indeed, that was the case with Harry and Alexandra. He planned on asking her to 'marry' him at one of the May Ball events under the fireworks but pulled out at the last minute. Instead, he picked up some cheap flowers from *Mainsbury's* and popped the question in the accommodation halls on the last day of first year. Harry's proposal certainly would not be going down in folklore.

The purpose of the college marriage was that you would get 'college kids' and show them the ropes of student life at Cambridge, similar to a buddying system, to ease them into what can be quite a daunting institution. The kids were allocated based on the parent's subjects, so Harry had one child studying Economics and another studying linguistics, Alexandra's major. Harry recalled being neglected by both of his college parents after the first week of term. His college mum did not even attend the first family dinner. For all Harry's promises not to do the same, he soon found out that in his second year, he had better things to do with his time than babysitting some freshers. Consequently, he did not spend much time with his college family at all. He had also grown somewhat apart from Alexandra after they kissed on a night out in second year and made things uncomfortable between the pair. In fact, Harry had not spoken to her since that night, so he was surprised when she had messaged him to ask him to accompany him to the formal dinner.

It turned out that the dinner was a 'college couples formal', and Alexandra did not want to show up alone. Harry did not know this until he arrived and may have changed his mind if he knew that Alexandra had an ulterior motive. Indeed, Harry was sceptical about the dinner to begin with. While his wife was easy on the eye, she lacked the ability to hold a meaningful conversation. The thing that swung it for him was that the dinner was Harry Potter themed. The comparison of Cambridge to Hogwarts hit the stereotype right on the head, particularly with the students in their gowns. Harry was intrigued to see what the evening would entail.

Harry was immensely impressed with Homerton College's Dining Hall and actually thought it rivalled Trinity's, although he did not care to admit that to any of the guests he was dining with. The four long dining tables were decorated in the colours of the Hogwarts houses (red, yellow, blue, and green), with long banners of each house draped from the balcony above their respective tables. There were several guests in the hall before Harry and Alexandra entered, and they were left with the choice of joining Ravenclaw or Hufflepuff as the red and green tables were already full.

A wand (or rather a twig collected from the college's orchid) was placed in front of each seat, with the tip glittered in the house's colour. Harry swung his wand around, and it snapped before they were even seated. He contemplated wrapping it together with tape to mimic Ronald Weasley but did not have the resources to do this. Harry scoffed his face with the Bertie Botts Jellybeans laid out on the table avoiding conversation with Alexandra and her Russian friends. The courses were Harry Potter themed, with the starter of a scotch egg, with two tasselled sticks poking out of it to replicate the golden snitch. Alcoholic Butterbeer was served throughout the night in the place of wine, with non-alcoholic Polyjuice Potion as an alternative option.

Harry surmised that Homerton had done a reasonably good job with the themed formal dinner but reflected that it had not been worth the taxi journey down. That was until a live barn owl was brought out in between the main course and dessert (a chocolate sorting hat cupcake). Harry sat in disbelief that an owl would be allowed to fly across the Great Hall as they dined. This certainly served to make the evening more memorable. After getting a photo with the brown and white barn owl following the conclusion of the meal, Harry had decided to call it a night and leave Alexandra to enjoy the rest of the evening with her friends.

In the end, Harry concluded that it was a delightful formal. Indeed, seeing the live owl was the only thing he talked of to his friends over the next couple of weeks. They did not quite share Harry's enthusiasm for seeing the strigiform. However, Harry revelled in the experience and continued to brag about it, showing anyone and everyone his Instagram picture of him posing with the wise old owl.

Sabrina held Harry's phone, staring at the screen, looking impressed, or at least giving that outward impression, as Raymond came moseying his way into the college bar. 'Christ, you cannot still be parading that bloody owl,' said Raymond in exasperation as he approached the duo on the sofa.

'I think it's so cool that Harry got to go to a Harry Potter formal,' said Sabrina admiring her crush, 'and this little snowy owl is just adorable.'

'Actually, it's a barn owl. A snowy owl is three times the size of that little thing,' said Harry. 'You should have seen the detail that they went into at the formal,' he said while taking his phone from Sabrina and pulling up some of the many photos he had taken that night. Raymond, at this point, had gone to the bar to get himself a pint of the college's own brewed lager, which was heavily subsidised at just two pounds twenty.

'Oh, I do like this one,' said Sabrina, as Harry stopped on a picture of a poster.

'Yes, it was a brilliant idea, they replaced Sirius Black with the Homerton principal in the most wanted poster. Very creative!' said Harry.

Raymond came over to join them, opting to sit on the armchair instead of squeezing all three of them onto the one sofa, although he did think of plonking himself between the pair just to wind up Sabrina. 'Right, Harry, I refuse to listen to any more stories about this Harry Potter formal. I'm sure it was amazing and I'm sure you had a great time, but you're actually banned from talking about it. At least in my presence,' said Raymond before taking a huge gulp of his draught lager.

Harry looked a little discontent at Raymond's bluntness, but they were such close friends by now and he knew that Raymond truly had no filter. 'On the beer are we Raymond?' said Harry, who looked surprised at his peer's choice.

'Indeed I am. I'd much rather have a whiskey, but the prices are just extortionate in here. An absolute rip off,' said Raymond.

'Right, well we can't have you drinking alone now can we, what with it being your last night and all. Sabrina, would you like a drink too?' asked Harry.

Sabrina contemplated the offer, not because she did not want a drink but because she felt uncomfortable accepting it. It was rare that a boy offered to buy her a drink. She accepted with hesitance, 'Yes please Harry, can I have a double vodka and lemonade. Diet lemonade.'

'You can indeed. Do you want to pass me your card so I can pay for it?' said Harry. Sabrina was mortified by Harry's response and the realisation that the drink would set her back a pretty penny. Raymond did not buy whiskey at the bar because it was too expensive and now, Sabrina had gone and ordered a double. It would be at least eight pounds, which was extortionate for a drink at any college bar.

Despite the fact that it was the last day of term, the bar was surprisingly quiet. The students were set to go home for the break for the next six weeks, but the city was already hollowing out as many left sporadically over the past few days. Indeed, Cuthbert and Mo had gone home yesterday, and Aaron went back three days ago when teaching finished. 'May I please have a pint of the college lager and a double vodka lemonade,' said Harry, who had forgotten that Sabrina had specifically asked for diet lemonade.

The bartender poured the two drinks and placed them on the bar before saying, 'Ten seventy.'

'Can I pay separately?' asked Harry to the inconvenience of the bartender. Harry tapped the two cards respectively on the contactless reader and headed back to join the other two. As he turned around he could see that Gertrude had arrived and taken his spot on the sofa. Harry placed both drinks on the coffee table in front of Sabrina, handed her card back to her and went to pull up a chair from a neighbouring table. Sabrina took a sip of her expensive drink and was ignorant that she had been given full-fat lemonade. Clearly, the placebo of drinking diet lemonade was enough to deceive her.

'Well, here's to our last night together! May everyone have

much success with their revision over the break. It's full steam ahead from here,' said Harry in what was meant to be an inspirational toast but only served to deliver the harsh reality of what they could all to expect over the next few months. Harry stood up and raised his pint glass above the coffee table. Raymond did the same from the other side of the table, and the two girls were last up. Sabrina clinked her glasses with the other two, and much to the entertainment of the other three, Gertrude pulled out her plastic water bottle from her bag to join in the celebration.

'I can't stay long,' said Gertrude, 'I still haven't packed yet and my train to Stansted leaves at five in the morning.'

'Yikes. My flight back to Italy isn't until two in the afternoon tomorrow, so thankfully I'm not in such a rush. I think I'll have a few beers as a little send off to the city.'

Sabrina suddenly felt as though she was being roped into a drinking session with the boys. At eight pounds and fifty pence per drink, a session would certainly hit her bank account hard, a small price to pay to be with Harry, so she decided to stick around.

'When are you guys heading back to London?' asked Raymond to Harry and Sabrina.

'My parents are picking me up tomorrow,' said Sabrina with a smile.

'I'm not going home over the break. I haven't exactly got the most suitable home working environment, so my parents are paying for me to stay in college over Easter,' said Harry. Raymond looked at Harry soulfully as though his family showed him no affection, and Harry continued to justify himself, 'It's just better that way. Plus, I have still got a serious amount of work to catch up on. I've still got an essay from week two to submit. The deadline for that one has been extended four times now,' said Harry with an empty chuckle.

Gertrude was shocked at Harry's lack of organisation with his university work, 'Really, are you that far behind?'

'I'm slowly getting back on track. Had a bit of a slow start to the term, but things are picking up now. I'm back in my stride. I've got three more essays to do and a hell of a lot of reading before I can actually get on with revision,' said Harry optimistically.

'Well, I, as we are supposed to, have handed in all of my essays and made a detailed revision timetable that schedules every single hour of my life from tomorrow right down until my final exam on June fourteenth,' said Gertrude in a snobbish tone, 'I am not leaving anything down to chance this year.' Raymond and Sabrina nodded along in support of Gertrude; they knew the importance of getting these next three months right. Strangely, at Cambridge, the result of the entire degree rested on the final exams in the last year. The culmination of all their studies depended on their performance in one short exam period. All or nothing. The stakes could not be higher. They were at the final stretch of their marathon of a degree, pushed to their limits for three years and could not afford to slip up now.

Gertrude's sobering comment, combined with the fact that she was steering clear of alcohol, left the other three thinking twice about drinking the evening away. Sabrina finished about half of her drink when she decided that it was probably best for her to leave with Gertrude. Harry and Raymond stayed a little while longer, simply because they had more liquid to consume in their pint glasses but headed back to their rooms immediately afterwards. As the two parted ways to retire to their own chambers for the evening, Harry called out, 'Night Raymond. I'll come over at ten tomorrow to give you a hand carrying your luggage to the Porter's Lodge.'

'Thanks Harry, sleep well mate,' said a grateful Raymond.

Harry woke up at around nine, and by the time he had eaten his breakfast and showered, there was not much time left to commence with work for the day. Instead, he decided that he would go up to Raymond's room a little earlier than planned. When he ascended the staircase, Raymond's door was already open, but Harry knocked anyway to signal his early arrival.

'Come on in,' said Raymond, who was sitting on a large suitcase trying to squeeze all of his possessions into it.

'Need a hand?' asked Harry

Forcefully dragging the zip around the case, he replied in a somewhat stressed tone, 'No, I've got it.' With one last tug of the pull tab, Raymond managed to close all of the teeth on the suitcase, which was now left bursting at the seams. Harry was worried that it might explode when Raymond stood up, but somehow it managed to stay in one piece. The room was naked and cold as Raymond had packed away the last of his belongings. 'Let's get a move on then, shall we,' said Raymond picking up his huge case. Harry opted for the smaller of the two cases and also left Raymond to carry his hand luggage. Raymond viewed the messy room as he closed his door; the bin was full, and the floor needed a good hoovering, but it was nothing that the cleaners could not sort.

When they got to the Great Court, they both opted to carry their suitcases in their hands instead of using the attached wheels to avoid dragging them along the cobblestone. Raymond handed his key into the Porters and signed the file to indicate the transaction that just took place. The pre-booked taxi was already waiting for Raymond on Trinity street, and the driver came out to help them with the bags. He loaded the larger of the cases in the boot and put the smaller one in the back seat of the cab.

'Have a good break Raymond. It's going to be weird not having you around in college,' said Harry with the sobering realisation of how lonely he was set to be over Easter.

'I'm always on the other side of a phone. Keep safe Harry,' said Raymond as he lumbered into the back seat to accompany his luggage, avoiding the front seat and any possibility of small talk with the driver. Harry stood on the street waving his friend off like a grandmother standing at the door waving away their family. And then there was one, just Harry remained out of all his friends.

Instead of retreating to the isolation of his room, Harry thought that he would have a quick stroll into town to enjoy the spring sunshine; work could wait another half an hour or so. It was indeed perfect weather to grab one of Harry's favourite freshly squeezed oranges from the market square, so Harry set off in a slow pursuit behind Raymond's taxi. He was walking in the middle of the road, and without realising it, he was behaving just like the tourists he had grown to hate, dawdling in the street as opposed to on the narrow pavements.

It was good to see that the market was fairly busy, although most of the clientele were older adults. Not just because adults are more likely to shop at the marginally more expensive market, but because the vast majority of the student population were on their way home today. The juice stall had a vintage green and white thick striped tarpaulin roof, which matched the design of the rest of the stalls. From the sky, the colourful polyester market roofs came together and resembled a slightly misshapen rainbow. Harry approached the vendor who was acclaiming the brilliance of her orange juice to the crowds. He happily paid his three pounds twenty for a small cup of the stuff. She was not wrong; the chilled beverage was refreshing, and Harry particularly liked the sweet juicy bits which came with it.

Feeling content with his purchase, Harry headed back to college through the market, observing what the vendors were trying to flog today. There was such a diversity of stalls, from fresh fruit and vegetables to trailer vans selling delicacies from all over the world. From sweets to cheese, artwork to books, household goods to bike repair stands, the market sold just about anything you could imagine. Unlike traditional markets, everything had a fixed price, and haggling was not an option. There was an extensive line already forming for the Chinese food trailer, and Harry waltzed his way around the hungry customers. He made his way to the honey stall, towards the edge of the market, and that was when he saw her: Elizabeth.

Harry did not know how to react and instinctively hid behind the stall selling jars of sweet nectar to avoid being seen. Elizabeth was as beautiful as ever, her curly blonde hair glistening in the March sunshine. She strode along the street with two of her friends, and all three of them were sporting their Girton College puffer jackets. It was clear that after two terms at Cambridge, she had now settled in and was growing in confidence. Harry could see this radiant self-assurance from the way she walked. Elizabeth appeared to crack a joke, and the other two laughed aloud. She really was the whole package, and Harry was not surprised that she was popular; she had an amazing personality, and her aura was hugely attractive.

He had not seen her since New Year's and had come so far to recuperate from that pain but seeing her brought all those agonising emotions rushing back. Harry wanted to rush over to her, kiss her, hold her, talk things through, and work it all out. He knew that this was a fairy-tale romance in his head. If she had been alone, he may have plucked up the courage to go over to her, but he was intimidated by her friends and continued to hide behind the stall. *The one that got away* had never been truer as she walked on past Harry's secret spot. Harry's eyes began to water, and a single teardrop rolled down his sullen cheek from his left eye.

21

The next couple of weeks were not easy for Harry, who was left moping around over his unrequited love. His heart was in agony, his mind tortured, and his soul was lost once more. All of Harry's endeavours to get over Elizabeth had been undone in a matter of seconds. He had spiralled into another bout of depression, but this time it felt as if his relapse was inescapable. The fire of grief burning within Harry was growing daily. It was as if his body was a crematorium, with the flames fuelled by the fact that he unblocked Elizabeth on Instagram. He had hoped that stalking her, admiring her beauty from afar, would help to ease his pain, or at least comfort him, but the photos of her expressing tenderness with Matt turned the fire into an inferno.

This streak of sorrow was worse than the last. Harry was left in arrant isolation. All of his friends had gone home for the break, and Harry's family did not send so much as a text message to check up on him. He wanted to scream for help, but the college was so empty that his bellows would not have been heard. With nobody to turn to, Harry turned to alcohol each night to help numb the agony. It started with a few beers in the evenings, but things hastily degenerated, with the drinking starting progressively earlier each day. It was soon the only thing on Harry's mind, and he would start drinking as soon as he woke up, which tended to be in the early afternoon. He decided that the best way to overcome his desolation was through swilling and snoozing. It was not long until he turned to whiskey since beer was no longer giving him the same buzz.

There was no perceivable way out of this slump for Harry. Last time he moved on from Elizabeth by going on a date; granted, it was not exactly the time of his life, but it was a welcome distraction. He also had the swap, which extinguished the conflagration. However, these diversions were no longer in Harry's arsenal since the city had been drained of its young scholars. Even when Easter term started again, and the students started flocking back to Cambridge, people would be far too busy revising to be going on first dates. The suffering worsened for Harry as the weeks passed by in solitude, which continued to adversely impact his studies.

Over the last few weeks of term, Harry had worked diligently to catch up on all of his work. The Easter break was set aside to complete his dissertation and revise for his hectic exam period. Alas, his concentration had been obliterated. He kept delaying starting on his thesis because of his mental incapacity, but the deadline was fast approaching. It was not until Friday 17th April, just two days before the hand in date, that Harry finally started writing up his research. As he scrambled away, writing thousands of words over the weekend, he realised that this was the distraction that he needed all along. But this realisation had been sluggish to slither to Harry, who had put together a half-hearted piece of work, which lagged ferociously below his usual high standards. It was inexorable that he would be penalised for his sloppy work, which would undoubtedly put him on the back foot for his exams.

Harry had burnt away his time over the break. Before he knew it, the final term of his Cambridge career was almost upon him, and he had drifted from his schedule again. For the good of his degree, he realised that he had to force himself to keep working, keep striving towards the end because he was so close after all. He had not completed a single day of revision over the past six weeks, and panic was setting in over the mountain of work that lay ahead of him. It had been the worst possible timing for heartbreak to hit him. Thankfully, he still had a few weeks left before his exams commenced. Harry cleared all the empty beer cans and bottles of whiskey from his room, gathered his plates stacked messily on his desk, and emptied the bin. He needed a fresh start, which began with tidying his room, hoping this would lead to the decluttering of his mind.

Raymond, the last to leave Cambridge, was the first back to the city, and Harry was glad of his arrival. He had gone many weeks without talking to anyone at all and was hugely relieved to have some company, even if it was only someone to speak to briefly between studying. Harry wasted no time in racing up to Raymond's room and observed him unpacking his things.

'You're looking rather tanned,' said Harry staring at Raymond's hairy forearms, which appeared to be a couple shades darker than when he had left Cambridge. Harry made himself comfy on Raymond's vibrant blue swivelling desk chair.

'Yeah, well we've had some nice weather these past couple weeks in Naples, so I decided to revise outside to catch some rays,' said Raymond, who was carrying his folded black jeans. He opened his wooden chest of drawers and dumped them in with the rest of his trousers.

Harry looked rather envious of the Italian sunshine that Raymond had been exposed to. He had been stuck in Cambridge, where it seemed to be raining relentlessly and was far too cold to be out and about. 'How's the revision coming along then?' asked Harry, hopeful that his peer would be in a similar boat to himself: slacking and wildly out of control of his studies.

However, this was not the case, 'I've been working really well. I handed the diss in last week, have finished taking all of my notes and now I'm doing past papers and sending them to my supervisor,' said Raymond, before adding, 'they do take quite a while to send back my essays though and I hate chasing them up on it.' Harry looked glum at Raymond's progression, contrite for wasting time talking to his pal right now. 'What's the matter? I take it by that look that your revision isn't quite going to plan then,' said Raymond.

'You can say that again. It's Elizabeth, I just can't get her out of my mind, no matter what I try,' said a disheartened Harry.

Raymond laid his white jumper made from Alpaca wool (which he had purchased from a family trip to Machu Picchu a couple summers ago) down on his bed and walked over to console Harry. He put his hand on Harry's shoulder, trying to come across as sensitive to the delicate matter, but instead sounding rather blunt, 'You need to get over her mate. Now is not the time to feel sorry for yourself. We have a few weeks left until exams start and that must be your number one priority. You can sit around and cry over her all you like when this is all done, but you cannot afford to do this now.'

Harry chimed in, 'But,'

Raymond quickly interjected, 'No buts. I'm saying this as your friend, forget about her. Girls will come and go in your life, but your degree is with you forever. Your grade is like hot iron, being burned onto your skin like branding a calf. You may be young now, but that shit stays with you for life.'

Harry smiled at the dark analogy, 'That's a sinister way of putting it. I'm with you on that. I know how important it is to smash these exams, but I'm just drowning in work at the moment. No matter how hard I try, I don't seem to be putting a dent on what I need to achieve. Even when I do try, my mind always drifts to her. I just can't focus,' said Harry exasperatedly, on the verge of another breakdown.

'Hey, hey, breathe, calm down,' said Raymond in a sooth-ing tone. Harry was thankful that he finally had someone to talk to about all of his stresses. Raymond took a short pause to allow Harry time to relax, 'Are you okay?' he asked, and Harry responded by nodding his head along. 'Look, I think I might have just the thing you need to get you through this. Leave it with me and come back to my room this evening,' said Raymond rather suspiciously.

'Right, thanks Raymond. I'll be sure to pop back later. I appreciate you listening to me and helping me through this. I'm sorry I'm such an emotional wreck, I just haven't had the chance to speak to anyone about this over the break. I ought to head to the library and get some work done, I feel guilty sitting around when I know how much I need to get through,' said Harry, who picked himself up from the chair and headed towards the door.

'See you later then Harry,' said Raymond.

As Harry made his way back down the staircase to his room, he was curious as to what Raymond had planned. *What on earth could he possibly have or do that could help?* This was all Harry could ponder on as he packed his bag and headed towards the college library. Indeed, even when Harry was in the Wren library, he was distracted by his conversation. It was just as intrusive in his thoughts as Elizabeth had been, and getting work accomplished today was as laborious of a task as ever. Harry spent a few hours in the library flicking through lecture slides and trying to take notes on presentations that he had not attended throughout the year, but it was hopeless. Not only did he fail to understand the complex formulas on the PowerPoint slides, but he simply could not concentrate and decided it was best to change his environment and work from his room instead.

It proved no use going back to his room; he felt claustrophobic despite all the space around him. He associated his chamber as a place of torture, given the despair he had been through in this exact location, thinking about Elizabeth. Instead of wasting more time failing to get any work done, Harry thought he would use his time in a productive way beyond studying. This entailed doing his washing up, which had been piling up for weeks and finally getting around to doing his laundry. He went on a treasure hunt around his bedroom, where the only prizes were his odorous garments! Harry placed them all into his personalised laundry bag, bearing a large red 'H' on it. At least getting these chores out of the way would mean that he could hit the ground running with revision tomorrow morning.

The evening soon came around, and it was another day squandered for Harry, who seemed to be slipping further and further away from where he needed to be. Nonetheless, he was excited to see what Raymond had in store for him as he bounded up the staircase. With a gentle knock on the door, Harry made his way into Raymond's room for the second time today.

Raymond was sat at his desk in his creative flow, working on yet another practice essay as he muttered, 'Come in,' not knowing that Harry was already halfway across his room. He tapped away at his keyboard on his Dell laptop to finish off his sentence, took out his noise-cancelling earbuds, and turned to Harry, who was standing precariously in the centre of the room. 'Take a seat,' said Raymond while gesturing his hands towards his bed for Harry to perch on.

Harry made his way over to the single bed, which was dressed in college-provided bedsheets and lay rather glum in the corner of the room. Harry could not hold in his curiosity any longer and blurted out, 'So, you said you had something that might help me with revision.'

'Ah, yes, I certainly do,' said Raymond, as he pulled open his desk draw. He rummaged around, making quite some racket, before eventually pulling out a small cardboard box. It looked as though it was a packet of paracetamol or ibuprofen; Harry could not quite tell. Raymond pushed off of his desk, still seated in his chair, and launched towards Harry. The wheeled desk chair flew across the hard wooden floor, and Raymond put his legs out and pushed off the bedframe to stop himself from colliding into Harry. Now seated next to Harry, he chucked him the box, which Harry fumbled before catching, and said, 'Here, take these.'

Upon closer inspection, Harry realised that it was neither paracetamol nor ibuprofen. In fact, he did not recognise what it was as at all, as he slowly read out the name on the box, 'Methylphenidate. What the hell is this?' asked a bewildered Harry.

'It's Ritalin,' said Raymond, but he could tell by Harry's blank face that he needed to explain further, 'it's a study drug. It basically just enhances your concentration and means that you can keep going for hours on end.'

'What, a bit like the movie Limitless,' said Harry, who was slowly coming to terms with the idea.

'Yeah, pretty similar to that. Just pop one of these bad boys into your system every few hours when you're studying and you're good to go,' said Raymond while swivelling from side to side on his chair.

Harry was still sceptical about the idea; he had never taken drugs to help him study. 'Is this not just cheating then?' asked Harry.

'Well, yes and no,' said Raymond, 'they're a performance enhancer, but they're not illegal or anything. Plus, everyone is taking them, you're at a disadvantage if you don't. There's thirty in the pack, so it should be enough to get you through to the end of exams.'

Harry held the box in his right hand and stroked his beard in thought with his other hand. His beard had grown wildly over the break, and he had no intention of shaving any time soon. This was yet another one of his ridiculous superstitions – he would not trim his beard or get a haircut until he had finished his exams since he believed that his wisdom lay in his hair. But for his smart shirt, Harry could have easily been mistaken for a homeless man or even a caveman, but that was the way he consistently chose to present himself over the exam period. 'Be honest, what else do I need to know about this 'study drug' of yours. Where did you even get it from?' asked Harry interrogatively.

Raymond took a moment to think about how best to convince Harry of its mystical powers and decided to skip the last question. He contemplated hiding the fact that it was a stimulant used to treat ADHD but knew that this was something that Harry would easily be able to discover himself. 'There is nothing wrong with Ritalin, it is just used for people with ADHD to improve their attention span. It's not that it automatically makes you more intelligent, it just assists you with your concentration and allows you to study for longer,' said Raymond in a severe tone replicative of a doctor. 'Just make sure that you are actually in front of your books. I remember when I took one last year, I spent four hours intensely scrolling through Twitter,' he said with a little chuckle, 'mind you, I do that more often than I like to admit.'

Harry was a little relieved to hear that Raymond had taken the drug before and said, 'It does sound very promising! How much do I owe you for them?'

Raymond wavered his hand at Harry, 'Don't worry about giving me any money. You're my friend and I just want to be here to help you through this difficult time. Just buy me a pint or ten when these wretched exams are done with.'

'Thanks man, I really appreciate your help,' said Harry, who picked himself up off of the bed and headed towards the door,

'I'll let you get back on with your work.' Raymond pushed himself off of the bedframe and went whizzing back towards his desk.

Harry was positively intrigued by what Raymond had given him. He did not know what to expect when Raymond said that he had something for him, but he certainly was not expecting study drugs. Harry's mind was too preoccupied to work when he got back to his room; he was fascinated by these small white pills and decided to do a little more research into precisely how they worked. The drug held the promise of enhanced productivity, greater focus, more hours in the library, and ultimately a better degree at the end of it all. It seemed all too good to be true. Harry read up on how Ritalin increases dopamine, a brain chemical responsible for attention span and was getting increasingly more convinced by what he read. There were, of course, some side effects, but all drugs have their side effects, and these were not sufficiently serious enough to deter Harry from deciding to take the drug.

A long night's sleep gave Harry enough time to consider the pros and cons of taking Ritalin, and he ultimately decided that it would be worthwhile. He had read that they were, in fact, illegal without a prescription, so he thought it best to take one before heading to the library. It was just after nine in the morning when Harry filled up his Chilly water bottle and popped a tablet out of the packet. While he had taken many drugs throughout his life, they were all recreational, for partying and having a good time. It seemed bizarre, even paradoxical, to take a drug to help him study, the only drug that makes you stay up all night so that you cannot have fun. Harry placed the tablet on his bone-dry tongue, and with a large gulp of water, the drug was washed away down his oesophagus. He had discovered that it takes approximately half an hour for the effects to kick in, so Harry swiftly packed his bag and headed to the Wren.

Harry thought it was nice to see people that he vaguely knew back in college since Trinity had felt so empty over the break. However, he did not stop to talk to them because he feared that the Ritalin would kick in, and he would be engaged in conversation for far too long. He could not afford to waste another day of revision; he was too far adrift as it was. There were only a few students in the library when Harry arrived in the morning, but he knew it would not be like this for many more days. The Wren was notoriously busy during Easter Term with everyone in panic over their forthcoming exams. Indeed, students would be lucky to get a seat in the library, so Harry tended to relocate to his room when it got to this stage. But with students still swarming back into Cambridge, the library had not reached this chaotic stage, and Harry was able to take up his favourite study spot.

Harry withdrew his laptop from his bag, put it on charge and opened up a PowerPoint slide from Michaelmas term for his Development Economics module. He was anxious, knowing that at any moment, the effects of the drugs would kick in and interfere with his neurons. His leg was shaking, drumming down on the wooden floor to match his racing heartbeat. As time passed, his mind went through a natural transition, and while he stopped fidgeting, his heart only pounded faster. Harry began to breathe a little quicker as his eyes locked onto his screen. Harry's surroundings seemed irrelevant. Not even the students getting up and walking around the library could distract Harry, who had developed tunnel vision, staring at the slides and absorbing the information like a sponge.

It was unbelievable, as if a switch had been flicked in Harry's brain, and all he was concerned about was the lecture in front of him. He whizzed through the content providing empirical studies of slum regeneration, and moved swiftly onto the next lecture. And the next one, and the next one. Before he knew it, it was two in the afternoon, and he had powered through four lectures. This was a totally unprecedented feat; he would usually only manage to go through a couple lectures each day. Harry was working so productively that he did not even want to stop for lunch but knew that he ought to regardless. Besides, he wanted to take another pill to help him plough through even more lectures in the afternoon.

Not wanting to waste valuable time cooking at lunch, Harry quickly made himself a wrap and filled it with the leftovers from his butter chicken curry last night. He heated it in the microwave before scoffing it down in his room, eager to return to the library. Harry consumed another pill to keep his buzz up and headed back to the library, where he laboured relentlessly, yet effortlessly, over the next few hours.

The sun was setting later as the summer months were quickly approaching in Cambridge, yet Harry persisted in the library until after dark. Once again, he headed back to his room to heat up a pasta dish that he bought from *Mainsbury's* for dinner, popped in another pill and made his way back to the library.

Harry's concentration was flawless. Raymond was indeed right; this is exactly what he needed to focus on his studies. The clock struck midnight, yet Harry felt that he was able to continue with his revision. He was euphoric about the progress he had made. By the time he finally clocked off at two in the morning, he was the last to leave the library and had managed to get through a whopping ten lectures. It was unimaginable that he would be able to get through more than an entire term of lectures for Development Economics in a single day!

When Harry finally retired to his bedroom for the night, his mind was still racing, thinking about all of the information he had just absorbed. It was inconceivable that he would go to sleep now, so he opened up his laptop once more, this time to watch some Netflix to help him relax before bed. He put on an episode of *Peep Show*, a series that he always turned to when he could not be bothered to invest himself in a new show, and after half an hour of uncomfortable humour, he was tired enough to call it a day.

Although he still had a long way to go with his revision, Harry was quickly getting into a routine with his work, albeit a drug-dependent one. He worked persistently throughout the days, without distraction, without even thinking about Elizabeth. Even with the support of the study drug, Harry's unabating work mentality was being matched by his peers around him. Everyone was revising an unhealthy amount, and the heat in Cambridge was beginning to rise, both in terms of work pressure and temperature. With this brought the tempting summer scents, making studying indoors even more torturous. The build-up to the exam season in Cambridge was always peculiar, as tourists seeking to explore the city displace the students who are locked away in the various libraries scattered across the East Anglian land.

Despite Harry's unparalleled focus, he still had a mountain to climb. He knew that it would not be possible to achieve the amount of revision he desired and decided that it was best to strategically revise for his exams. He needed to take a gamble and pick a few topics to study in great detail, hoping that they would appear in the exam. It really was his only option at this point and would be much better than spreading his efforts across all of the potential topics.

There were now just seven days until the exam season commenced, and Gertrude had suggested that the group had a brisk luncheon together on Monday afternoon. This was met with profuse approval since they had all lacked human contact over the past month or so. Everyone, except Cuthbert, who said he was *too busy* with revision to have lunch, met in the hall at midday. The sunshine was bursting through the stained-glass windows, leaving colourful patterns on the stone flooring. It was a glorious day in Cambridge, not the kind of day you would choose to be stuck in a library, but sadly that was the fate of all of the students.

'Shall we eat outside on the benches in the avenue?' suggested Gertrude openly to the group.

'I haven't got time for that,' said Raymond dismissively as he picked up a brown plastic tray for his food.

'What do you mean haven't got time for that? It literally takes the same amount of time,' replied Gertrude in protest.

'It's all the faffing around, and getting the food in a takeaway box, and using plastic cutlery, and eating on the grass. I just want to sit in the hall, have a quick spot of lunch and get back into the library, okay!' said Raymond, who was clearly quite stressed over his intensive work schedule. Gertrude did not respond; instead, slipping quietly into the queue and grabbing her tray.

They all got their food from the catering staff, with everyone except Sabrina opting for the smoked salmon option. She just decided to get a bowl full of salad to have a lighter lunch and drizzled it with Caesar dressing. Aaron picked up a fluffy tiramisu to accompany his meal and justified it as 'brain food' to help him study.

The six took their seats on the red upholstery fabric chairs with the Trinity crest carefully stitched onto them, and Gertrude kicked off the conversation, 'How's everyone's revision coming along?'

Aaron was quick to bark back at her, 'Please, can we talk about anything other than studying.' It was clear that everyone was on edge, short-fused and ready to explode!

'Well, all we've been doing these past few months is studying. So, I don't think there is much else that we can talk about,' said Mo while using his hand to sloppily cram down a handful of baby potatoes.

'It sure as hell is the only thing that's been on my mind,' said Harry. Even sitting down to have lunch made Harry feel rueful as he felt that this was time that could be better spent with his nose in a book. It was a rushed lunch all-around but a welcome break for their sanity. Everyone had finished eating, except Aaron, who was tucking into his tiramisu. Wasting time was not an option for them, so the group got up and left the straggler behind to finish his dessert alone.

As they were heading out of the hall, Harry grabbed Raymond's arm and said, 'Mate, I need a quick word with you.'

Raymond was caught off guard and mumbled something along the lines of, 'What's up?'

Harry came across agitated, 'Pills. I need more of them. I need them now. I don't how much they cost; I just need them immediately.' He was almost shaky in desperation.

'Alright relax,' said Raymond, 'I've got some more in my room that I can give you for now and I'll get some more in for us both. But go easy on them, they're not candy.'

- 22 -

If you look up 'dependence' in the Oxford dictionary, it will tell you that it is 'the state of needing the help and support of something in order to be successful', and this one word described Harry's situation entirely. He had become completely hooked on Ritalin, the only thing that was fuelling him to power through with his revision. In the week building up to his first exam, he had doubled his dosage of the drug to keep up the effects. In fact, he started taking in so much that it began to impact his sleeping. Harry had started to suffer from insomnia since his mind was in a constantly active state. But of course, he had found a solution: more drugs. He was taking one Nytol, a sleeping tablet, to help him drift off to sleep each evening after a long day of studying.

Harry now worked exclusively from his room since he did not want to take the risk of heading to the library only to find out that there was no space available for him. The only time he left his room was to grab food from the hall (since this was more efficient than shopping and cooking for himself) or to have a stress cigarette. Sunday evening came around fast, and Harry did not even find time to check the Chelsea score. Instead, he used his last day to cram as much as possible for his Development Economics paper the following day. His stress was bubbling, and he felt sick to the pit of his stomach as the sun disappeared for the day. The next time the star rose, Harry would sit his exam. He got through nearly an entire packet of cigarettes that night in an attempt to calm his nerves.

Regardless of how much time Harry had expended on revising for his exam, he still felt underprepared. This always seemed to be the case for university students; there was always more that could be done, always a further paper to read, always another lecture to re-watch. When it reached midnight, Harry was sat at his desk, staring at the two different drugs available to him. He contemplated taking another Ritalin and pulling an all-nighter in preparation for his exam. However, he came to his senses; his exam was at nine the following day, and a good night's sleep would do him a world of good. He took an extra Nytol to ensure no difficulties in falling asleep and, as per his routine, put on Netflix while the drug kicked in.

The day was finally here, and it came as somewhat of a paradox. He had been dreading this day, fearful of not putting in a good performance, but equally, it meant that he was one step closer to finishing his degree. He rose at 8am sharp and chose not to snooze his alarm. Despite the roasting temperature outside, he put on a pair of tracksuit bottoms and a hoodie. He wanted to make sure he was comfortable for the exam and poured himself a bountiful bowl of Coco Pops. After devouring his cereal, he ate an overly ripe banana, of which the skin was almost entirely brown. Harry pushed another Ritalin tablet out of the packet and consumed it with some water. His initial dubiousness about taking the drug for the exam was quickly overcome; it had been so effective in helping him revise that it was a no-brainer. He stormed through the plodge and thought it best to cycle to his exam to save time. Naturally, Harry took his trusty satchel with him, filled with all of his notes, even though he would not have the time to look at them when he arrived.

The exam was taking place in the Mill Lane lecture theatre, not far from college, but Harry thought that the cycle would do him good. He had arrived in good time and locked his bike. Plentiful economics students were gathered outside of the hall with little chatter – they were clearly too focused on the test that awaited them. Harry spotted Mo over by the doors but decided not to talk to him. He did not want any distraction whatsoever before his examination, so instead rushed over to the toilets to alleviate his bladder while he had the chance.

It was clear that many of the other students had the same idea as Harry, and he had to queue to use the urinal. He thought about going for a nervous poo, but there was only one cubical with too many people waiting in line. When he got to the front of the queue, he stood next to someone he recognised from his course, but there was no conversation between them. One of the unwritten men's toilet rules had already been broken as no urinal was left between each user, and they were not prepared to break another by engaging in chit-chat. Harry unzipped his flies and stared straight at the white tiled wall in front of him. He was struck with a little stage fright, which he just put down to the nerves of the exam, but after about ten seconds, he began to alleviate himself.

By the time he had left the toilet, there was approximately ten minutes to go until the start of the exam, and people were making their way into the hall. Harry chucked his satchel on the floor outside and grabbed his see-through pencil case before he joined the back of yet another queue and made his way in too. He paraded up and down the hall, looking for the candidate number that matched his own, 8642C, and eventually found the space allocated to him. He withdrew his CAMcard from his wallet and placed it next to the green card displaying his candidate number as proof of identity.

The head invigilator stormed down to the bottom of the lecture hall, with his gown flowing graciously behind him. Exams in Cambridge were incredibly formal, as per the rest of life in the institution, and all of the invigilators were required to wear their academic gowns. Addressing the entire theatre, the head invigilator announced, 'Do not open the question paper until I instruct you to do so. You are now under exam conditions,' he continued to ramble on the usual spiel, which the students had heard far too many times over the past three years. Harry's entire body was now trembling, shaking as if he had Parkinson's disease. His hand became sweaty, and his heart was pounding harder than it ever had before. He fiddled with his pen, as a coping mechanism, since he simply did not know what else to do. He looked around to see what others were doing. Some were engaged in silent prayer, others sitting calmly, composing themselves for the three-hour exam ahead, others still were panicking, and some were even trying to read the questions through the thin sheet of A4 paper to gain an advantage moments before the exam was about to begin.

'The start time is nine o'clock and the finish time is twelve o'clock. I will let you know when there are five minutes left of the exam,' said the invigilator. The silence was deafening as everyone stared at the large clock behind the man in the cape as it ticked slowly towards nine o'clock. When the thin second hand struck twelve to meet the minute hand, the invigilator said, 'You may open your question papers and begin.'

The time for nerves were now over, and these were rapidly replaced with determination as the students scoured through the questions to select which ones they preferred answering. They had a choice of ten essay questions and had to answer just four of them. As usual, picking the first three was easy for Harry; he had studied these topics in great detail and was comfortable answering them. It was deciding which one to attack last that proved tricky as he weighed up between a few competing options. He made plans for his first three essays to give him time to consider which one to leave until the end. Using the scrap paper provided, he generated mind maps to create skeletal essay plans, one sheet per question, so that he had enough room to add to them as the exam progressed.

Surprisingly, the exam was going incredibly well for Harry, and rather unsurprisingly, given the pressure of the situation and the Ritalin that was consumed, Harry was incredibly focused on each essay he produced, engaging deeply with the rigorous question at hand. If anything, he was too deeply absorbed in his work; by the time he had finished his third essay, he had just thirty minutes left to write up the last one. He had not planned it at all, nor had he decided which one it was to be, so he just chose the first one that he could see from the three he was deliberating over.

His spontaneous efforts were proving fruitful, and he wasted no time in getting his thoughts down on the paper. The final essay may not have been so coherent and well-shaped as the other three, but there were some phenomenal pieces of raw analytical work that would serve to stand it out as a magnificent essay. When the invigilator broke the three-hour silence and announced, 'The exam has finished, stop writing and put your pens down,' Harry was yet to write his conclusion and continued scribbling away. He added a couple sentences to sum it all up and would have kept writing if it was not for one of the co-invigilators walking over to him specifically and taking the pen out of his hand. Harry's handwriting had become increasingly sloppy as the exam went on, and he did not even manage to finish his last sentence, but he was convinced that his writing was so illegible by this point that the examiner would not have known. He was just grateful to only receive a slap on the wrists for writing beyond the time allocated.

When he was finally released from the exam hall, Harry breathed a huge sigh of relief. He caught Mo gathering his belongings outside the hall and headed over to see how he found it. The post-exam analysis was always an exciting part of the exam period for Harry. He always wanted to see how others found it in comparison and wanted to discuss what questions people took. 'Thumbs up or down then?' asked Harry as he approached Mo.

Harry could see from Mo's reaction that things had not gone quite as well for him; he looked distraught as he slowly pointed his thumb towards the floor. 'Fucking bullshit man. That paper was an absolute joke. Literally none of the topics I prepared for came up. Genuinely reckon I'd be lucky if I pulled out a two-one in it.'

Harry did not know how to react to Mo's disappointment but tried to quickly distract him, 'Well, there's no time to dwell on it. Macroeconomics exam tomorrow.'

His words clearly served to pain Mo further, 'I'm so done with this shit man. Are you walking back to college?' asked Mo, as the pair headed out of the exit.

'I'm cycling mate,' said a relieved Harry. He could not think of anything worse than having to listen to Mo whining about the paper. Plus, he did not want to throw away any more time than he had to. The rest of the day was set to be another long one, stuffing as much information into his brain as possible. Luckily enough, it was an afternoon exam, so Harry could work into the early hours of the morning.

It would have been tough work for Harry to motivate himself and study again after his long exam, but for the assistance of the magic white pills. He allowed himself an hour break at lunch to clear his mind of all the knowledge he needed this morning before taking two Ritalin pills. He thought that he would head to the library to change his environment and was lucky enough to find a study space to claim as his own for the entire day. Again, he worked non-stop throughout the day, and he did not even have to leave the library for dinner this time as he brought a bottle of Vanilla Huel with him to get him through the night. He did, however, head to the college bar on two separate occasions to fuel his caffeine addiction.

The next exam was yet another remarkable success for Harry, and he was delighted that Mo had been just as positive about it. The stress had certainly toned down after the first exam, and the end was in sight; two down, two to go. Harry's exam schedule was farcical. After having two exams in quick succession, he had to wait a whole three weeks until the next one, which was again followed up immediately by his Microeconomics exam. He did not allow himself to slack off over the next three weeks, despite his peers finishing all around him. He was envious of those who had been given an early release from the shackles of the exam period. They ran wild in the college and were partying into the early hours of the morning; Harry had been tempted to join them on a night out or even at a pre-drinks to participate in the celebrations, but stayed strong and committed to his studies. His time would come.

The silver lining of a select proportion of students finishing early was that there was now always space for Harry to study in the library, and stoked up on Ritalin, he spent many a long night in the growingly glum study space. As each day passed, the number of students in the Wren continued to drop off as more and more students finished their Cambridge careers. Harry found himself working increasingly longer hours, and often, he would be leaving the library as students would come stumbling back into Trinity, merry after a night of clubbing. If anything, seeing the jubilation of those around them celebrating the end of the exam term only served to spur Harry on. It was just three days until he could join them in rejoicing freedom.

The night before their penultimate exam, Regional Economics, Mo and Harry decided that it would be mutually beneficial to revise together. Mo had asked if they could work together in his room, but Harry was quite adamant that the study session should take place at his place instead. He could not bear to spend any more time than he had to in Mo's cramped, lifeless room. Mo came by at about nine in the evening, after they had both had dinner and had gone through what they wanted to achieve for the day. 'Right, so how should we do this then?' asked Mo, who clearly had not planned anything for this cooperative session.

On the other hand, Harry was well prepared and had an agenda of precisely what he wanted to get out of this. 'Well, firstly, we need to list what topics we chose to study for this exam. That way we can whittle down what ones we are both interested in,' said Harry.

Mo interjected, 'I've actually decided to cover all the topics for this exam. After being caught out in the Development Economic paper, I did not want to take any chances again.'

'That's quite preposterous,' said Harry in an outraged voice, 'what a foolish way to approach an exam.'

Mo was quite riled up by Harry's response, 'Look, I did not come here to be lectured about my exam technique. We both got into Cambridge, which means that we both know how to do well in exams. You do your thing and I'll do mine.'

'Right you are,' said Harry with raised eyebrows, 'well then, let's just cover the topics that I've focused on, since I don't want to waste my time hearing you babble on about things that are utterly irrelevant to me. I was thinking that we could test each other on the readings, quotes, abstracts, you know the drill.'

The boys proceeded to have a chaotic quiz, testing every nuanced detail about what could come up in the exam. There was no way that the test would require such niche knowledge and specificity of the topics, but that did not stop the boys from pushing each other's capabilities. It was clear that they both knew their stuff exceptionally well, but that did not mean they would pass the exam in flying colours. Cambridge examinations are known for throwing a variety of curveballs at the students, to test how they apply their knowledge and to put them under pressure to see how they can adapt to difficult circumstances. It is one thing to memorise lectures, readings, and textbooks, but another thing to apply this knowledge in a creative and original manner. It is this originality that stands students out from the competitive crowd. The quiz went on until two in the morning, when Mo decided to call it a day; he was exhausted and wanted to be well-rested for tomorrow afternoon. Harry, on the other hand, powered on for another two hours to refresh his memory on his notes one last time.

The exam was to take place at the David Attenborough building on Pembroke Street, a modern building with a colossal lecture hall. The only issue is that the hall was clearly built for lectures, not exams. Students shared long desks, which spanned across the entire length of the hall, and there was a serious design flaw to these desks. While they may have been ideal for laptops, they were far too thin and, as a result, could not fit on an entire sheet of A4 paper. This meant that the students had to keep adjusting their pages as they proceeded, somewhat of an inconvenience for the stressed finalists, of which there were over a hundred of them for that exam. Nonetheless, having overcome the challenge of physically writing on the exam, both Harry and Mo had come through relatively unscathed and were now less than 24 hours away from liberty.

Mo was on the verge of collapsing; he was so drained physically and mentally from the gruelling exam period. Whereas Harry was running on pure adrenaline, which helped him get through the final evening of revision. The only issue was that he had spent so much time preparing for the first three exams that he had somewhat neglected Microeconomics. He was naturally gifted in this paper and relied a little too heavily on that fact. It was only when he started mulling his way through his notes, which he had stored on his Google Drive that he realised how unprepared he was.

Harry was finding it incredibly difficult to focus, with all of the students being so raucous in their rooms around him. He could hear music blazing from Raymond's room and had to go up to tell him to turn it down. It was not their fault that they were noisy; they were celebrating, and rightly so. But given Harry's lack of preparation, he became increasingly ratty as the night went on. Even taking an extra Ritalin was not enough to keep his concentration. Perhaps at this point, his body had become so used to the drug that it had minimal effects on him.

It was a late one again for Harry, but nowhere near as late as it was for Mo. When Harry woke up, he had received a voice note from an unbelievably stressed-out Mo, which had come through to Harry's inbox at five in the morning. He was blabbering on about how unprepared he was and how many coffees he had consumed to enable him to keep on powering through. It was clear that Mo had been pushed to the limits and wanted to give his all for this last exam. Mo's lack of preparation made Harry feel somewhat better – misery loves company after all.

Nobody could have predicted the carnage that this exam was about to spew out. As Harry was lining up to enter, he lingered around the back to give himself as much time as possible to stare intensely at the notes on his Google Drive on his phone and take in as much as he could before entering the exam hall. The test itself was taking place in the Guildhall, a monstrosity of a building lying right in the centre of the city, adjacent to the market square. Instead of putting his phone in his bag, as usual, Harry put it on silent and slipped it into his pocket. The hall was set up in a vintage style; the seating plan was militant, with students sat equidistant apart on wooden desks to minimise the possibility of cheating. Harry thought that this was a befitting end to his Cambridge career. Just three hours to go until it was all over.

The head invigilator was reading through the instructions, 'You are not allowed to have any unauthorised items in the exam room. If you have any unauthorised items, including mobile phones or any kind of electronic device you must hand them in now. If you do not hand them in, you may be disqualified from this examination.' These words sent a guilty shiver down Harry's spine. Of course, he had no intention of checking his phone; it was more of a precautionary measure. However, when Harry turned the page at the start of the assessment, he realised just how much trouble he was in. It was a sinking feeling when he read through all of the questions and realised that he would be able to answer two of them at most. He started panicking; one bad exam could completely throw his chances of getting a first-class degree. Deciding to stay calm in this horrendous situation he found himself in, Harry planned out the first essay and wrote it straight away.

Around fifty minutes had passed when the first dramatic event had taken place. Mo came storming into the back of the huge hall, panting for breath. He had clearly run or even cycled over to the Guildhall; it was too close for him to get a taxi. His entrance had caused a great disturbance to the examination, as necks swivelled around to see who the latecomer was, before immediately looking back to their paper and continuing with their work. The closest invigilator stomped over to Mo and told him to be quiet, 'You need to come outside with me right now,' she said in a low but authoritative voice, 'you are more than thirty minutes late to this exam and we cannot allow you to sit it.' This was another one of Cambridge's stringent rules that was inflexible to the ever-changing times. Mo pleaded her, but it was of no use, 'We can discuss this outside.' It was clear that the invigilator was becoming more severe in her tone and not wanting to upset her further, in the hope that he would somehow manage to convince her to let him sit the exam, Mo obliged.

Harry felt devastated for his peer. He knew that he had no chance of getting any sympathy from the invigilator. Yet, Harry had his own issues to focus on. Almost an hour had gone by, and he had still only written one essay. His mind was completely blank on what else to write, and if he did not come up with something fast, he would be in the same boat of failing this exam as Mo. He had to do something, and he had to do it now. He raised his hand like a dart in the air to attract the attention of a nearby invigilator who was strolling the aisles like a security guard. When the invigilator arrived next to Harry, he whispered, 'I need to go to the toilet.' The gowned man tilted his head and pointed towards the door at the end of the hall. Harry rushed out of his seat and bombed in the direction of the toilets.

Upon leaving the hall, Harry heard the invigilator saying to Mo, 'I am afraid that there really is nothing we can do for you. I suggest that you contact your tutor and see if you can take up your extenuating circumstances with the exam board.' Mo was distraught and began sobbing away at this news. When the invigilator left him, he walked over and slowly collapsed by the wall. He was wailing away, unsure what to do as his entire world was caving in on him, and Harry thought that this would definitely be a distraction for all of those inside the hall. He wanted to console his peer but now was not the time. He would have plenty of time for that when he had finished in less than two hours.

Harry walked straight past Mo, went down the stairs and entered a cubicle in the toilet, pulling out his phone. He had no intention whatsoever of cheating at the start of the exam, but things were not going as planned. The Eduroam Wi-Fi was too slow, so Harry switched to his 4G to get up his notes. He began scouring through his notes on the essay questions, realising that there was a trade-off between digesting this information and writing the exam itself. Flicking through the pages, he slowly gathered the information he needed, and his memory was being refreshed with each additional page. He was starting to relax a bit more, when suddenly someone was banging on the bathroom door. 'What are you doing in there?' barked a blood-thirsty invigilator, clearly excited by the prospect of catching a cheater red-handed. 'Come out immediately!' he ordered. *It could not end like this, please no*, thought Harry as he slipped his phone into his pocket.

'I'm coming out now, give me a minute,' said Harry, who flushed the toilet to give off the impression that he was using the cubicle for its intended purpose. If there had been a window, he would have for sure chucked his phone out of it without any hesitation, but he thought that attempting to flush it away was completely non-sensical. Harry held his head low as the invigilator stood before him, gritting his teeth.

'I am going to have to search you,' he said.

Harry tried to maintain his act of innocence, right until the very end, 'What do you mean search me? What on earth for?'

'You know exactly what for.'

Harry acted confused, 'I have no idea what you are going on about, but at least let me wash my hands first.' Harry applied soap and rubbed his hands extensively to bide his time while he came up with a plan to get himself out of this sticky situation. He went over to the drier and held his hands underneath it until it automatically switched off for being on too long. This was it; it was all over for Harry. This was not what was written in the script. Harry slowly walked over to the invigilator and put his arms out wide to allow the search to take place.

Christ, what a mistake Harry had made, and now he was set to pay the ultimate price. The invigilator began by patting Harry's outstretched arms and was about to make his way to his ankles, when suddenly Mo came bundling in. He was now fully red-faced and screaming at his predicament and decided to go to the toilets to get some tissue to wipe away his tears.

This was Harry's chance to get away, the diversion that he had so desperately needed. He did not know if Mo had come in deliberately to his rescue, but either way, it was an opportunity not to be wasted. Harry stormed out of the bathroom, and the invigilator shouted after him, 'Oi, get back here at once!'

When he arrived at the door, Harry shouted without turning back, 'I have an exam to finish. You can search me after if you so desperately desire.' As soon as he was outside of the bathroom, Harry's brisk walk turned into a full-on sprint as he pegged it up the stairs. He tossed his phone into his satchel, not bothering to zip it back up, before entering the exam hall once again. It was now Harry who found himself exhausted, panting to take as much oxygen into his lungs. It was a truly miraculous event, and Harry was unsure if he would even get away with it. When the invigilator re-entered the hall, he looked exasperated but left Harry to get on with the rest of his paper undisturbed. His answers were not perfect by any stretch; he had only briefly looked at his phone and now had an added time constraint, but at least he got something down on the paper. When Harry's paper had been handed in, he wasted no time in loitering around to gossip with the rest of the students outside of the hall. Instead, he headed straight to the exit to avoid encountering the angry invigilator.

- 23 -

The pressure was building, escalating so rapidly that it was increasingly difficult to bottle it all up. No matter how hard it tried to fight against it, this was a battle that would inevitably be lost, and sure enough, it all got too much. The cork went soaring through the sky, and the champagne started flowing uncontrollably out of the bottle. The bottle was really a pressure vessel masquerading as a drink's container. The others had followed Raymond in unleashing the pent-up energy from their bottles, firing the cannon, and running up to Harry to spray him with alcohol in celebration of finishing his degree. In many ways, the popping of the cork was symbolic of Harry's life over the past few months. He had been working relentlessly to get to this point, cramming in as much information into his brain as physically possible, and now his cork had popped. The final exam was over, and Harry felt just about every emotion possible as his friends covered him in sticky liquid, which was actually rather refreshing in the beating summer heat. His emotions were all blended in to make a remarkable cocktail, a splash of exhaustion with how challenging the past few months (and indeed past three years) had been, an abundance of euphoria to have completed his degree, a shot of sadness in the realisation that his life in Cambridge was coming to an end and sprinkled with a hint of relief that he had not been caught cheating at the final hurdle.

Harry grabbed the bottles, or what was left of them and began to polish off their contents. Champagne had never tasted sweeter, and it did not matter that the time had only just passed midday; it had been his first drop of alcohol in quite some time, and it sure as hell was not going to be his last tonight. He was carefree and ready to rejoice. 'I'm fucking done!' roared Harry while slapping his now sodden grey t-shirt. The market square was filled with animated students ready to give their peers the same reception. Harry was shaking in disbelief and almost brought to tears at the buzzy atmosphere outside the towering Guildhall. He could not believe it. It was all over. It was all *finally over*!

'Congratulations, you're now officially unemployed!' said Raymond in a jokey fashion.

The others were all jumping and celebrating around Harry, pulling out their second bottles, ready to bask in Mo's glory. 'Where's old Mohammed then?' asked Aaron. Harry pulled a grimacing face, which was enough to inform them that something was unapt. As he proceeded to explain what had happened, Sabrina began to slowly put her bottle of champagne back into her bright orange Sainsbury's bag. It was certainly not the news that they were expecting to hear and was at great odds with the jubilant scenes around them. Gertrude headed back to Trinity to console Mo, but it was no use. He said he wanted to be left alone for now as he had a lot to sort out, so she obliged. She could only imagine the horror of the phone call back home to his parents; they would have been expecting to applaud their son on his tremendous achievement, but instead, would be finding out that everything, even his graduation was up in the air.

Mo's shocking news certainly dampened the mood, but it was not enough to stop the planned proceedings, and after a few drinks on the green near Scudamore's, the saga was quickly forgotten. The gang watched as tourists and students fought with their long poles to navigate their punts down the River Cam towards Grantchester Meadows, colliding into banks and boats alike in the process. There were several trips to and fro *Sainsbury's* to replenish the stock of bubbly, although, after the initial spraying, they had switched to Prosecco to save some money. Cows prodded their way across the green, dropping monumental faecal matter on the very grass that they were consuming. As the day wore on and Harry became increasingly intoxicated, he plucked up the courage to stroke the friendly beasts and remarked that they were effectively just big dogs. Harry was *udderly* exhausted by the time the sun had started to go down at around nine o'clock, a mixture of day drinking as well as months of hard work and sleepless nights, but that did not stop him from going to Fleek Fridays in Cindies that evening. Over the next three days, Harry and co were living out Sean Kingston's song of sleeping all day and partying all night.

It was a hectic schedule of relaxation over the weekend, and indeed this was the tempo that was to be set for the rest of May Week, a one-week bender where students righteously bathe in their glory of getting through another year at Cambridge.

Not a single conscious moment was to be spent sober this week, and drinking at any hour of the day was considered acceptable, indeed encouraged. Themed garden parties were particularly fashionable, sipping Pimm's in the sunshine, playing croquet, dancing to live music. The unlimited drink and food made these parties good value for money, and at around thirty pounds per event were a much cheaper alternative to the ludicrously expensive May Balls. Nonetheless, it was Harry and his friends' final year, and no expense was to be spared on this week. It was their last hurrah at Cambridge, and they had booked on to the most sought-after events. The invoice for all of these garden parties and balls came to around one thousand pounds, which Harry's friends could quite comfortably afford, but he himself thought was an excessive amount. In spite of this, he convinced himself that the memories would be worth the money and the FOMO was enough to justify the cash.

As Trinity students, they were able to secure tickets to May Week's centrepiece occasion, the Trinity May Ball, which welcomed around 2,500 guests into the college on the Monday evening. These tickets were like gold dust, and without good connections, were near on impossible to secure. Most students never had the opportunity to attend this spectacle; it was something they spoke about in admiration or even jealousy. While the majority of colleges held a ball, Trinity's was by far the most extravagant, obsessing over consummate quality. White tie may not have been compulsory as it was at Magdalene college, but guests certainly did not look casual in their tuxedos and ball dresses. The Trinity May ball was the first Cambridge ball, founded in 1866 and has undergone a dazzling transformation since its inception. Over one and a half centuries, the ball had only been interrupted by the death of a monarch and the Second World War. No expenses were spared at this extravaganza, and consequently, the punters were willing the price.

It pained Harry to splurge two hundred and fifty pounds on his VIP ticket. He would have opted for a regular ticket if it was not for the fact that the tickets had to be bought in pairs and he could not convince anyone else to join him at the lower price.

Cuthbert was the first of the group ready and waited outside in the Great Court as the time approached six on the night of the Trinity May Ball. Harry was out not long after, and he was in hysterics when he saw his friend wearing a single, golden rimmed monocle. 'Fuck off,' said Harry as he approached Cuthbert, 'I didn't realise Mr Monopoly was coming to the ball tonight.'

Cuthbert was shocked at Harry's foul language, 'Well, if you are referring to Rich Uncle Pennybags, the mascot from Monopoly, I think you'll find that he does not have a monocle.'

'Shut up,' said Harry in disbelief, 'I've played Monopoly for years, of course he does.' Harry withdrew his phone from his tight suit trouser pocket and searched 'Monopoly' in Google to prove Cuthbert wrong. He stared blankly at his phone before saying, 'Nah, that has to be the biggest Mandela Effect ever!' Cuthbert stood smug at Harry's revelation. 'Since when did you need glasses anyway?' asked Harry quickly to move past his embarrassment.

'You've known me for three years now. How do you not know that I'm long-sighted?' asked Cuthbert rhetorically. Harry chose to ignore the question.

Over the next ten minutes or so, Mo, Raymond, and Aaron had joined the pair already waiting in the glorious sunshine.

Mo had spoken to his tutor about his situation, and they subsequently organised a meeting with the exam committee tomorrow morning to see if his predicament could be resolved. There was nothing he could do about it right now, and he realised that there was nothing to be gained from sulking. 'Why on earth have we bought VIP tickets?' asked a disgruntled Harry flagrantly to the group.

'Well, it means that we can enter the ball an hour early. Ample time to explore before the masses start flocking in,' said Aaron. 'Plus, we don't have to wait in the queue with all the shitmunchers!'

Harry could not help but break a smile at this amusing term, but he progressed to his argument, 'Yeah but the ball goes on until six in the bloody morning, what benefit is an extra hour. Plus, I honestly wouldn't mind queuing on a day like today.'

Raymond came in to support Aaron's case, 'Don't forget the champagne reception for the VIP guests. And the fact that we get to call ourselves 'very important' for the night.'

'Get your head out of your arse will you. We get served unlimited champagne all throughout the night. This VIP malarkey is all one big scam if you ask me. We've paid forty-five quid more, for absolutely nothing. Very Important Person, more like Very Ignorant Person if you ask me,' said Harry. While he was clearly over-exaggerating his frustration, perhaps for comical value, it was undoubtedly something that had been on his mind for quite some time. The boys nattered for some time over whether it was a good decision to pay extra for their VIP tickets and came to the general consensus that only time will tell if they made the right decision.

Despite beginning to get ready at four in the afternoon,

Sabrina and Gertrude were taking an absolute age to join the boys, and Harry awkwardly joked that they would be the last ones to enter the ball at this rate. It was around six-thirty, and the queue was already beginning to form by the time the girls emerged from the other side of the courtyard. Cuthbert spotted them first and remarked, 'There they are, lets head over to them.'

The sun was beating down on the men from behind, putting them in pursuit of their own shadows as they made their way over to the fountain in the centre of the Great Court. Harry imprudently said to Cuthbert, 'Didn't fancy using that monocle of yours then?'

To which Cuthbert replied, 'You really are a bumbling baboon. I am long-sighted. I have difficulty seeing things that are close to me.' Harry was left feeling rather foolish once more as he navigated his way around the students looking for the perfect picture, to encapsulate the memories of this night forever.

It was no wonder that the girls took an eternity to get ready; they looked astonishing. While the boys recently had the revelation of Gertrude's beauty, it was not until now that Sabrina came out of her comfort zone. As a devout Catholic, Sabrina tended to dress conservatively, but not tonight. Much to Gertrude's dissatisfaction, Sabrina stole the limelight as the boys were left gawping at her stunning backless emerald velvet dress. Sabrina's cleavage was on full display, and, with Gertrude's assistance, she used boob tape for the first time to boost her perky breasts. She was trying one last time to impress Harry and hoped that after three years of desiring him, tonight would finally be the night that something happened between the two. As she confidently strode over, the slit in her dress revealed her powerful thighs, and she certainly caught Harry's attention.

The sound of their stilettos clattering the stone slabs echoed across the quadrangle as they approached the boys eagerly waiting by the fountain. Sabrina wore six-inch black Jimmy Choo shoes with a deep rouge sole. For someone who did not wear high heels often, she had spent a considerable amount of money on them.

'Come on, let's get a photo by the fountain,' said Raymond, waving the two ladies over. This was to be the first photo of many taken that evening. *What good is going to a May Ball if you do not have a bazillion photos to show for it?* Sabrina was eager to stand next to Harry, perhaps a little too eager. It was when she switched from the flat slabs to walking on the cobblestone that disaster struck. Her long heel got caught in a crevasse between stones and snapped violently as she tried to walk forwards. Sabrina ended up rolling her ankle on the uneven surface and took a hard tumble onto the firm ground.

It was Harry who led the way in laughing at her misfortune, and quickly after, the rest of the boys joined in. Sabrina burst into tears, and mascara came running down her cheeks, ruining her make-up which she had spent hours perfecting. She did not know what hurt more, her fall onto the surface or the public humiliation with everyone around guffawing at her. Sabrina unbuckled her broken heel and stood back up. Now wearing only one shoe and standing slightly lop-sided, she said to Harry, 'You're such a fucking obnoxious little prick. I've wasted the last three years trying to get you to like me, but I'm glad that I'm not with a little shit like you.' It was strange to see Sabrina so illustrated, so harsh in her tone. Naturally, her words were tainted by her embarrassment, but it was clear that she was done chasing after Harry.

Harry persisted with his laughter, which acted as a catalyst for Sabrina's rage. If they had not been in public, there would have been a good chance that she would have taken a swing at him. Harry leaned over to Raymond and tapped him on the shoulder with the back of his right hand, 'Oops, it must be that time of the month again,' he said. Raymond offered a slight chuckle in support of his friend, but the rest of the boys did not find Harry's comment appropriate.

Thankfully, Sabrina, who at this point had turned away from the group, did not hear the comment, or god knows what she would have done. Gertrude, on the other hand, did hear Harry's throwaway remark, 'That is not funny,' she said in an earnest tone before walking over to assist the hobbling Sabrina.

It certainly was not the start to the ball that anyone had hoped for or had been expecting, and Harry felt somewhat guilty for causing the divide between the sexes. Alas, the night was still young, and the boys did not see the point in letting this minor incident ruin their evening. They decided that it was not really suitable timing to get a photograph by the fountain and instead decided that they would venture into the ball. As they were walking over to collect their wristbands, there was still tension in the air, which Harry tried to break by saying, 'Look lads, I'm sorry for all that. To make up for it, the first drink is on me.' His joke was met with rapturous laughter, tonight was an evening where no more money would be exchanged, but countless drinks would be consumed.

The worker tightened Harry's wristband slightly too much,

and it was at a point where it was a little uncomfortable to wear, with the metal clip scratching harshly against the veins on his wrist. 'Any chance I can get this replaced, it's hurting my wrists,' said Harry.

The unenthused worker looked back at him and replied in a scripted manner, 'Unfortunately, it is the May Ball policy that we are only allowed to hand out one wristband per guest.' It was clear that Harry had not been the first guest to ask for a replacement and would not be the last either. The employee already looked fed up to be working despite the long twelve-hour shift ahead of him. Each college's May Ball had strict security measures, but given the extravagance of Trinity's event, security was at another level. Indeed, there were the most ludicrous stories of people breaking into the ball, from people punting into the college to others literally swimming their way in, as well as people hiding in the college all day to enjoy the festivities. It was, therefore, no surprise that there were two security guards on each doorway checking that people had their wristbands on since they did not want students to be sponging from the evening's entertainment.

Once their wristbands were secured, the boys made their way through the college. Harry's bedroom was on full display to the guests through his large windows; knowing this, Harry took extra effort to ensure his room was immaculate. They made their way out of the Great Court and headed into Nevile's Court. Harry was examining the programme as they made their way through the cloisters. A shadow was cast over the booklet every few steps as a column would block the rays of sunshine. Even the programme was of excessive calibre. The card used for the cover was navy blue to match Trinity's colours, and on the front, below a picture of the college, in shiny gold, was the writing, 'The first and third May Ball – Second to none'. Harry thought this was a creative slogan and flicked through the pages to see what events they could expect in the night ahead. There was a myriad of entertainment, from chart-topping stars to world-class comedians to the finest classical and jazz musicians.

Nevile's Court was relatively empty, and the boys were not sure what to explore first. They felt like royalty as they walked across the red carpet which had been laid across the grass in the quad. This was the only day of the year that students could walk on the impeccable lawns, which was in itself a real treat. Despite all of the suggestions of what to do first, it was unsurprising that Cuthbert's suggestion came out on top, 'Right, we had better get ourselves some fresh oysters. I have been desperate to try these West Mersea wild Pacific oysters for weeks, my parents tell me that they are to die for.'

On they went to try their first delicacy for the evening. Harry had never eaten an oyster before and had no idea what to expect. Each of the boys grabbed a flute of Bollinger Champagne from a waitress walking around with them on a silver tray. There was no queue for the oysters, and the well-presented oysterman explained where this batch had come from, before advising the boys how they were to be consumed. 'You want to eat the oyster naked, so that you can really taste the region and the sea water from where they oyster is derived. Take it to your mouth and tip it all in in one go. But do not swallow it, as you need to chew it to release the full flavour.'

Before trying the oyster, Harry wanted to get a snap for his Instagram story. Raymond took the photo for him, and it captured the pique of privilege. A Cambridge student in a tuxedo, in one of the oldest colleges, bearing champagne in one hand and an oyster in the other. 'There you go bud,' said Raymond while handing Harry's phone back to him. Harry put down his flute and pocketed his phone.

With one big swig, the salt-water bivalve mollusc entered Harry's mouth, and he began frantically chewing away. As soon as the juice hit his tastebuds, he began gagging. He disagreed with the briny taste and started retching while pacing away from the others. Harry was eager to get it down, given his surroundings. No sooner had he swallowed it did the oyster come right back up, along with the rest of his insides, which he spewed onto the freshly mown grass. Harry's eyes watered as he threw up. His friends showed no sympathy as they started filming Harry. One thing is for sure; this would not be going up on his Instagram story.

- 24 -

When Harry had finished barfing, he re-joined the others who were still in hysterics at his reaction to the oyster. Harry grabbed his champagne flute and slammed it all down in one. 'Jesus, that was horrific,' said Harry to the others, offending the oysterman with no contrition in the process, 'let's go get some proper grub!' Harry was grateful that the ball was not yet in full swing; otherwise, his antics would have been a source of entertainment for all.

They decided to head out past the Wren library to get some food from one of the trucks lined along the riverfront, showing the security guards their wristbands as they did so. Harry went straight to the Argentine grill and picked himself up a kebab with all the dressings. The steak was tender, juicy, and loaded with flavour, much more to Harry's preference than the oysters he had tried and failed to consume. Raymond accompanied Harry, and they grabbed a cocktail from the bar set up next to the trailer. Harry decided that since he had paid so much for his ticket, he would be sticking exclusively to cocktails and champagne throughout the evening to really get his money's worth. He could never usually afford to splash out on fancy cocktails, generally sticking to beers, which made him feel like a bit of a part-timer on the juicy beverages tonight. Harry picked out a Hemingway Daiquiri, which was rather interestingly topped with candyfloss, and Raymond went for a Vesper Martini, which was, of course, shaken, not stirred.

The group reconvened and headed over the Avenue bridge, which was dressed up in fairy lights for the evening, yet it was still too bright outside for them to have full effect. The majority of the ball was to take place on the South Paddock lawn, which was usually a broad open green, but tonight was littered with different stalls and tents. 'Where to next?' asked Aaron, scoffing some upmarket Mac and Cheese into his mouth. Once again, they all had different ideas on what freshly cooked food to try, but instead of picking just one stall, they were all determined to sample everything on offer, to abate their fears of missing out. This was one of the first world problems of May Balls; they feed gluttonous behaviour. They are not dissimilar to staying at an all-inclusive hotel, or better still, a music festival, where everything is complimentary. The students' greed manifests and they gorge on as much food and drink as humanly possible. Regardless of how bloated they became, those sugary doughnuts or some Jack's Gelato ice cream were a must.

It turns out that buying the VIP tickets was not a terrible idea after all. The boys were completely stuffed by the time the ravenous masses started flooding in, and the long queues soon began to form once again at the different food stalls. Queuing was certainly a prominent feature of any May Ball as students were desperate to justify their vast expenditure. Indeed, there is almost a pressure to enjoy oneself. You *had to* take lots of photos; you *were obliged to* taste all the food; you *must* try out all of the amusement rides; you *were compelled to* get unbelievably drunk; you *needed to* attend the headliner. Despite the longevity of the evening, spilling into the early hours of the morning, every second was crucial, not to be wasted.

As the evening wore on and the light began to fade, so too did the queues for the food stalls. The initial excitement and panic began to die down, allowing people's stomachs the chance to digest the excessive amounts of food that had been consumed. The boys had spent the last hour ferociously laughing away at a comedian in the performance tent. Harry looked at his schedule and saw that a drag show was set to follow the comedian and said, 'Right, let's get the hell out of here.'

'Uncomfortable with gender expression are we Harry?' said Cuthbert, who looked remarkably relaxed in his chair with no intention of leaving.

Harry looked uneasy, 'No, it's not that. We've just been sat here for ages now. Don't want to spend my entire night in this tent, there's so much more of the ball to explore.' He was right, there was always something new to discover, and his argument convinced Raymond, Aaron, and Mo, leaving Cuthbert finally outnumbered and outvoted.

All of the guests were now at the ball, and it was increasingly resembling a music festival. There were six colossal tents set out on the paddock, four of which offered different live music. 'Who fancies a boogey then?' asked Mo, who was relatively intoxicated already.

'That works for me,' said Raymond.

'Before all that, lets grab some drinks to take with us,' said

Harry, who had been gasping for a beverage. He only had one cocktail during the comedy show, and with all the food he consumed was beginning to sober up.

'I'm okay,' said Mo, 'I'll just head straight to dance. Shall we head to the main stage?' he asked.

'Nah, I wouldn't bother going this early. They've got nobody good on yet. Things will start heating up at two A.M. when RAYE comes on! Probably best if we wait until then,' said Harry, who by this point had almost memorised the schedule of events.

'Come on, let's go to the jazz tent,' said Cuthbert to Mo. From the look on Mo's face, you could tell that this was not exactly the type of music he wanted to listen to, considering he fancied a dance. However Mo knew how set in his ways Cuthbert was and did not fancy challenging him.

The group split up, with Aaron and Raymond accompanying Harry to the rooftop bar, set up to overlook the river. RnB music was blasting from the bar, which offered a wonderful vantage point of the rest of the ball. In fact, it was probably the second-best view of the evening as it unfolded, behind being at the zenith of the Ferris Wheel. Harry thought that Mo would have likely been much happier up here than down below in the jazz tent, and the three boys were in no rush to get back to the Cuthbert and Mo. Harry's craving for a beer finally got the better of him, and he was convinced that the cocktails were more sugar than alcohol – slowing him down on his venture to get intoxicated.

'What are you two getting then?' asked Harry as he took a sip of his locally brewed IPA.

Aaron answered Harry's question with one of his own, 'Ooh,

what's that you've got? I wouldn't mind a nice ale myself.'

'Fuck it, yeah get me one as well,' said Raymond to Aaron as he approached the front of the queue. 'Wait, hang on a minute, what's all this about?'

A woman, who was quite clearly an employee, given her slightly more casual clothing, came parading up the stairs with two other workers. Each was parading a bottle of Bollinger, with sparklers emitting flickering flames, in a similar fashion to bottle servers at nightclubs, but with a difference. The lead woman was carrying a thin long silver sword, which she unleashed it from its sleeve when she reached the rooftop. In normal circumstances, if someone were to pull a sword out on you, a quick exit would be had. However, there was no hostility whatsoever from the woman, and she certainly drew the attention of the ball-goers.

It was clearly a planned act; the music was cut, and three bar staff approached with trays of empty gasses. The woman continued and ran the sword along the neck of the bottle in an attempt to dislodge the cork. The first attempt failed, as did the second. On her third attempt, she took a bit too much of the bottle and took the neck clean off, spilling both champagne and glass onto the floor. Her success in gaining access to the alcohol released a raucous cheer from all those around. Several guests remained confused as to what had just happened before them, until they were enlightened by the woman of the sabrage technique used to open champagne bottles at ceremonial occasions. The woman proceeded to slice open the next two bottles and poured their contents into the flutes to be served to the guests.

'Sack that beer,' said Raymond, who clearly fancied himself a bit of the posh drop, 'I'm having one of these.'

Aaron stood with a pint in each hand and said, 'What am I supposed to do with this then?'

'I'll grab it off of you,' said Harry, who by this point had almost finished his own beer. The boys finished their drinks and grabbed another one for the journey over to Mo and Cuthbert. They felt guilty that they had taken so long, and by the time they had arrived, Mo was anxious to leave the jazz gig.

'How about we head to the hall?' suggested Cuthbert, 'I hear that they've got ballroom dancing on there at the minute. Could be fun.'

'Absolutely not,' said Mo, who did not want to be dragged along to another pompous activity. Thankfully for Mo, neither of the other three were too keen on the idea, and, instead, they decided to head to the casino in the transparent tent set up in Nevile's Court. Unsurprisingly, real money was not exchanged at the casino; rather, chips were used by the professional dealers to deliver a swanky image and experience. Harry thought that if the students were playing for money, there undoubtedly would have been some high rollers here tonight. It was not long until the boys got bored of the dissimulate casino; the thrill was non-existent when playing for fake money. Besides, it was not long until the fireworks were set to go off, which, at the cost of around twenty thousand pounds, were often considered the highlight of the evening. Indeed, Trinity certainly had a lucrative budget to spend on its one-night spectacle and spend it did!

The lawn outside of the Wren Library was mobbed! All the guests had assembled in this small space, and it was quite some challenge for the boys to weave their way to the low-lying fence by the riverbank. Cuthbert was adamant that they should take up a spot right at the front, insisting that it was the best view for the fireworks. Cuthbert jokingly used the argument that he was a VIP guest to push his way to the front and the other guests were displeased with the shoving they received. At last, they made it. A waitress was making her way around the cramped lawn, carrying more flutes of champagne, and Harry insisted that she made her way over to the boys so that they could sip a beverage while watching the display. Withdrawing his pocket watch from his jacket, which was attached to his waistcoat by a short golden chain, Cuthbert informed the others, 'It is ten twenty-nine, only a few seconds to go now.'

If it was busy up on the lawn, it was nothing compared to the carnage taking place on the River Cam, which was packed with people in punts. It seemed as though all of the punts in the city were rammed into this tight space on the river. These were predominantly tourists who would have paid a premium for their tickets, but there was still a clear divide between the students and visitors. Cuthbert literally and figuratively looked down on them as he said, 'Bloody commoners, sponging on our college's May Ball. It's an utter disgrace if you ask me. They did not get into Cambridge; they did not earn the right to enjoy the firework display. These *punters* are just leeches and should be damned right banned. I hope they all get neck pain from staring up at the sky.'

There was no doubt that Cuthbert would have continued his rant if it was not for eight huge fire machines simultaneously blasting their roaring flames on the other side of the river to indicate the start of proceedings. The fire was enough to seize everyone's attention, and the silence that followed was enough to catch their curiosity. A solitary rocket whizzed through the air; its eruption of neon pink sparks lit up the entire night sky. When it exploded, it set off the pumping music, which was ablaze in perfect synchronisation with the fireworks that were to come.

The black canvas was painted with silver sparkles, vivid colours and a musky mist below. The enormity of the fireworks being set off at once, presumably under some sort of timer, made it difficult to take it all in. The thunderous explosions certainly would have been a real disturbance for many of the locals and of particular annoyance of those trying to revise for their A-levels on a Monday evening. None of this mattered to the guests, who were in awe of the visual spectacle that the pyrotechnics offered.

Midway through the display, things came to a halt again. Both the fireworks and music stopped momentarily, and the crowd was left unsure whether that was their lot. Some guests started clapping at the brilliant exhibition, yet just as the applause was beginning to build, another single firework headed in the guests' direction. Many were panicked for their safety, but thankfully it did not fly directly at the students, instead slightly above them. Everyone's eye was now fixated on the rocket, which exploded just above the Wren library, at which point the building lit up for an illumination lights display. The transition was remarkable. The projected lights gave a whisked history of the college where they were all standing; Sir Christopher Wren certainly would have been proud of the effort.

After the illumination intermission, the fireworks and blasting music continued from the North Paddock. The second act of fireworks seemed even more extravagant than the last, and indeed the display lived up to its reputation. This truly was the pinnacle of the boys' three years at Cambridge and potentially even their entire existence. They were finally stress-free; they had made it through the most challenging years of their life and now found themselves with a Cambridge degree. An education that provided a passport to travel wherever they wanted to go in life and immense achievements would certainly be expected from these men.

When the fireworks finally finished, Raymond's eyes began to water. He had been taken away from the emotional display. It enabled him to reflect on his academic achievements. 'That was amazing,' said Raymond, wiping the tear that was falling down his cheek.

'You can't be serious,' said Harry, 'what on earth are you crying about?'

'I just want to hold on to this moment forever. I can't believe we've all done it,' said Raymond.

Mo looked a little sheepish since he did not know what lay ahead in his future, but he did not want to say anything to ruin the moment. Instead, he deflected the conversation, steering it towards a safer topic, 'Come on, let's grab some drinks and head to the punting station before everyone else has the same idea.'

After even more cocktails, the river had slowly been cleared of all tourists, and the traffic quickly dispersed. Those renting the punts only had a license to watch the display and then had to be taken straight back to the punting stations. It was strange how quickly Cuthbert's tune changed when he and the boys opted to go punting. While the tourists were regarded as peasants, the chauffeured tour was a special treat for the boys, who thoroughly enjoyed the experience.

As hoped, there was only a short queue when the boys headed over across Brewhouse Lawn and towards the college punts, but by the time it was their turn to get on the vessel, the queue had grown exponentially. Harry was surprised Mo would choose to get in a punt with him again after the previous incident on the River Cam. But lightning would not strike twice, especially as they were all passengers this time, with an employee to take them down towards St John's College.

The punt glided effortlessly down the opaque river. The trees lining the banks were decorated elegantly in fairy lights, which glimmered brightly on the water's surface. On their left, a sophisticated water feature was spewing out water high into the air. Beyond the fountain, on the South Paddock, were three igloo-styled pods, offering a peaceful bubble to relax from the carnage of the May Ball. 'This is romantic isn't it. Nobody else I'd rather be floating down the Cam with than you boys,' said Aaron. In punts around them, couples were kissing and cuddling, and it was true that being in the punt was the ultimate romantic setting. Harry thought that there was someone that he would rather be sharing this punt with but did not allow this distraction to ruin his evening.

The boys were not on the river for long, but by the time they were back on dry land, it was approaching midnight. At this stage of the night, things started to become a little more casual and indeed served to blossom romance further. People had taken the majority of their photos for the evening and were now keen to loosen up and enjoy all of the remarkable events that the night had to offer. Many women switched from their heels to flats; they were done parading around and sought comfort ahead of formality. Similarly, the men undone their bow ties, laying them across their shoulders. That was the look that Harry adopted, unlike Cuthbert who was adamant about keeping his tie in place. Mo, who had not learned how to tie a dickie bow, was wearing a clip-on and stored a matching tie in his pocket just so that he could rock this casual look.

The boys made their way over to the South Paddock aiming to enjoy some more food from the new stalls that had been set up since the turn of the day. They were mostly dessert stalls, and Harry was adamant that his warm gooey brownie was the best he had had in his life. Time flew by, as it always does when having fun, and the temperature began to drop as the early hours of the morning were among the boys. It was not uncommon for the men to chivalrously give their dinner jackets to their partners to keep them snug, adding to the contrasting casual vibe of the formal ball.

It was not too long until two in the morning when Harry said, 'Come on, let's head over to the main tent; RAYE is coming out shortly. We don't want to miss that!' They headed for a quick pit stop to the portaloos, which added to the festival feel of the May Ball. However, these portable toilets are nothing like the retched ones that you would find at a festival like Reading. They were more luxurious and honestly better than standard bathrooms despite their compact nature. After the boys' bowels were alleviated, they grabbed some VKs from a nearby stall and headed into the enormous red and yellow striped tent. It was much more practical to grab some bottled drinks rather than carrying open cocktail glasses and should provide enough booze to get them through the hour-long set.

The main stage was erected in a similar fashion to a music festival, which was most fitting for RAYE since she was a big-time artist after all. The kind of artist whose name you would faintly recognise but would definitely be familiar with her songs. RAYE had never had a UK number one hit, but she was always flirting in the charts and was prominent enough to draw the students to the tent, like an eclipse of moths to a flame. 'Mate, I'm so pumped,' said Aaron.

Raymond nodded his head in agreement, 'I've been listening to her tunes all week. She actually has so many bangers!' The boys again pushed their way through the ever-growing crowd until they got to an area that was no longer permeable. They found themselves very central, right in the midst of the throng. 'Let's try and get to the front,' shouted Raymond over the chattering crowd.

Harry shouted back, 'I don't think I fancy replicating the Hillsborough disaster. I'm good just here.'

By the time RAYE had walked out onto the stage, the tent was at maximum capacity, spilling out at the exits with the Cambridge students desperate to hear the artist live. This would have been a great time to explore the rest of the ball since any queues would have dissipated, but clearly, this was the place to be for the next hour or so. Never before had there been a higher concentration of intellectuals crammed into such a confined space. RAYE started with her smash hit 'Decline', and the crowd went absolutely ballistic, chanting along with the lyrics as she sang them. She was much more than an incredibly talented singer; she was a performer, bringing copious amounts of energy to the stage.

It was when she dropped her tune with Jax Jones, 'You Don't

Know Me', that she got the biggest response from the audience. She was hitting every beat, and when she was mid-way through the song, the smoke machines propelled clouds of smoke into the air in a similar way to the fire machines. At the same time, confetti guns were set off, and small pieces of coloured paper began raining down on the students, who were simply loving life.

It was difficult to fathom that the firework display could be topped, but this performance certainly provided some competition. RAYE may have taken the edge, given the euphoric state of the students who had consumed more alcohol at this point in the evening, but it was a tough call. Everyone around had their phones out filming the concert, and Harry was actually streaming the performance live on his Instagram story to show the rest of the world what an unbelievable night he was having.

RAYE was singing her latest smash hit, 'Secrets', when Harry's screen blacked out. 'Ahh for fuck sake,' said Harry in response to his phone running out of battery, although it was so clamorous in the tent that his frustration could not be heard. Harry was a little disappointed that he could not record the rest of the session, but this gave him the chance to actually enjoy the music instead.

When the hour slot was up, everyone was screaming for an encore, wanting just one more song from the superstar. But it was evident that she was only under contract for sixty minutes and did not want to spend any longer on the stage than she had to. Besides, another artist was lining up to come on after her. The next performance was not a big headliner, and most of the students dispersed from the tent, rushing to the different stalls to capitalise on the lack of queues. A few stuck around, but Harry and the others thought it best to join the mass evacuation.

'Christ, I think I love her,' said Raymond in complete admiration, 'I just want her to be my wife.'

'Yeah, that definitely lived up to its expectation,' said Mo.

'Right, where to next?' asked Cuthbert.

It was strange for Cuthbert to consider what the others wanted to do, but maybe it was because he was constantly outnumbered that he had given up trying to get his own way. 'Let's get some more booze, grab some food, and head over to the silent disco,' said Raymond authoritatively.

'My phone has just died,' said Harry showing the others the black screen on his iPhone, 'I'm going to quickly nip back over to my room and grab my portable charger and I'll meet you guys at the silent disco? Can you grab me a drink though?'

'What do you want?' asked Raymond.

'Just grab me whatever you're having. I'll be quick so don't you guys go dallying on too long,' said Harry before jogging his way across the paddock, eager not to squander too much time. There certainly was a thinning effect as Harry got further and further away from the main tent, a clear indication of quite how popular RAYE had been. He continued scampering over the bridge until he got to the Wren library, where he quickly found himself out of breath. Perhaps it had been all the food and drink he had excessively consumed, but he could feel a stitch beginning to form, so he thought it was best to revert back to a walk. He raised his right arm to show off his wristband to security and made his way down the cloisters back towards the Great Court.

He proceeded now to a brisk march; his rigid heel clicked against the stone flooring. Harry checked his watch to see how he was doing for time, and when he looked up, he saw her. There was nowhere to hide this time, and he was not particularly in the mood for cowering away. She stood in isolation as if lost in the boundless college, looking around for anyone she knew. Harry had wanted to speak to her for so long, she had been running around his mind all year, and he was not going to squander this golden opportunity. As he approached her, he called out, 'Elizabeth'.

25

Elizabeth turned around and seemed relieved to see a familiar face. She felt comfort in Harry's unexpected presence. Elizabeth was as stunning as ever, wearing a sparkly sapphire long-sleeve dress, which brought out her vibrant eyes. The dress was short, revealing her long, tanned legs, and was perhaps a little informal for an event like tonight. This would have been her first May Ball after all, so maybe she was not familiar with the dress code, but nonetheless, her rose gold clutch made her look the part. Harry's heart was pounding, but her affectionate smile helped to settle his nerves. He had so much that he wanted to say yet finding words in this instant was challenging for Harry, who decided to ease himself into the conversation.

'How are you doing?' asked Harry, 'You look gorgeous too may I add.' Harry was apprehensive with his latter remark, not sure if it overstepped the mark. Thankfully Elizabeth was incredibly receptive to this compliment.

'Thank you. You polish up pretty well yourself. How come you're all alone?' Elizabeth asked politely.

'I could ask you the same thing,' said Harry cheekily.

Elizabeth's face dropped a little, 'I've actually lost all of my friends. Shameful I know, but I'll go out now and look for them. This college is so big that I have no chance of finding them,' she said, before repeating her question, 'So, why are you by yourself then?'

Harry fumbled his words under the pressure of Elizabeth's gaze, 'Me. Oh, I'm just heading back to my room to grab my portable charger.' Seeing the potential to get some alone time with Elizabeth, Harry pounced, 'Why don't you walk back with me, then I can help you find your friends after?'

Elizabeth was just grateful to see someone she knew and decided to accompany Harry back to his room, 'Sounds like a fair deal to me. I could certainly use a little break from this wild night. I do want to make it to the survivor's photo at six.'

Harry gave Elizabeth a short tour of the college and informed her of its rich history as the pair walked back towards the Great Court, where the eve had begun all those hours ago. Elizabeth was impressed by what she saw, fascinated by the intricate details of the college with each corner they turned. 'If you think all this is impressive, wait until you see my room. It's far better than the sort of accommodation you would have at Girton college,' said Harry braggingly.

Elizabeth was least pleased with Harry's last remark, but when she entered the room, she was amazed by the splendour of it all. 'And this is all yours?' she asked in disbelief as she began floating around the room.

'Yep, it's all mine. Have a look at the bedroom, it's marvellous,' said Harry leading her over to the wooden door at the end of the room. He entered first and drew the blinds for privacy,

'I do hate that anyone can just look into my bedroom though, that's the only downside. Feel like I always have to draw these whenever I'm in here.'

Elizabeth made her way into the centre of the room and was once again gobsmacked. It certainly did trump her small Girtonian room. 'Sit on the bed. You won't believe how comfortable it is,' said Harry with an outstretched arm pointing towards his ancient four-poster bed frame.

'I'm okay, thank you,' said Elizabeth courteously.

Harry now paced over to the door, and belligerently slammed it shut, 'I said, sit on the bed.' He was now insistent, and Elizabeth, all of a sudden, felt rather uncomfortable. Harry's eyes turned sinister, and Elizabeth felt claustrophobic in the large room. She felt completely trapped and obliged to obey Harry's command in trepidation.

Elizabeth's body tensed up as she slowly took a seat on the mattress without making a comment. She started to tremble as Harry sat next to her. Harry lunged in to kiss her, and she instinctively dodged away to avoid it. 'Harry, I have a boyfriend. I'm sorry,' said Elizabeth, who felt that she had to justify her action.

This did not deter Harry, 'You know you want it,' he said menacingly. He once again lunged onto Elizabeth and forced his lips onto hers. By this point, Elizabeth had been pushed down onto the bed, and Harry grabbed her wrists to pin her to the mattress.

'Stop, Harry,' said Elizabeth, who felt increasingly powerless as the situation spiralled out of control. But Harry ignored her, thinking that she was playing games. In his head, Elizabeth desired him so desperately. Harry grappled with her, picking her up by the torso and thrust her onto the middle of the bed.

It was when Harry put his hand onto her inner thigh and started running it up her leg that Elizabeth completely froze. She wanted to scream out, but her lungs evaded her. Besides, even if she had bellowed for help, it is unlikely that she would have been heard. They were so isolated, so far away from the rest of the May Ball taking place.

Harry put his hand onto her soft knickers and forcefully began to yank them down, ripping them as he did so. With one hand, Harry unbuckled his belt and pulled down his trousers slightly. He forced himself into Elizabeth's lifeless body, slowly at first, but then he started pounding at her corpse relentlessly. The attack was ruthless, and Harry continued to bear down on her. His weight almost squeezed the soul out of her, as Elizabeth had an out-of-body experience. It was as if she was watching herself from across the room, lying there helplessly as Harry molested her.

Harry continued to persist brutally until, eventually, he was satisfied with his act. It was not until Harry had climaxed and rolled onto his back that Elizabeth finally found the courage to move. Her wrists were red raw as she pulled up her torn underwear. Without saying a word, she crawled off the bed and headed straight to the door.

'Elizabeth, where are you going?' asked a bewildered Harry. By the time she had reached the exit, tears were now flooding down her face. It was not the first time that Harry had made a girl cry this evening. 'Elizabeth,' called Harry again, trying to seize her attention.

Elizabeth opened the door and turned slowly towards him. She could not even look him in the eye, 'I said no!' she shouted out before turning back and charging off to escape this living nightmare.

These three words were enough to send chills throughout Harry's entire body. Only now did he have the realisation of what he had done. Culpability began to flood into his body at this unwelcomed revelation.

26

The burning sensation of the boiling hot water swiftly faded away, and Elizabeth soon felt numb and lonesome in the bathtub. No matter how much she scrubbed her body, she still felt dirty and wondered if she would ever feel clean again. The water turned icy as she sat there for hours on end, turning into a complete prune until the sun began to rise. She gradually sobered up, and the events of the evening were starting to sink in. Traumatised, she had now moved beyond tears and stared blankly at the white bathroom wall, acting as a blank canvas to replay Harry's vulgar act. The flashbacks were too much for her to handle alone, and she felt as though she needed to tell someone about the incident.

Elizabeth considered talking to her boyfriend, Matt, but she could not bring herself to tell him what had happened. That another man had been inside of her. She was mortified that he would be overcome with a flurry of rage and that he would end things with her on the spot. She now felt like damaged goods, undesirable and fit for disposal. Elizabeth decided against talking to Matt about this just yet and instead pondered letting her friends from college know. However, they were all asleep at this point, recovering from the May Ball that they had just attended. Even then, while she got on well with them, she had only known them for a year and did not yet feel comfortable talking about a situation as traumatic as the one she had just been through. Elizabeth wanted to talk to someone she felt unreservedly comfortable around, someone she could trust and be completely open with. In the end, she decided that it would be best to call her brother Daniel.

Fortunately, Daniel was awake at eight in the morning when Elizabeth called, getting ready for a day's work ahead of him. It felt like the phone was ringing for an eternity before her brother picked up, and with each ring, she contemplated hanging up the phone and keeping the secret to herself. When he answered, Elizabeth was silent, and it was not until she heard his comforting voice that she felt confident enough to speak.

'What a lovely surprise this is,' said Daniel in a chirpy voice, unaware of the car crash news that was about to hit him.

The emotions all came back as she started sobbing away to her brother, explaining exactly what had just happened to her. Daniel could not believe that his best friend would do this to his little sister and while he was boiling up on the inside, he stayed composed to support his sister. Daniel comforted Elizabeth, as it was clear that she was in grief. He was her older brother; it was his job, after all, to protect her and look after her, yet he had failed in this duty. Daniel had never felt more betrayed by the vile actions of Harry, what a befoul monster he was.

'Don't worry, I'll take care of all of this,' said Daniel before hanging up the phone. After the call had ended, Daniel started to breathe a lot heavier. He was nearly fully dressed for work, but he did not bother putting his tie on; he would not be going into the office today. He stormed straight downstairs, ignoring his mother's greeting from the upstairs bathroom, and headed to the kitchen. He raided the drawers, looking for the biggest knife he could find, and eventually pulled out a sharp bladed chef knife with a matte black handle. Daniel did not bother with breakfast. Instead, he grabbed his car keys and got straight into his red Ford Focus.

His temper was flaring as he entered the driver's seat, placing the weapon next to him on the passenger's position. He pulled out his iPhone and clamped it into the holder to give him the directions for Trinity College. He was coming for Harry; he would have his revenge. Daniel was not the violent type, but if anyone caused harm to his sister, he would not sit back and let them get away with it. The sun was beaming harshly that morning as Daniel made his way up the A1 from Hatch End, so he pulled down the sun visor. The knife shined brightly, reflecting the sun's rays. He drove in deathly silence, undeterred and focusing on only one thing. Some doubts crept into his mind on the journey, but he pushed those thoughts to one side and carried on without remorse.

Daniel spent the entire journey in the fast lane, driving obscenely above the speed limit. He thought that he had been flashed twice by speed cameras, but that issue did not command sufficient attention to occupy his thoughts. When he got into the city, he ignored the traffic system in place that allowed only taxis to travel down certain streets. As he drove down Sidney Street, past *Mainsbury's*, he began to get nervous, questioning whether what he was doing was the right thing. Perhaps he should have given himself a little time to think about what he was planning to do. It was as if he had an angel on one shoulder, warning him of the consequences of his proposed actions. However, it was the devil on the other shoulder which came up trumps, egging him on. Besides, he had driven all the way up to Cambridge; he was not exactly going to turn back now.

It was just before ten in the morning that he pulled onto St John's street. Fortunately, he had arrived before the barriers were put up to pedestrianize the road. He drove down the narrow-bricked road, his entire body jiggling from the uneven surface, which was already lined with tourists looking to explore the city, taking photos of the marvellous colleges. Hundreds of bikes were parked up outside of the two most prominent colleges, Trinity and St Johns. Daniel nearly ran over a Chinese tourist, who began shouting loudly at him as he pulled into the driveway for Trinity College, but Daniel completely ignore the complaints. He was in a rush and wanted to waste no time.

The tourist had approached the car to continue his rant. Daniel grabbed the knife and rose from the car, towering above the Chinese man seeking confrontation. When he saw the weapon in Daniel's hand, the tourist hastily apologised and stepped backwards away from him. No further words were exchanged, and the tourist was petrified, grateful to get away with his life. Daniel tucked the blade into his pants and covered the handle with his t-shirt as he made his way towards the Great gate.

He did not really plan how he would get past the porters but was hoping that he could just walk right through. Daniel was twenty-two and could easily have passed as a Cambridge student, and that was the alibi that he was going to stick with. However, in the summer months, the porters were more stringent and stopped everyone coming into the college to check their CAMcard.

Daniel avoided eye contact as he walked on through the lodge. 'Sir, sir, can we see some ID please,' said the older balding porter from behind the desk. This was when Daniel panicked. Little did he know that he could buy a ticket to enter the grounds, but he carried on walking, pretending that he did not hear the request. 'Sir,' he repeated louder, now standing up from his office chair.

The porter's movement acted as a catalyst for Daniel, who suddenly switched from a confident stroll to a full-on sprint. He did not bother sticking to the designated path. Instead, he dashed straight across the immaculately mown lawn, kicking over the small black 'Do not walk on the grass' sign as he did so. The men behind the desk, whose job it was to control entry into the college, were slow off the mark in pursuing Daniel. By the time they had made it out of the lodge, Daniel was already across the other side of the court, heading straight for Harry's room. The porters stuck to the path, trudging after Daniel. The Great Court was remarkably quiet, given that everyone was still sleeping, recovering from the ball last night.

Daniel swiftly got to Harry's room; he remembered where it was from when he came up for his birthday, which felt so long ago now. He pushed against the door, which appeared to be locked. It was clear that Harry was hiding inside. Worried about the porters coming after him, he took a run up and flew through the air to attack the door. Daniel had gathered enough force to swing the door wide open. The flimsy latch was perhaps one of the most significant disadvantages of having such an ancient room. The security of the room depended entirely on just two feeble rusty screws.

After barging down the door, Daniel was quick to get back to his feet and withdrew the knife from his trousers. A quick scan of the room informed him that Harry was nowhere to be seen. He glanced over to the desk, which oddly enough had no chair parked underneath it, before creeping over towards the fireplace in case he was cowering away behind the settee. Harry certainly was not in the living room, and Daniel was beginning to doubt whether he was in his room at all. This was when Daniel assumed that he was most likely sleeping, beyond the door at the end of the room.

It was not exactly how Daniel wanted to kill him. He wanted Harry to be awake, to see him squealing away for mercy. But perhaps this way would be easier; Harry would at least be an easier target. As Daniel inched towards the bedroom door, he firmly gripped the knife in his stronger right hand, holding the weapon with a bent arm at shoulder height, ready to pounce on Harry. He grabbed the cold black handle and pulled it downwards slowly. Daniel's heart was racing, but he had little time to think. The door creaked as it opened, and Daniel invited himself into the room with one last deep breath. This was it. When he was completely in the room, Daniel could not believe what he saw before his eyes.

27

'Please, you can't do this,' he said in a distraught tone, 'there must be some other solution we can come to'. It could not end like this, surely not. He felt trapped in the room, which felt as though it was shrinking by the second. There was no way out, and he began to panic, suffocated by his surroundings. Mo's meeting with the exam board was not going as planned, and he began to hyperventilate, scrambling for a solution.

The stern woman across the long oak table started to show an ounce of sympathy for the first time, 'I'm sorry Mo, there is just nothing else we can do. It is university policy that any student failing an exam in tripos will not be allowed to graduate. We cannot make exceptions to this.' The other two sitting opposite Mo, including his tutor, remained silent, and that was when he knew it was all over. *Not all stories have the happy endings that we desperately desire.*

Mo's entire world was crumbling around him. It did not help that he was only running on a few hours of sleep. Mo had made his case, but it was ultimately down to him that he was late for his exam – no one else was to blame. His excuse of the alarm not going off did not hold any weight in the discussion. Mo was quivering as he stood up and made his way to the door. When he left the room, he was unreservedly distraught. He had worked assiduously, invested the last three years of his life, as well as thousands of pounds; *all for what?* Failing his degree and having this stamp marked against him for the rest of his days.

The meeting had taken place in the seminar room at the top of the tower in Trinity College, and Mo was too shocked to muster up any tears as he made his way down the spiralling stone staircase. It was a beautiful day, yet Mo had absolutely no idea of what to do with himself. He had tickets for yet another Garden party but was in no mood for celebrations. How could he be? Mo had never felt so astray in his life. When Mo had made his way out onto the Great Court, his shock was displaced with tentative curiosity. There appeared to be a bunch of mortified looking students gathered across the other side of the quadrangle. There were screams and shouts and, instead of heading back to his accommodation block across the road, he thought he would head over to check out what all the commotion was about.

It turns out that they were all huddled up peering into Harry's bedroom window, which Mo thought was most strange. Perhaps an even bigger shock to Mo as he crossed past the fountain were the police officers storming into college. This informed him that something serious had taken place, and he was afraid to find out what that was. As he approached the outside of Harry's room, there were too many bodies blocking the view, so Mo decided that he would head around to his room to check out the scene for himself.

As he walked towards the building, one of the officers author-itatively spoke out to him, 'Stay back, nobody is allowed to come through here.' Mo kept his composure and confidently conjured up an excuse that he lived in the building and just needed to nip in to grab his stuff. The police officer was scepti-cal but allowed Mo entry on the condition that he just headed straight to his room. Mo pretended to walk towards where he claimed his room to be but side-stepped in the other direction when the officer turned his back to control the existing crowd that was building up outside.

A chill ran through Mo's body as he made his way down the naturally heated corridor. He slowed as he approached Harry's room, expecting that he would be denied entry, but nobody was guarding the door. Everyone was preoccupied with what had happened in the bedroom. In fact, nobody even noticed Mo as he traversed the living room.

Just as he approached the bedroom door, he saw it and was left absolutely horrified. No wonder there had been such a vast crowd of onlookers outside. Harry's body was hanging lifelessly from one of the posts on his bed. The desk chair was lying flat on the floor. Presumably, he had kicked it away once he had fastened the belt, acting as a noose, around his neck. He was still in his tuxedo from the night before. His head tilted forwards, and his arms drooped down by his side. Mo was on the verge of throwing up at what he saw – one of his closest friends asphyxiated by the leather strap.

Mo had wondered why on earth the curtains had insensi-tively been drawn, they were not left open when he came into college earlier, but that was the least of his concerns. The porters consoled a man, who Mo recognised to be Daniel, who was on the sofa, bawling his eyes out. They were completely oblivious that he was there to murder Harry, yet seeing the dead body drew all sorts of emotions out of him. Daniel wanted to be the one to stick the knife into Harry, to see him squeal like a pig, and bleed a slow and painful death, but he was too late. In his eyes, Harry had cowardly taken his own life to evade taking accountability for his actions. But Daniel was still in disbelief seeing Harry's body hanging; they were still friends after all.

One of the porters, the older of the two, patted Daniel on the back in an attempt to comfort the wailing man. The other porter looked as though he needed someone to support him as well. Both of the porters were left gobsmacked; this was far beyond the remit of their regular duties.

Mo wandered slowly past Daniel into the bedroom, where the police officers were now examining the scene. Perhaps they thought that Mo was part of the investigation team because they did nothing to stop him from coming in. Mo felt as though he had to pinch himself; this could not be real. *Why on earth would Harry take his own life?* The timing was nonsensical. He had just been through the most stressful months of his life, and when he came through the other side, he decided to top himself. *Was it perhaps because his life now felt meaningless? Had he reached the pinnacle of his life and thought that it could not get any better?* The Trinity May Ball had been sensational, but there would be other astonishing things to come in the future!

Mo was baffled as he stared deep into Harry's partially open eyes. He looked at ease. All Mo could think about was the waste of potential that he saw before him. Seventeen years of education. Harry was the smartest man that Mo knew, yet his raw talent was now worthless. A life that had been cut short, just as it was beginning. A life never truly lived.

Mo could not rack his brain around the situation, that was until he strode over to Harry's dressing table. Placed above it was a piece of plain paper folded neatly into quarters. Mo knew that it was something that he should not be touching, but he had to know what was written on it. He clasped at the paper and subtly slid it into his trouser pocket. He could not bear to be in the room any longer and headed back out to the courtyard, where the police officer faced quite some task of keeping people from passing through.

Mo felt discombobulated as he made his way into the sunshine, and this lost feeling was not just his hangover kicking in. He slowly paced towards the Porter's Lodge and withdrew the note from his pocket. Mo stood completely still to read its contents, hoping to uncover the reason for Harry's suicide.

I'm sorry Elizabeth, I got it wrong.

He stared at the scruffy black ink for a few seconds, hoping that somehow more writing would appear, but it did not. Mo was still astray as to what the message meant until he eventually recognised the name. Elizabeth had been the girl that Harry had been so heartbroken over at the start of the year, the girl he so dearly yearned for. Mo had assumed that Harry had been rejected again, and this rejection was too much for him to handle. He was devastated at the loss of his dear friend, but little did he know that the world was now a better place.

The travesty put everything into perspective for Mo. No matter how tough his situation was, that he would not be graduating, things could be far worse. Even though he did not know the whole story, he thought about how much agony Harry must have been in to take his own life, having nowhere or nobody to turn to. Sure, Mo was devastated right now, but time is the greatest healer. Unlike Harry, Mo still had the rest of his life ahead of him, and failing his degree was not the end for him. This sombre conclusion to his Cambridge career was not what Mo had expected, but the tragic event helped him gain a fresh outlook on life. Life is too short to dwell on the negatives, each and every day should be lived to its fullest, and this was certainly the ethos that Mo was to take going forwards.

THE END

@hayes_writes is on Instagram

YouTube channel Hayes Writes